DIVISION

For treasured friendship —

Best always,

Pat

DIVISION

or

FORGIVENESS IN CHICAGO

a novel by

PATRICK CREEVY

Division or Forgiveness in Chicago © Copyright 2020, Patrick Creevy

All rights reserved. No part of this book may be used or reproduced in any manner whatsoever without written permission from the publisher, except in the case of brief quotations in critical articles and reviews.

This book is a work of fiction. However, settings are based on real places in Chicago. The Teague Funeral Home in this book is modeled on the Griffin Funeral Home, but the character of Maurice Teague is entirely fictional. Ernest A. Griffin directed the Griffin Funeral Home in the Douglas community on south Martin Luther King Drive in Chicago. In 1990 he designed the Heritage Memorial Wall on the site of Camp Douglas, an infamous Civil War prison on Chicago's South Side. Griffin's memorial to the Confederate prisoners who died at Camp Douglas included a Confederate flag, which he flew at half-staff. All other names, characters, places, and incidents either are products of the author's imagination or are used fictitiously. Any resemblance to actual events or locales or persons, living or dead, is entirely coincidental.

First Edition   ISBN 13: 978-1-937484-71-2

AMIKA PRESS   466 Central AVE #23 Northfield IL 60093   847 920 8084
info@amikapress.com   Available for purchase on amikapress.com
Cover design by Francie Bala.

FOR SUSIE
IN OUR FIFTY-SEVENTH YEAR

CONTENTS

ix Acknowledgements

x Author's Preface

1 What Can I Get Started for Ya?

8 We Do

19 A Catholic Family

29 Soul Coast and Gold Coast

39 We Don't Want This

48 One Hour Earlier

57 Where Did it Start?

66 Still the Innocent Son of Maurice Teague

77 No Dream

85 Mother And Son

93 Good Morning, America, How Are Ya?

102 The White Community

112 Couldn't You Be Somebody Else?

121 When to Open and When to Close

132 She Brings it All Togetha

141 Communication

152 CCDOC: Division One

160 More Loving than Loved

170 The Real Girl

181	Lovemaking
191	She Say You Coulda Been a Preacher Man
199	Confiding
212	Heart of Darkness
221	I Am Here with You
230	Personhood
239	CCDOC: Division One to Division Nine
249	Duty
261	The Braided Necklace
274	Doorways
284	The Source of Self-Respect
290	Mother and Child
298	Robert Teague
307	Olivet
316	In the Place of American Pain and Sin
325	The Names
336	The Whole Truth
347	Closure
359	In the Kingdom of Heaven
374	What Will You Do?
388	We Do

ACKNOWLEDGEMENTS

For his wisdom, his fierce intelligence and his tireless efforts to make a good thing of *Division,* as well as for conversations I will treasure always, I thank first and foremost John Manos. I thank Sarah Koz for the sensitive, skilled way in which she has put together *Division* as a physical book. I thank Francie Bala for the remarkable gift of her art, shown here again in this third cover she has done for me. And I thank Jay Amberg for letting me publish now a second time with Amika Press, and especially for the way the press personalizes, always, for its authors the very hard business of bringing out a book.

For the truly invaluable help they gave me in their introduction of me to the operations of the criminal justice system in the Cook County Criminal Courts and at the Cook County Department of Corrections, I would like to express my sincerest gratitude to Michael Morrissey, Director of the Chicago Public Defenders Office, now retired; Crystal Marchigiani, Chief of the Office's Murder Task Force, now retired; and Rich "Spike" Siegel, investigator for the Office's Bond Court Unit, now retired. For his most generous help in introducing me to the ways in which the Chicago Police Department would operate in the investigation of a homicide, I want to thank Sergeant Ken Epich of the CPD, now retired. I want to extend my sincere thanks as well to Jim O'Connor for sending me his extraordinary unpublished piece "County Time," of which I made close use in my accounts of life in "County." Also, I have taken from the Home Page of the Gangster Disciples (gd7414.weeblie. com/index.html), in some cases in verbatim transcriptions, the wording of statements of the gang's philosophy and of its initiation oath.

AUTHOR'S PREFACE

I finished the first full version of *Division* quite a long time ago—nearly five years. After finishing it, I spent close to two years just sitting on the book, doing nothing with it, thinking for most of that time that I might not ever try to get it published—for not long after I had typed my final period on a story which not without prominence features a very particular memorializing of the Confederate dead, white supremacist Dylann Roof carried out his hellish massacre at the Emanuel African Methodist Church in Charleston. Not a month later, for every right reason, Governor Nikki Haley ordered that the Confederate flag flying at the South Carolina State House be taken down for the last time. And in the years immediately following, if not without resistance, the removal of Confederate monuments would gain momentum across the South, most noticeably in Louisiana, where New Orleans Mayor Mitch Landrieu both took courageous action and spoke out eloquently for the need. Civil War historian Eleanor Harvey, with respect to the South's public memorialization of the Confederacy and of the dark potential that was always in this, and that has lately been so grimly realized, states in succinct terms what has for many become the obvious: "If white nationalists and neo-Nazis are now claiming this as part of their heritage, they have essentially co-opted those images and those statues beyond any capacity to neutralize them again." And then—still before I could muster any real will at all to publish *Division*—there came history-changing Charlottesville and the infamous Unite the Right rally, which might have put beyond any capacity in us to hear again in the way we once did the voice of Shelby Foote, Ken Burns's *Civil War* narrator, as he says that in battle after battle of the Civil War, remarkable valor was shown on both sides.

Nor did it relax my uneasiness or, indeed, unwillingness to attempt to get *Division* published that I had, in my close consideration of the divisions in a Catholic family, presented, on the charged subject of abortion, a perspective that is multi-sided—and that hence would be satisfactory to no one.

But always I had had "Forgiveness in Chicago" in mind for a subtitle for *Division,* which is after all *meant* to explore those things that separate us—for I wanted to suggest as well what might help bring us back together. And perhaps nothing has helped more to restore an author's resolution in me to work toward publication than the interview that Hoda Kotb had with the three African-American women of "Mother Emanuel" who survived the murderous violence of Dylann Roof— Felicia Sanders, who lay that evening over her granddaughter's body to save the little girl's life but whose son Roof shot and whom she saw take his last breath; Jennifer Pinckney, whose husband, Clementa, Pastor of Emanuel A.M.E. and South Carolina State Senator, Roof murdered; and Polly Sheppard, whom Roof told he would not shoot because, intending to kill himself, he needed a survivor, presumably in order to tell the story of his attempt, by means of a horrific mass murder, to help start an American race war. But the story that would be told by these surviving women was by no means, as Roof no doubt hoped it would be, dramatically inflammatory, warlike in vengeful anger, rather it was one of a quietness bordering on mystic silence that entered that room at Emanuel, even amidst Roof's relentless gunfire; of a white light that descended; and of their profoundly Christlike forgiveness of the utterly lost Dylann Roof.

And more recently now there has been that moment in that courtroom in Dallas when, as he gave his victim's impact statement after the conviction of Amber Guyger, a white police officer, for the murder of Botham Jean, his brother, the black Brandt Jean, both forgave her and asked the judge for permission to hold Officer Guyger, for a moment, in a forgiving embrace. The image of this momentarily division-ending embrace, in which Officer Guyger wept profoundly on Brandt Jean's shoulder, has proven to Americans who have seen it to be deeply, even historically inspiring but also, for many, in communities both white and black, perhaps just as confusing—for we will ever have a need for strict justice as well as mercy. Or because the deepest sanity of God must always seem some kind of madness in the eyes of the world.

—Patrick Creevy, 2020

WHAT CAN I GET STARTED FOR YA?

"Welcome to Starbucks," she said, in that warm-civil way that customers, or most, anyhow, appreciate. A dark-skinned black, maybe about her age, twenty-two, who had been last in a six- or seven-person late-afternoon line, was coming up to the counter. She'd been studying him, in glances, from the start. He had this hard, thick-muscular power to him that his jacket, a seeming-expensive, black leather, three-quarter cut, didn't hide. Also black-bandana-ed, un-smiling, he bore no innocent look of some school athlete—so possibly bulked and toned, she'd let herself think, in some weight room behind bars. How would he sound? You just couldn't tell with these project blacks, her experience had proven: a powerful, intense-seeming presence like this one's, intelligent-looking, beautiful-handsome, could open his mouth and out might come nothing—an ungrammatical and borderline-worthless ninth-grade education, sounding itself out in southern-rooted mumbles she'd need a cultural linguist to explain the reason for: did they just plain determine never in their lives to speak white, or were they just so cut off that they could never really hear it—and so never spoke the language of the country they lived in? Yet in this one's eyes—penetrating and...perhaps, if given his chance, charismatic—there was, she'd been feeling more and more as he approached, something possibly really different: he didn't read easily as your common gangbangin' thug, with his powerful man's body, make him 6'2", the dark-beautiful face, and those deep, dark-browed eyes—didn't read as just one more empty *gold-toother* (which would be the heading that, in ever-growing contempt now, she'd been placing all the standard-thug types under).

She'd marked what she'd thought a representative sampling of these types in the six months she'd barrista'ed at what her old North Shore boyfriend, in a half-respectful nod to the venturesomeness of gentrifying pioneers, had called Fort Apache: the new Starbucks at Clybourn and Division. And there it was—this miracle, this brave, new, white-world outpost set right in the infamous dark shadows of Cabrini Green, nineteen-story shadows that were then, early spring of '99, beginning to let in some light at last: for the City's wrecking ball (though Richard M's great Plan for Transformation was only in its invisible embryonic stages) had already swung hard into its work, taking down some of the darkest death-traps in "the Greens," first "the Castle," then "1157," and now "Bank Roll" and "the Rock." And with every single high-rise on both sides of Cabrini's notorious two-sided battleground, both south of Division and north—every last Red, every last White—now deemed "non-viable"—everyone wondered when that wrecking ball would start adding to its history.

VL's, Mickey Cobras, GD's. In ways no white girl normally would, she (instructed by her co-workers Clarice and Ayisha, both such delightful girls, and her good friends) really did kind of know the differing homeboys now. Or she could in a surface way make out, at least, one gangsta tribe from anotha, maybe even call beforehand the direction one of this denomination, or of that, would take away from the shop, when out on Division—or the direction he wouldn't take. Never had there been any violence, nor ever even any sign-flashing, not in the new, white coffee shop, guarded as it always was by one or more CPD patrol cars parked in front of its doors, often with a bulky-vested officer outside a car, on hard watch, radio ready (and she did love these cops for keeping their eyes on her, or for following her some in the car, when she got off work and walked back homeward into Old Town, up Clybourn and then east, on Goethe). And things like the war paint—

2

the tattoos—she really did know now, even to the point of not caring that much anymore to notice who wore what.

But somehow, now, *not*—not with this one at last now right before her, standing there close, maybe even too close, at the counter. Somehow, with this one—and she felt it now even with a slight loss of breath, or even with some palpable loss of all her life's courage—there was nothing not to be noticed when her eye caught the X-crossed pitchforks cut across his throat. GD. God Damned. Gangster Disciple. A young white woman, she could immediately, in a flash, imagine this young black man, her age, standing so close before her now, under the tattoo needle and gun, thinking what Clarice said all the young gamers think: *Everybody's gotta die sometime.* But this one wouldn't be like the rest; for this one, she felt suddenly, deep inside her, would think of death with the last full measure of devotion to it. Nor would he back off from what it stood for—that indelible six-pronged symbol X'ed above the neckline of his dark blue t-shirt. Disarmed, she felt herself warming both beneath her breasts and in her face. She hoped she showed nothing; but how did she look and sound, as her own throat went tight, and she asked him what she'd been asking customers all day every day for six months straight: that Starbucks colloquial, comfortable, "What can I get started for ya?"

He said nothing. Expressionless, in a strange, fraught pause, suggesting to her that he'd sensed the white girl's uneasiness and that he enjoyed the scent of it, he ran his eyes over her, warm. And uncivilized? as if he wasn't any different after all?—as if out on the street he'd just come up and lift her skirt and take a look inside, the way one of them had once? He turned his mouth down. Then, in a firm, quiet voice, toneless but now surely hard-aggressive—even of a same spirit with the war paint on his neck: "Y'all got it started good now already, I believe." She played dumb, tilted her head as if to describe a question mark. "Y'all"—"it"—"started good now already"—what did he mean? But she knew what he meant—here on this intense frontier, where every white and every black knew every minute of every hour that that large change of worlds, black to white, Soul Coast to Gold Coast, had gotten started, and good.

Yet what really did he want? Playing her like this? Throwing his aggressive mysterious-yet-in-fact-transparent stuff at her like this? What would he really like?—to follow me out of here and slit my throat? or to come with me to my place and fuck me good and sweet? Her mind went that fast to the eternal borderland question—that double question—kill me? or make love to me?—which right there, at that Starbucks, she thought had maybe the single answer *yes*. But she pinched up her face, as if still puzzled, and asked, "Sorry?" He ignored hard, however, this second act of her polite masquerade, and, as a customer who knew this place well enough already, he said, "Black coffee, make it grande." And in cooler return now—fuck him—she just nodded, unfitting a green-logo'ed paper cup from the grande stack, and a white plastic Solo sipping cap; but when at the spout she was doing the hot pour, she turned, stopping before finishing, and asked, over her shoulder, "Leave room for mixing in cream?" And she did—she actually did then imagine—as she smiled at him over her shoulder, a cloud of thick white cream floating, and breaking, in hot black coffee—and then its being wholly suffused, white with black, when stirred by the stick—and she kind of lurched, restrainedly, cup still in hand, with a half-suppressed laugh. But fuck him again, for he could read her body language, she was sure. He knew why she'd laughed. Yet he just said to any idea of a happy, transcendent, borderless white-black integration: now and forever *no*. Just a cold uncivil, "No, keep it black." So fuck him. She finished the pour, took his pay, then made change. Then she firmed the Solo cap on the grande cup and sleeved it. But as she handed him his coffee, and before she turned to take the order of her next in line, she said with an aggressive-soft smile to his dark GD self, "Don't blame me."

Don't blame nobody but you, nigga! Got damn gangsta motherfuckers! Killin' peoples. Killin' ya own. Killin' black children. You see them white peoples ridin' they curly-handled bicycles down this side now a Orleans. Down Division to get they coffee and they movies at Blockbuster. They comin', motherfucker. And we gone. And don't you blame nobody but you. His grandmother—hollerin' bitch calls herself an activist—for her *community*—where she's lived all but twelve of her sixty-one years of life—comin' down on him just an hour ago, blamin' him 'cause she won't get qualified herself for the mixed housing that's goin' up. Got her own sheet. Got her own bad credit. So she's gon' be moved the fuck out when they bring this place all the fuck down and she won't know where the fuck she'll be goin'. All her bitchin' about them needin' to screen people before they let 'em in the Greens. Select and eject. That's what she's said long's he can remember. And it bein' the downfall a this place 'cause they haven't screened since the time

WHAT CAN I GET STARTED FOR YA?

after they shot King dead and all the crazy niggas tore up the West Side—and then with no screenin' they brought a million crazy West Side niggas over here, all of 'em gangbangin' fools—like your fucked-up daddy she says. And now she's bein' screened outa here her black-ass self with them rebuildin' for mixed peoples. And that's all his fault. Shiiit. And now this sassy-jittery white bitch. Pretty white cream. Leave room for it, boy. Got somethin' for you, little girl, upside my belt, you want it. And fuck her scaredy white ass anyhow, sassin' me.

Sitting now at a table, waiting for his homeboy Tumbler, comin' over this way up Orleans past Camp Ball in the Reds (he came himself from Tha Jube, in the Whites, 3-5-4, my brotha, right down Division like always, representin' nation), he blew into the sip-cup top to cool his coffee and looked again at the sweet-fleshed white thing at the counter, with her purplish lipstick and dyed-dark hair, with purple in it too, and the metal in her tongue (for ticklin' other white things' pussy?), and those sweet titties showin' under her apron whenever she turns sideways. Her and her comin' at him all mysterious with her *I know you want this white pussy* whisper and her "Don't blame me" bullshit. All those white words in her pretty head, he knew, but he could tell she didn't know the word *hustle*. Never looked at that white cream in the mirror and said I gotta hustle this thing. Like some white ladies he knew. *Don't blame me.*

And so who *is* gon' take responsibility? his nasty-ass grandmamma says. They comin'. And we gone. Now these whites, this pretty-assed white bitch, gon' take his hustle. Take his work. Sell her coffee where he's been sellin' since he worked "S" along Big-D's sidewalks, one bad-ass shorty motherfucker. No yella-ass buster even a day of his life. Not afraid to pull that trigger and blow off the smoke. And the OG's knew it, so they give him real work, age ten, when they said he's now a ward of Tha Jube, his sorry-ass hypin' fucked-up ho mama found dead on the floor, by him, her throat all slit—by somebody. He found her there, all cut and dead in her blood. Same room he was born in, when the ambulance never came to help her when he's bein' born out of her. Never forget seein' her dead like that. Come at him when he's walkin' just about anywhere. Just about not a night, neither, when he doesn't retaliate on somebody in his dreams. His grandmother, she says she wants him after that, but he never believed her—so he never came to her.

He took a touch of hot coffee now on his tongue and put down the

cup. When he leaned forward, he could feel the Glock 19 press hard
against his abdomen. He sat up then, but as he did, he tapped, and
then squeezed with his palm the right pocket in his leather coat. One
full-up thirty-plus mag—all nine inches, good and stiff. No bullshit
goin' down tonight. He wrapped his hand round the hot sleeved cup,
then let it go. Then he started studyin' again on his mama's mama—and
what she said when he warned her and told her he made up, this time,
on her tax with the Folks, not payin' her percents on that hairstylin'
thing she's doin'. Made it up, he told her, out of his own work money.

Work, she said—ol' sharp-tongued bitch—like spittin' it right out of
her mouth at his face. I know what y'all mean by work, ahright. Ya
mean dope. Sellin' dope. Killin' y'all selves. Killin' children. Givin'
white peoples what they want, bringin' this place down so's it cain't
never be fix. I tell you what—them white peoples got a plan—always
had they big plan. 'Cause we sittin' on a gold mine here, boy, right next
the Gold Coast, and they wants it back. So now you don't—do ya?—see
no meedya comin' in here reportin' for white folks' enjoyment just the
bad shit. Cabrini Green. Cabrini Green. Nineteen stories a shit piled
up them elevator shafts and dead peoples everwhere. Crazy niggas
ain't human. Ain't never been equal 'cause they just animals, livin' in
them cages, which wasn't there 'til they started throwin' other niggas
over the rails, up them high ramps, and shootin' down, killin' them
two po-lices with rifles, and Dantrell jus' goin' t'school with his mama,
eight years old, and rapin' little Girl X so turrible. Way the news always
was for years, even though there been so many good peoples in this
community and not just y'all ignorant gangbangin' fools and black-
nosed dope fiends and sassy-mouthed babies havin' they babies, more'n
Jesus could count. But now it's all good shit the meedya be sayin' 'cause
they don't want to scare no white peoples off now. 'Cause they comin'.
And it's over. Just a matter a time. And ain't nothin' we can do about
it—though I hear enough ignorant black folk says they got *squatter's*
rights here. Ain't got no rights. Not 'til you owns what you's standin'
on. And we ain't ownin' nothin' a this. Never a day.

So, he thought now, who's she?—who the fuck is she, sayin' he's got
to turn things around and take responsibility for his life and control it
and make it good when she says she can't control a thing? When she
says *THEY* tell her she can't stay here no more, and *THEY* gon' tell her
where she goes, and when she goes, and ain't nothin' she can do about
it, and better grab her her Section-8 and go on off now, 'cause *THEY*

WHAT CAN I GET STARTED FOR YA?

gon' renege that too, quick enough. Then she changes up and bows
her head down and starts cryin' all hard. Cryin', shakin' her head and
sayin' she can't control nothin' in her life. And then she looks up at him
with all the tears all over her face, and she says why he cain't do nothin'? Handsome, beautiful boy, she says, cryin' so hard. Most beautiful
strong man. Smartest she's ever seen, words, numbers, even though
he ain't been to no school but gotdamn Division St. since the day
his mama pass. Cain't he help her some way, 'sides with them strong-
armin', thievin' gangsta thugs and they so-called taxes, just 'cause she
help some girls look pretty sometimes? Cain't he help her some better
way'n that? Some good way at las'?

But then she stopped. She put her face down once more in her hands
and all quiet-like into her hands she said, "Watt." Then nothin', just
silence, a long time. Then all hella hard she wiped her face and she
looked up, hard. "I know why they call you *Watt*, motherfucker," she
said. "Call you that so long don't nobody know your real name. Call
you that 'cause when you don't come to me and you livin' in crack
rooms and sleepin' in piss-pool stairwells with dopin' hos and they
scrufty-ass drunk pimps, night after night, you wake up mornin' after
mornin', when you's a kid, and, just like them thugs tell you to, you
take your broomstick and you bust out light after light, all up and
down everwhere, so don't nobody have no peace, and don't never no
po-lices come, or the outside worl'. *Watt,* be short for Hundred Watt,
I know all 'bout that—'cause you done bust more light bulbs than any
a them ignorant fools who be makin' the life a good peoples here
hell on earth. And truth, truth, truth, motherfucker: all that you is, is
darkness."

WE DO

Tumbler, steering clear of the VL's 364, headed toward what was now a safe route out on Orleans—'cause with the Cobras' Rock all demo'ed down, Orleans was GD-safe. He had just passed under old St. Dominic's, the huge, long-ago boarded-up Italian church, which still stood in the middle of the Greens—the big empty place, now mostly a bat house, that his mama said got left behind when the Italians moved out 'cause too many blacks had moved up from the South. Mother Cabrini was a nun who worked here with the Italians, tryin' to help make peace when they called this place "Little Hell" and, right where Dantrell got shot, it was called "Death Corner", 'cause more Italians killed Italians than blacks are now killin' blacks. Turf fightin'. And then retaliations. Street justice, then and now, white same as black.

They called him Tumbler because, for the four years he was with 'em, he was the number-one best of the famed Jesse White Tumblers. Wasn't anything he couldn't do. The real showpiece boy, flyin' sky high everywhere they went. And he'd been a lotta places with Mr. Jesse, not like most Cabrini boys, who some of 'em had never even been

WE DO

downtown in Chicago, though they lived a mile and a half from it all their lives. All over the country he went for the NBA, NFL, and college games—and one time to Tokyo, Japan—because Mr. Jesse got that done, too, believin' it would make his young men think big all their lives, fillin' their hearts with dreams. And now Mr. White's become Secretary of State, even though he grew up with nothin', just like the rest of them, right down here on Division St. His mama told him to mark that down, so he would always know what was possible. But it had been three years now since he tumbled with Mr. Jesse's team, and his horizons had been shrinkin' for a long time—so he'd gone Folks now, and lately he'd smoked a little rock and had sold some too, to get himself a little more, out front of Camp Ball—not down the Rows, where his mama's place was.

Camp Ball's where he met Watt, who fixed him up, and then got him up with a sweet, sweet lady too, one of the gentleman's club girls from over at V.I.P.'s who work for Watt. Not soon to be forgotten, that evening with Sara Lee! Not soon at all. And some other evenings, too, my brotha. And for other reasons besides, he and Watt now were gone deep with their thing. Watt got him, too, to cut out all that crack smokin', 'fore he ever really got started, 'cause he was gonna be needin' his brains, for all the big things ahead. Got us a future, my brotha Tumbler, Watt said; build us a kingdom 'fore we die! Mr. Jesse always made sure his tumblers stayed in school and kept up their grades. So there he was, just about the last of the boys to stick it out at school, graduating from Wells—doin' that for his mama. Education, she said every day he could recall, is the only way out. Hadn't gotten him out, though, or proved much use. But now he was gonna use that education, all right—just not for things his mama needed to know.

Not tall or heavy, rather lithe, athletic, and light as a dancer in his Air-J's, baggy pants hanging low, Tumbler came out onto busy Orleans, his black White Sox cap turned backward and the collar of his silver and royal-blue Wells track-team jacket turned up just right—the left wing of the W on its breast an eagle's wing. He turned north up Orleans toward Division, heading toward the sidewalk shadow of Camp Ball as it fell over St. Luke's Church of God in Christ.

These boys have *good* minds, *good* hearts, *good* souls, he could hear Mr. Jesse say—but they need to know it—they need examples to show it. Their mothers they might see, but not their fathers. So I want to be there—to show them. Because what these black boys do see is hopeless

9

DIVISION

black men and defeated, black men gone wrong, or just gone. Gone so they can't ever be seen—to prison, or death, or drugs, or to just plain nowhere (that just plain nowhere, Tumbler thought, that his own father disappeared to so long back he couldn't picture the man). And just as gone is *respect*. It's not enough to show a boy an example, to let him see what he can be. He's got to respect what he sees. Look at is one thing. Look up to is another.

The MB Union, his mama's church (and his, too, though he'd had to repaint in his mind the face of Jesus), was just past the Church of God in Christ; and the MB Union too, along with St. Matthew's United Methodist, the third church of three in a row here—all these three churches standing together on Orleans, Locust to just north of Oak— fell now under that wide late-afternoon shadow of towering Camp Ball. And now, as Tumbler came up Orleans toward Oak, at the same time, coming out from "the Camp," 'tween the MB and St. Matthew's, were some ten gangin' shorties, half of 'em sportin' the dark blue bandana. Most crazy-dangerous, war-startin' motherfuckers on God's earth; but he knew all these young Folkin' homeboys now, and they knew him. So if there was the fork thrown up from two or three, as they nodded at him in silence, it was just S'up Tumbler, Hey yo, S'ahright, yeah, S'ahright, Tumbler—comin' from the rest—and S'ahright, my young brothas, comin' back at them all from the nodding Tumbler—as he continued north, crossing Oak, and they then all turned as one and swung south. *Respect.* True and deep. Kneel-down-and-bow-your-head deep. He thought how all these young ruthless motherfuckers showed it to Watt, like religion all right—and the respect of these dangerous-ass Disciple foot soldiers was deeper than any he'd known as a Jesse White Tumbler, no matter how far away it was from Cabrini Green to Tokyo, Japan.

His mama told him who the nun Cabrini was. She said to him, you learn the names. You learn who Mr. Jenner was, who they named the school after, 'cause he cured diseases kill more peoples than guns do, small pox, so bad, which this city had back in the day. And Mr. Schiller, they name the other school and the street after, he's a poet who wrote things for the human soul. Mr. Seward and Mr. Stanton, they name the parks down here after, worked for Mr. Abraham Lincoln. These streets are livin' with all that hist'ry, so important to black peoples, mens fightin' and dyin' for freedom and equality, black mens in the fight too, instead of mens killin' each other, like nowadays, for the

WE DO

blood money and the drugs. You learn Mr. Byrd he flew over the North Pole—and whenever you walk down here you fly up in your mind, 'cause those names make you think it. Don't you walk these streets a blind man. You learn sister Sojourner Truth, who they name that other school after, out by Stanton Park. Sister *Truth,* she's a slave up north, 'fore abolition, 'cause they had slaves up north s'well as south, and maybe still do, I'd say. And she fought for freedom and for rights of womens, too—'cause she's a black slave woman and she knows what it means to have no rights a'tall in this tearful world. Fought capital punishment, too, and *all* killin'. She said she hated white peoples 'til she found her master in the white man Jesus, which changed Sister Truth and set her walking in the Lord, like Dr. King, who couldn't of been what he was if he thought there's just this world.

And don't you ever walk past St. Matthew's, Marcus Sabbs, out t'Orleans, without thinkin' how your mama stood right there when Dr. King came and twenty-five thousand peoples stood there and then went with him to Soldiers Field, when he talked about fair housin' and the right to live where anyone else had a right to live, no borderlines anywhere—but about how the CHA's build up the high-rises 'cause they don't want black peoples movin' outwards, into the white territories. So they put all the black peoples up the sky 'til it all would come crashin' down like Babel Tower, which we see here every day. Dr. King—even with bad mens' guns pointed on his heart *all* the time—he preached non-violence—so good a man, a true man of Jesus, with the courage and the faith, and the love for his enemies—and forgiveness; and he got more done than anyone ever did who carried a gun and has no forgiveness. Worse thing they ever did when they killed that man. But you stop every time, Marcus, and you think of him when you pass by St. Matthew's. You stop on those streets there, and you give that place Dr. King's name, every time you pass. And you hear him in your mind, and you listen to him with your soul. And then you know the way. Not like the ones who got so *bad,* bad as the man who killed him, that Earl Ray, and out of retaliation they just tore this place up after Dr. King died and brought on the National Guards and the tanks, with mens firing guns down on those army mens right out the high-rise buildings. And then all the stores leaving. Del Farms. Pioneers. And all the hope leaving. And they're thinkin' then black peoples' just animals, fit for cages. Been crazy down here ever since, and gunfire still comin' down out these buildings. Even with so many peoples gone

11

away from these projects, we can still see it nights, and hear it roarin', just like hell's own Independence Day. And it breaks my heart *so* bad t'see what was so beautiful in the beginnin'—like heaven on earth after what we's use to—now's all so long-gone filthy.

Tumbler did his duty by his mama—now taking a pause, and reciting, but in a kind of mental slurring together, as if he were quick-mumbling an automatic prayer, a few familiar phrases of Dr. King's about justice and equality, at the corner of Oak and Orleans—same words he'd said every day all those years he'd gone to school to the Catholics across the street at St. Joseph's, where his mama (with help from her brother Maurice, who'd made good money as an undertaker and was a good, kind man) had sent him to school, hoping, she said, to save his life. Tumbler'd stayed at St. Joseph's 'til he'd been worked on enough by a few last school-goin' friends in the Rows who'd gotten him to transfer from the Catholics to Wells, some three years back now, when he's sixteen. It'd about broken his mama's heart when he switched (she havin' seen none of her first four finish school or come to much good—Johnnie B already dead, and his three sisters now all long gone off to California and not much heard from since, except when Tina needed money for a lawyer), and he wondered now, if he'd stayed at St. Joe's, would he be headin' where he was headed this evening?—to hang with Watt.

Tonight, Watt said, he'd tell him how they'd be taking over Camp Ball in the upcomin' time—said he'd be layin' out for him his grand plan for fillin' the power vacuum. The power vacuum, Watt said, was spreadin' everywhere in GD nation, which he said was breakin' up block by block, building by building, every main playa now playin' for himself, since they long-term RICO-ed those thirty-eight execs back three years now, super-maxing, too, Chairman Hoover himself. Ain't no phone calls, Watt said, comin' out that Rocky Mountain Alcatraz. And Watt'd made clear what power he's relying on in himself. It's only one way to come out on top in this dangerous motherfucker of a world, he said: and that's not fearin' whether or not you leave it. And that day, back two weeks now, with all the homies old and young just standing around in the lobby of Camp Ball, next all the dangling, broken up mail boxes, some just drinkin' wine, some smokin' weed and waitin' on custom, the "S" boys all gone lazy pitchin' nickels up to cracks in that piss-smellin' concrete lobby floor—out the eyes in the back of his head, Watt sees a car rollin' slow into the Camp lot. He caught it movin' in past the old Buick Riviera that for years had stood

WE DO

cockeyed there on three rusted hubs, its shit-filthy vinyl top all peeled up like some skin disease and its windows all gunned out long ago. It was a chromed-up Lincoln Town Car, silver-gray with shining spoked wheels, comin' slow and dramatic round that old rust-bucket Riviera. And it was carryin', Watt could see, a full-up carload of OG Cobras. Truly ruthless, murderin', stick-hot-nails-up-your-dick motherfuckers —who'd been thinkin', word was, that they just might make some headway into the Camp, seein' how they just lost the Rock, their home base for near thirty years.

It had been his conversion, Tumbler was feeling—full conversion right then, and *forever* ('less Watt's action was just about suicide?)— when right before his eyes it's Watt, sayin', all calm, 'Scuse me, my brothas, and then reachin' in for the pump-action sawed-off they kept inside the broken-down elevator door, and walkin' out the lobby into the lot with those Cobras comin'. Everybody else was now turning and looking and then was taking a knee, prayin' all right, but mostly, Tumbler knew, getting ready to hit that floor and piss a little more stink into the cracks. But Watt just went out there, holding the sawed-off across his waist. And sure as hell fearless, it must be, as some black Jesus on the stormin' waves—he stood in front of that car and stopped it. He took the short double barrel of the sawed-off in his left hand, gripping the pump handle, and then set his trigger finger round the front trigger—and spread and braced his legs. Then calm as hell he asked those murderin' motherfuckers if any of 'em was as unafraid of dyin' as he was. Or if any of 'em was to live, if they thought they'd come out alive next time they came this way. *That* was seein' something, Tumbler was sure—an example, all right, of somethin' he'd never in his life seen. And he could think that not even God would disrespect him if he hung with Watt, no more than those Cobras, who drove out a whole lot faster than they drove in, and hadn't been back since—would be disrespectin' Watt.

As he walked past the Seward Park field house, across from the drunk shelter, used to be something else—that big old building that had "Divine Providence" carved in stone across its top—Tumbler, suddenly feeling heavier on his light feet, was looking ahead at the new condos they put up where Carson Field used to be—but where white people lived now, right on Division, *west* side of the "L." And beneath and beyond the tracks, just this side of Sammy's Red Hots, he saw the new library, which they built now that white people were comin' in. And

13

he thought of the new police station they were puttin' up over on Lar-
rabee, which they needed long time ago, but now that white people
were comin', they were building fast as could be. He saw white people on bicycles and white people walkin' in Seward Park, which was
all fixed up now, but not for black people. It mixed him up, because
he'd known good white people at St. Joe's, he could admit, but mostly
it all just made him angrier than burnin' fire—even if he thought this
place might become more beautiful now, and safer, and stores were
comin' back—'cause he wasn't any white person, which is also why he
left St. Joe's for Wells. Money, Watt said, is the only place it's at. And
there's only one way to it for a black man, which ain't gon' be through
your mama's Jesus. You feelin' me, my little brotha? That's the world
we're livin' in. Truth.

St. Joseph—he ain't the same as St. Charles, is he? Watt laughed
when he said this. But he didn't laugh when he said St. Charles had
been his school, all right—though he wore a hard kind of grin when he
started thinking about how he'd gotten there. That Juvy judge he knew
me so well, every time I come up to 1100 S. Hamilton to say hello, sir,
he jus' says back, "Where's your grandmother, son?" And the mitigation man he says, one more time, she's indisposed, your honor. And the
judge he says, "What else is new!" And 'course he tells me I got to go
to school, all those times near after my mama died. And the next time
I'm up, the mitigation man says, he's goin' to school, your honor. And
the judge he about laughed, 'cause he says, "Going to school, indeed,
but with a loaded .38 in his jacket!" But the las' time, it's about eleven
times of broken probation by now, and two, three times out to Hart-
grave for checkin' out my mind, after he ax that same question 'bout
my fucked-up, indisposed ol' ho of a grandmamma (she says she's too
scared to get down all those flights a stairs in Tha Jube without an elevator, but she's just too morbid fat)—and he gets the same ol' answer,
'bout where she is and where she isn't, he jus shakes his head and he
says, "It's over, son, too many violations, too many broken promises,
and now with you riding one more time in a stolen vehicle, this time
after sitting lookout in a robbery. It's over. It's St. Charles." And he
tells me then the sentence it's indeterminate. Nine months out there
and the rest is up to me. Depends on my behavior. Took me eighteen
to get out, 'cause I was learnin' out there what it really means, down
the last place in your gut, to represent your side 'gin th'other—which
understandin', my brotha Tumbler, I took with me for those full two

at Stateville. B. O. S., Brothas of the Struggle—out t' Joliet you learn deeper'n your life what that means. And what GD means. And you learn the *book,* harder'n you gon' learn books at St. Joseph.

When Watt told him about gang taxes—on stairwell squatters, on crack heads usin' crack rooms, on all the hos regular and visitin', on all the hustlers hustlin' whatever—from candy store hustles and handy-man repairs and car wash work and hairstylin' work—and then on all the booster sales of everything from pants suits to pampers—and on and on—and then about the drug trade, from wholesale buyin' to street retailin'—he showed Tumbler a mind for numbers like Tumbler had never seen before. Past the speed of lightning, Watt could figure per-cents on a number, but more than that, he could tell you what percent of one number another one was and what number it would take to make the same percent of any other number, pull it right out of the sky fast as you like. And now Tumbler smiled with admiration, too, thinkin' about the three or four times he'd sat at a poker table with Watt and seen him all night long just be the king—laughin' at his fools. Money, Tumbler, my man, Watt said—if you gon' make it grow, you got t'know how it come and how it go. And you, brotha T, gon' be the one who keeps track of it for me on a computer and prints it out, so I can know jus' where and when to apply the right amount of *presh*-a. And you ain't, my little brotha, ever gon' have to be somethin' you ain't—which means you ain't even gon' have to *see* any violations handed out, to say nothin' of handin' any out yourself—no bloodshed witnessin' for you. And you listen up now—this thing we're sellin', it's no different than alcohol: there's them that knows how to use it for recreation and relaxation and there's them ain't got enough sense to know when to stop, just like drunks. But it ain't legal, what we're sellin'. So *we're* the law regulates it. And I don't want you pretendin', ever one time, 'bout you don' know how bein' the law it takes bloodshed. No actin' like you ain't heard about that. No innocent bystandin'. You hearin' me? Else you're shit-phony and you ain't my man.

Watt had taken him to the top of Camp Ball, to an abandoned floor of vacant apartments, everywhere GD graffiti-scrawled, passages punched out between all the apartments for rapid movement—just in case, Watt said, any fool five-o's brought a ram to a door, or mother-fuckin' VL's were tryin' to pin down a sniper. Standing before a black-charred wall and at a broken-out window that looked on the whole huge city of white Chicago money beyond, the John Hancock rising up behind him, Watt, turning his back to the window, looked Tumbler hard in the eye. Watt crossed his arms and with his hands took his t-shirt and stripped the dark blue shirt off, showing a thick, hard body even more powerful than Tumbler's own was beautiful. Then Tumbler saw it all. Beneath the double forks across Watt's neck was a six-point star with wings coming out each side and in the star's center the bold letters V L K. And cut across rippling stomach muscle, beneath the "shine of the six," there was a full sneering devil's face, with the words MONEY MACK MURDER written across its forehead. Watt now touched his two middle fingers together before his chest and then slowly brought his two palms down over his chest and then over his stomach as he said in a cold flat voice, "All this rightyeah—it's the law." Then he took his right pointer finger, and not ever looking down at his chest, but still staring Tumbler hard in the eye, he began to go slowly round that six-point star, saying as he touched each new point, a different word: Love, Life, Loyalty, Wisdom, Understanding, Knowledge. Watt stopped then, waited a moment; then he reached out his hands and touched Tumbler's two shoulders and with no pull, just a kind of silent magic, sat him down on the bare floor. Then, saying nothing, Watt sat down himself cross-legged before Tumbler, and he pointed, still staring hard at Tumbler, to those letters V L K in the center of the six-point star. At last he said, "I want you to tell me now out loud, clear, and slow, what those letters stand for—because you know. And you make it like you're performin' hard on the trigger yourself with each word you say."

Yes. Tumbler knew. And it all now was like that first night with Sara Lee, half white, half black, all beautiful, face and body past heaven, handing him the reefer they shared—for he felt the hot spell of a sex thrill come over him when he said, slow and clear as he was told, imagining he was pulling his finger, first degree, three times on the trigger of a gun: "VICE LORD KILLER." "Good," Watt said. "Good. Jus' so you know it real clear, brotha Tumbler. Six, no love for five. No changin', *ever,* what you are, and what you aren't. And jus' so you know clear how the law—it sometimes has to hand out the maximum: full-out capital punishment."

Not then into the business book—but into the *book,* the Bible of the Disciples, old testament as well as the King's New Concept, Growth and Development, little brotha, that's what GD stands for now—Watt took Tumbler step by step. Repeat after me, he said: "The night I was

WE DO

born Folks was the night I died." And Tumbler, with a rush again of a sex thrill, as if he were touching his mouth to the soft-lipped mouth of Sara Lee, tasting her glistening lipstick, warm, and wet, did it, as told. Then again, after Watt, "As my brethren cast my body into the lake of Fire and Knowledge, I was baptized." And then again, "With a Pitchfork in my hand and a Six on my chest." And finally, even slowing and deepening his voice as Watt had his, "Others will speak my name and know the name of Death." Then, after a silence, Watt closed his eyes and spoke out by himself what he told Tumbler was the Pledge of the Disciple, come from the King. And he sounded like he'd gone to a white man's college, or like any time he wanted to, he could talk any way he wanted to: "I am the courage that creates resolution in man. I am the source that provokes originality of thought. I am the hand that moves man's hands. I am Gangster Everlasting! I am the Gangster that creeps in the night to do the work of many. In fear of me they will travel to places of worship to condemn me or places of vice to submit to my will. The woman who prays in the silence of the night to keep me from her bed is like the whore who invites me to her chamber! I am Gangster Everlasting! I am the heart of evil; I am the father and mother of all sin. I am Gangster Everlasting and Forevermore!"

All for one, and one for all. But it's all gone, brotha Tumbler, Watt said now. The King he's gone to Colorado, and ain't nobody settin' the rules any more. The King is dead, long live the king. But who's the one? Who's gon' set the rules? Muscles now rippling as he gathered himself, Watt stood up from the floor, and, still shirtless, in all his black power, he turned to the window, "Tell you what," he said, "ain't gon' be some pussy-shit *askin'* what's right and what's wrong. It's gon' be somebody who *says* it, right out his own mind!" He looked out then on the white man's Gold Coast, from his burned-out hole up top of Camp Ball, and he said, "Money. Ain't gon' be any growth and development, my brotha, without it." Then, once more in that different voice, from the King's book: "Knowledge. It is making us see what our natural enemy has always had in store for us. And it's not Freedom, Justice and Equality. It's now as it's always been, Slavery, Suffering, and Death!"

Tumbler had said fuck the Don't Walk signal at Orleans and Division and had just walked out. "You could get killed doin' that, buddy!" —he'd heard a voice shout out the window of a car he'd held up. But he took his time, thank you, motherfucker. And on the north side of Division, walking past those new, white-folks condos, he'd fixed his

17

face, and his walk, and, though he wore no nation colors (for the blue of his track-team jacket would be no blue in a GD's eyes), he'd put his mind on representin'. And now turning up Clybourn, he could see, in the window of Starbucks, tilting back a coffee for a last sip, Watt.

As Tumbler came up, their eyes met, and they each grinned and nodded. Tumbler pumped his fist, and Watt, still nodding but now turning down his mouth, tapped the bottom of his cup, two, three times on the table—then he left the empty there as he rose. But now through the window he signaled to Tumbler with his hand, flipping it back, directing Tumbler to come in, which Tumbler did, catching then the reflection of his own face and his Sox cap as he pulled on the suck of the insulated glass door. When Tumbler passed into the shop, Watt said nothing— but then, for some reason, he flipped his hand back again, signaling for Tumbler to come forward. And then in a way that left Tumbler confused, and which Watt would never explain, Watt took him up to the counter, where there was this white chick workin'. She had real white skin and real dark hair, with purple mixed in it. Maybe she was pretty, but she was kinda funky lookin', with that white skin and black-purple hair. But now gettin' Tumbler in on something he never once would understand, Watt put his arm around Tumbler's shoulder, and standing there together with his little brotha, Watt looked cold at that funky, pretty white girl, and he just said, outa nowhere, "We do."

A CATHOLIC FAMILY

"What say, Con, we get the hell outa here!" Jack Riordan, handsome, tight-end big, and tall, black-haired, dark-browed, his dark-Irish cheeks always tan-colored, now flushed—was home from Holy Cross for spring break. He'd been shaking his head and squeezing a fist, all the way from the front room of the Riordans' Lincoln Park West brownstone, where he'd been with his father, whom right now he really couldn't take, and his mother—through the long, coffered-ceilinged, chandeliered dining room and on back to the kitchen. Under the variously angled beams of a five-fixtured track light, his younger brother sat at the black-walnut kitchen table—Jane Longden—its surface a sculpted kidney shape, with an apron-inlay of blonde teak defining its elegant form. The table, soft-glowing in the dimmered light, was their mother's latest gift to herself (for she'd won three multi-million dollar cases in eighteen months for Lucas and Winston)—and a last touch to her new, high-end designer kitchen. De Giulio. Connor had been bent over his father's copy of *Adam Bede*—its margins marked thick with professor's notes, which jottings Con had been turning the book to follow. Connor Riordan was tall, too, but

19

DIVISION

slighter of build than his brother, and more fair-skinned, but with even deeper blue eyes. His hair looser-cut, blonde-brown, he was handsome in his mother's way, while Jack had all his father's dark-browed, dark-haired features. Connor was home for his ten-day break from Cal Berkeley—where, following in Tom Riordan's footsteps, he was majoring in English and American lit—and getting himself noticed, his father had been told—by the likes of Cavalieri, Harper, others too. He'd looked up when Jack, still squeezing his fist, passed through the columned lintel into the kitchen; and, though Con could see that some kind of thing must just have happened out in the front room, he snapped his father's book shut. "Hell yeah," he said; for he loved it when Jacko was fired up. The guy's life was just *big*—and Con loved getting swept up, too, in the energy, no matter where it might take things, or almost no matter where—for there were times, with the women.... Insane. But maybe tonight it would be just plain awesome, maybe crawlin' the bars on East Division.

"Fuckin' A," Jack said, as he strapped an arm around his brother's shoulder; for it had forever been a pure *back at ya* when it came to their love. But, as the Riordan boys made ready to march on out of their Lincoln Park back door into that big city night, the throb of which they could feel every time after sundown when they looked south along the opening given by the old-bricked alley behind the house to the huge, hovering Chicago skyline, with its lights shining—they heard a sound behind them. Separating before the door—they turned round. Their mother, in her suit still from work, soft gray, with a cream-colored blouse and a necklace of braided gold, stood in the passage between the kitchen and dining room. Yet so strange, Connor thought—the way she looked—all pale, like a beautiful ghost, but with her eyeliner oddly darkened. Jacqueline Riordan, Jackie—and it had been said of her that, in her high-cheek-boned beauty, she was like a lighter-haired version of Mrs. Kennedy-Onassis—was strangely just *there*, too, not saying a word. She stood against one of the burnished-brown columns, and—so weird, Con found it—the way she now touched, as if in some kind of need (she'd never showed need in her life!) and then held the fluted column, her left hand in front, which displayed her wedding rings. Like some mysterious, challenging portrait meant to suggest personality's unknown depths, this picture of her seemed made for some kind of never-ending preservation—framed the way it was by the lintel, against the backdrop receding through the rooms to where his father sat, be-

20

A CATHOLIC FAMILY

fore the front window, his head half turned. And for certain it would stick with Connor, this picture, for long nights and days to come. So clearly he would remember how his mother wore a strange look of what he could see was some kind of grieving sympathy. And how she—the famed hard litigator, sharp, tough, never once by Connor seen crying— looked like she might break into tears. And how she set her eyes not on him but only on his brother. So bewildering, too, how Jack wrapped him under his arm again then and just swept him out the backdoor, like they were right back on track for a big night—everything just fine. And like their mother hadn't been there, looking at Jack with that look —and about to break down and cry!

Behind the Riordans', a gravel path led through a spot-lighted ever-green garden back to an iron gate that opened to their three-car parking pad, set on the bricked alley that separated the backs of the homes on Lincoln Park West from the backs of those on North Orleans. But not two steps along the night-lighted path, Connor said, "Excuse me, Jacko, but what in *the* fuck was *that?*"

Jack, walking ahead, didn't look back. He just said, "Nothing. *Nothin'.*" But after a few more steps, he slowed. Then, "Just the old man preaching away on the full-out Catholic thing, like he never walked a *step* in anybody else's moccasins." Then nothing more 'til he came to the gate. But as he lifted and pulled back the bolt, he turned round. "Murder, he calls it. We're talking about abortion—don't ask me why. And he has to call it *murder.* I say I have friends that I know, girls that I know— and so maybe he could use another word." He pulled the heavy, self-closing iron gate open and, as he walked through, swung it back so Con could get hold of it. "But, even after I tell him that!—after I do everything but name names—of people *he* knows too—all he says is 'Circumlocution, euphemism—finding other words for things! Pro-*choice,*' he says, 'that term might represent the single greatest exercise in indirection in the history of goddamned mankind. I'm serious,' he says, '—the single greatest, and most cynically calculated.'" And now Jack imitated Tom Riordan's voice in a mocking tone that rose to a bitter pitch. "'And if we weren't afraid to use *real* words,' he says, 'and never used convenient evasions—I'll tell you what—you might not know people and you might not have friends who'd had abortions. And maybe we'd find ourselves at the *real* heart of ethics!' Christ almighty! I had to get out. The real heart of ethics. *Real* words."

Connor stood still in the gateway, holding the gate back against its

21

spring. And all along he'd been thinking okay—this is *very* fucked up now because here's my own brother—and on top of it with some bitter-as-shit sarcasm—sounding like it's not the case that all the Riordans have always been pro-life! Without a single day's exception! And he was thinking no the hell wonder his father was goin' full-out nuts as he—who'd kept the faith even at Berkeley—was blown away himself by Jack's position, which was sure as hell *new*. And he wanted to stop his brother's mouth and say—So what are you saying? that you've had your conversion experience! And maybe to throw in that hadn't they more than once agreed that the particular conversion in question was as big a moral alteration as maybe the world had ever known—though so many of even their Catholic friends had just walked over to the other side like it was no more than crossing the street? But pressing even harder on his now fully messed-up mind, and making him really lose it—was this thing with their mother, whom Jack had still not even mentioned. This—all of it now—was disturbing him with some dim and yet already live suspicion. And anger. So as he released the gate and heard it click itself fixed behind him, he crossed over the car pad's empty third space right up to Jack, who, in the evening darkness, which was lighted here by the alley lamp, his head bowed, arms folded over his chest, was leaning his big frame against their mother's new silver-gray Mercedes S, parked this side of the old man's '89 Audi.

"Okay," Connor said, "what you're saying is freakin' me out bad enough—as you know! And I find it hard to believe that you're pissed about what Dad was saying, given what you've said yourself a million times. And what's with that weird-as-hell shit with Mom? Honest to God, Jack, I feel like my life is about to change but for reasons other people know and I don't. So I'm pissed as shit as well as goddamned bewildered. And I mean what *was* that, with Mom?!" But more than with questions, Connor's mind was alive with the first movements of a suspicious conception, which he wanted to abort sure as hell, before it ever came out, but which he also wanted to see fully born.

Jack had kept his head bowed and had said nothing, which only angered Connor more. And now still saying nothing, Jack unfolded his arms and dug into his jeans' pocket and got out his keys. Still he kept silent, but maybe *because* now his silence would cause the explosion that would bring everything out—the explosion that he knew he'd already sparked the fuse for. And hell if he didn't *want* it to happen— Yes! And for what? His freedom from living a lie? YES!—he wanted

A CATHOLIC FAMILY

to bring things to the full breaking point—to the point of revelation, and *liberation*. And he could see how his brother was getting angrier every second that he put him off, which he now kept on doing as he pressed the car key, one time, to open the driver's-side door. But as he got in and sat, and Con then came hard round to the other door and started rapping on the glass, and then slapping it, Jack thought—suddenly struggling, as an intense guilt awakened in him, and divided him—about what all his brother did not know about his father, his mother, and now him—and a certain girl. And he wondered now why in *hell* he'd raised things up to this heat and if he shouldn't—if at this point he even could—try to cool things off, with some kind of evasion. He lifted his hand to his door-handle panel and clicked open the passenger-side door.

"Fuck you!" Con said, as he got in and slammed the door, his mind now racing, rapidly constructing things, pushing buttons no matter how dangerous. "What do you know that I don't? This isn't about the word *murder*. You've used that word yourself, for Christ sake. And not just about late-term, or partial birth. *Double murder* I've heard you call it, JACK, when a woman gets murdered when she's carrying a child. And don't deny, either, that you've used the term *murder* talking about the basic run-of-the-mill abortion! And don't try to tell me that that look on Mom's face and that weird-as-hell shit with her standing there —the killer lawyer—looking like a fucking specter with a broken heart was about Dad's using the word *murder,* as if she'd never heard him use it before. Fuck you, if you treat me like some puppy and try to put me off."

"All right!" Jack said, impelled to go on—if also knowing that what he was doing would begin something, and end something forever, with his brother, the brother he loved. And because, too, the smoke from Connor's sacrifice had always risen heavenward? But to hell with it, he took the knife to his brother's heart, though he never looked at him, just stared ahead. "All right, little brother! I'm sure something you've never known—is *this:* Mom and Dad got married because they had to —because Mom got knocked up."

And indeed Connor felt this as a shocking wound, for he had never suspected anything like this, now, or ever in his life. But he hated, too, *hated,* that it was his brother telling him—that his brother somehow knew about this and he didn't.

"She wasn't in high school. She was twenty-two. So it wasn't that hard

23

DIVISION

to hide, especially because they were in California at the time and they were able to just lie about when it was that they actually got married —so there'd be no knowing that little me came into this beautiful world some seven months after the real marriage date."

Jesus *Christ!* Connor kept thinking—how in hell does this guy know all this—and I don't? But he knew, he dead knew, that the answer lay in that look that his mother gave only Jack, in the kitchen. And somehow, as his mind shot to a night when Jack stranded him at Butch McGuire's, leaving with some girls, particularly one.... Fuck life! and all worst possibilities...he had some dark prophetic sense of exactly what beast it was that slouched toward Bethlehem to be born.

And now Jack, still impelled, "But Mom told me she has *never* been able to get past the feelings that come with being forced into marriage. And she is not happy! Ya glad to hear that, too? Are ya?" Jack knew he had his little brother in the dust, and bleeding. But he kept on, feeling he was getting himself free, bringing things out of hiding—if at the expense of something like Connor's soul's life—and so he also despised himself. "She says she can't even remember when she was happy! She resents her marriage! Deeply, she says! Because she was *forced* into it. And she's thinking about making a change now, while she still has a chance! Do ya hear me? And she changed her views on abortion—yes —*abortion!*—years ago! She's only quiet about it to keep the peace, but she's more and more not even giving a damn about that!"

Connor, his face contorted in pain, had begun shaking his head back and forth—as it all was coming clearer and clearer to him—for he was no sorry fool—about Jack—and his mother, who had already become to him this whole new person, and a dangerous total stranger, whom his brother knew all about. And there was more—he *knew.* More than just these deadly, heartbreaking things about his mother, which he had not at all foreseen. There would be other things, which he felt he had a sick but real clairvoyance of—things that would be as crushing to him as the revelations about his mother, and that he was becoming sure were *connected* to those deadly, life-changing revelations. He was saying low, "Fuck you," over and over, chanting, "Fuck you and fuck her and fuck everybody...." And now, "GOD DAMN YOU! Exactly *when* and exactly *WHY* did she tell *any* of this to *YOU!* Don't lie to me! Tell me why she told you this shit! Why did you even have this conversation? I'm already guessing, real clear—so don't lie!"

Jack still didn't look at his brother. He just grabbed the steering wheel

24

with both hands and squeezed it tight. He said, "Okay, you wanna know so bad, little boy—I GOT SOMEBODY PREGNANT—which I'm sure is what you've guessed. And Mom overheard me talking to her. And she helped me. She helped me make the choice. Helped us make it. And she paid for it, Connor, because she *wanted* to!"

"You tell me *this*," Connor said, almost breathless in his pain, for this emphatic involvement of his mother he had also not foreseen, "did she think to mention, as she helped you *choose,* and as she *paid* for it, because she *wanted* to, that, if she'd made the same choice herself, the one person who would not be here now to make his own choices, and to live his *life,* would be you! Did she notice *that* little irony? And what does she mean—*making a change while life still offers her the chance?* Is she fucking someone behind Dad's back? Christ all fucking mighty! Did she share *that* with you? And seeing how you're telling me everything there is, and that you're glad to do so, why not go ahead and tell me WHO IT IS you helped make the *choice?*"

Furious too, wanting now not to protect his brother but to kill him— which the things he was about to say *would do*—Jack let go the steering wheel and began to pound on it hard with his fists. "Yes!" he said, "She's found someone! She doesn't know that I know. But I do. I guessed it. And then I saw her with him, sitting in that park near her office—and then the two of them leaving together, in this car. I don't know him. But I've heard her, too, on the phone with him. So are you happy now? And since you wanna know also, SO FUCKING BAD, the girl is Ellie Shea! So now you know that, too! And are ya happy?"

"Oh, Christ," Connor said, and, as he buried his face in his hands, "I knew it. I knew it. Shit on this earth! I *knew* it!" Then, "God Jesus, Jack, I want to kill you. I want to *kill* you!" That is what he said, even as he thought, too, thank God Ellie didn't have his child. Thank God for that.

Tom Riordan had waited some minutes after his sons were gone—before making his way back to the kitchen, where his wife now sat at the table, under the softened light, resting her cheek in her right hand as with her ringed left she tapped listlessly on the shut cover of her husband's *Adam Bede.* When he pulled back a felt-padded chair on the hardwood floor, stained in golden mahogany, and he sat down next to her, she didn't look up. "He knows," he said, "he *knows* what a betrayal I would find it if he changed his mind on a principle that he *knows* I put at the center of the moral world—and yet he expects *me* to use delicate language! And do you know what else he knows! He knows that if I use the strongest language in the condemnation of what abortion really is that I do *not* condemn the woman who has had one—that I do *not* find a complete condemnation of the sin and a complete love for and forgiveness of the sinner to be a contradiction, *at all!* He acts as if I don't know that in every room I walk into there could be a woman with a secret—and that she could be a woman whom I've known and loved for years. And does he think I don't utterly forgive that woman, as I pray she forgives herself? Or that I would stop loving her? Honest to God! And do you know what *else,* Jackie? I really would not mind it if you looked the hell up and maybe at least pretended that someone was sitting next to you and expressing feelings that go deep as his life!"

Jackie lifted her cheek from her right hand and looked up. She set her right hand then over her left, which she kept on the book—and so stopped tapping the book. But still she said nothing. And still Tom was angry, and getting angrier, at her—and at everything. "How many times have I said it? The deep and real contradiction lies right at the heart of this goddammed schizoid country." But he'd indeed said just these same words, in the front room, with Jack—which Jackie as much as said to him, by still keeping silent—and by, once more now, lowering her eyes. Tom wanted just to walk off. He pushed back his chair, yet remained at the table. But he couldn't help it. Angry, not speaking any more now himself, just staring out at nothing, he still kept hard within his mental groove. This damned schizoid, split-headed country. Right wingers, ever so horrified over abortion, are just as ready to start wars against everybody from here to hell and gone, as well as to sell guns to everybody and his little sister, and then to execute people they sold the guns to. And they wear their crucifixes as if the cross were not itself an instrument of execution, which was used to kill the same Jesus they would have killed themselves! And left wingers, ever so sensitive on capital punishment, ever so dovish, ever so ready to save the whales and the spotted owls, are fine with a million children killed every year. And they passionately espouse—*liberals* espouse the abortion cause as if abortion weren't the ultimate *conservative* act! What lies at the absolute and hideous heart of reactionary conservatism but the desire—for the sake of the convenience of the self-interested damned *self*—to kill all new and inconvenient life? Infant-killing Herod with a bloody sword in his hand! That's what conservatism *is*—and what do liberals do now but stand ever-vigilant in the protection of Herod's *right* to wield that sword! I've read their sophistical essays. Potentiality does not have the same moral standing as actuality. No deeper conservative sin than to argue that—and to kill in the name of that! Or killing in the name of property or privacy rights! Who invented that but Tories from the pits of hell! Slave holders love that filth! Or even worse—coming up with names, godforsaken nouns to kill verbs—the insultingly abruptive, dismissive noun *fetus*—to stop and kill as it comes every unwanted leaf on the Tree of Life, conveniently dismissing its living potentiality as an unreality—because its full life can't yet be *seen!* Do they not know how in just about every book they venerate that living only in the visible is the original sin? And to pretend that their murderous dissection, their using the knife of the name *fetus* is any different from the killing of black life and its endless unseen potential with the murderous noun *nigger*—or to kill all the as-yet-unseen potentialities of an entire gender with the fixed noun *woman?* "And now," he said out loud, "you've got goddam Jocelyn Elders saying we've got to get over our love affair with the fetus."

And to break, to *end,* what had become to him an intolerable silence, Tom spoke out now more firmly still, and bitterly. "Does she, a black woman, for Christ sake, not hear the George Wallace in her voice, or know that the secret glee of the white American Herod is the high rate of abortion among blacks? Can she not hear the great white genocidal sigh of relief? And here's her boss, Clinton, going to Missouri and making a speech defending a woman's right to choose while at the same time—in the very same speech—supporting capital punishment. But of course you're some kind of illiberal Neanderthal if you think the Pope has seen the light—the Pope who goes to St. Louis at exactly the same moment as Clinton and says that what you create with abortion on demand and goddamned capital punishment is a culture of death. And the day after he speaks against abortion *and* against capital punishment—in a true Christian consistency that our country, neither right nor left, can make *any* claim to—he goes over to see Governor Carnahan and gets him to commute the sentences of several of the condemned. Right there—*That!*—is what Christ is to me—a voice forever against godforsaken right-wingers and against equally godforsaken left-wingers—against death!—*period*. But at the same time *always* for forgiveness. Seventy times seven. Which only the blockheaded mind of a right-wing moron would think equals just four hundred and ninety."

Still Jackie said nothing. And she now took her cheek in her right

DIVISION

hand again, and she began once more to tap with the fingers of her other hand upon the *Adam Bede*. She knew well what he'd been thinking. And still now she resisted with silent resentment his every spoken syllable that might cut her heart—and her silence had put ever greater heat into his anger, she knew. She knew exactly what she was doing, more and more firing his anger as she let him go on, and on. But it had perhaps, at last, come time to bring things to a crisis, and to let him know everything she had been keeping secret. All the seventy times seven things she had been keeping to herself, now for years, and lately for months...six months...and more. And for her the idea that he would forgive these secret things was not disputable. He could not, and would not, for all his talk. But she had long moved in deepest conviction beyond the reach of his moral world. And she didn't care anymore what he condemned or what he forgave. So she knew it was time —and that with just a handful of words, right now, she would bring to an end their more than twenty years.

SOUL COAST
AND GOLD COAST

Watt had told Tumbler that he some-
times liked to do his thinking while walking. But as he'd led Tumbler
east on Division, to where it started to be all white peoples' restaurants
and shops and bars, and then east and more east, to where everything
was all just for richer white people and richer (even though still so
close to the Greens: richest in Chicago livin' up against poorest, "in a
way oughta set somethin' on fire," Tumbler had heard a sweet little ol'
Cabrini lady say once)—during that whole time that they'd kept on
movin' east-ways down Division, Watt hadn't talked at all about what
he'd said he'd be talking about this evening: the way they'd take control of Camp Ball, and then go on from there, buildin' up that kingdom before they died. And he never told Tumbler what he'd meant
by that mysterious "We do." All's he'd said—if he'd done any talkin'
at all—was some few things about his mama. They were sad and terrible things, but which he let Tumbler know, by the way he kept on
walkin' after he said 'em, he didn't want anybody else's thoughts on.
And then, as they'd come up on North State Parkway, in the heart now
of the white man's Gold Coast, and had turned north toward Lincoln

29

DIVISION

Park, it had been a word or two about his grandmother, 'cause Watt, like it's his only goal now, had walked them right up to this rich white people's home that his gramma'd worked in, before she got fired for stealin'. It was this multi-million-dollar, three-story place, with stone walls and pillars and round-topped windows, with black-iron balconies and a black-iron fence, 'tween Schiller and Goethe streets. And through those fence bars you could look right into the place and see things, especially now that the sun was down and the house lights were on. There were paintings on the walls. And there was a woman—and though she was mostly turned away, you could see her bracelets and the glass of her watch glittering. She was spreading flowers around in a bowl, which she'd set on the table under this big fancy light, all shining.

It had been right out of nowhere, when they'd first begun to move into that all-white world (and, truth to tell, Tumbler had enjoyed the feeling of walking with a black man who made white people as uncomfortable as he could see Watt made 'em, young and old, with the way he looked—like the spittin'-image son of Jim Brown, but tattooed, and sportin' his black leather and his blue-black bandana, and with never a trace of a let's-all-get-integrated smile). Right between Wells and La Salle they were, in front of this fancy white-folks dress shop with white manikin ladies in the window, wearin' the fine dresses and the jewels—and Watt just suddenly says how ten years old he'd come up on his mama killed, lyin' dead on the floor up sixteen stories in Tha Jube. She's lyin' there in a red pool of her own blood, he said, with her throat slit clean across, cut deep and wide. It was in the same room as he's born in, 'cause back in '77 the ambulances had already started not comin' to Cabrini, and his mama, just fifteen, was all alone when she lost her water—and all alone, not long later, when he came into this world. Right there where ten years later she died, lookin', with her eyes all wide open, like she's still terrified a the one who did it to her, and like maybe even on the other side the grave, she's gonna stay terrified of that bloody murderer 'til somethin' got done to him (which Watt said like he knew who it was—and like he's gonna make that motherfucker bleed if it's the last thing he ever did). And when they were passin' the Butch McGuire bar, just west of North State, Watt said, right outa nowhere, too, *Fuckyeah!,* and made a fist, with no explanation—but Tumbler put it together that he was thinkin' still about the one who killed his mama and what he intended to do about that, for justice. And now at last, as they were still standin' out front of that mansion his grand-

30

SOUL COAST AND GOLD COAST

mamma got fired from, lookin' still at the white lady, Watt did say that when the good, good money started comin' in from their "operation," he's gon' fix his grandmamma all up with a big house in Cal Heights, "right with all the other mamas got fixed up by their gangsta boys. So she won't have t'worry about what they're gonna make her do and she can't do a thing about it." Then, as he laughed and put his arm around Tumbler, "We'll see then, my brotha T, if that ol' hollerin' bitch ax me questions 'bout gangsta tax dollars." And Tumbler smiled, even as he could feel something hard under Watt's coat, right at the belt.

But as he stood there with Watt on exclusive North State, looking still into that glowing mansion (and he had wondered a moment if Watt brought his gun for maybe breakin' into that iron-gated palace), Tumbler was suddenly surprised to hear his name called out—"Hey, Marcus! Marcus Sabbs!" The evening light was still clear enough so that when he looked up he could make out—of all people—his cousin Robert Teague, his uncle Maurice's son. Robert Teague was closest to Tumbler of all his cousins, the two of them being just a year apart and always having gotten along real good—though their worlds were so different. "Robert Teague! Is that you?" Robert Teague came up quickly, smiling. "I'm just gonna ask one thing, Marcus, and that's what the hell are we doin' *here?!*" Robert Teague laughed as he stepped up to his cousin and thumb-locked his palm into Tumbler's and shook with him, palm in palm. Then Tumbler said, as he stepped back and let his two companions look at each other, "Watt, my cousin Robert Teague. Robert, this is Watt."

Robert Teague, his hair clean cropped, his mustache tight and close cut, wore wire-rimmed glasses and had on a dark-green down vest. He was built lean like his cousin but hadn't the same hard acrobat's and track man's body. The soft, coffee-colored flesh of his face suggested even that in not too many years he might go fat. And as he and Watt nodded and thumb-locked their palms, shaking, even before Robert had said the first thing, Watt could tell that Robert Teague was a rich man's book-learned boy. But Watt would never have heard of St. Ignatius High School, where Robert every semester made first honors, even though it was just over at Roosevelt Road and Blue Island, nor be able to say where DePaul University was, where Robert was now in his third year, majoring in African-American studies and looking to move on to law school, preferably at the University of Chicago—a goal that Watt would never have known how to imagine, though he'd seen what

31

lawyers were and what the law was. And if Robert Teague couldn't see in the growing dark the double pitchforks on Watt's neck, he could read the man's garb and wasn't blind to the fact before him: that his cousin Marcus had taken the step his family had forever tried to prevent his taking—into the gang life. But immediately, even as he could see himself reporting in sorrow to family the defeat of all their good efforts, Robert, as he and Watt stood there looking at each other, felt drawn himself to this no-doubt hard-core gangbanger, by the power in his eyes and by his look, which suggested an irresistible force of mind, and by the impression of strength that he gave, silent in that body which bespoke not just physical power but an unyielding iron discipline. And immediately now, too, because of something that in recent days had set him against his own father—and made him ashamed of a man he'd quarreled, argued with often enough but never not respected, loved—Robert Teague found himself wanting to say, and especially to say out loud to Watt, why it was that he was there on North State Parkway, just south of Lincoln Park, even though he had been swallowing down his anger in shamed silence ever since Maurice Teague had done what he did.

"Marcus," Robert said, "the fact is you and Watt won't believe why I'm here. You just won't. My father, Watt, is a mortician." And now Robert Teague stepped back northward, and motioned with his hand, coaxing his companions back toward the park, where he'd just been. Tumbler and Watt stepped along—although Watt let it be known with cold body language and an unresponsive look that he didn't follow anybody for long. "So," Robert said, "Maurice Teague does think about how people get buried. But you won't believe the Uncle Tom shit he's pulled." Watt gave now just this slightest nod, as Robert, turning to Tumbler, to include him, said, "I mean, Marcus, you won't want to know him as your uncle, I swear to God, same as I can't believe I'm his son." Tumbler smiled. "That'd be a switch—me disappointed in Uncle Maurice." Watt, still silent, thought how these schoolboy motherfuckers, when it comes to turnin' hard on their daddies, don't know first dead shit. But all three kept moving toward the park. And Robert Teague said, as they started to come up toward Burton Place, "There's this plaque at the park and it marks where the Chicago City Graveyard used to be.... And who got buried there, in the thousands, at the time of the Civil War, were Confederate POW's who'd been brought up to be held in this Union war prison out on the South Side, called

Camp Douglas, and they died in large numbers at this place because it was a torture chamber and shithole of filth, so they died of things like cholera, small pox and malnutrition, besides plain brutality. And then what happened, after those thousands of dead Southern Rebels were buried in the City Graveyard, was that when storms riled up the Lake, the overflow would float up the bodies from the shallow graves they got thrown in. And this remained a disgrace for the City of Chicago until they just dug up all the bodies and moved the now-scattered remains, which couldn't anymore be identified, bone by bone out to a big hole at Oak Woods cemetery on the South Side. But if you're saying 'Why should I give a goddamn what happened to the bones of those Southern slave masters, who after all just got what was comin' to 'em...?'" At last now, with a cold passion, Watt spoke: "I'd like to thrown those motherfuckers out the Lake first thing they got here." "Then, Watt," Robert Teague said, "you'd be just like me—and just that different from my father."

The three passed the Cardinal's Mansion, which imposing old estate, all lighted, for a moment Watt looked hard at. And then as they crossed the wealthy-residential, quiet eastern terminus of North Avenue and came into Lincoln Park's south end, Robert Teague said, "You can see the plaque right over there. It has a title line that says 'The Hidden Truth,' but I'm gonna tell you this truth about my father that I'd like to hide all right, if I only could." He looked past Tumbler to Watt, who looked back with his mouth turned down, but who then nodded, thoughtful—and who seemed now to Robert Teague as if maybe he was saying *All right—I'll give it to ya—you've got me curious.* Robert then said, "Come on up to the Lincoln statue; there's seats around it where we can sit." And as they walked up the promenade to the St. Gauden's statue of Lincoln, Robert Teague said, as if he had a thorn sticking in his heart, and it tore and pained him, "They fill this park up with their all-white history, starting with their white Abraham—and then all their white poets and writers—statues everywhere. And I hate it—because it's like this sick feeling that they've laid on you and you'd just like to shake it off—but I feel it every time that I walk through Lincoln Park, which I'll do to kill time between classes at school—I mean I feel this anger when I come to this place, which isn't all that different from all the rest of pure-white America—*anger* that they ripped us away from *all* of our history and stuck us right in the middle of theirs and said be inspired by it. Lincoln and all his men—that's all we need to look to

DIVISION

for heroes when it comes to those hell-dark days of slavery."

Tumbler now made it clear *he'd* been made curious for sure—and that he wanted it known he was part of things here. He said, "And don't forget how they get us to worship the white man Jesus while we're at it."

"No shit, my cousin," Robert Teague said, touching Tumbler's shoulder as they came up now to the statue of Lincoln, risen from his chair, holding his lapel and stepping out over the stone base he stands on, "and that would bring me straight to the point." They sat down on the stone bench that half surrounds the statue and that has carved into it those well-known words about malice toward none and charity for all and about the faith that right makes might and about doing our duty in that faith. Robert Teague said, "So here it is, in all its Christian piety —for what my Jesus-lovin' father finds out when he's reading this book about Camp Douglas is that *our* funeral home, the Teague Funeral Home, happens to sit exactly on the site of this shithole war prison where all those sons of the South happened to bite the dust. And what then does my turn-the-other-cheek of a house-nigger daddy do but go out and get himself a Confederate *battle flag* and raise that piece of filth up the flagpole in our funeral parlor parking lot! Right in the middle of the black South Side of Chicago, this black man whose son I am, runs this X-crossed rag up as if it's not as bad as running up a swastika where they gassed the Jews."

"I've seen enough a both on peckerwoods' arms at Joliet," Watt now said, deep voiced, but dead toned, not looking at anyone, "swastikas and stars and bars. Aryan Brotherhood. Every one of those motherfuckers got some kind a shit like that on 'em." Now, though, he turned and looked right at Robert Teague, with an intensity that if it excited the university student also disturbed him, making him wish he had *not* spoken out to Watt about his father, and yet also excited that he had. "Maybe," Watt said, still looking at Robert Teague, "you mention that some time to that mortician."

That mortician—despite all his anger at his father, Robert disliked the way Watt said this—and he was about even to say something. But he suppressed it as he was thinking how completely unsurprised he was to hear that Watt had done hard time—and as he was thinking, too, with real fear but also excitement, even with a strange arousal, that he could be sitting next to a man who had killed someone. And he preferred, to having spoken up for his father, or half preferred, the strange warm feeling of dark excitement that he felt now.

34

But Tumbler, in a way that made Robert Teague both not glad and also glad, did now say something for his uncle. "The man," he said, "is gonna have his reasons. I know my Uncle Maurice, and the man, Robert, is gonna have his reasons."

And now Robert did speak up. He said, "He does, Marcus. Of course he does. Before they were sons of men, Robert Teague, he said to me, they were sons of God. They were persons. And they were not respected as persons, cared for or fed as persons, or buried as persons—when they lived right here and when they died here. And who should understand the horror of that more than a black man?—and especially a black man who has given his entire adult life to making sure that honor and respect are paid to the personhood of the dead? But that's when I lost it. I said to him, God damn it to hell!—the very cause that those so-called sons of God died for was to keep enshrined the notion that a black man is not a person! That you are not a person. That I am not a person. And that, *not created equal*, we can be bought and sold and killed and disposed of any way that the person who owns us non-persons, whose *property* we are, wants to kill us or to throw us on a garbage heap—which was the law they made and the law they lived by in this country of theirs not ours for two hundred and fifty years! And to this day, after another hundred years of apartheid, what that rag you've hung up in our parking lot, in front of our neighborhood's eyes, so we won't be living down the shame of it any time soon—what that filth *still* says is that we are not persons, that, birth to death and beyond, black men and women are not human beings!

"But now, Marcus, Watt, he goes into his forgiveness thing. Forgive us our trespasses as we forgive others. For without forgiveness, there is no future. Just ask Desmond Tutu. And then it's his kingdom-of-heaven thing and about how hard it is to find it and about how forgiveness has *got* to be the key to it; for our vengeful anger, he says, our refusing to forgive and wanting forever to retaliate is *the* thing that locks us out of the kingdom. And I say to him, angry as hell and proud *of it,* that this forgiveness he's preaching can be the deepest insult to justice—and the deepest insult to the personhood of all those whom those sons of God enslaved and killed, for it says they didn't *matter*—and even, I said, your forgiveness can insult the personhood of those criminals you want to fly their flag for because forgiving them says they weren't personally responsible for what they did but were just innocent products of their time, doing what circumstances made them do. And he just looks

35

DIVISION

at me like nothing I've said matters the first thing to him and he says, ever so pious, Love thine enemies is not a suggestion, it's a command —Go thou and do likewise is not a suggestion, it's a command—and if mercy, Robert Teague, doesn't look like madness, it hasn't gone deep enough. But then I said his mercy *was* madness, and I walked out and haven't been back since—three days. Could *not* walk back and see that filthy rag-flag still flying over the place that has my family's name over it. And, Christ, if *I* want to kill him, just think what the neighborhood would like to do. There's people there who *will* put a bullet in the man."

"I do believe," Tumbler said, "that that is some crazy shit Uncle Maurice is into. No doubt about that. Crazy shit. But the man is not crazy. And you got to give him credit, Robert Teague, for not givin' one damn what people think! And credit for some crazy-ass courage, too!" Tumbler shook his head and, smiling, said, "Hell yes you do. Talkin' crazy-ass balls, man!" But then he got serious, and thoughtful. He said, " Remember this, too—people always were tellin' Martin Luther King that everything he did was crazy. So I don't know, I think about where I'd be, Robert, if I didn't disrespect Uncle Maurice. I think about that often enough, I guess. And I love the man, same as my mother does. And I'm hopin' you won't turn this thing into the end of the world 'tween you two. The man's got reasons. You know he does."

Robert Teague smiled at Tumbler. "I know he does, Marcus. I know. The crazy motherfucker." He set his elbows on his knees and his chin on his folded hands. But then he raised his head again. "Your talking about MLK, though—it makes me think about all that Jesus stuff about how the meek are supposed to inherit the earth and about love and integration and all that likely wrongheaded faith of King's that if he never did anything violent, if he kept things Christian and didn't fight, guns blazin', for *revolution* that the white world would come around out of pure moral respect—that the black man's goodness would bring out the white man's and that all that black goodness plus all that white goodness would change the world. I'm sorry but I think that's just pie-in-the-sky. Neo-slavery. Economic slavery. It's taken the place of old-time chattel slavery. And just as it took war to get rid of the first kind, it's going to take war to get rid of the second. It's going to take complete change of the system. Capitalism on its own won't redistribute a thing. Just say the word *redistribute* in this country, just speak of spreading the wealth—or in other words, just preach the real message of the gospel of Christ—and in this country you're a sinner and

36

SOUL COAST AND GOLD COAST

criminal. Anti-religion is the real religion in this fucked-up Ameri*k*a. And before it spread the wealth in order to change the world, the anti-Christ of capitalism would stay happy 'til the hell it's created froze three times over."

Though it was one he'd made many times in his own mind, and often enough at school, as he made now this speech, Robert Teague felt, and felt more as he kept going, that it was as if he were on a stage—as if he were auditioning—for only a single director, a judge, who would choose him, or not—and that that director-judge was not his cousin Marcus but the prison-hardened and possibly murderous gangster who sat next to him, someone whose dark presence made him warm to his performance so that he found himself taking it up to a whole new level, which, however, he was sure was one where he was discovering a real truth. "And what it's gonna take to change things," he said, squeezing a fist and setting it hard on his knee, "isn't anything King spoke about. What it's gonna take is a gun to the head."

Clap, clap, clap. Watt, as if he'd been reading Robert Teague's mind, now applauded—clapping three times slow. "Didn't know, Cousin Teague," he said, turning to Robert and looking at him cold, "if you didn't come here to shed some tears yourself for those sorry motherfuckers got washed up here from their graves." But then he smiled at Robert, nodding his head. Then, thoughtful, his mouth turning down, *"Revolution.* Same's the word *money.* No growth, no development without money. Been hungry enough to know. And the system ain't never gon' cough up their money, just like you say. *Redistribute,* ain't never on its own gon' happen in this world. And good things won't come to those who wait. So we make our own system. Hell to their heaven. Ain't gon' be there neither for him's afraid to cross the line, him's afraid to die, him's lookin' for somebody else t'make the rules. And it ain't never gon' be an organization if everybody's lookin' round for somebody else to start it up. And it ain't never gon' be the right one t'start it up 'less somebody look inside himself like some bad-ass gangsta motherfucker and he blows away all the things holdin' him back. All the things that ain't *him.* 'Cause you got to go deep, Cousin Teague, if you're gon' make history and get people to come along with it. If you want your own statue in the park and your own motherfuckin' park. Martin King, the man went jus' as deep as his sweet Jesus gon' let him go. The man ain't afraid to die—but he don't wanna kill nobody, neither. And they ain't gon' be no second Fourth of July if you countin'

37

DIVISION

forever on the goodness a them's fuckin' you over, buildin' their ten thousand jails and prisons just for you when you don't build a single one for them. Or if you gon' be afraid 'til the end a time to jus' pull that fuckin' trigger, like the shot heard round the world. And don't know if you really hearin' that, Cousin Teague. But now I jus' been feelin', all the sudden, like I wanna do somethin' tonight for the son of the all's-forgiven, flag-flyin' gravedigger, 'cause I been thinkin' we run into him for a reason."

Watt reached into his coat pocket and pulled out his cell. When Tumbler saw this, he thought for a moment that that was all it was, the hard thing by Watt's belt, though he knew that couldn't be true. Then he was thinking, too, about all that Watt had said, and about Dr. King, and about his Uncle Maurice, and about his own mama. But now Tumbler, as he was looking also at Robert Teague, who'd said nothing yet but who seemed like maybe he wanted to get out of here and go home, to his father—and yet at the same time to stay—heard Watt ask him, "My Brother T, what say we introduce Cousin Teague to the sweet charms of Miss Sara Lee?"

38

WE DON'T WANT THIS

Watt knew what would happen. Just put the pussy nickel in bro Tumbler and make the boy a fast-talkin' pimp. Shit's fun to watch. And which way Cousin Teague gon' go? Back home to his Jesus-lovin' daddy flyin' the Stars and Bars? Or out for a sweet, sweet evenin' under all these city lights shinin'? Never, the man says, underestimate the power a pussy—'specially if it's some God's own fine Halle Berry tang, way his cousin Tumbler put it now to Teague. Don't need to say a thing, Brotha T—just let you do *all* the talkin'! Just let you mix all that sweet white cream up into it and stir it up slow and fine, Halle-Berry style. *Don't blame me.* Watt suddenly now said this again to himself, in his mind. Then, out loud, "We do." But as the three young men, having passed the Chicago History Museum, all now crossed LaSalle, the two cousins, playfully punching at each other, were too lost to their new excitement to have heard what Watt had said or to have picked up on the changed look on his face.

But still as they stepped back up into the park again, Watt felt that he just might work in a little more recruitment time with these two cousins, even all juicy-ed up and distracted like they were now, before that sweet evenin' appointment he'd set up for 'em ("And y'all gon' find out how Miss Sara Lee brings it *all* togetha!"). So rather than split now to his other business, he just gave a check-tap to the thirty-plus magazine in his pocket, then kept on walking through the park with the two cousins—past the Franklin monument, along the path bordering Stockton Drive. Got to invest, he said to himself. And got to keep on investin', even though the future can't be told. But it's gon' come a time, he really was thinking now, as he'd seen things in not just Tumbler but cousin Teague, the book-learned revolutionary, when these schoolboys'll be useful to me in ways no ignorant thug ever could. But can't be some all-the-sudden baptizin' in the burnin' fire two boys never had to sell their soul, or hustle their body, just to stay alive, and never done hard time of any kind, in prison or out. And never been standin' with blood all over their shoes and blood on their hands and knees from kneelin' in it and sayin' to themselves won't be no killin', ever, and no dyin', gon' keep me from a full mother*fuckin' payback.* Got to go slow with these boys. Full up convertin' to what all the salvation-seekin', chicken-shit motherfuckers call *evil,* instead a callin' it war, like it is—full up committin' to this—in the way there's *no* comin' back from—it takes lead-up time. So these boys never gon' hear what I drove by tonight, down t' Camp Ball. And they won't be with me when I get a car. Just some sweet mack's what we start it with. Plant the seed with that sweet love thang.

But do somebody listen up to this Teague again, Watt said to himself, smiling, as he heard Robert start once more to speechify about a black revolution (and Watt noticed, too, that the book boy ain't changed his mind 'bout his sweet appointment with Miss Sara—still goin' with the program, 'stead a goin' home—which fact Watt took an even warmer pleasure in, thinkin' how he'd greased the wheel some, ahright). And he ain't puttin' on this show a his for brotha Tumbler, Watt could see. It's all for me. But truth of it is, don't mind havin' m'own wheel greased some by this book-readin' brotha—'cause the boy got some *game* when he's paintin' the big picture. And he's got that game a his *on nah,* walkin' through this park he says he doesn't cater to, struttin' the stage again, whoopin' it up now like a preacher. Only he ain't spoutin' no Jesus sermon—but things make us think the boy's knowin', somewhere down deep, that place, all the lights struck out, where you gon' find inside you the Gangster Everlasting.

"I mean it. We've got to wake the hell up," Robert Teague said, as they started now to circle the park's South Pond. "We've got to see the system. How we get formed by it—get made into neo-slaves ripe for prison or death—or, worse—for compromise and cooperation—for the old *if you can't lick* the black-man-destroying bullshit, just give up and *join it*—like one good Christian black man I know. And we've got to stop feeling that *we* have failed but see how history has failed us. They call black men criminals but the so-called black criminal is the product of centuries of white corruption. And he's not the one who needs to be forgiven. *They're* the ones! They cut us off from our origins—from the things that give us a chance at pride and hope. And it's a fool's game to think they're not going to keep on exonerating themselves, letting themselves off the hook, century after century, saying that whatever wrong was done, was all done long ago and not by them but by people whose names are all forgotten and whose actions they can't be blamed for. They'll never see their every-minute-of-the-day involvement and responsibility without some kind of eruption that *makes* them see. Look at all those penthouses and doorman buildings over there. Look up at all the shining lights. The imbalances of wealth and quality of life that we have to stare at everywhere we walk in this city, and everywhere we walk in this so-called America the Beautiful, are not natural. But the system, which is just another name for motherfucking money, makes the unnatural appear natural. It made slavery seem *natural!* All that filth of calling black men and women property and not equal but partial persons—it made all that seem *natural*. And the system, the money system, the property system, the inheritance system, the legal system that preserves it all, and the schooling system, the good old boy system —it's so wide and deep and goddamned strong that there is no fucking chance that some turn-the-other-cheek religion is going to get things changed."

"Gon' take that gun to the head, ain't it," Watt said, and, as he saw that Robert Teague was looking at him past Tumbler, he added, smiling, "but money ain't the problem, Cousin Teague. It's not havin' it that's the problem. And not havin' any way to get to it, lest, that is, you make y'own way. Revolution, it ain't gon' come cheap."

But now Watt stopped. He thought—gon' say somethin' real to this boy with the wire glasses, 'cause it just might be another good moment for it. He turned and faced the schoolboy in his iron-strong body, tall, thick. He set his jaw hard, showing Robert Teague all of his real black power. In the lamp light, traces of his war paint, if indecipherable, were nonetheless perceivable between the black-leather wings of his coat collar. He said in a voice deep, deliberate, "But it won't come, my brotha, without all six a the six burned into you in the lake a fire, where you been baptized to the death in *brotherhood:* Love, Life, Loyalty, Wisdom, Understanding, Knowledge. And that *knowledge,* it's knowledge a that system you're talkin' about—deep-down-in-the-blood knowledge a what it's done to you. And I don't know how many souls your daddy buried, Cousin Teague, who say, when they're goin' down, *If I die, show no pity, bury me in a gangsta city*—but it's gon' take them who say it and mean it, sayin' live free or die, motherfucker, with hearts stone fuckin' hard—or you ain't never gon' get your revolution done. Not without the ones say Fuck the salvation's gon' cost me what I want." But now he stopped, and, as if he were deciding then by slow degrees to be amused by his own words, Watt let a smile come slowly over his face again. And then he laughed. "But first things first!" he said, "and first things is keepin' a date with a lady gon' change your life for *real,* my brotha."

"FOR *REAL!*" Tumbler chimed in, as if relieved by the change in the tone of things, "and I was about to *say,* let's get it on!"

Robert Teague was still emerging from one state of mind to another, coming up like a swimmer from deep in the water into the air. But now he shook his head with a laugh, took a breath, and said, smiling, laughing again, "Lead the way!"

Then the two cousins, once more slapping each other's backs, headed west out of the park with Watt, who, still amused, still had time to kill before his Camp Ball business—and so he continued to keep these boys company. And now, Watt in the lead, they would make their way through the Lincoln Park neighborhood and all its million-dollar brownstones toward Sara Lee's place on N. Mohawk, in the no-man's land between Cabrini's north edge and the white world of west Old Town. Sara Lee lived and entertained in her house with two other ladies Watt pimped for, all three working at V.I.P.'s, a few blocks west of Sara Lee's.

Watt didn't want to say, with Cousin Teague maybe sensitive for ladies' *rights* (he smiled thinkin' this), how he liked the way he kept these three, and kept 'em tight on the short chain, with a full-reliable supply of H and cocaine, sweet stream of both that bad 'boy' and that good 'girl,' weed too, and nice gentleman custom (not that these ladies don't

WE DON'T WANT THIS

have their own magnetism), and the best 9-1-1 service bitches ever gon' find. Bam! Motherfucker! But he'd mention none a that now.

He thought, though, that he might just set the scene himself a little for Cousin Teague. So he did—he started pimpin' it all up, with brother Tumbler all noddin' and grinnin', throwin' in the *oh yeahs,* 'bout the way Sara Lee she's *so* fuckin' beautiful in that creamy-tan skin, that Halle Berry face a hers comin' straight outa heaven above, with them big eyes, blue, no shit, and dark lashes all touched up jus' right, and that body so fuckin' fine. Can't be decidin' which you most favor, them perfect sweet T's or that hold-*on*-to-it A! Jesus be praised! or them legs, jus' keep goin' and goin' all up to that sweet place—so sweet, and so sensitive. And she gon' light up some candles as she's movin' around all graceful like a dancin' lady, with this sweet soft voice all the time— till later, that is, when it's shut the fuckin' door, my brotha! Cause Miss Sara she ain't in it for show. She's in it to be *in* it! But maybe she's gon' get some incense first and spark her a little reefer for all to share, or get her this water pipe she likes, and she gon' put on the right music, and take care t'look perfect, dress t'show *all* she gon give you, she bein' so generous, and beautiful, with her long, soft hair fallin' down and her lips so fine, all touched up and wet t'kiss....ooooh, don't *know* if I can go *on!*

They'd come off the 5-points where Wisconsin runs into Lincoln Ave. and then had headed south down Lincoln Park West, to where the short access alley connects to the main back alley, which runs between the backs of the brownstones on Lincoln Park West and the backs of those on N. Orleans. Watt, even as he entertained his boys, fueling those good love flames, had with deliberate consideration made the move toward the back alley because he thought he might find a car there, nice and lonely in the dark—one he might come back for. The old-bricked alley was dark, except for where a lamp was lit on the north end, where they now were, and then where there was another lamp, down near the south end of the block. The way the alley opened things up, you could see clear out the south end to all the big lights of the city, rising to the sky.

And it just hit the juiced-up Tumbler some way, lookin' down that long straight alley and then up from it into the big city lights. So all of a sudden he stopped. "Hold up!" he said—in a way that made even Watt do it. He took off his White Sox cap and handed it to Robert Teague. He unzipped his Wells track-team jacket with the eagle-wing

43

emblem and took it off, too, handing it to Robert. He hitched up his baggy pants. He bent his body forward and spit into his hands and rubbed them together. Then he took off, to the delight of both Robert Teague and Watt—and dove onto his hands and then sprang off his hands and backflipped high into a hand spring, throwing his feet over himself in a lightning whip, and then he dove again into another hand spring, backflipping high and whipping his feet over himself in the air, and then again into another hand spring, and then another, and another, and another! As if he was out to prove he'd lost not a single thing since his days with the Jesse White Tumblers!

"Got damn!" Watt said, laughing hard as Tumbler finally stopped about halfway down the alley, "sign that nigga up for somethin'!" And Robert Teague, as he and Watt walked down toward Tumbler, who was standing in mid-alley, smiling, doing a little triumph shuffle, was truly proud of his cousin's talent. And he brought his Sox cap to him and his jacket in this gracious, even deferential manner, just to show his cousin Marcus Sabbs his respect.

But as Robert Teague held Tumbler's jacket for him to put it on, and then handed him his cap, Watt's eye caught over the cousins' shoulders a set of cars parked side by side under the south-end alley lamp. He couldn't make out the second, but the first was a silver-gray Mercedes. A nineteen hundred and ninety-nine "Model S"! Shiiiit! Gon' look into it. Gon' look *into* this motherfucker. The cousins, the one wearing wire-rimmed glasses, and wearing a green down vest, and the other wearing a White Sox cap, fitted backwards, and a blue jacket with an eagle's wing on its breast—both laughing, happy, thinking again of Miss Sara Lee, who tonight was their true destination, moved now with Watt down the brick alley toward its second lamp. Gon' shed these two, Watt thought, soon's we get out this alley. Gon' send these motherfuckers on their merry way. Circle back then n' get me a set a wheels fine as they come—for the big occasion. *Fuckyeah!* Leadership at Camp Ball—it gon' change up tonight. Whole world gon' change up—weak t'strong. But jus gon' take a look first into this pretty vehicle. Check me out the sticka price.

To the two cousins, so soon to be sent off on a separate way, Watt had given no idea what was going through his mind. But now he said, "Will y'all jus' lookyheah!" as he steered the two toward the silver-gray Mercedes, glowing in the light of the alley lamp. And the two cousins, too excited to think about whatever suspicions they at that moment might

WE DON'T WANT THIS

or might not have had, went along, walking with Watt toward the car.

But now—shit too sweet!—Watt saw that the car was occupied! Some white dude sittin' in the driver's seat! Instantly he thought he'd jack this motherfucker. Keys every time over the wedge, hanger and Swiss knife—and no matter these innocent little niggas are with me. Tumbler, though he'd moved forward right with Watt, had noticed no one in the car. Robert Teague, having seen no one inside yet either, and now for fun acting the rich white privileged-class customer, placed his chin in his hand, and walked around to the other side of the car, nodding his approval.

But suddenly Tumbler felt the rush—as Watt stepped fast to the car window. And immediately Tumbler knew—knew all that was goin' down as soon as he saw that white boy's face in the driver's window. But he couldn't run. He didn't want to be here at all! But he couldn't run. And Robert Teague, he could sense immediately too some terrible danger as he saw Watt stepping fast to the car—and he knew it was bad, maybe bad as death when he heard Watt pound his hand like a hammer on the car roof! Robert now looked into the car, as he saw movement—someone in the car, who looked his way before turning back the other! He saw the face in the passenger-side window! And he knew that face! Connor Riordan. He knew this guy from St. Ignatius. One of the good ones. Con Riordan!

"Get out the car, both you motherfuckers!" Watt, as he now hammer-fisted the driver's-side window, gave his commands. In no time the passenger-side door opened and Connor Riordan got out, though he stayed bent toward the interior and was pleading, "Jack, do as he says! Just do it! Get out!" But the driver's-side door did not open. Only a voice: "Fuck him! And fuck you!"

Watt again hammered his fist down furiously on the roof of the car. He said into the closed window, "You gon' be brave, motherfucker?! You gon' get brave on me, big fella?! Best you listen to this chicken-shit other motherfucker who knows the value a life! And lookin' like you don't! Get out the fuckin' car! NOW!"

"Please, Jack! Do as he says! Please!" Connor Riordan, still leaning into the interior, was pleading to Jack in wild fear and desperation.

But only the window opened on the driver's side. And a white face then looked up into a black one. A terrifying black one. But out of some deep bottom of dark fury a voice came out from the car: "You think you have some right to steal from whites! You think you're fucking

45

owed! You think you can blame *me* for your worthless fucking life. There's not a soul on this earth to blame for the shit you are but you! So *you* get out! *You* get the fuck out! And get your hands off what doesn't belong to you!"

Watt said nothing. He just stood up straight and smiled—then turned his mouth down in pure ferocity. He unbuttoned his mid-coat button and reached inside his black leather to where his gun was tucked in his belt—then pulled out the 19. He spread his legs and with two hands held the gun up and pointed it into Jack's face. Tumbler, who had never moved, cried out "No! No! It's not worth it! Nothin's worth this! We don't want this! We don't!" Then Tumbler took off running in all his lightning speed south out toward the alley's end. Robert Teague, even as his cousin flew by, stayed where he was and cried out, "No! For the love of Jesus, NO! NO!"

But Robert Teague's words were lost in the terrifying firecrack of the gun. Only God knew how many times it lit the dark with flame, before it stopped. And now at last, the one on the passenger side backed fully out of the car. Connor Riordan, covered in blood, his face, his clothes, red, dripping with Jack's blood, backed out and away from the car—in mute shock and horror. Robert Teague, in a shock and terror nearly as deep, couldn't think. He could only cry out the words that his mind found for him: "Connor, Connor Riordan, Connor!" And now he said, to a shocked face, all covered in blood, that stared at him, "Connor, I am so sorry! I'm so sorry! Oh my God I am so sorry!" Then Connor saw that voice, that face, the one he could only stare at, turn and run.

But now a shout, chasing that running body, chasing whoever it was who called out his name—down the alley as he ran: "You know this motherfucker! You know this shit fuckin' chicken!"

Connor looked back to see a black man, tall, big, dark-faced, in a black leather coat, with a black-silky bandana. He had a gun. He was leaning to his side and reaching into his pocket. And he now slapped what he found there hard up into the handle of the gun. A black gun. He was raising the gun, with this long projection now at the handle's base—and pointing this thing at him! But now Connor heard, "Boys! Boys! Jacko! Con! What in hell!!" It was his father. He was coming. From the house. And his shouted words made this dark black man with the gun lower it. He said, "Fuck y'all motherfuckers forever!" And then he walked off, right past Connor, with a killing look, before he spat on the ground, and then walked off fast, and then at last ran—

WE DON'T WANT THIS

the same way that the person who'd called his name had run. He told him he was sorry. He was from Ignatius. Robert Teague. It was Robert Teague. He knew him!

The back gate opened. Connor looked, saw his mother as well as his father. She wore that suit, that blouse, that gold necklace. His father came to him and held him. But as he held on to his father, he heard his mother scream. And he moved with his father, who never let him go, toward the car, and saw his mother sitting, right where he had sat with Jack, holding Jack in her arms, her dead son, destroyed, all blood, his body destroyed; and with his blood pouring over her. She was wailing, as she held him in her arms, rocking with his dead, bleeding body in her arms, wailing "My son! Oh dear God.... Dearest, dearest God!"

ONE HOUR EARLIER

In the third-floor turret room, his library, atop his home on S. Calumet, around the corner from his mortuary on Martin Luther King, Maurice Teague was meditating on history —as a first step in a spiritual exercise directed toward freeing his soul from it. He was thinking of the spring day, thirty years back, and of his excitement, when in this room, armed with a claw hammer and crow bar, he began to strip off the cheap paneling that, wholly unbeknownst to him, had been covering over beautiful and extensive, floor-to-ceiling library shelving, which all round the room was broken up rhythmically by columns and by arched niches for objets d'art. The shelves and niches—set in by some skilled artisan who had worked with the original architect to create, with the beautifully proportioned arches and pilastered columns, echoes of the home's Richardson-style neo-Romanesque forms—had been built for the first owner of the home, back in the 1880's. And now it held Maurice's own library of several hundred volumes. Maurice was trying to recapture the feeling of delicacy that came into his fingers and hands as, thirty years ago, he continued to take down the crude covering that had been used to convert this once (and now once more) beautiful library into bedrooms, or bunkrooms—back at the turn of the nineteenth into the twentieth century, when what once were the most stylish homes in all of Chicago were first sold off to slum-hustlers who partitioned them up into ten- to twelve-apartment warrens for the African Americans surging north in the early waves of the Great Migration.

In the years after the bloody Chicago race riot of 1919, with all the killings and the homes of a thousand black families torched, this place was abandoned altogether and then stood empty for over twenty years, when a new generation of slum barons came in and fitted it out for the next great waves of the Migration, which came after the Second World War, and which all also, in Chicago, got herded tight into the segregated Black Belt—but this time to the absolute bursting point; for the numbers were in the hundreds of thousands.

Maurice now put his memory's eyes up to the cracks in the wall of the rusty-tin-roofed shotgun shack in Artesia, Mississippi, and looked out to the fields, which, when he grew up there, all were cotton, but which had all long gone over to pasture—and he let himself see what he'd seen there as a boy, and let himself, in this meditation on all that history which wouldn't let him go, feel the dark agony, the terror, the rage.

There had been no escaping the curse of it when his family came to Chicago in 1947, when Maurice Teague was twelve and a half—and all the eight of his family who remained moved into a two-room cell in this very home on Calumet, no less afraid and even more crowded than in that unpainted, listing shack in Artesia, surrounded by Mr. Mac Randall's cotton fields and set up tight against the pen where Maurice's father raised pigs. But from the start, Maurice seized hard upon the chances given him here, and not there, finishing at Du Sable High (and while he could always sense trouble in any claim-staking about who was first here or first there—and this especially now as he put his mind on the more than hundred-year history of his Calumet Ave. home and on the history of its varied ownerships—Maurice let himself feel once again the pride he felt that first time he heard that the first nonnative settler of Chicago was a black man, Du Sable—and he thought of how he and his little sister Dosey would talk about how you could learn so much from the names of things around you, like a school or a street, and how once you'd learned what the names named, your mind could come alive as you walked among the things).

Maurice had studied music at Du Sable under the famed Walter Dyett,

DIVISION

who showed *the unbreakable relation between beauty and discipline!* to him and to his remarkable friends Eddie Harris and Julien Priester, boys of such breathtaking gifts that it brought a tear of pride to his eye to think of all that they could do (and of all that they did do with their music, learned in the same Bronzeville high school where, under the same remarkable teacher and disciplinarian, Nat King Cole and Dinah Washington had learned theirs). Then in 1956 he took his bachelor's degree in history from Roosevelt University (named for Franklin Delano and Eleanor Roosevelt and housed in the Auditorium Building, designed by Louis Sullivan, whose work was of a spirit with Richardson's, just like the work of the architect who designed the house Maurice now lived in, and the library where he now sat, meditating—on things too, now, like Louis Sullivan's own library, preserved in a room atop the Auditorium Building, where Sullivan lived—a late-nineteenth-century white man's library quite likely similar to that of the white man who first lived in this house and had set his books where Maurice now set his different books—by authors just as often black as white).

Maurice Teague, who'd recovered this grand old house on Calumet, rehabilitated it all the way back to what it first was, with his hard work, and his hard-earned money, let himself feel now a pride of ownership. He thought back on how many times he and his mother, Tillie Early Dawn Teague, when the family all lived here—1947 to 1950—maybe noticing a panel of the original lead-mullioned cut glass as its prisms cast rainbows on the wall, or the still-fine quality of the woodwork of an old columned lintel with its plinth blocks, or the frieze-work of some sculpted molding before that old molding, now slap-painted over, got abortively cut off by a cheap new partition wall—how many times the two of them would say that this place, all so cut up then, and crowded, filthy-dangerous, not fit for human habitation, but good enough for the Black Belt, must once have been beautiful.

Maurice Teague, child of Mississippi, went to a shelf now for his many-times read first edition of *Native Son,* and he looked, a long time, at the black back of his hand before taking the book from the shelf. What different books would be here when he was gone? Twenty years? Fifteen? And would it be a white hand that reached for them as it was a white hand that had reached for those different books long ago? The progeny of Bigger Thomas, gang insignias on their necks and chests, tears tattooed to the corners of their eyes, now in their poverty and rage look out the windows of that once-undivided mansion on Drexel

50

Blvd. where Bigger in his Othello's panic murdered white Mary Dalton and decapitated and incinerated her dead body.

God's vengeance on owners, on division: if you want no partitions, no dismemberments, then create none, cut none. There are no owners in the kingdom of heaven. No landlords, only the Lord God—and may His kingdom come and His will be done. The blessed meek—they alone inherit the earth. Shut your eyes and ears, Maurice Teague. Only the eyes perceive black and white; only the ears can hear the identifying sounds, the accents, of black and white. Shut down the senses. They produce the divisions that make us the fools we are. They make us form hard, partisan identities, black or white, and take sides to the death, all in a fool's accord with what we look and sound like. The senses never show us our invisible souls but just our bodies that die— and so every minute that we so-called live, our senses make us afraid of dying, of sacrifice, of change, of difference, of what is not us—or what we think is us—for they never let us see who we really are. The musically proportioned shelving in this quiet room never will mind what books it holds, this man's or that's, nor did it ever complain when it was covered up; and as he returned Richard Wright's great book to its place on its shelf, Maurice Teague smiled to think of the racial innocence of alphabetical order, for Wright's *Native Son* took its place in his library next to Whitman's *Leaves of Grass,* a book he deeply loved, and which he bought because he'd seen it on the shelves of Sullivan's library atop the Auditorium Building, which became his university's home, Roosevelt, dedicated to the promulgation of social justice. And in all great human books, beyond the white paper and black ink that the eyes show us, is the invisible and indivisible human soul.

Maurice Teague had not heard from his son, Robert, in nearly four days. "Could you please, Daddy, just call him? Please!" His daughter, Carolyn, had begged him, saying she *knew* that a single call was all it would take. "That and a promise you'll take down that *thing* you've decided to call attention to yourself with! That's right!—to call attention to yourself!" Mary Tate, his wife, never before not on his side, gave him no quarter when it came to this action he'd taken now two and a half weeks back, and which no doubt he should have discussed with her before just doing it—but then he did just do it because he foresaw, for all her life-long loyalty to him, that she would try to stop him, and he trembled enough at the act without hearing her objections, which were sharply, sharply pointed. "Attention to yourself and also to your family. And it's unwanted attention, I promise you! Because, Maurice, you can count sneers and threatening looks and someone's spitting at the ground as I walk by among the things I don't care for in this life, and especially when I can't answer this treatment with an unashamed look of my own pride. I know what you're saying to yourself, Maurice Teague. I know. Blessed are they who suffer persecution for righteousness' sake! And all I say to that is how many self-congratulating fools who have done foolish or plain wrong things have taken the world's judgment that they're nothing but a pack of damned fools or cads not as a sign of how wrong they are but of how wise and good!"

With his imagination's eye, Maurice could see Mr. Mac Randall's face, blue-eyed, with a high forehead and thinned brown hair, though he was only maybe thirty—and already with thin white lines running across the skin on his neck, where the sun couldn't reach. And Maurice could hear the man's voice—and exactly what it said that day, fifty-three years ago, Maurice not yet twelve. A black man's dog will bark as hard at a white man as a white man's will at a black. His brother Jesse's best-ever hunting dog, Old Cuba, the Chesapeake pointer, when Maurice found him, two weeks missing, gone off, everyone thought, with Jesse to who knew where, just lay there, not barking, or moving. His muzzle set up on his crossed paws, atop the bank of the deep, dry creek bed that for thought and quiet Maurice had been walking, Old Cuba stayed silent, unmoving—even as Maurice shouted out his name, so surprised to see his brother's dog after all that time. But then suddenly the dog sprang down the ten-foot bank, tumbling over himself into the creek bed, barking and snarling, and then tearing, head bent, right past Maurice. Huge naked river-tree roots in all their wild forms hung there into the creek bed—and now as Old Cuba, slowing at last, baring his teeth, snarling, began to poise his trembling, leaf-covered body for a spring—the butt of a gun bent back one of those snakelike overhanging roots, and, as if from behind a curtain, Mr. Mac Randall stepped. The white man surprised Maurice completely, even though all of the dog's wild attack action, had let him know that some hostile thing, feral boar maybe, or bobcat, must be close by.

But why was Old Cuba out there, and maybe *right* there—maybe for all of the two weeks since Jesse had disappeared? And what was Mr. Mac doing there, Maurice had thought, following me?—for surely he had been tailing him.

"Maurice Teague, what in *the* hell!" The white man, gun at his waist, one hand set over the stock, the other gripped on the barrel, now stepped into the open space past the screen of overhanging roots. Then, looking up at Maurice, "You tell me, boy, you don't know come end a March, right down this creek bed, Mac Randall's out for turkey! You out' that nigger mind a yours, son! I cain't see your black face in this shade! See black movin' down here, I think it's a gobbler. Turkey don't give you no time, neither—it's all just quick shoot and think later. And hell*fire,* boy, if I's not about to raise my gun on you! Hadn't been for this dog, mighta raised and pulled the trigger too. So you listen good: Y'all git your black behind off this property, and y'all take that dog right with ya. And y'all put that ol' boy up good, too, and keep him full out these parts, which is posted clear."

Old Cuba—as Mac Randall now looked at the dog hard, threatening, raising some at him the stock of the gun—barked twice loud and then lowered and poised himself again, snarling. "And you git the boy's jaw shut, too, right nah, or he'll feel the butt a this gun."

"Yessuh, Mr. Mac." Maurice knelt down beside Old Cuba and wrapped his arms around his brother's dog's neck, and whispered softly under the flap of the pointer's ear, "Sssshhh. Hush nah, Cuba. You hush nah, ol' boy. Hussshhh. Hussshhh." And as the dog began to relax and go quiet and then lick his face, Maurice said, "Come ohn nah, boy, les' get on outa heah. Come ohn."

Mac Randall, as Maurice still held the dog in his arms, stepped around boy and dog and, with his shotgun slung under his right arm, began to walk down the creek bed. Maurice, rising to his feet and loosening his hold on Old Cuba's neck, began to call the dog, trying to coax him back through that curtain of river roots, "Come ohn nah, Cuba boy. You come ohn with me." But now Mac Randall, as he'd come right even with that place where Old Cuba had for who knew how long been keeping his silent watch, now turned to Maurice and said, with a new ferocity, "I see you or that dog aroun' this place, *any* future time, jus' gon' tell people ah thought you's a bird when I shot you."

Maurice, as the dog had begun to bristle and bark again with the sound of the white man's voice, had taken tighter hold of Old Cuba and tried to hold him—but the powerful dog was too strong and now broke free and darted at the white man in full fury, teeth bared. Mac Randall, as the dog came on, raised up high the butt of his gun and brought it down with all his force on Old Cuba's head as the dog came up to attack. Old Cuba fell stunned. But then slow, unsteady, he rose,

DIVISION

blood now running over his eyes from a deep gash in mid brow. He
didn't try again to attack. Rather he turned to the steep bank and, right
at that spot where Maurice had first seen him, tried to claw his way
up from the dry bottom to that place where he'd been lying, all quiet
at the creek bed's edge. But as the great pointer, beautiful brown
Chessie, scratched and clawed, too weak to get himself more than half-
way back up the bank, Mac Randall raised his gun and, when the dog
had clambered to a man's eye level, put a shell-full of pellet in his back.

Maurice, when the dog had broken free, had backed up behind the
screen of roots. But he'd stayed and looked and seen it all, and now
he saw the dog, not sliding down but staying hung as if nailed in his
blood to the creek bank.

For fifty-three years the image of Old Cuba, shot wide open to the
gut and bone, for it was no bird gun the white man had been carrying, had haunted Maurice. And the sound of the white man's voice—
"You seein' your nigger future. You come back this way, you can expect
the same!"

Maurice was terrified. As he turned, though, and ran back through
the creek bed, dodging, leaping roots, not stopping or looking back,
he still marked in his mind's eye the spot where Cuba had lain in his
watch and then died. So that even if the dog's shattered remains were
gone when he came back—and he would come back—he would know
exactly where to look. The time came soon enough. Not three days later,
Maurice heard Mr. Mac's daddy say Mac Randall was gone to Columbus for business that might take all the day. So Maurice made fast for
the bridge and cut down into the creek bed on the sloped footpath
that he would take to get into the bed for his thinking walks. There'd
been no rain, so the bed was still dry. And down in the bottom, Maurice moved quickly, not stopping to gaze upon the mysterious giant
root forms. He feared now every crazy thing—like he might just have
been tricked by Mr. Mac's daddy, or that even from Columbus Mac
Randall could see him. And he felt a sick dread over the *not*-crazy possibility that what he would find, at the place where Old Cuba had kept
watch and then died, would be something terrible. His legs trembled
as he knew that around the next bend he would see that curtain of roots,
which Mac Randall had opened with his gun and stepped through,
coming on him by surprise, having no doubt tailed him, maybe just
to scare him or maybe just full-out kill him.

Maurice turned the bend—and there it was, not thirty yards, the

54

curtain of roots. He came up toward it cautiously, fearing everything—that he could be heard, that he could be seen, that Mac Randall, never gone to Columbus, was waiting on the other side of the root-curtain, pulling back the hammer of his gun. And it was a true terror that Maurice did feel, fifty-three years ago, when he at last pulled back the dangling roots and saw, staring at him, two great birds, black vultures, eagle sized—one claw-perched on Old Cuba's back and the other standing on that ridge of the bank where the dog had first been seen—and then the dark-black birds turning and breaking away on their wide wings, flapping down the open creek bed and at last climbing the air up onto some high dead limbs of an old cottonwood, from which they could keep a hard eye on their claim.

Those three stories up, in his quiet library on S. Calumet, Maurice Teague now moved to the front window and looked northeast to the parking lot of his mortuary, just a few hundred yards away on MLK. And there it was, slow billowing northward in the south breeze, spotlighted, at half-staff for the six thousand who died right there. Sons of God before they were sons of men. They received no respect—as persons. No nourishment or care. And no proper burial when they died here, from starvation, preventable disease, and inhuman abuse. Treated worse than animals, they perished in the thousands, only to be buried worse than animals. Think of it, Maurice Teague; take your soul through the deepest exercises of sympathy—right past every discrimination to the oneness that lies on the other side of original sin. Forgetting is one thing, but being able to forgive, that gift, it lies at the end of a long, chosen journey, awaiting the arrival of the soul driven by every sick agony that is its unforgiving hatred, that is division, division, division, and the sick desire to kill the offender in violent retribution, *lex talionis,* and so to speed on the cycle of violence. Original sin, it lives on, and on—just steps from the Tree of Life. But those few steps—they take so many years. More than fifty now. Oh, my Lord Christ, help me put down the flaming sword of my detestation and anger. Closure, the word is filth if it means just the false satisfaction that comes with vengeful retaliation, with winning over a jury to retaliatory wrath by ripping open your shirt and showing your scars. Victim's rights—demanded only outside the Gates of Eden.

Maurice, standing before his high window, let himself feel the bark of the vine he grabbed when he pulled himself up, past the death stare of Old Cuba, whose teeth were still bared in his frozen last look—and

DIVISION

up over the creek bank to the ledge where the dog had lain in watch
and where the one black vulture had been perched. He let himself feel
how he had stood there in the quiet, listening for a man with a gun,
and looking about him—into the surrounding tangle of underbrush.
He let himself feel again the sting in his hand—and hear the sound—as
he cracked off a dry but strong pine branch that was pronged—and so
good for digging. And then down that worn path in his mind, for the
thousandth time, he let his memory take those few steps to where he
saw it—the low dirt mound that was the length of a man, in that space
where the brush had been broken away. And he let himself feel the frenzy
and then—as he came upon something—the unbearable delicacy and
heartbroken, loving care in his hands and arms as he dug away the
dirt to find him, Jesse, his strong, kind, courageous brother, who stood
nothing from the white man, no matter the danger, ever, and who had
promised he would take Maurice away from here one day, lying there
still open-eyed, unburied, only just hidden in the shallow dirt, and
with the death stare on him like his brave dog's, and, no doubt in this
world, shot dead by the same gun. Two wounds, so terrible to see, unforgettable, one had torn open Jesse's chest, and a second....

Never would Maurice Teague want anyone to suffer the loss of a
brother still in his youth or young manhood. Pain so terrible. Everlasting. But when it's murder...and desecrating mutilation! On top of
the unbearable grief comes the rage. And when it's a white man who
does this to your black brother, the rage can widen 'til it covers the
whole of the white race, and can deepen 'til it erases all starting and
ending points and makes all whites the same, in a collective guilt running back to when the first of them saw he was different from the race
of Ham and called himself better. Nor had there been any justice for
Jesse...or funeral, or proper burial. No cross of sticks, even. For Maurice had feared to leave a sign that he'd been there. And when he finally found the courage to tell his mother about Old Cuba and Mac
Randall...and all that he'd found...she made him swear on the family
Bible, before a candle in a dark room, never in his life to tell his father,
or anyone else. And he never did—always believing that Early Dawn
was right when she said, "Won't come to no good, only more evil."
But as he stood now at his window, looking at the slow-billowing flag,
spot-lighted for the night, flying at half-staff for the dead, he determined that it was time to call his son.

WHERE DID IT START?

POLICE LINE DO NOT CROSS PO-
LICE LINE DO NOT CROSS POLICE: the yellow plastic of the
crime-scene tape, triple strung, closed off both ends of the alley that
ran between the backs of the homes on Lincoln Park West and of those
on N. Orleans. Calls had flooded the 911 lines. Numbers of neighborhood people had heard the shouting and the cracking gunfire. And
now pairs of Area 3 detectives were working their way up the 1400
blocks of both Lincoln Park West and N. Orleans, knocking on doors,
taking down statements. Lights were on everywhere. Home lights,
shining up above the alley, revealed faces in window after window.
Patrol car blues were flashing at both ends of the alley. Blue magnetic
rooftop lights were turning atop two unmarked cars, pulled up near
the Riordan Mercedes. The ambulance light, filling the alley with its
strong rotating beam, was encrimsoning gates, garages, and the coats
and faces of the police. Forensic lights had been set glowing by the
lab boys, who were all three kneeling in the alley, looking for more
shell casings, having tweezered and zip-locked seven. The press were

DIVISION

already at the tape, at both ends of the alley. Crowds, too, had gathered around both ends, and were growing. John Brenner, the 18th District Watch Commander, stood near the ambulance with three of his uniformed officers, Cristol, Morrissey, and Rudkus. Five Tac-teamers from the 18th were there as well—because this was a real heater: brutal black-on-white homicide; highest-profile, wealthy white real estate— the kind that had to be protected, for the sake of the city's name and wellbeing. The two beat officers first at the scene were also still there, and one was heading now to the south end of the alley to take back the tape for the ambulance, which at last was shutting down its rotating red light, and, silent, no siren necessary, and no speed, was beginning its trip to 2121 W. Harrison.

Jackie Riordan's sisters, Bridgid and Celeste, had come immediately when Tom Riordan called. They sat by her bed now, as Jackie, sedated by the paramedics, had for a while been gone into full sleep. It wasn't until she had become groggy in the sedation that they had been able to touch her. But now they had washed her and had taken her bracelets and necklace and washed the blood from them. The police said they would not need her clothes, so Celeste, when she and Bree took off Jackie's blood-covered blouse and suit, asked one of the uniformed policemen, officer Rudkus, if he could take them where they would never be seen again.

Bree, who now held her sleeping sister's hand, had not spoken for a long time. Her eyes were raw from weeping. Her lips were pursed tight as she just moaned and rocked her upper body and bobbed her head. She was thinking, over and over, of how she had said to Jackie, just days ago, that even still, with her own son Billy dead a full four years, she would get up every morning feeling that the only reason she was still alive was that she hadn't died. She had lost him, only eleven years old, in a terrible accident, hit by a speeding boat, in Michigan. And she had been waiting ever since in some kind of heartbroken, empty faith for the message from God that would tell her what she was supposed to make of her grief. She thought every day that God had been more generous to Billy, whom mercifully he'd taken away from this world.

And where will this take Jackie?—Bree now asked of that darkness beneath her shut eyes that she had spoken to, out loud in the car, in her bedroom, in her kitchen, and in silence everywhere, every day since her own child had died. How is she supposed to stop the birth of monsters in her brain? What kind of cancer has already been conceived

58

WHERE DID IT START?

in her mind, and is now growing, even as she sleeps? And she'll wake screaming, you know this—if not for anyone to hear, then deep in her heart, maybe 'til the day she dies. The sick distaste, too—for people, good people, who try to offer words of comfort—for everyone associated with this moment, even Tom, and for Connor, who lived and didn't die, and for herself, her house, her life here? And why was it *murder!?* When it's *murder*—of her *son*—how is she supposed not to hate? You tell me, God. How does she keep her life from becoming just a relentless, vengeful anger? How does she keep herself from hating black people—*all* black people? Because you, God, have allowed racial cancers to be able to spread into hatred for whole peoples! And this one so easily could! I hate the Michigan beaches! I hate them all! And why does it not matter that we know such animosities are insane? Why, when we know this, can't we stop them from growing! Why can't we suction them out—these...sweeping, all-inclusive hatreds? And our sorrow, which you give *life* to—like some deadly tumor, it wraps itself around the brain stem of our souls, as if you told it exactly how to make itself inoperable?! How do we stop the life of such a thing—and just plain love again? Do we have to die first? Only the dead can be forgiven. I keep saying that line from that poem. When his father told him to fight, to hang on, Billy told him he couldn't; his last words, as his father held him in his arms, were "I'm sorry, Dad." How can I live with this? Were you with me when I removed the things from his room? When I took his clothes from his closet? When I took down his posters? Were you with me? Or was I alone? My beautiful sister—I beg you from a broken heart to help her. Help me. And help Jackie...before she wakes. She needs one of your miracles. She'll need one every day. A miracle to kill her sorrow.

"Do these things get carried into eternity? The last thing we did was quarrel! About abortion. A goddamned *sensitive subject.* Just another name for the things people tear each other apart over. He walked out in anger—because of the way I put things to him. He would have stayed in, and not been in that car. And this is what I have as a last memory. That we fought and he walked out, because of the way I spoke to him." Tom Riordan, elbows on his knees, the fingers of both hands run back through his still-thick gray-black hair, was sitting again in the window chair in the front room of the Riordan home, but bent over now, his eyes, moist and red, fixed on the floor. Detective John Touhy, thick set, with a shadow of late-day whisker, looking in his blue sweater and

59

open-collared blue-gray shirt even like a close-in-age brother of Tom Riordan, sat where young Jack Riordan had been sitting just an hour and a half ago. He had asked the father if there was any reason that Jack had gone out, having begun now with Professor Riordan because the other son, Connor, who sat across the room, looking out the window, had just stared at him when he asked if there was anything he could tell him about the shooting. Time pressed. He would need to get to Connor, who was right there in the car with Jack when he was killed, so he saw it all, saw the faces—but he had to give the shocked young man a little more time to regather his mind.

"Is there any reason," he asked, turning back to Tom, "to think Jack knew his killer? that he would have been in any way connected to him?"

"I can't imagine. Can't begin to imagine Jack connected to this person—I have to think, from Cabrini. And a murderer. Connected to a murderer? No. And it's not like I didn't know my son. It isn't like that. He led a full, high-energy life. But he never got into anything that was even close to truly wrong—never stepped over the line.... But he wouldn't take things lying down. Yet why...why didn't he tonight? God help me...I hope our quarrel...." Tom Riordan now just buried his face in his hands.

John Touhy waited a long moment, respectful. At last then, "No history between them. We see it that way, Professor Riordan. We do. We always need to know the beginnings of things. But this was all just right here—a carjacking from the start. It's just—please forgive me—that when the attack is so violent, we need to ask if there was anything between victim and killer." John Touhy, a father of two himself, a boy and a girl, about the ages of Jack and Connor Riordan, had begun graying early, like Tom Riordan—in the way black-haired men often will. God help this poor man, he thought, knowing his detective's inquiries might do no more for this father except further tear his heart—and now as for a brief terrible moment he imagined his Sean Michael killed the way Jack Riordan had been killed. Shot again and again in the face. Ripped apart beyond all recognition. God Jesus help us in this life—and in this godforsaken city.

Turned sideways in the armless chair nearest the fireplace, Connor Riordan, fairer than his father, more like his mother, looked out the front-room window, sitting on his hands, now all hot and sweated under his thighs, rocking slightly and nodding to the pulses of blue light coming from the patrol car that blocked the access alley up the street.

WHERE DID IT START?

Pulse after pulse of the blue light, blue and again blue. But words now came to Connor, his father's words. And suddenly he broke his silence. "I got him angry. *I was the one!*"

Tom Riordan took his face out of his hands. John Touhy turned and looked, and then rose, not standing, only stooping—but now he lifted his chair under him and turned it and moved it toward Connor's. He said, gently, "Can you tell me more, son—about what happened? Anything more, about how it began, about who was there?" Connor didn't turn. Still facing the window, he kept nodding in time with the pulses of blue light, kept rocking slightly, his hands under his thighs. But then, "You say you want to know the beginnings. How does a thing get started? When? Where? It wasn't you, Dad! Jacko and I fought, too, tonight. And it was worse! The last thing I said to him, before they got there, was that I wanted to kill him! The last thing before that big black guy came up, in the coat, with the bandana, shiny, like black silk. And Robert. The guy slammed the roof with his hand, like a bomb. I got out. I was telling Jacko to get out. Robert told me he was sorry. He said Connor Riordan, Connor, I'm so sorry. And he ran after the other one. He said we don't want this. We don't. I heard that. It's not worth this, the other one said. Nothing is. But I was a chickenshit. Jack told the big black guy with the gun in his hand he had nobody to blame but himself for his fucked-up life. He told him he had no right to steal from white people. He said get your hands off what doesn't belong to you. Get your fucking hands off. In the name of Jesus no. He was so sorry. Robert said he was so sorry. Then he ran."

John Touhy had risen from his chair. He had walked over to Connor. He didn't touch him. He just knelt now on one knee beside him. He said, gently, "Who is Robert, son? Connor, Con, can you tell me, son— who is Robert?"

"It wasn't you, Dad," Connor said again. "It wasn't you. It was Mom. Ellie. Ellie Shea. He stepped over the line. Jacko did. Maybe *murder* is not the word. Maybe it's the wrong word. That was murder—what that black guy did to Jacko. *That* was murder. But it wasn't you, Dad. It was Mom. She did it because she wanted to. She wanted some fucking change in her life! I told him I wanted to kill him. I said it! Those were my last words before that black guy slammed the roof, like a fucking bomb. I was the one who made this happen. You know this shit fuckin' chicken? he said. Fuck y'all motherfuckers forever! But Robert was so sorry."

61

DIVISION

John Touhy, still kneeling beside him, now touched Connor's arm softly. He set his left hand gently around the back of the boy's right arm. He said, "Con, who is Robert?" He pressed his fingers just slightly tighter round the back of Connor's arm. "You spoke of Robert, Con. Who is Robert?"

"I knew it was Ellie. I *knew* it. That night at Butch's. I *knew* it! I told him I wanted to kill him! He crossed the line, with Ellie. Mom. Her gold necklace. Like a brokenhearted ghost. Is it equal? Equal? Equal! Equal! If you say it's equal, what then? If you say it isn't, what then? Killing is killing. What the black guy did was commit murder. *That* was murder. And I was the one. I told him I wanted to kill him!"

Tom Riordan—even as his mind, against his will, began to pursue the hints in his son's garbled speech as these fragments flew here and there, not believing he could be distracted by such things, or conflicted, with his other son just killed, murdered—still pleaded with Connor to concentrate if he could. "Con, think. Is Robert someone you know? Someone you've seen before?" Yet still as he spoke, knowing that getting Con to concentrate must right now be *the* important thing, he couldn't will out of his mind the things Connor had babbled about a girl Tom Riordan was sure he knew, a girl in his class at DePaul, Ellie Shea, he knew her, and things about Jackie, whatever those things might be or would ever come to, nothing, or something, from years ago? from now? and about Jack. He must be dead. It must be true. This is why this detective is here, asking about Robert. Robert who? Connor needed to concentrate and say who he was. "Robert *who?* Con. Can you tell us?"

"The one who said he was sorry. Who is he? Robert?" John Touhy held Connor's arm still more tightly. He lifted himself into a squat beside the boy and gently pulled his arm to turn him to him just slightly —to get him to look at him. "The one who said he was sorry, Connor. Who is he? Robert? Who is *Robert?!*"

"Teague. Robert Teague," Connor said—and blinked, and shook his head—as if he'd awakened himself with saying the name, though still he looked ahead, rather than down at the man beside him. "We went to Ignatius together. His sister, too, Carolyn. They live in Bronzeville. Their father is a mortician. But Robert didn't do anything. It was the big guy in the leather coat, with the gun. The silk bandana. Robert didn't do anything."

"But Robert was there tonight? One of three?" John Touhy had now brought out from his pocket a notebook and pen. "T-E-A-G-U-E?"

62

WHERE DID IT START?

Connor now turned to John Touhy, who was rising to his feet beside him. He looked up at the man. "Robert didn't start it. You're looking for the start of things. You've got to separate Robert out. He didn't do it. And the other one, who ran. It isn't all just one in the same. You've gotta separate things out. Five feet, two feet—it doesn't matter! They can be worlds apart. Not connected. Totally different people!!"

"His father is a mortician in Bronzeville?"

"On Martin Luther King. But he didn't do it. The whole time, nothing!"

"Their home is on Martin Luther King?"

"The funeral home. But Robert is innocent!"

"T-E-A-G-U-E?"

"Yes! But he and the one who ran. They're not the same as the one with the gun! They weren't in it!"

John Touhy had his pen still in his right hand, notebook in his left. "Justice, Connor," he said, "sorts things out. Robert Teague is not the same as the one with the black leather coat. Justice will see that. But we need to talk to Robert about the one in the coat, so we can bring this one who killed your brother to justice. Can you tell me where Robert lives?"

Connor fell into confusion again as he looked up at this man now hovering over him. Was he the one asking questions? But now Connor saw it again—the flash of the gun! and then again! and again! The blinding flash! The cracking sound! And the smell! And heard he was a chicken shit who valued life. And he said, "I told him I wanted to kill him. I was the one! Because of Ellie. He stepped over the line. But what that black guy did was murder. And Mom because she wanted to. She paid. She wanted a change in her life. I was so angry—at everyone. At Mom. At Jack. I said I wanted to kill him!"

"Where, Connor, does Robert Teague live? Can you tell me?" John Touhy was ready to go. He could in short order find out where this Teague lived, but if the boy could tell him, it would make things go still faster.

"Where does Robert live, Con? Detective Touhy needs to know. He needs to ask Robert who it was who was the real one—the one who *did* kill Jack." Tom Riordan now got up too and walked over to Connor. He touched his son on the shoulder. Then the father knelt down before his boy and took his son's cheeks gently in his hands and lifted his face to him. "Can you tell us where he lives, Con?" But Connor only buried his face now in his father's chest and held him tight. "It wasn't

63

you, Dad," he said. "I was the one who made Jack get angry. And it killed him. I was the one!" "Later, Con," Tom Riordan said. "We'll talk about that later, and so many other things. But now...." And the father now took his son by the shoulders and, gently, moved him away to arm's length. "Now we need to know where Robert Teague lives. Tell us where he lives if you know." "He wasn't in it," Connor said. "He didn't do it, Dad. And the other one, he was innocent, too!" "Where, Con? Where does Robert Teague live?" Connor bowed his head and looked at the floor—and, for a long moment, said nothing. Then, "In this beautiful house. Carolyn had a party." "Where, Con? Where is the Teagues' beautiful house?" With his head still bowed, eyes still on the floor, the boy said, "Around the corner. From the funeral home. 33rd and Calumet." He looked up—to John Touhy. "Don't do anything to him. I'd be sorry for the rest of my life if anything bad were done to Robert. He's already sorry for the rest of *his* life. He's not lying about that! And the other one; he did nothing. He *said,* the other one, 'We don't want this! We *don't!*' "

John Touhy without looking was scribbling "33 Calumet" in his notebook, and at the same time he was saying, as he looked down at the boy, "This other one, Connor. Can you tell me what he looked like? What he was wearing?"

Again Connor went silent—and his face went blank, but now this blank look seemed to signal a kind of sinking of his whole being into a memory. The boy began audibly to moan in short moans, like those of someone in intense physical pain. His father put his arms around his son and took him back to him in both arms and held him against his chest—until at last he was just breathing deeply against his father's chest.

"You have helped us so much, Connor," John Touhy said now. "You have given us what we need, son. And we will bring the right one to justice. Robert will help us, too. I'm sure you're right about Robert Teague—and that he'll help us." As John Touhy turned then to go, he said to Tom Riordan, "Professor Riordan, with your permission, I'm going to order Officer George Rudkus to remain in the house 'til morning, as a very dangerous man, who knows your son can identify him, is still at large. Officer Rudkus would be ready as well to answer any need your family might have for the securing of emergency services."

"Thank you," Tom Riordan said. "We are grateful."

John Touhy touched Tom Riordan's shoulder and gently squeezed

WHERE DID IT START?

it, before turning to go. But now, as the detective moved off toward the dining room, and, eager to get out to the Commander and the Tac-team boys, was looking across that chandeliered room through the passage that led into the kitchen, Connor Riordan, with the side of his face still held against his father's chest, said, "There was a W on his jacket, a sports letter, with a wing. And he wore a White Sox cap, backwards."

John Touhy stopped, and turned, but did not take out his notebook, rather made only a clear mental note—then said, "Thank you, son, so much. We will bring the right one to justice. I promise that to you and to your family. And it will not be long." Then quickly the detective made his way through the dining room toward the kitchen and the back door. But as he passed under the lintel into the kitchen, he heard a shattering cry come from the boy, and then another, and then hard, loud sobs; and he looked back to see the father holding the son still, and rocking his boy to comfort him in an agony that in deep and terrible ways, the detective knew, would remain unrelievable forever.

STILL THE INNOCENT SON OF MAURICE TEAGUE

He couldn't go home—Connor Riordan would say where he lived, but, terrified, Robert Teague didn't know where else to go. On North Ave., too afraid to think of anything but getting away from where he was, he walked as fast as he could without making himself look like a criminal on the run—west to the station at Clybourn—and took the "L" south. When, out past the canyons of the Loop, the train stood a moment at Roosevelt Rd., he could see the steeple of Holy Family Church, and the silhouetted block of St. Ignatius, his old high school, and Connor Riordan's...and his brother's. He got off at Comiskey Park/35thSt., his usual stop, and walked east, as always, past the narrow-belted, miles-long City of the Dead that had been the infamous State St. Corridor, along what remained of that particular grim run of it that had been Stateway Gardens (a wrecking ball, hanging from a towering crane, was there ready to swing into the morning's first ten-thousand-pound blow). But he didn't turn north on Calumet Ave., toward his home, rather kept walking 'til he came to MLK, and then turned north two blocks to the Teague Funeral Home—where, in the parking lot, there it still was, spotlighted in the dark, floating at half-staff, with its stars and X-crossed bars on its red ground. As he'd come down MLK, he'd suddenly worked up a superstition that if that thing was still there, then *all* was real, not just some nightmare in which insane things like those he went through to-night get connected with more insane things into an insane story. No. Not just an empty superstition. Or an insane dream. He'd had those—plenty of those black man's bad American dreams. But this was real. Connor Riordan's brother was dead.

Jack Riordan. Jacko. Big football player. Loud laugher. Never liked him. Never knew if he was one of the good ones. But what do I know about him? Connor loved his brother. And he's dead. Never another day of life. Like winning five consecutive lotteries, our coming into life. Maybe ten. Twenty. The chances in this universe that any of us would ever come into life. And he won't have another second of it. Shot in his face—by that gun that wouldn't stop! Watt's gun! Christ help us!—what is he?—Watt?

Robert had a key to the mortuary (which looked like a home, his father having had it built to look like some American-dream home)—and, taking now a last look down MLK for signs of the law, expecting flashing blue lights at any moment, or would it be a detective in an un-marked car?—he stepped into the shadow of the building's eaves, be-yond the reach of the light shining on that flag—which he could see was *still* there! He opened the mortuary's south door and made his way into the silent building, dark but for the outside lights' casting a beam through the small high windows of the door, which he now pulled tight behind him. Turning on no inside light, he made his way down the entry corridor to the first open room, the south visitation room. On a stand at the entrance a black letter board had on it a white-lettered name, which in the dimness he couldn't make out; and at the north end of the room, opposite that of the parking-lot picture window (which was draped, so no sign of that flag could be made out through it—though some of the spotlight's beam was breaking in where the drapes were slightly parted), a closed casket rested on its bier. And the person whose name was on the letter board, and who tomorrow would fill that coffin, would be resting now in the dark of the base-ment morgue room. Robert Teague had sometimes been the one who turned out the lights down there—not once without feeling a wrench of loneliness, thinking about what we are, and what we think we are.

Flowers would deck the table, too, in the middle of the room, and on

DIVISION

the display easels would be pictures of whoever that person was in the morgue room, who would be waked here tomorrow (for the community hadn't yet shunned the mortuary of a man who, if he hung up that X-crossed flag, had also waked Elijah Mohammed). His father would be gracious to the mourners—and respectful. Every day the man saw it all—from people going through the motions to people suffering real and unbearable grief. Robert wanted to call him. He had come here, he could feel now, not for no reason, but to be as close to his father as he could without bringing the law down on Maurice Teague's door. Because he wasn't hiding. He would be caught. Just a matter of time. And the best thing now would be to turn himself in—to call the police and tell them where he was. He knew—but was afraid.

Along the west wall, beside the empty easel boards, there was an upholstered settle-bench, and Robert walked to it now and sat—about evenly between, at one end of the silent room, the empty casket, and, at the other, the draped parking-lot window, through which those few shafts of the spotlight's beams were breaking. And still there, beyond the drapes, that X-crossed insult. Forgiveness. The key to the King-dom of Heaven. Your forgiveness isn't forgiveness until it has the look of madness. But Christian meekness could never make a revolution. You inherit *nothing* of the earth under the laws in this country, if you're black. He'd said these things to Watt, and it all came in the end to a gun to the head. He knew that still on his deathbed he'd be asking himself if Jacko Riordan would have lived, had he never said to Watt the things he said. An accomplice. Would the police ask if he provoked the killer? Would he be grilled on this—if he had to take the stand? Do not testify in your own defense. Do not take a lie-detector test (be-cause uncontainable words can start up uncontrollable trains of asso-ciation in the mind, provoking who knows what responses). Anything you say can be used against you in a court of law. Property law. Ninety percent of it. Keep-things-as-they-are-law. Redistribution across every line of division. He'd said—so that Watt could hear it—that it would take a gun to the head. He'd said, to impress Watt, to get himself *in* with Watt, to bring himself *together* with Watt, not Marcus, that his fa-ther, Maurice Teague, did some shameful, unmentionable shit.

Because he'd found out that our family's funeral home sat where the Civil War prison Camp Douglas (and *naturally* the land *right here along Martin Luther King Drive!* was owned by that anti-equality, pro-slavery, pro-Dred Scot, pro-universal-and-eternal denial of the person-

68

hood of black men, women, and children Stephen A. Fucking Douglas, who's got his pillar still here looking out over Lake Shore Drive!)—because Maurice Teague read in a history book that exactly where our black funeral home was, was where the Union brutalized thousands of Confederate prisoners, a full six thousand of whom died—because he read about this crime against humanity and found out too that if the Union didn't throw them in the cholera yard, it dumped the bodies of the Confederates in the City Grave Yard, where their bones then got washed up by Lake Michigan until those bones were, by an embarrassed Chicago, dragged up from the muck and hauled in a mass undifferentiated heap over to Oak Woods, where they got shoveled into a hole that sits now under another tall pillar and has four Civil War cannons around it and pyramid-stacked cannon balls, and a flag of the United States (all of this obscure, forgotten site now darkened in the surrounding gloom-shadow of that other forgotten American refuse heap that is Greater Grand Crossing, deepest dirt-poor Chicago ghetto, where on a daily basis lost black folk just eat each other alive)—that because my father read in his history book, *To Die in Chicago,* all about this Camp Douglas, and because he has given his life to the proper burial of the dead and because his Christian soul was offended by the disrespect shown to the personhood of these Confederates and so-called rebels (who called oppressive the government that demanded of them that they end their own hideous oppressions)—because he was so ghost-haunted by the inhuman disrespect shown to the personhood of these fucking pseudo-rebels, who, every one, for this Christian Maurice Teague, *was a son of God before he was a son of man*—because of *all* this, this self-abnegating Christian madman, my father, set out that X-crossed battle flag. A black man did this right in the soul's center of black Chicago, Bronzeville, not the "Douglas" neighborhood, on Martin Luther King Drive.

Jacko Riordan would never be waked in this black funeral home, not in this capital city of divisions. Tell that mortician that on one arm of the white prison population it was always the Stars and Bars, and, on the other, the Swastika. Kikes, niggers, non-persons—gas chambers and the slave trade, commodities, mere contents of conception, buy 'em, sell 'em, degrade 'em—'til the one called Watt values himself so little that he becomes a walking murder-suicide, but still with all the raw power God gave him, including especially that of mind. When I die, show no pity. Hardened killer, unafraid to die, or kill—because he values life so little. But no better than Marcus, I might have followed that man's black-gangster power—all the way until I crossed some un-re-passable line. The way he looked at me. To convert me. The way he told me what it really takes. The Six. Were you, Robert Teague, in any way in partnership, in league, with this *Watt* when he shot Jack Riordan in the head?

That moment before Watt's gun went off—it was loaded with the history of America. But, Christ, I fucking *despise* history. The bullshit that supposedly makes me this or makes me that. Determines outcomes. Fuck history. And let all black people say *fuck* history, if we don't own it. I am me. And Watt is Watt. But if we're free agents, true persons personally responsible for what we are, then we can't blame anyone but ourselves for what we do, not white people, not anyone else present or past but only our own present selves, the way Jacko Riordan said before he died—his last words, the ones that got him shot in the head.

But where does it *start*—the way a person acts? lives? To understand all is to forgive all. History is forgiveness, when it takes all we've come from, the poverty and abuse, into account. But, NO, goddammit, forgiveness is not exoneration. It is not saying that the free person is after all not a person but a mere product of history—and therefore, as a no-person, forever blameless. Forgiveness is the forgiveness of *sins*. The law knows we are free, and personally responsible—capable of *sin*. The law deals in eternity, and our free and immediate relation to it, not history. Watt knew what he was doing. And I was there, with him. Not because I wanted Sara Lee, or just because I wanted her. But O God *Christ* how much better my life would be if I were with Sara Lee now—which is where I would have been, touching that beauty, closing my eyes and feeling her kiss, instead of here, with my life in fucking ruins, neither a hardened criminal, nor, anymore, my father's good son.

And my father's life. God help me. And forgive me. And Connor, forgive me. That good white kid, Connor Riordan, whose life will never be the same. Not an hour. And who was I to have changed Connor's life forever, or even for a minute—or the lives of his family. To have been there, been part of it, when his brother, Jack, whom I never knew the first thing about, was destroyed—for a car! A gun to his head, fired again and again, tearing apart a life!

The willful ignorance of what life is, the closing of the eyes to *that*. O Jesus God I am so sorry. I am so fucking sorry! Connor, I am so sorry. If there is an afterlife—then it has to be some kind of life in which Jack

Riordan could forgive me, forgive Watt, even as if it were nothing. It wouldn't be worth living if it weren't that. Infinitely better to be blank dead forever than to be forever unforgiving, even of some lynch mob of slave masters who would laugh in front of some festive crowd when they strung up a teenage boy, having cut off his testicles and penis and stuffed them in his mouth.

Sitting still on the settle bench, his eyes having adjusted to the darkness as it mixed with that light breaking in from the parking lot, Robert Teague now determined to call his father and tell him everything, and then to go to him and to call the police. For three days, he had had his phone silenced against all calls from his father, though he had checked numerous times—and found no record of voicemails or calls received from Maurice Teague. There'd been a number of voicemails from his sister, Carolyn—pleas to him to come home.

But now when he opened his phone, he saw in its screen light that just two hours ago, his father had called him. He felt a rush of grief. Two hours ago—I was making my way home, maybe, and hadn't yet seen Marcus—or Watt. The world was so different, from what it is now —and will be now. If I hadn't shut my ringer off, and had answered my father, I would not be part of a horrible murder. I'd have been the innocent son still of Maurice Teague, who has given me all, who has spent his life on ending, with *me,* cycles of poverty...and violence.

Robert had his phone still opened in his hand, and now he bowed his head and waved the still-lighted phone over himself, back and forth, in another rush of grief. As tears now began to gather in his eyes, he rose. He walked to the window and pulled back the drapes. And now he stood in the wide un-draped window, his phone light still shining, he himself lighted now in the glass by the light shining on the Stars and Bars.

"There he is! In the window!"

Robert Teague heard the shout, and, wiping his eyes, now saw running across the parking lot two uniformed Chicago cops, bulletproof-vested, in ball caps, and two more in overcoats, all with guns drawn. The two in vests were already at the south door of the mortuary, pounding on it, shouting out "Robert Teague! Come out with your hands up, Teague!" One of the overcoats had made his way toward the window, ready any second, Robert knew, to turn into the picture window with arms up and outstretched, his gun raised in his two hands, set to fire. The other was heading round the western edge of the building—

71

DIVISION

to cover any escape he might try out the north door. And now sirens were loud out east on MLK. And already he was hearing these sirens' last weird whoop. Car doors slammed. And now—but at the east door, on MLK—more loud pounding—his name being shouted—his being told to come out! with his hands over his head!

He had no wish to die. He dropped his phone where he stood (Amadou Diallo), shouted loud, "Don't shoot! I'm coming out. I have no weapon!" He made his way to the visitation-room entrance, where now he hit the light switch, so he could be seen clearly when he came out the south door—which slowly he did then—but then quickly, as he let go the handle, raising both his arms over his head. Immediately as he stepped out he was grabbed, one arm taken by each of the two in uniform and vests, and yanked out into the light and, near the base of the flag, slammed to his knees and then shoved face-first onto the concrete. His hands were pulled behind his back and he was cuffed with a knee between his shoulder blades as he was pressed to the pavement.

"Robert Teague, you're under arrest for the murder of Jack Riordan!"

One of the two plainclothes re-holstered his gun and bent down to stare close into Robert's face as the uniform who had handcuffed him pulled him back to his knees. This plainclothes now mockingly set Robert's glasses, which had been knocked awry, back straight—and looked brutally into his face. "You have the right to remain silent, Teague, and all that other shit." As now he was hauled up to his feet, Robert, feeling a sick fear of all the newest realities of his life, said nothing, keeping his eyes up and away from the plainclothes, this reader, mocker of his rights, who he feared might pistol whip him or even gun him down if he so much as said a word, and instead followed the spotlight up to the red and blue, X-crossed flag. Indelible stain. Tattoo of death. "Christ," the plainclothes said now, "if I don't hate every last one of these motherfuckers—South Side fucking youths."

You wanna fix what's wrong? Execution. Fear a God. Only thing's gonna stop this shit. Cruel and unusual? Cruel and unusual would be what the Riordan boy got. So give it right back. An eye for an eye. Thank *Christ* for the death penalty. And let the family be there. For closure. But you tell me how ya ever get enough closure—to stop that family's goddam pain? Maybe feed the killer's body to the fucking crows.

Robert Teague kept hearing the like from the two arresting uniforms of the 21st District as he sat cuffed and screen-caged in the back of the squad in which they transported him from E. 29th St. to "Violent

72

STILL THE INNOCENT SON OF MAURICE TEAGUE

Crimes" at Western and Belmont. And again and again, as they drove across the city, he'd turned these cops, big, thick-bodied white guys, into jurors, judges, prosecutors. Silver stars on their jacket chests. The four-starred flag of Chicago on the arms. The checker-banded hats of the Chicago police.

And now these hours. How many hours had he been left alone since they took and left him here, in this unpainted concrete-block what? holding room? shackled to this iron-stapled bench, listening to the buzzing of the fluorescent lights, watching them blink, struggle. Tactics. Scare tactics, from the start, with all that talk in the car, and now the two? three? hours sitting here, chained, waiting for something to happen.

If I say the name *Watt,* what will they say? Do they know him as Watt? Do they know there were three? I won't give Marcus away. Did Connor Riordan see that there were three? Did anyone, up in a window? I won't give Marcus away. If I say there were only two and someone saw that there were three? Will they trap me? What will happen if I lie?

These had been Robert Teague's questions to himself, for hours. He couldn't get past them. He wanted his father. He hadn't been given his call. He had a call—a right to one telephone call—and to a lawyer. But there hadn't even been a sound at the door. He was afraid to rattle his chains. He was afraid for his life. And no clock here. At least if there were a clock. Or some kind of change.

More time passed. And more. Then, at last—after how many hours?— a turning of the handle of the room's single door. A white man, gray-white whiskers and hair, a blue sweater, not a uniform sweater, his shirt blue but not uniform, and no tie. He said some words to someone outside the door—as if there were more urgent matters outside than in— and then entered, closing the door behind him. No gun, just a notebook in his hand. He didn't look at Robert, rather kept his eyes on the notebook as, from the side of the room opposite the bench, he took up in his free hand a folding chair and then brought it over before Robert —at last, while still looking only at his notes, seating himself before the boy shackled to the bench.

"St. Ignatius," he said, now finally looking up. "Great school. And your sister, Carolyn, went there too?"

"Yes." This night was so strange and terrible—so far out of the realm of all his experience. But Robert felt immediately the comfort of a simple truth. Yes. For the first time in so many hours, a trace of comfort.

73

DIVISION

To keep feeling it, this peace and comfort, he wanted now to keep telling nothing but the simple truth—to let all defenses go, and to speak the truth to this man. Was he a detective? He wasn't like the others. He was good. He had to be.

"My kids have friends who went there. I have a son about your age. And a daughter who would maybe be Carolyn's. If I had it to do over again, Robert, I'd have had them go to Iggy for sure."

"My father wanted us to go there."

"He wanted the best for you."

"Yes."

"Sean Michael, and Janey. Those are my kids. Touhy. Our name is Touhy. I'm John Touhy. I'm a detective, Robert, with the Chicago Police Department."

"Yes."

"You guessed that."

"Yes."

"Robert, will you do me the great favor of not saying 'It depends' when I ask you a question?"

Robert smiled and said, "It d..."

"Nah ah ah ah. Let's not get off on a wrong foot." John Touhy smiled, then hunched his chair a bit closer and bent his head closer. "Let me just ask you, Robert, to *try* not to say 'It depends,' okay? Here's the truth as I see it right now, son—about an issue we haven't yet broached. With respect to this issue, to this case we have here, you can be a suspect —or you can be a witness. And in a case like this case, it will make a very big difference for you—suspect or witness. So here's my question, and no 'It depends,' okay? Will you be a witness?"

Comfort gone, confusion spread immediately through his thinking and feeling—but Robert Teague, hoping still for some peace, some freedom from fear, from being thought a criminal...at Violent Crimes, said, "I will."

John Touhy didn't move in his chair, or change his expression. He looked carefully in Robert's face. He smiled slightly. Then, "When the time comes, son, the fact that you didn't lie, and that you helped us— this will help you more than you could believe." He looked down now at his notebook, turned over a page, and without looking back up, asked, "How many were you tonight, Robert, in that alley?"

Robert didn't answer. He felt a sudden dread and a need to explain.

74

He said, "I had just decided to turn myself in. But then they came. They found me when I was just about to turn myself in."

"How many were you, Robert, in that alley tonight? *How many?*" John Touhy, who had not once changed the tone of his voice until now, said this with a voice just noticeably raised. But then, back again in the quieter voice he'd been using before, "Tell me, Robert, was it just the two of you?"

Robert thought of Marcus. Maybe no one had seen Marcus. But if he told a lie now, if he was being tricked into lying, and he was caught lying, he might spend the rest of his life in prison. Or lose it, an eye for an eye. "There were," he said, feeling a sudden sick shame, "three of us."

"One wore a lettered jacket and a ball cap, backwards."

"Yes." Robert, as he answered, thanked God he hadn't lied. This guy knew far more than he was saying. He wouldn't lie now. He could die if he lied.

"I need his name. Do not lie to me, Robert Teague, and tell me you *don't know* his name. Do not lie to me!" John Touhy looked fiercely at Robert. He leaned forward, close to his face.

"Marcus. His name is Marcus."

"Marcus who, Robert? And do not tell me you don't know Marcus who! Do not lie to me, Robert Teague!"

"Sabbs, Marcus Sabbs; he's my cousin. I ran into him tonight. Just an accident—over near Lincoln Park. That's how we came together!"

John Touhy ignored the explanations. "Just tell me where he lives, Robert. Tell me where your cousin Marcus Sabbs lives!"

He had already spilled his guts. Robert felt the shame, the dishonor, of being known as one—of being mocked as one—who just instantly spilled his guts, giving up his cousin. But still so afraid for his life, he said, "Marcus lives in Cabrini—in the Row Houses, on Cambridge, with his mother, my aunt Dosey Sabbs."

John Touhy had withdrawn a pen from the spiraling wire of his notebook and, having clicked out the ball point, he rapidly noted down the location and the names, hard scoring an underline beneath them.

"But he did nothing!" Robert cried in a new sick misery, and fear. "He didn't do it! Marcus didn't do it!"

"Well then," John Touhy said, placing his left hand with the notebook on his left knee and his right hand with the pen on his right, "that leaves you and the third one." He leaned again forward, right into Robert's face, his own face wearing the look of someone who wanted

DIVISION

it understood that he could say life or death with respect to the future of any detainee he held under his power. "Who is he? If not you, Robert Teague, who used the gun? Name him, Robert, name that one with the black leather coat and the blue-black bandana! Name him—or be complicit with him—in a capital crime—because we *will* charge you with capital murder!"

"Watt! That's all I know! Marcus just called him Watt!"

"Jesus Christ!" John Touhy said, now standing, pushing back his chair with the back of his legs, "how did you get tied up with that homicidal animal? Did you say anything that brought him to that alley— behind the home of two boys you went to school with? Did you say anything that made him fire that gun, right into the head of a boy you went to school with! What got it started? What?"

"I didn't! I had nothing to do with it! I swear! Whatever he did, he did it himself! I had no part of it!"

John Touhy had turned away from Robert Teague. He had walked away from him toward the door and now rushed out, letting the metal door shut itself behind him, leaving the pleading boy alone, shackled to the iron-stapled bench, in the concrete-block holding room at "Violent Crimes," with no clock.

NO DREAM

The paramedics had taken his shirt and sweater. They'd washed his face and neck and hands—and examined him further, head to foot, to see if any traces of his brother's blood remained on his clothes or shoes. When they asked for and got for him fresh jeans and shoes and socks, he took off his old things and put on the new. But he hadn't let them stick a needle in his arm and had taken no pills to sleep. And now somewhere in the middle of the night, never having gone to bed, just having for hours paced his room (though for a time he'd stopped and watched as a police tow truck winched up his mother's Mercedes), Connor Riordan stood before his bathroom mirror, with only the sconce light on, shining low like a candle. As he stared into the mirror, he now pulled fiercely on the neck of the fresh t-shirt—imagining they'd missed spots of Jack's blood and that when he pulled down on the shirt, there they would be.

But nothing there. So maybe it hadn't happened. But now suddenly he was down in the alley, sitting in the car with Jack, raging over what Jack let out about their mother, telling Jack he wanted to kill him over what happened with Ellie Shea—and now hearing that hard rapping at the window and the terrifying pounding on the roof—and as, right then, he was getting out of the car, fast, Jack was staying where he was and putting down the window—Why!—Did he want not to live?—and telling the black guy he had no right to steal from whites, that he had no one to blame but himself for what he was, and to take his hands off what didn't belong to him—and now that murderer, like some dark terror in a nightmare, was taking up his gun and filling the car with flame and the deafening gunfire and smoke and the stink of matches, and Jack's blood, all that wet blood. Connor could see it in the mirror —on his chest where he pulled on the neck of his shirt, so hard he now ripped it. With two hands, he tore the t-shirt off and threw it to the floor—and in the mirror he saw his chest blood-covered—and he hoped that the blood was his own.

Tom Riordan, lying wide-eyed beside his deep-sedated wife, had for a long time been listening to the footsteps of his son crossing and re-crossing the floor in the room above. He hadn't gone up. Jack had died, had been brutally slaughtered, tonight, God almighty help us— and he hadn't gone up to talk to Connor, though he had been listening to his pacing and pacing. But now the pacing had stopped, and Tom Riordan hoped that maybe Connor had given in to exhaustion. But so unbelievable—it was things that Con had said, incoherently uttered in a kind of babble, that had been pressing on his mind and breaking through his grief almost to the point of dominating all feeling. It can't be helped—*feeling*. But the voice of your feelings, if you can't silence it, you can ignore it. You can *do* the right thing, no matter what you might feel. He now touched his wife's hair, lifting it back from where in dis-array it had fallen over her face, so beautiful, but which even in sleep seemed tortured out of its beauty by a harsh new reality that would never let her be the same again.

He inhaled deeply in shocked pain and closed his eyes. He took his hand back from Jackie's face and again lay on his back, opening his eyes on the ceiling but hearing still nothing above. What had Con meant when he said *she* was the one—Jackie, *Mom,* was the one—that she'd crossed the line—and that Jack had crossed the line, with Ellie Shea? *Equal*—all killing was equal. Con, his son who lived, said again and again *equal*. He'd talked with him about equality—about how the denial of it can lead to sexism, slavery, abortion. Slavery works from the denial of equality. And abortion works from it. He'd talked about

NO DREAM

this with Con, just yesterday. The fetus isn't equal to a full person, just like a Jew to a German, a black to a white, a woman to a man. The argument with Jack tonight, their last words with each other. Jackie's silence.

He pictured now Ellie Shea. He thought about all he didn't know about the lives of his students. But maybe he would have remembered Ellie Shea, even years after—the girl with the dark red hair, cut in a stylish way, rounded, cut evenly on both sides—that framed her face, very pretty. But so many were pretty. And smart—she was one of the very good ones. But A students didn't get especially remembered. Most likely he would have wholly forgotten her. But not now, not until the day he died, would he ever not think of Ellie Shea as the girl who for some time had carried the child of his son—the son who died young, who was murdered, all his beautiful, immeasurable potential cut off! Not another hour of seeing, hearing, thinking, of being with people who loved him! Jesus Christ, help me! And would he, when he saw her again, see Ellie Shea's face now as beautiful, not pretty but beautiful? He imagined himself looking at her face now and telling her, in some way that might help all her days, that he would remember her always.

It was unbearable—the grief. And how could he teach *Adam Bede* to that class she was in? He would not. Hetty Sorrel. To be hanged for infanticide. While you pity Hetty and would never have condemned her to die—do you condone infanticide? Would you not say to Hetty that we love you and understand your misery and that you cannot handle this having birthed a child, and we will help you, take the child for you, and we would never hang you—but we cannot condone your killing of your newborn. We cannot call this permissible....

He couldn't believe he was thinking these things. The professor, thinking these things, even now. But it couldn't be helped. Thoughts—just like feelings. You can't stop the things that come up in your brain—come up even as you follow your son's coffin to the grave. But you can cancel the reading of *Adam Bede*. This you can do. You cannot *make* feeling do the right thing—even as you lie next to your wife on the night your son was killed. Horrible shit comes up. But you can wait until the feelings of love return. This is marriage, a vow. It means waiting—until the feelings of love return—again and again waiting—because they *will* return. But had she...waited? As she vowed she always would? Or had she crossed the line—and done impermissible fucking shit? What had she done with Jack and Ellie Shea? And what else had she done—

79

because she needed a change in her life! Who doesn't sometimes want change! Want out! He couldn't believe the shit his life had become. The pain. The unbearable confusion. As if his son's dying—his being murdered—just hours ago!—Jack gone forever!—that beautiful, strong boy, good boy, with so much life in him!—as if this weren't enough!

And the rage! What was he supposed to do with the rage that he knew he would feel, more and more, the rage against the killer of his son, the desire to murder this murderer—to execute him with his own hands! Sweet closure—by the neck until dead! And he was black! Of course he was! Jesus Christ! He looked again at Jackie asleep beside him. Could he feel more grief—more anger? Not possible! But there are things I could be wrong about. Ellie Shea. Jack. Jackie. I will need to talk to Con—because I could be so wrong. I have got to have Con tell me what the truth is. But I could no more ask him now than die. And whatever the right thing is to do, in the hell of this unbearable heartbreak...and rage, I do not know.

Would the sun ever come up? Connor had sunk to the bathroom floor. He sat, eyes closed, his face in his hands. From the first moment —at Ignatius, the first day freshman year, when he saw her. And all those days in the classes they took together. He wouldn't look. Never would look. But what he felt whenever she came in, or when she was there when he came in. And every time she spoke, her voice…. And the things she said—even though he never showed a response—how they would, at times, almost seem even physically to touch him…the more he tried not to show a thing. And never a change except a greater deepening of his feelings, over the four years, which seemed now to have passed in a day. But so unbelievable now—that first time he saw her, Ellie was walking down the corridor at Ignatius with Carolyn Teague. Closest friends still. Carolyn Teague—Robert's sister! How does this all happen, as if in a dream-story! And he'd *told* it to Jack— told Jack that he was so in love with Ellie Shea that he could never let it be known that he even cared for her, just on the chance that she might hint that she could never care for him in the same way. Was it only once he'd told this to Jack? Or more than once? Had he put it exactly this way? Fucking *yes,* he had. Or maybe not. Maybe he had never said it would kill him—that he could die from it, the way he loved her. No one should love so much. Because the one you love so much might sleep with your brother, who didn't, when he slept with her—once?— more than once?—fifty times?!—give one goddamned shit what that would mean to you or her! Or maybe he did give a shit. Maybe he did what he did *deliberately*. Premeditated. Did he want to kill me? I said I wanted to kill him. The last words he heard from me! But maybe he'd done, with Ellie, nothing except what I was too chickenshit to do—me the chickenshit, who knows the value of life!—and maybe done it innocently. Christ, how do I get out of this! Mom helped us make the choice, he said! She paid for it—because she wanted to! Jesus fucking Christ! Mom! Who are you?! I can't picture it! I cannot picture the shit of it! And Jacko is dead the way I need to be dead. Gone—like Jack. Forever. But I know the value of life! But how do I get out! How on this shit fuck earth do I get out?

That murderer. Where are you when you can murder! *What* took you there? But if he'd just killed me. All solved. I'm out. Ended. That black man with his gun ended Jacko for me the way that that abortion.... Closed it all off. No more consequence of Jack's sleeping with Ellie. Fucking her. No more wanting to kill my brother all the rest of my days. Because he's dead. Such a convenience. And I can go about my life—without him, without his and Ellie's child. Christ, how can it ever begin, absolution? How will I fucking *ever* get out of this shit that is my so-called life? I'll walk down the street—and it will come back, years and years from now, if I live that long—that stink and blood and Jack's life over, in an instant, that deafening gun. Where did he go the instant that first bullet hit his face? To what kind of place? Or to what nothingness? And where do I go to get out? That one word—*sorry*. Who was Jack, my brother? Maybe I never knew—what he was. But Robert said he was sorry. Robert Teague. Why was he there? I don't know how this happened—that that black guy was where he was and I was where I was and Jack was where he was. Too fucking much to say where things begin—or how or why they come together. Take your pick, and blame what you want.

But I have to say I know Robert. I have to say *hard* that Robert Teague is not the kind who would murder—that he's innocent. What does it matter that he was there? *He* wasn't there—Robert, the real Robert. He said the word *sorry*. Everything that he is, was in that word. But why was he there? Can't ask that. Can't let that question set off a thousand fucking possibilities until I don't know who Robert is or who I am or what any goddam thing is. I've got to cut off the fucking endless suggestions that can make anything into anything—and just *say* that Robert had no part in this. I've gotta do this. Or somebody else

DIVISION

will come in and just *say* that he's guilty and deserves to die. And if somebody asks me whether by helping Robert I'm failing to give my own brother justice, I just won't watch as the ripples from that stone go on and on, suggesting endless things, going everywhere. That other guy, too, I know enough about him. I heard him. He said *We don't want this!* No! We don't want this! I heard that—and I will fucking *say* that I heard it—and that I saw him run. But it won't help me. No doubt it won't. Not for shit it won't. Nor will the voices in my head ever stop asking why those two were there. But I won't listen to those voices—even though not listening won't fucking help. But it will never do me any good, either, when they catch that guy who pulled the trigger. Called me chickenshit. And when they convict that violent murderous fuck and set him on the gurney—it will bring no good to me—though voices in me will whoop out some pathetic worthless war cry. Closure! Hoo-fucking-ray!—which shit will all just go dead silent and show its total worthlessness—when I try to sleep. And can't. Justice solves nothing. Neither does mercy.

Still sitting on the bathroom floor, Connor closed his eyes and again covered his face with his hands. The house was silent. In the silence and darkness, he thought of death—and considered whether, if for some continuing time he were to keep his eyes closed and make no sound, he might just fade into nothingness. He couldn't tell how much time was passing, without event. But at last he heard a sound, a voice talking—not his mother's or father's—rather a stranger's voice, coming from the first floor—the kitchen—he could tell, in the otherwise perfect quiet. Only one voice, a man's—so someone down there, some guy, on the phone? Connor lifted his head—but couldn't make out the words, which however now came louder. He rose to his feet, straining to hear the words, to make them out—not in a dream. The sounds were real. Some man was on the phone in their kitchen. He stepped out from the bathroom and began to walk down, past now his parents' room. He could hear the words more clearly—and still more clearly as he made his way to the bottom of the stairs.

"I'm sorry. It is terrible. Really bad. I should have let you sleep. But you'd told me you knew him. You'd talked about him, all those times. I never asked, but I figured you two had a history.... Yeah...I'm really sorry.... Yes, I'm here now... Yes, Lincoln Park West. I'm sitting at their kitchen table right now—because the guy who did it—he's still out there —and because the brother... Connor, yes, he saw him. There were three.

82

NO DREAM

Connor saw all three—and he knew one of them, a kid, black guy, someone he knew... I don't know... No, Ellie, I didn't hear the name. But
we got the name... Ignatius? No... I don't know. Pretty unlikely, don't
you think?... Yeah...very unlikely."

Having made his way past the front room, Connor was standing in
the unlighted dining room, looking into the kitchen, where under the
track lights, sitting at his mother's new table, a uniformed police officer,
his cap hanging on the finial of the chair he sat on, was talking on the
phone. The cord was drawn across the table, and the cop was turning
his father's book on the table's surface, with his forefinger and thumb.
Connor had heard every word the cop had just said. And now, "Ellie,
Ellie... No need to thank me. I thought you might have been upset
if I didn't call you—if I waited... Yes... He was there, Connor... Yes,
in the car... As soon as I can, yes. I promise I'll come as soon as I can."

Connor was still standing in the dining room, now just staring at the
cop, who, as he hung up, now turned in the chair and sat up straight, so
that Connor could see his face in profile—light-browed, his hair blond-
ish, blonde-whiskered, strong-jawed, not fleshy in the face—strong—
young, not much older than he was, maybe twenty-five—so someone
she could in reality be seeing—though this had to be a dream. Connor
moved—took an audible step toward the kitchen to prove that this was
a dream—and to make it end with a real sound, which would wake him
from it. But when he moved, the cop, really there, turned full-face to
him. He rose then and looked into the dining room. He saw Connor.
"Rudkus," he said, "Officer George Rudkus. And you're Connor. I'm
here to watch for the night, Connor. Anything you need—just name
it. I'm here to help."

"Who were you talking to?"

"Just my girlfriend. So sorry if I woke you. Really so very sorry."

Connor looked now at the cop's face—at his jaw, at his hair, blue
eyes, blonde whiskers, an Eastern European face, strong, intelligent.
But now saying nothing, Connor turned back to the stairs and headed
back up toward his room, determining perhaps never to come out of
that room alive.

Then, however, in this real nightmare, as he passed his parents' room,
he heard his father, "Con, is that you? Con?" And now his mother—
from out of the darkness, perhaps wakened by his father's calling out
to him—first groaning, then groaning again deeply, and turning in the
bed. Now she cried out. No words, just a wild cry, which subsided at

83

DIVISION

last back into a groan—as his father said to her, "Jackie, Jackie—it's me, Tom"—and then kept saying to her, "I am with you. I am with you. Right here with you, Jackie"—which Connor kept hearing as he made his way again now up the stairs, not knowing what in this life he could believe.

MOTHER
AND SON

         Sometime past five in the morning, but still in darkness, a patrol car out of the 18th, carrying two vested officers from the District's Tac Team, one armed with a Mossberg 12-gauge, had come to Cambridge St., at the south end of the Cabrini Green Row Houses, and then had waited for the team's second car as it made its way to the north end. In the second car were four vested officers, two with Mossbergs, a third with a battering ram. The fourth, a sergeant, carried a warrant for the arrest of Marcus Sabbs on a charge of murder. As at last the two cars, moving, one north, one south, slowly, no flashing lights, came together on Cambridge and, quietly, the six Tac officers emerged and then surrounded 921, three to the back, three to the front, sixty-year old Dosey Sabbs was sleeping, though not soundly.

    Her baby, Marcus, had not come home. There had been other nights when he didn't come home and some when he did but came home high. About this, there was no use lyin' to Dosey Sabbs, or tryin' to hide what she could tell from ten mile away—what with all her other children and their doin's, especially Johnnie B, who's shot dead 'cause a the drugs now seven years back, and with that long-gone daddy a

Marcus's, most likely dead now too, for all she knew—what with every last *one* of 'em having deep-lessoned her in just about every kind a heartbreakin' lie. And the girls sellin' themselves for it. She knew that, too. And now in California, sellin' their bodies for it, most likely. Never did matter how hard she might have tried to get any of 'em safe or keep 'em free, or how many times she'd prayed—the only prayers matterin' in the end bein' the ones for their souls on the other side. Sweet Jesus, Lord! Please help Dosey Sabbs in this tearful world.

But with her Marcus it was only those few times a him bein' messed-up stoned—and lately, no times—though the way he'd grown distant, not attendin' service much anymore over t' the Union, and when he *was* home, not lookin' her way, or talkin' to her much, just lookin' off like he's dreamin', though not happy dreams, 'cause there's never a smile on his face—it all had her sick worried.

She couldn't lose this last one. Couldn't live her whole life tryin' to save 'em and then one after another lose 'em all to the streets—to the game, the way they call it now-days, to the life—which ain't nothin' but death. She couldn't lose this boy. He's *always* her sweetest child, Marcus. Her respectful one. Even when he hurt her so bad and left the Catholics for Wells, he kept his promises, and worked at his books, every night after school and the practices, when he'd come home all wore out. And all those beautiful years with Mr. White, who took her baby all the way crost the world. With all the pro teams, football, basketball, once't they'd seen him a first time, they'd wait for Marcus Sabbs to come up again, 'cause he's the best. "Tumbler," they call him. But she wouldn't. Only Marcus, the name she give him for pride. But in her prayers she'd sometime whisper to God, "for Tumbler," 'cause that little secret she shared with the Lord made happy tears come up in her eyes—like as if that word "Tumbler" knew just how to go through all the things inside her mind and down to the angel in charge of her tears, who'd hear the signal and say to the waters in her heart, "Flow on up, you tears a pride, to the eyes a Dosey Sabbs." She couldn't lose him, her most special child, the one most like his mama. All those cartwheels, all day highflyin' cartwheels, and the cheer team at DuSable, where she was the best, so many years ago, 'fore she's carryin' her first. But long before that, the cartwheels, way back t'Artesia, all day *long* she'd be flyin'—*Mercy!* Early Dawn say—'til one day she flew right into that Mr. Mac himself, who said when he caught her up by the legs, out the end a that old dusty drive-up road, him lookin' down on her like she's a

MOTHER AND SON

dead bird hangin' upside down: "Whoa up, little nigga gal, jus' where in this world you think you goin' to?" Only white peoples' words she remembered out a Mississippi, 'fore they left, back when Jesse went off. Don't remember Jesse well. Not like Maurice does. Just his walkin' with her one time down a road in winter—give her his hat, she recalled, and him laughin' when it came down over her eyes. So long ago.

But what's now, is this Watt. Who *is* he, and where'd he come from?—this one calls Marcus these days, and who he's gone off with tonight—says only, "Tell 'im Watt wants 'im"—and then hangs up 'fore you can ask him *what* he wants. But I know. And I know where he comes from. But what it is makes him so strong?—against a mama's whole life tryin' to keep her boy safe? What—when I've been preachin' ever since he's a baby that it's only one direction the gangs gon' take you—exact same direction they been takin' this place used to be a *home* to peoples, where the young would listen to their parents with respect, and they'd listen to other parents, too, with respect—'cause everybody's workin' together to make this a community—and peoples all cared about how beautiful this place was and took care a the grass and the flowers, 'cause it mattered to 'em, the beauty—and they could leave out their laundry and leave open their back doors 'cause everybody was lookin' out for everybody else as a community, like nothin' any of us ever had.

And there was safety. And workin' families, fathers workin'—'til they made all the families with income get up and leave and make room for those without—which turned out so bad, no matter if it was good intentions. But the gangs, all the babies without any mama or daddy controllin' 'em, babies a babies, inmates runnin' the asylum, fifteen stories below whoever it is they call mama, her drunk or high or layin' down, and all of 'em turned hard as stone—they started the life here in a different direction. And you can tell what direction that'd be from the ugliness, the dirt, the graffiti everywhere, the broken everything without out a single thing gettin' fixed, not even light bulbs—and no beauty. All a Cabrini just movin' in one direction, just like that poor mama I saw. Never forget it. Marcie Dean. Knew her. Knew how she tried. And I saw it all. Saw it with my own eyes when high, high up, all nineteen stories, some five gangster boys they take her screamin' to the ramp rails, 'fore they screened the ramps all up, and hold her over and she's holdin' on to the rails but they's beatin' her hands and prisin' loose her fingers 'til she loses hold, and then all her screamin' gets lost in the wind of her fallin' and turnin' in the air as she's fallin'—all in one

87

DIVISION

direction. Marcie Dean. Saw her numerous times at the Wayman AME when Ramsey Lewis played there. It was his family's church. So many wonderful musicians grew up here, when this was a community. Curtis Mayfield. Jerry Butler. The Impressions. People Get Ready, so fine and beautiful, those boys voices. But since the gangs, just that one direction, like Marcie's fallin', 'cause she talked to the police about things, tryin' to stop things from goin' so bad. Can't stop none of it now, no more than she could, for all her turnin' in the air, lookin' like she'd like t' grab onto somethin' but nothin' there to grab onto. And now this whole place won't be here much longer, comin' down too, 'cause a this bad nigger says, "Tell 'im Watt wants 'im."

Sgt. James Gaverin, his men in place, guns trained on the exits back and front, patrolman Bobby Rizzo ready with the ram, stepped quietly up the three-step, un-banistered concrete stoop at 921 Cambridge— a street that even in front looked like a back alley—and standing under the small, flat door-overhang, pounded with the hammer-end of his fist—BAM! BAM!—on the windowless black metal door—one of the few un-boarded, un-spray-painted entrances in this stretch of the Cambridge St. Rows. Christ, these people. Probably some buck-naked pickaninny'll answer. Or this motherfucker Sabbs, too fucked up to value my life or his, ready to end everything in a blaze of stupidity. BAM! BAM! BAM! Gaverin pounded the black metal door again. Then, "Open up! Police!" Lights came on up and down Cambridge where windows were un-boarded. No window got raised, though, nor could anyone be seen looking out. Then, "Marcus Sabbs, open up!" Gaverin called again, "Marcus Sabbs!" as he hand-signaled to Patrolman Rizzo to mount the steps with the ram. But then a woman's voice from behind the door, "Marcus isn't here." "Open up! Or we'll ram down this door! We have a warrant for the arrest of Marcus Sabbs! Open up *now!*"

As the door handle began to turn, Gaverin moved away from the jamb-side of the door, where it would open, and, drawing his .38, set his back against the door's frame at the hinges. Patrolman Rizzo, still holding the ram, set himself behind Gaverin, and now Patrolman James Echols, waved up by Gaverin, moved forward and stood before the entrance with his Mossberg pumped-ready and raised to fire. But now, when the door opened a crack, it was just that same woman's voice, saying, "Marcus didn't come home tonight. I'm his mother. What do you want?" Gaverin lowered his pistol. "We're gonna need to come in and see, Ma'am. And we're gonna need to talk to you. So I'm gonna ask

MOTHER AND SON

you to open the door slowly and to show us your hands. Just do as I say. Open the door slowly. And keep your hands where we can see them."

When she opened the door, Dosey Sabbs, wearing a tight-sashed robe over her still-lean frame, showing her hands out and empty, presented to the police, as she looked down the barrel of the shotgun, a face that might have been pretty once but now drooped with the fatigue of a life lived in poverty and struggle, and with the look of one who'd now discovered that her last and most earnest prayer, like all her prayers for all her children's lives, had fallen on deaf ears—a look that might have said to Patrolman Echols, whose pumped 12-gauge was still raised, "Go on ahead and take me, white police man. Never was meant, anyhow, to journey this world."

Gaverin, fourteen years with the force, the last ten with the 18th, in truth expected not to find Marcus Sabbs at his home. But when he and his men went into 921, checking the closets, checking under the beds, pulling out the couch's pull-out bed, inspecting the apartment everywhere, what Gaverin saw made him think. Nothing was out of place, nothing un-dusted, every room spotless; the smell of deep cleanliness, of care, of pride, right in the middle of Cabrini's hell and stink of decay, its violence and death. He could feel in this small, clean island here, how it wasn't the expense of things but the way they were kept and placed that mattered. With honest respect, he thought *this* is where it starts—right here—not with government handouts but with this kind of pride and determination—found in a good person's soul— and nowhere else. There was, not some tacky Jesus painting come out of a truck stop, but a simple flat-toned metal crucifix hung on the wall over this woman's bed. It starts with this, too, he thought, as for a moment he closed his eyes. Forgive us our trespasses, as we forgive those who trespass against us. But when he looked at the computer, set on the neat desk in Marcus's room, he thought, God damn *life*—how do we get from here to bloody murder? How in *hell* does Marcus Sabbs come to be where he was tonight? Is it just *impossible* to resist the pull of whatever it is that drags these people down? How do ya stop it before it starts?—and where does it end?

"Ms. Sabbs," Gaverin said, when at last he sat down with her, armchair to armchair, in the small, first-floor front room, his gun re-holstered, "did Marcus say where he'd be going tonight?"

Dosey Sabbs, her gray-white hair pulled back tight, her arms folded tightly, uncomfortably, over her light blue nightgown, which had a

89

DIVISION

floral print, white, quiet, on its collars, intended not to say a word without thinking. She looked at Gaverin, eyes and brows dark as a black man's, thirty-five, olive-skinned, maybe some Greek or Italian in him, "No," she now said. "Marcus didn't tell me where he was going."

"Did he say who he'd be meeting?"

Dosey didn't answer. She tightened her arms yet more and asked, "What's this all about? What is it you have a warrant for? What is it Marcus is supposed to have done? He's never been in trouble in his life."

Gaverin didn't want to lose her by getting aggressive, but, ignoring her questions, he did ask her again, "Did he *say* who he'd be meeting?" And then, when she answered nothing, he asked, "Did he say he would be meeting his cousin Robert Teague tonight?"

Again Gaverin got nothing. But now this Mrs. Sabbs was changing. Her lips trembled. She still said nothing—but now she raised her hands and took the two sides of the collar of her robe and pulled them up and buried the lower half of her face in the wings of her collar and in her tight-closed hands, locked together now in front of her mouth.

"Ma'am," Gaverin said, hoping just to re-engage her. But she ignored him. She bowed her head lower—as now tears came to her eyes. And for a time, head bowed, she just shed tears. At last she unlocked her hands from before her mouth—but then, still not looking up, she broke into sobs. She just sobbed, hard—'til at last she did look up, but not at Gaverin, rather blankly at nothing. Then, "Maurice! Oh Lord! First day we come—it's worse. Worse than Artesia. More than fifty years now. But Maurice he says to me, first day, that it's *Here! Chicago! Here,* he says, is where it's gonna start. Gotta chance here, and I'm gonna take it. And he did. He made good on it. He raised those kids good. Both those beautiful children. And so many times he says to me, Dosey, you gotta get out the Greens. Live with us. I'll get you a place where we live. I'll take care of you, Dosey. I won't ever fail you. And so many times he saved my life. Swear I'd be dead without Maurice. But I say to him I can't go—'cause this place here is home. Been here since I was sixteen. Forty-four years. Been here from the start a black peoples comin' here. And I know it's so bad now. But it's home."

She stopped a moment—then looked at Gaverin. "And now," she said, "it looks like *nowhere* is good! Do you know what that is, sir! Nowhere on this tearful earth is good for us." She stopped—and again looked off. "Chicago no different. Over by Maurice, no better than here. It's all just nowhere for us. Robert Teague. Lord Jesus, don't you

MOTHER AND SON

tell me that boy's in trouble. Don't tell me there's nothin' we can do—that there's nowhere anywhere anytime we can change it before dyin' out this world. Got to have hope. Got to somewhere find it. Can't lose hope everywhere, for all our time. My sweet Marcus and Robert Teague and Carolyn. Can't tell it to me that it's all just the same, wherever you go. Please, Lord, don't tell it to me." She now sank to her knees, right before Gaverin, nearly touching him, though with her head again down, and she cried out, "Don't be deaf to me, Jesus! Don't all my life be deaf to me! Don't make it so's I have to forgive you, Lord. 'Cause I don't know if I could."

As the sun now rose over Lake Michigan and began to shine across Chicago, breaking through the city's skyline—all hunched up on the broken concrete floor, the Tumbler sat with his back pressed against the charred wall of that burnt-out apartment at the top of Camp Ball, nineteen stories up, where he'd been baptized by Watt in the faith of the Gangster Disciples. He still wore his Wells jacket, though he'd taken off his Sox cap now and set it beside him. Growth and Development. Knowledge. The Everlasting Gangster. *Money.* He raised his head and looked at the wall before him, opposite the un-boarded east window—which let in now the full shining of the morning. Twin three-pronged pitchforks rising up out of the Star of David, with a 6 in the center of the six-pointed star—wings spreading up and out too from the star's upper bar. Every gang's got its artists—boys who can do feathered wings with a can a spray paint, and the face a the devil—who can do the block letters that slant just right as they say Money, Mack, Murder. We don't want this! We don't! He could hear himself again—the words he shouted to Watt before he ran. Before the gun went off, no cell phone—how many times! And that white boy—why couldn't he give up! That car! Why'd he have to go and challenge Watt—and now he's dead? Couldn't stay and see that. The blood and death. Just ran. Like all the people who never *do* anything. How'd that white boy get where he got—Lincoln-Park rich? 'Cause some white man long back *did* things, which is always killin' and takin'—and callin' it *mine*. Watt does things. Get your hands off what doesn't belong to you. I said, shouted it—We don't want this! But Watt didn't hear a word of that. We *do*. That's what he said, back at the Starbucks—don't know what he meant. Just know that Watt *does* things.

World's never gon' change for us without puttin' a gun to somebody's head. Robert Teague. He knew that white boy. And Watt knows that that white boy knows Robert, my cousin. Capital punishment. We're gonna face it if they call us part a that killin'. And it won't be us who decides who was part a what—and what started what. Watt said to me don't ever pretend one time that I don't know nothin' about the things it takes—to make our kingdom. Capital punishment. Watt would say there's no difference between what he did tonight and what the white man does when he sticks the needle in your arm. All just gang religion, theirs and ours. Power—and the one who's gon' have it's the one who doesn't run off, sayin' We don't want this!

MLK and Uncle Maurice. Even though they don't believe in pullin' any trigger, got to believe they could see somethin' in Watt to respect. Got to believe it that—even if they see the face a Satan on his chest, they somewhere in secret respect him. If they saw, too, Watt standin' there when those ruthless motherfuckin' Mickey C's come up and he faces 'em, dead on, with that shotgun. Conversion time for me, it was. But that faith a the devil, power religion, no sweet Jesus in it—it's got to go deeper than carin' that that white boy is a human being. And it can't do that, Watt. Can't go deeper than that. It's like killin' yourself, you kill someone. Uncle Maurice did a crazy thing. But not like your crazy. And who's it gon' be saves me from dyin'—gon' be you? You like to kill Robert 'cause the law's gon' bring him in and he's gon' be told it's his life or yours. Or his life or mine? Robert gon' be brave enough to give his life for me? Not name me? Would Watt ever name me to the police, even if they put the gun to *his* head? We don't want this! I said. Did anyone hear it? Will anyone say I said it? That other white boy—he gon' say I said it? Or even if he heard it, he gon' keep it quiet 'cause a black man killed that other white boy—maybe his brother? Shot him so many times! Wouldn't stop, like he wants to kill every white person in the world. It's gon' be Uncle Maurice. And mama. Only ones gon' help me now.

Still sitting hunched up on the concrete floor, with his back against the charred wall, Marcus Sabbs, the Tumbler, now wanted for murder, with tears of a most desperate sorrow and fear welling in his eyes, stared now through his tears at the spray-painted six-point star on the opposite wall before him—with its wings and pitchforks and the number 6, all the significance of which he knew but, now, felt himself utterly divided from, untouched by.

GOOD MORNING, AMERICA, HOW ARE YA?

Still in his blue-black bandana and leather coat, Watt sat in the Union Station, holding a two-way ticket for the City of New Orleans, No. 58, to Greenwood, Mississippi—and back, next night, on No. 59. Eight hundred remained in his billfold—from the thousand he'd gotten off Lonnie D. Soft-shit Lonnie D, ignorant fool, whose whole bank we weren't gonna be askin' for last night but were jus' gonna wrap up in that motherfucker's scalp. But then things went t' shit. In his coat pocket his thirty-plus mag remained, and in his belt the Glock 19 (reloaded), which pressed once more against his abdomen. In his gym bag he'd quick packed a one-night change of clothes. And, wrapped inside his socks and shirt, resting now in its sheave, was his nine-inch fishing knife, cut-through-the-bone keen as he'd always kept it—for when the time finally came.

Rams and they shotguns, Slick Boys and all them other motherfuckers outa Eighteen—all that shit goin' up my ass 'fore the cock crow three time. And what it gon' cost *me* when the game's shut down a week or two or three? What it gon' cost *me*—'cause some crazy nigga smoke some white boy? And what it is? Young Caucasian man don't

DIVISION

wanna give up his automobile? Crazy shorty shit, my brotha—jackin'
a fuckin' car. Unreasonable shit. Gon' bring the house down kinda shit.
And gon' cost Lonnie D considerable. So why he don't just call the police? Why he don't jus' say I got that crazy carjackin' nigga rightyeah,
Mr. Po-lice-man—so y'all jus' leave them bullhorns and shotguns at
the station and call off the invasion. No need for no D-Day, Officer
sir, 'cause I got that carjacker rightyeah; and he's yours for the takin'.
Why don't he? *Loyalty,* my brotha Watt. All for one and one for all. And
it's one expensive motherfucker, loyalty. Jus' want you to think about
that. And Lonnie D ain't talkin' about this thousand dolla. He's talkin'
about the game—about *work.* Talkin' about the whole sweet motherfucker gettin' suspended for a good time. And about good time bein'
good money. Which brotha Watt don't think about when he pull back
on that trigga. And Lonnie D, he gon' say now to his brotha Watt, who
didn't use his head, unloadin' that dangerous firearm on a Lincoln
Park white boy: what you done, my brotha, ain't puttin' them bullets
in that honkey boy so much as puttin' 'em inta ya own skull. Don't
like to say that—but it's truth all the same. Suicide, my man. Capital
punishment on ya own self.

And for a moment he'd thought—no comin' back—not after that
Lincoln Park bloodshed last night. Thought about a one-way ticket—
outa Chi Town, never to return, or not for some good long time. But
he shook it off—and bought a fast round trip. Still got that gotdamned
future—and right here. Not some place where we haven't laid down
the groundwork, and the law. Show you what loyalty means, motherfucka, in the *respect* of a hundred bandanas gon' fuck you up you don't
say the Six is Watt.

But it's time now, all the same, for a walk down Avenue G, Greenwood, Miss'ippi. Fourth piece-a-shit shack out back the Lusco restaurant, facin' the shut-down tin warehouses, on the fucked-up side the
Yazoo, where the sorry-ass niggas still shuffle along, and one dopin'
drunk in particular, used to be a gangbangin' murderer. Tore Chicago's West Side all up, back when King died—and then burned that
West Side down. Pitched fire bottles at the army tanks. Gasoline Man.
Truth, truth, truth, motherfucker. There's not a soul to blame for the
shit you are but you. And get your hands off what doesn't belong to
you. And can I get something started for ya? But don't blame me. You
think you're owed. *Fuckyeah.* An eye for an eye. They're the ones who
should ask for forgiveness—ones up the doorman buildings. Revolu-

94

tion. Reparation. Redistribution. Revenge. It's *knowledge*. Taste the metal runnin' through her tongue—feel those sweet white titties and taste 'em. Press her against the wall and fuck her 'til she's cryin' out she wants to be this black man's *slave*. Wailin' Fuck me like a gangster man! Take this white cream and demon-fuck it 'til it dies! White motherfucker just wanted to die. Suicide by black man. Just do what he says, the other peckerwood says. But for some white-boy reason, goin' back to who knows where, he doesn't. And 'cause a that, if we're gon' get all we need, gon' have to go all Capone on that other peckerwood and on our own homeboy Tumbler and on the schoolboy Cousin Teague, son of that gravedigger.

Gasoline Man. White law don't know where he gone to. Cain't know nothin' if you don' care nothin'. Just another dead nigga gal slashed crost the throat. Cain't give it no time, white polices say. Got betta things to do. His grandmama took his face in those big warm hands a hers—then—seven years back—and she says, close up, eye to his eye: But if you *be* carin', you gon' *know* where he gone to.

He could see her now, feel her. Lookin' t' stare right down t' where my heart was poundin', me jus' fifteen. He could hear her say: "He gone to Avenue G, Greenwood, Miss'ippi." He could feel her again putting two hundred-dollar bills in his hand. Those big hands, she takes 'em and closes up m'hand all tight on the money. And then nothin' more but she walks off t' where she sleeps...and closes the door.

Same then as now in this waitin' lobby: twenty-two tracks out the window. White kids here—most of 'em gon' get off in Urbana-Champaign, and then the rest come Carbondale. And jus' like now, back then wearin' ball caps on backwards and with Walkmans all plugged in—one of 'em bobbin' on his candy ass, eyes all closed up, to 'Fuck da Po-lice'—make ya wanna laugh, and spit. And again here, about an equal number of sourpussed niggas all gon' ride down to Memphis or into some shitbag town in Miss'ippi, where they got their people—people who never left Miss'ippi, waitin' in their junk heaps on these ones who did leave, but lookin' none the better for havin' done so; or they gon' ride all the way to New Orleans, where their people live below sea level. Maybe I'll go down there for a time. Lay low. Below sea level. Or maybe *not*. Rather be stone fuckin' dead.

Boarding now for the City of New Orleans. Track Nineteen. Nineteen. Please have your tickets ready and out at the waiting room exit door.

All of them—all the white college students—as well as all the black

DIVISION

folks heading south along that hundred-year familiar line between Chicago and Mississippi (either to visit family in Mississippi or to head back to Mississippi from visiting family on the South Side, including some who could well recall changing at the Illinois-Kentucky border to the negro cars)—all of them, whites and blacks, because they could feel his pitchforked neck, his black-leathered presence, his gangbanger's bandana, as a powerful dark trouble—kept their distance from Watt.

And it was the same when they boarded. AMTRAK's now egalitarian, borderless coach seating, with not a single seat assigned, an arrangement whereby, when the seat scramble was settled, you simply sat with the one you ended up next to—and in which you would sit all night with him or her, and would sleep next to him or her as you sat-slept with your head resting on the single skimpy, gauze-covered pillow you were given, and in which, too, somehow, even as you slept, you would remain conscious the entire time of both your cool not-touching of that him or her or of your sudden, warm touching as the rattling train kept swaying and lurching, all night long breaking apart and bonding bodies—none of this came anywhere near Watt. Not a soul, white or black, ever took the seat next to him.

He slept after Champaign—but woke at Carbondale and was wide awake when at Cairo they passed over the bridge where the big rivers meet. In the moonlight he could see the Ohio coming in from the east and north and then the Mississippi swallowing up the Ohio and heading on south with it all sucked up into its giant bloodstream. Then once more he slept, not to wake again until Memphis, where the train, just as he'd remembered from before, clanked in slow along the river and then, exactly like seven years back, stayed a long time at the station before clanking slow again out of the city and then at last beginning to roll deeper south into Mississippi swamp and cotton land. It was past dawn by the time they hit Memphis, and breakfast had been called, but he stayed put, having poured himself a coffee in the lounge car. While the vibrating engine idled up the track, in the shadows of what was left of old Cotton Row warehouses, he held the Styrofoam cup in two hands and blew on his coffee to cool it.

So many times like to kill her myself, she bein' strung out so bad. He was thinking of his mother—and he brought his complaint close, protesting as if there were some listener inside him, an inner companion of his soul...right with him for the final stretch of this southbound ride. One minute she's lookin' at the TV so close she could take a bite

96

GOOD MORNING, AMERICA, HOW ARE YA?

out the people on it—then she jus' sleeps for whole days, then she's talkin' only with her lips, which were all cracked up and her mouth smack dry and her eyes gone smaller'n a snake's—and then the pukin' and screamin', and takin' half a day to shit out her brains. And her sayin' she doesn't know who she can't stand more, her own self or her gotdamned devil child, callin' her own child that, when she gets bad, and for no reason. And that child havin' to eat food right off her burnt spoons—if there's any food to eat, which she doesn't care if there is. And every time he gets some money, she finds and steals it. And then lies about it—like she lies about everything. Got so bad you jus' ask her if it's night or day she looks right out the window and tells you it's the one when it's the other. And her arms all black-purple bruised, so she won't go out but in long sleeves, long's that boy can remember. And she cares about nothin', ever any time. But then somehow she pulls herself all together and gets her hair right and perfume and lipstick on and washes out her smack-dry mouth 'cause she's got a man comin' and she's gon' entertain this gentleman, if it's jus' one, which it might not be, and she's doin' her so-called work, all laughin', and then the moanin' and hollerin' while her own child's in the next room, where he's got to shut the fuck up and keep out the way.

But then—and his thoughts now, if they had hands, might have taken that person inside him by the coat, because there was *another side* to this story—all the other times, when she's cryin', after she pukes out her guts, and she says she's gon' get straight, and she's gon' get her life together. And times when she sits with me, with the arithmetic flash cards, which she's been savin' since she's a little girl at school, where she won all the stars 'fore she's carryin' a child and then havin' him. And she works with that child a hers, sittin' down on the floor, and gets him goin' faster'n faster—till the two of 'em jus' laughin' he gets so fast. And she kisses him and calls him Boy Wonder! And then though he's but eight or nine, she teaches him everything she learned up to when she's carryin' him, in the ninth grade. And they read books together, which she says got no black boys in 'em but they're good books jus' the same, if you imagine the boys black.

And then *he* comes in. And not just one time or two but seems like ten, twenty, and he sees what mama and her little boy are up to and he kicks 'em apart. He jus' kicks that little boy to the wall, sayin' ah show you you po-tential, little worthless motherfucker, tear you limb from limb, and then he kicks him against the wall as many times's he needs 'til he's satisfied, and then he goes over to her there still on the floor and he kicks the shit outa her maybe all the ten or twenty times, and not one time but maybe five times that little boy *knows,* he jus' then drags her into the bedroom and rapes her 'til she's screamin' and cryin' and he hits her sayin' things like he gon' show her who the smart one, gon' show her some school, all right, gon' show her what it gon' cost her she go to them job programs over t' Sunshine, or them back t' gotdamn school programs, gon' show her what it gon' *cost* her she quit seein' them gentlemens he be sendin' her way, and gon' show her what it gon' *cost* her when she get off his program and try to get on h'own! And every time, he brings the dope. Sometimes he jus' tosses the plastic bags on her, maybe after he rapes her, and she's lyin' there bleedin'. Sometimes he goes t' the kitchen and cooks the shit up himself and then wraps the rubber round her arm and sticks her in the vein. Tells her how good she gon' feel now. She's back to herself now. She's a good girl now. She ain't gon' do no more evil to him, ain't gon' sin against him no more, goin' to them classes. Gon' be righteous now. And him holdin' her now like a baby. And she's cryin' and tellin' him how sorry she is. Sayin' she won't do him evil again. Like a good slave, sayin yes, massah, suh—feelin' that dope runnin' through her brain.

But all those other times, too—times she goes straight for a while—and her son, he gets to see her face. When they're sittin' on the floor. And not the face she puts on for slick johns, and scrufty johns, too, toothless motherfuckers, stinkin' drunks. Beautiful face. Beautiful black angel. Same dark eyebrows like her boy's and the high cheek bones, and her skin all perfect, and her smile.

Face you sometimes see too in her mama, for all that she's sick obese and diabetic, never movin' out that apartment sixteen stories up the Jube, lest it's some meetin' about not tearin' the project down, and not lettin' the CHA's ruin the community with their Great Transformation, gon' fuck the niggas some whole new way, after first fuckin' with the homeboys' money train. Still gon' get her out that place a dyin' and set her up in Cal City.

Three times the train whistle blew loud, drowning out the deep bass of the vibrating engine, and resounding through the empty warehouses of still derelict Cotton Row. He remembered that a white lady, dressed like Islam Nation, said she was a nun, sat next to him seven years ago—and that she said, "The day that Dr. King was killed here was the day that Memphis died, too. The city's never been the same since—almost twenty-five years. And only the Lord knows how long it will take for the wounds to heal. Detroit. Chicago. So much changed that day, with a bullet of pure American sin. Dr. King died for our great sin. But, dear God help us, I'm not sure he saved us from it."

Gasoline Man. To that invisible listener inside him he spoke now about the day that, every single day, would just come to his mind, whenever it wanted—the day when he saw that murderer in the stairwell, up above him on the landing. Elevator never works. So one more time we're walkin' all up the sixteen stories, lookin' out for human shit like the stairway's a sidewalk full a dogs with the skitters—only the piss won't disappear into the ground in a concrete stairwell, so it stinks even worse. And it's Lover's Lane, too, with the suckin' and fuckin' sounds you can hear in the dark. And other sounds, too—maybe a boy scout troupe a homeboys—they see you, gon' fuck you up jus' for bein' alive. So you duck out quiet to a corridor, you hear those boys comin', and you don't duck back 'til you hear 'em long gon'. Gun goes off in here might make you stone deaf, so you hear fightin', you duck down low and put ya hands over ya ears. Saw a dead man once, had to step right over 'im and his blown-up head, after watchin' the dude who killed him runnin' down the stairs too fas' to see if anybody's crouchin' down in the dark.

A few patches a light come out a slit-window here and there, if you're walkin' up the well 'fore dark. And that day, twelve years back, that kid who we were he's lookin' up the stairs just short the thirteenth story—and, in a patch a light, he sees him up above, comin' down. Jus' like that big motherfucker knew someone's there, so he stops on the landing, with that light all lightin' him up from behind—makes him seem ten times bigger. And now when he sees his own *son*—his son, ten years old, who he never one time called "son"—standin' down those stink-shit stairs in the half-way dark, he says, "Well, well, and straight out the fire a fuckin' hell, ain't this little motherfucker jus' gettin' hisself in mah way again." Then he starts steppin' down slow, and he says, as he's comin' down, makin' everything into his big, dark shadow, "Like I always tell his ignorant, sinful baby mama, shoulda jus' had this little bait grub dropped in the clinic bucket 'fore he's born." And now that huge shadow with that mouth and those arms, he quickens up. And in one hand, he's holdin' a blade! "But it ain't *never* too late! It ain't *never, ever* too late!!" And for real he looks this time t' end that boy's life! So that little boy he cuts out flyin' down those stairs with

DIVISION

that murderin' so-called father a shadow all up over him, intending to terminate his own boy's life—'fore he takes himself to Greenwood, where a dozen years now he's layin' low. And with that man right on him, that boy sees now that there's homeboys comin' up those stairs! And in the three-quarter dark, those homeboys they see runnin' down hard at 'em this scared-shit little shorty they called Watt—and right there on his tail they make out this old monster-fuckin' OG they know. But this bad-ass monster man's not declared himself in any way for the Six. So they quick let little Watt pass on through 'em—and then they close all up again, so they're a wall no shadow can find a crack in. And the drawin' of a gun or two makes that shadow put his knife back in his pocket and take a step back. So now he starts yellin' down the stairs, while those boys press him back, "Gon' split yo skull and pull yo fuckin' brains out, you little shit motherfucker. Gon' pull yo brains out!" But it's way more like to get *him* killed, all his crazy yellin', than's gon' have any effect on that little boy, who jus' kept on runnin' down 'til he hit sixth floor and he knows where the closet is he keeps his broomstick in and where he can hide and close the door behind him and pull the string of a light. And he waits behind that door 'til enough time passes, and then he comes out. And then up the stairs he goes again, all quiet—'til he makes it up to sixteen—and behind his home door, he finds his beautiful mama, beautiful black angel, worked all those times to teach him things, layin' in her blood.

As the train had clanked slow out of the Memphis station, he'd kept the cup of hot coffee down between his thighs. But he sipped it now as the train began to roll faster south into the Mississippi Delta: first stop—just two hours now—Greenwood—9:10 arrival. He would stay nowhere. Same as last time, jus' change clothes and clean up here on the train. A good clean shave this time, didn't need one at fifteen. Too small for the job, too scared. Walked around that block a shacks all day waitin' to see him come out. Too scared to jus' go up t' doors and knock 'til he came out a one. Jus' more and more times around that block, 'til we musta been seen by everybody livin' on G and F, too. Every last nigga in that broke-down hood a shacks musta seen us but him. 'Cause nothin' came outa that leanin'-over shithole he's livin' in—'til maybe the fiftieth time. And then there he was. Fourth shack out behind the Lusco restaurant, so at least we know now which one. But couldn't do it then. Jus' saw him there and it stopped me. Jus' hoped he didn't see me. Jus' turned around then and started walkin' 'round the block

GOOD MORNING, AMERICA, HOW ARE YA?

the other way. Maybe come up behind him if he's still there. But when we came 'round that other way, he's gone. And though we know now where he is, can't do a thing about it. Jus' walked on off into Greenwood city and walked around 'til time for the return train, 7:37, same as tonight. Only law's the one you gon' take in ya own hands, grandmamma say. But I couldn't take it into m'hands—too afraid back then a that man killed mama so violent, her head about hangin' off, in all that blood. And couldn't face grandmamma for near a year after comin' back. Jus' one time slipped work money under her door t'pay her back.

Same's las' time. Swamps. And trees growin' up out of 'em. And the flat cotton fields, stretchin' out, stinkin' like shit, nothin' yet comin' up in any of 'em, jus' rows and rows where it's all gon' be. Time goes slow when you think about it, fast when you don't. Makes no difference. Train keeps rollin'—exactly like makin' things right, which won't get off its line a rails, Mama, 'til the job is done. But there will be justice 'fore this day's done. Delayed won't mean denied. I promise you.

He'd taken off his leather coat in the night and had set it on the unoccupied seat beside him. The loaded 19 was wrapped up inside it. His gym bag with the nine-inch blade hidden in his change of clothes sat on the floor. In a kit in his bag he kept his toiletries and a razor. He looked at his watch. But he knew. Time had come.

He gathered up his things and rose as the rocking, speeding train cut through shadowy pinewoods, steep banks rising on both sides of the tracks adding dark to the darkness, and made his way to the broom-closet door of the train lavatory, not losing his gun as he ducked and squeezed his tall, thick-muscled body inside, and locked the door. He set his coat and gun on the vanity, took out his kit, and set his bag on the floor. He stripped off his t-shirt and, on balanced legs, bending forward, looked at his man's face and at that fear-striking, prison-tattooed body in the mirror. Gangster Everlasting. Fear a the Six. Money, Mack, Murder and the face a the VL-killin' devil. The law. Not afraid to die. Or to kill. He shaved and then changed, setting his sheaved knife on the vanity. He unwrapped his coat and took out his gun and the thirty-plus mag. But now he wrapped the gun up again, and the magazine, inside his old clothes, and put all these things down in his bag. In his belt, where his Glock had been, he stuck the sheaved blade. He put his coat on over the knife, zipped and took up his bag, and went out.

THE WHITE COMMUNITY

Jack Riordan's friends had come from everywhere, from Holy Cross, almost the entire rugby team, and HC girls too; and almost everyone Jacko knew from St. Ignatius, more than a hundred; and friends from St. Clement's grammar school, and their families; as well as just about every friend his parents had ever had, old friends, colleagues and business friends and acquaintances, his father's students, current ones, old ones; and Connor's friends, too, even some from the West Coast, as well as every relative of the Riordan and Connaughton families still living in the Chicago area, and many, too, from out of town; and just people who knew *of* the Riordans, from the present or the past, and felt connected, were part of the Riordans' wide, wide community. Donnellan's Funeral Home in Skokie had two policemen directing in-and-out traffic on Skokie Blvd., and attendants were working cars in and out not just of the Donnellan lot but of the adjacent store and restaurant lots. The line of mourners had split, one branch out around the building north and the other south. Ushers at the door asked people, discreetly, as they welcomed them from one

THE WHITE COMMUNITY

line and the other, please to consider the many other mourners as they paid their respects to the Riordan family.

Connor stood last of the now three Riordans, next to his mother; his father was first, standing just the other side of the closed coffin from the endless approaching line of mourners, whom one by one his father and then his mother would greet for over seven hours. Con, as he stood there, often sweating, feeling pressed by this mass of people, from whom he wanted just to get away, was relieved at least by this: his parents' saying the names of people whom they greeted made it possible for him, with their names just put in his ear, to greet and thank people that he might not have been able to name, no matter how long he might have known them, in some cases even his own friends.

What thoughts did they, *could* they have?—all these people, as they each one knelt and bowed his or her head for that moment before the closed casket? Could even a single one not think of what Jack Riordan's face, so well-known for its dark-Irish handsomeness, looked like beneath the closed lid?—for the word had spread everywhere about the nature of the murder? Could they just *not* think of the horror? Closest-range shooting, so many gun shots, right at the window—the savagery? Or could they escape feeling at least some kind of racial animosity along with their dread? Could they just cut off the life of every fertile seed of racial anger? This white world of circumspect people, good people, as they spoke to those before and behind them, was it possible for them not to start at least some discussion of the fact that the three involved all were black—or if they didn't discuss it, was it possible for them not to think about it, maybe even more intensely, as they repressed it? If a measure were taken of the full white-cultural depth and breadth of all that was either whispered, or that got intensified by repression—what would the overall spiritual mass of this invisible but monstrously powerful thing come to? Or was there even a single one of these good white people, virtually all of whom had lived their whole lives without once openly insulting a black person or taking action prejudicial or harmful to a single black person, ever, and not a few of whom had taken significant action to better the condition of the African-American under-privileged—was there a single one, no matter how good, who didn't feel in some secret place, when it came to this violent killing, so senseless but also seemingly so hate-driven, the little automatic rush of satisfaction that comes when a confident prejudgment about blacks is proven to be accurate, one more time? Or

103

any who didn't have some feeling—of discomfort, of admiration, of admiration mixed with discomfort, of admiration mixed with unpreventable prejudice—as he or she caught a glance of—and then looked away from, or looked a moment longer at—the several black friends of the Riordans who had—was it the courage?—to come, and who might well have felt, as they stood in that line, a self-consciousness beyond any they had felt in their whole lives of trying to rise up over exclusive divisions, in every attempt finding that racial self-consciousness produces, every time, some form or other of spiritual sickness?—some kind of immediate manifestation of that most intransigent soul's disease of all: original sin? Indelible stain.

But maybe more than any other white soul there, Connor, when he saw any black face had to look away—because for him that rush of feeling he had had on his bathroom floor—the feeling that he was right back in the alley, would start to come. He already knew the signs of its approach, the aura. He hadn't known before what the words *panic attack* meant—but he knew now, in his sweat glands, in the tips of his fingers as they pressed against his sweating palms—and in his need to get himself alone.

Mr. and Mrs. Creadon. He had heard the names. "Mr. and Mrs. Creadon, thank you for coming. We are so grateful."

"Oh, Connor, we are so heartbroken for you and your mom and dad. We are just so heartbroken. Everyone is so shocked and heartbroken."

He wanted out. He wanted to get alone, away from everyone, from these noises. But he wasn't so lost yet that he couldn't recover himself —for his brother—and remain in the line, for the hours of his brother's wake, next to his mother. Who is this woman, his mother?—who spoke now with Ken O'Brien and Maryanne. Yes, Ken and Maryanne. My mother, who held Jacko slaughtered, in the front seat of her Mercedes. Her clothes were covered in his blood, her first child's, all over her. Who is she? "Mr. and Mrs. O'Brien, thank you so much for coming." "Connor, we are so sorry. That's all we can say—just that we are so incredibly sorry for you and your family." His mother—her whole life forever changed. She wanted a change. My mother, standing here next to me, so beautiful. Cleaned. She gave me life. The sound of her voice, saying thank you now to the Rathjes, Terry and Monica. I can hear those names. Her fragrance, her bracelet's glitter, her wedding rings, her wonderful bright mind, not to be opposed. What on this fucking earth does it take to get away from things, to get rid of dark thoughts,

THE WHITE COMMUNITY

that just keep growing—that take on a life—that take your life away from you? And the pictures. What right do these things have to grow and live in *your* brain, as if they owned what used to be you? What were these people's names again? "Thank you. Thank you so much for coming." Who were they again, those two? My mother, speaking to someone else now. And I missed it. Who are they? God, the giver of life—often enough the giver of life to the thoughts that murder body and soul. Thoughts and pictures. God would give life to them as soon as to anything else—put 'em right in your heart and say live for as long as you want! Giver of life! Fucking perverse! "Thank you. Thank you so much for coming."

Officer Rudkus, George Rudkus, hundreds of names stayed down in his mind, lost in places that got cut off by the sounds of that gun, by the blood that obscured, flooded over these places where the names were lost, maybe forever—his own name, he might, if asked, have to think before it came to him—but *George Rudkus,* it came to him the second he saw him. Not padded, those shoulders, maybe not the suit you'd expect a cop to wear, out of uniform, fresh-pressed, tan-colored, no dumb pinstripes, no overdone, over-sharp shit like a collar pin—but was there a gun under his jacket's breast? Six feet. The Eastern-European face, strong cut, the blonde hair short, not crew but short, so a barmaid or call girl might think cop the second she saw him—but not everyone would. Off duty. His face, that of an actual person, just like everyone here, a person with a life, and soul. "Thank you. Thank you for coming. We are very grateful. Thank you so much."

And with him?...coming out past that table, and the vases, with the flowers? Christ help me, it was true. It was her. She was there. Her hair...the beautiful dark red. Her pale face. So beautiful. And everything, all of it, came with her as she stepped clear of those flowers—the first sight of her, at Ignatius, which always came back if ever he saw her, anywhere, and now the revelations, the way Jack stabbed him in the fucking heart, the images of her with Jack, making love with Jack, who *knew* how much his own brother loved her, he knew it, and he fucked her, and how many times would they come in the future, *endless times*—the thought, the picture of Jack's fucking her, of her fucking Jack. "Yes. Thank you for coming. Thank you so much. We are so grateful." The pain, the physical pain, the anger, like an eternal curse, all confused with the fact that Jack was gone, never another day of life in this world. My last words to him were that I wanted to kill him. This

DIVISION

shouldn't happen; in a good world it would never happen that you couldn't get rid of the anger at the person you will miss every day for the rest of your life, because you love him utterly, your brother, who stuck up for you every single time since the day you could walk. He's gone, and I'm still here. Jesus Fucking Christ. That fucking abortion. "Thank you. Thank you so much for coming. We are so grateful."

She and Jack—they made the *choice*. His mother helped them. My mother, standing next to me, her perfume, her gold bracelets, the sound of her voice, which she had given now to someone new. John and Ellen Gleason. Ethics. Can't think of ethics. Takes energy of mind. But it's my own mother, and brother, and *her* that I'm talking about, not just empty names. My people. So close. But can't give my mind to anything, except the shit that comes up on its own. Comes when it will and then goes. Because my mind does not belong to me. Who owns it? Where does the shit-flow that runs through your mind start? There is no beginning. And no end. "Thank you so much, Mr. and Mrs. Gleason. Thank you for coming. We are so grateful."

When she kneels at that kneeler, what will she be thinking? Her face, the beautiful lines and turns of her mouth, no smile now—but he could see her smile any place, any time, just with a closing of his eyes. What all will be going through her mind? She doesn't know that I know about the abortion. What names are getting said now? And my father. How will she come up to him? And to my mother? How will she and my mother greet each other? Will they come to tears? Sob in a sisterhood of grief? Or pretend they need to be introduced? Will she say, "Ellie Shea, Mrs. Riordan, I was a friend of Jack's," as if my mother would need to be told?—all so that my father won't become aware that there's a bond between them, the fucking sisterhood, the sisterhood of fucking?! "Thank you. Thank you so much for coming. We are so grateful."

Will she be embarrassed that she's here with another guy?—embarrassed that it was that easy for her to become someone else's lover, if she was ever Jack's lover, or just someone who fucked him after a night at a bar—and which would be worse, real love, or a casual fuck—which would more painfully rip my brain in two? Even here, in this place and moment—this funeral line for someone whose child was conceived in her—will she feel the easy freedom that comes from the death of others, of that child, and of the one who fucked her and started the life of that child, both gone for good—out of the picture—and she free of it all? Mr. and Mrs. Katzmark. Tom and Jennifer. But who am I to judge, particu-

106

THE WHITE COMMUNITY

larly about that child gone, and even about Jack gone? Still, will she be ashamed when she sees me, thinking that I know? Or not, even if she does think I know? Will she be ashamed that she involved my mother in something that, if my father were to know of it, the knowledge would destroy him? Does she know that? Would she be ashamed? Rudkus, George Rudkus, he called her his girlfriend. "Thank you so much, Mr. and Mrs. Katzmark. We are so grateful you have come." He said *girl-friend*. So they must have made love by now. She has made love with George Rudkus. So he cannot *not* have a good soul. He must have a soul—a good soul. Her boyfriend. If he died. Could she move on if he died, this cop she met *how*—in this never-ending nightmare story of my life? George Rudkus and Ellie Shea—the future, my future, if they are for real, if they last. George and Ellie, 'til I die—'til death do me part—from all future time. "Thank you. Thank you so much for coming. We are so grateful." How do I get out of this shit? If I died. If I *weren't* still here. Would she come to my funeral? Would she be shocked if I told her I have loved her every day since the first moment I saw her? Would she feel fear? Or fucking pity?

"Would you like, Con, honey, for me to spell you for a while?" It was Bree, his mother's sister, now come up behind him. She had said she'd be looking to see if any of them needed a break—such a good person, who'd suffered the worst, the loss of a child, my cousin Billy, sweetest, best kid in the world, and now her sister has lost a child, the worst that can happen. No worst, there is none. Pangs—schooled at forepangs, herds long gather in a main, inside our sweating selves. What stops it! *What?* "Do let me stand in for ya for a bit, sweetheart."

He didn't answer right away. He looked to see where she was. How long would it take her to get to the kneeler? What would it mean, for the whole rest of his life, if he missed her—if when she came up, he wasn't there? It could never be that George Rudkus, the cop with the good soul, *maybe* a good soul, that this cop, her new lover, could ever see in Ellie Shea all that Connor Riordan saw—would ever lose his breath like this, feel this pain just seeing the way her dress rested on her softly, so beautiful, fucking God, or the way the light changed on her hair. Could ever be willing to die for her the way Connor Riordan would, if anyone ever threatened to harm her.

"Con? Honey? We've set up a refreshments table in the back room. Why don't you get yourself a soft drink, or a bite? Give yourself a little break?"

107

DIVISION

Bree still stood behind him, and now he did turn to her. He smiled and hugged her, twisting his head again back, though, to measure any change in the line—wondering how long exactly he could be gone without missing the moment she would come up. Then he said, "Thanks," to Bree, and, "Yeah, it would be nice—for a moment. I could use a little break. Thanks, Bree, so much." Stepping aside, then, to let his aunt, his mother's sister, take his place next to his mother, he did turn toward that back room, thinking, yeah, an iced coke and maybe a finger sandwich—there'd be time for that. But right away, as the door of it opened, he could see that the refreshments room was packed solid. So no fucking way. He'd suffocate. And all these people everywhere. Christ. Out in the corridor, he saw a single door under a red EXIT sign. He made no contact with another face, taking, with relief, the privilege he was given to be left to himself, the brother who was right next to Jack when he was murdered—and he took the exit door. The parking lot, though still filled with cars, was for the moment empty of people. A spotlighted American flag flapped in the breeze, but as Connor lifted his eyes to it, he caught the OPEN sign in the window of EJ's Bar and Grill. How many breath mints would it take, he thought, to kill the fragrance of a shot of Jameson? Or two, or three shots?—and as he began now to wind his way through the parked cars toward the bar, he thought or five? or ten? And maybe I don't come back to the people-parade at all. Just get hammered—'til the sweat stops in my hands. And the shit-flow in my head. And if I miss her now and for the rest of my life, she'll always have Officer Rudkus, who can have her if he wants, for all future time. Every change of light in her hair.

The line moved slowly toward the closed casket, but it moved. On a night like this, everyone would have been thinking of everyone else, even had the ushers not touched them with that gentle reminder of a special need for mutual courtesies. Still there would be bursts of grief, people's just being overcome—in ways that kind politeness could never hurry. For anyone at all, moving finally toward the kneeler at the coffin, it might prove impossible to get free of dulling self-preoccupation, concern about manner or appearance, which will just come at times like this, exactly, perversely, because, they should not—but a deep politeness, here, would make anyone in this community respect, with a silent patience, always, the grieving of others—even should it break from the quietly established pace of things, or when there had best be a looking away.

108

THE WHITE COMMUNITY

Ellie Shea, coming closer and closer to the casket, now gripped tighter the handkerchief she'd taken from her purse. And now she looked away as Teresa Scannell, a good friend, came up to Mrs. Riordan. She knew they were hugging, but likely not both in tears—for she had over a good time now taken glances at Mrs. Riordan, Jackie, and hadn't seen her once break down. She knew so well, too, that Connor had left the line—and that still he wasn't back. Professor Riordan was there. Why had she taken his class? To try to make everything seem all right, all normal, no issues? Just to say there's nothing to it? For the purpose of completing her self-exoneration? Or as an act of defiance—against the gods, of what?—of those wells inside her where all the tears came from, for those days and days after? Or as a propitiation of those gods? Or to see where the mysterious, distant Connor Riordan—the one she had had such intense feelings for, for years, but who never once gave her the time of day—actually came from? And will he come back now? Why did he leave? And what did Jack say about him—his little brother, that night? I know. Why ever pretend I don't know exactly what he said? He whispered it softly to the air, as we were doing what we did. But I could have made it out from the roar of everything else in the world. "Little brother," he whispered, "don't you wish this was you?"

She looked back at the coffin, gripping her handkerchief. No one has ever celebrated, in happiness marked down, to be remembered, the day she had an abortion. Prayer—the secret hope that someone, something, will help you, if you make yourself open to the help—if you believe that by opening yourself to it, it will come. But if you fear that that someone or something has seen what in deepest secrecy you have done—if what you *believe* is that the help you need will somewhere deep inside you be cut off before it starts by that something or someone who answers prayers, or doesn't—the result is you just won't pray. And I can't remember the last time, Jack, I even tried. It's just me, no God around, for worse or better. Divided from the divine. But you know, Jack Riordan, what it was and wasn't. I was nineteen. It wasn't love. It wasn't even like—for either of us. You knew it, and I knew it. We just wanted to cross the line that night—just the way we did—until the line was gone and we were bored. I know the reasons.... And could I ever make go away the way we both talked about Connor, working ourselves up in an intimacy of shared resentment, drinking, laughing. Did I *laugh?* So incredibly painful to think I laughed. All because I thought Connor would *never*.... And why is he gone now?

DIVISION

The last person before her had blessed herself at the kneeler and was rising. Georgie laid his hand gently on her shoulder. He wouldn't go to the kneeler with her, respecting her need to go by herself. So many things she did like about Georgie, the way he called her that night and the way he told her. That touch of his hand now, too. Oh, Jack Riordan. Oh, Jack. She at last walked up now and knelt before the casket and bowed her head. Jack, if you can hear me—no matter what it was, or wasn't, between us, you were good to me. You didn't abandon me. You didn't flinch from responsibility when I told you—not for a moment. You didn't go silent and never talk to me again, or insult me by asking me if I was sure you were the one. You talked to me again, so many times. You came to see me, more than once. You took me that day. You waited for me. You took me home. You stayed with me and talked to me. And other days, afterward, you talked to me, to see how I was. All of it gesture, not needed—but *good*. And all of it, so there would be no more—which was also good. No lingering bitterness. Nothing to forgive. Nothing.... It is so, so terrible, Jack, so beyond-belief terrible, what happened to you. So terrifying. That someone saw you as nothing, saw your life as nothing.... I cannot think. And why you? What made such a terrible thing happen—to you? You were a good, good person. And you were what I wanted that night, for reasons I don't want to think about. And God help me, you were beautiful—and wild, which helped.... If there is a God, he knows how good you were. This is so terrible. But whatever there is to be forgiven, please, Jack, know that I do forgive it. What we did, I have thought now many times, it was the *opposite* of love, the *opposite* of commitment. But from opposites—you learn the real thing.... So I have that in my heart: a sense of the real thing, because of our mistake, for which I forever forgive you. And if you can hear me, if anyone, anywhere can hear me, may I please some time in this life be forgiven too.

Tighter and tighter she had gripped her handkerchief as she did pray this last prayer for forgiveness, and now, as she rose from the kneeler, she took the handkerchief to her eyes. The gods who move the tears of compunction were not to be defied. She waited for Georgie, the touch of his hand. But once more now she had to step out alone.

"Ellie Shea, thank you so much, Ellie, for coming."

Not having known that Ellie Shea was now taking her husband's class, Jackie Riordan was surprised to see he knew her, though she made no sign of surprise.

THE WHITE COMMUNITY

"Professor Riordan, I am so, so sorry. This is so heartbreaking. I don't know if you know—but I was a friend of Jack's. We went to St. Ignatius together. And I, I would see him still." So much for her—too much. Besides this terrible death, so many secrets. Thomas Riordan. Professor Riordan. Every reason she had for taking his class. Connor. Connor Riordan. Little brother. She was crying again now, and suddenly now hard, maybe crying out of her soul every secret that weighed on her, smothering her life. Her lips, wet from her tears, said nothing—but her tears cried out her secrets.

Tom Riordan waited. He wondered how ever he could have missed it—the deep beauty of this young woman, standing before him now, in tears. But there was something he would do, because he knew, now, that he had been right about everything—every fragment which came that night from Con in his frightened misery—that he had put every bit of Con's jumbled words together, and was right, about Jack, and this girl, and all the things that might well overset completely his own life, which for days now he had felt breaking apart: "Ellie," he said, when she'd caught her breath and dried her face and could look at him: "Could you do me a favor? I won't be at class for some days. I wonder if you could help me?"

"Of course. Anything. I would be so happy to help you."

"Just a simple thing. If you could go to the class, both next time and the time after, and tell those who come that the syllabus will remain the same—except for the *Adam Bede*. We'll remove *Adam Bede* from our reading list, and that's how we'll handle the days I miss."

"Of course, absolutely. I'd be so happy to do that. And if there's anything more, please just tell me. And... I guess I have just missed Connor. If, Professor Riordan, you could please tell him, for me...that I am so very sorry. So terribly sorry."

"Of course, I will, Ellie. I'll be sure to tell him."

Jack Riordan would never now have a child, never leave a child behind him. The thought had come to her before, and as she turned to Jackie Riordan, it came again. It was what she was thinking as she said, "Oh, Mrs. Riordan, what can I say? I am so sorry. I am so sorry... I just don't know what to say." Then, with her heart breaking, she reached out and hugged the mother—to share for a brief moment an unspeakable grief and weight of secrets. But she got no feeling, from the unresponsive arms of a silent Jackie Riordan, that the grief and the weight of all their secrets were felt by the two of them in the same way.

111

COULDN'T YOU BE SOMEBODY ELSE?

4 A.M. Jackie Riordan, having turned away long since from her sleeping husband, lay on her side, wide awake. She reached to her night stand and reversed the face of the electric clock. But now there was its red light, glowing on the wall before her. She tried to calm her breathing, in hopes that her exhaustion might at last gain upon her ceaseless agitation—and put to rest her fierce, irrepressible anger at her son Connor—the one who survived, and who just *left* the wake of his brother—an anger which she did not need. But she couldn't stop it. So much unbearable grief—and anger, reaching everywhere—to that dead-souled black murderer, no face to him yet, just his blackness—black America, come to murder her son, not knowing the difference between Jack Riordan and any other white face—just that he was white: that was all that that ignorance needed. And the images of her holding her murdered son, red, glaring pictures painted in some madhouse in hell, where parts of her mind were condemned to suffer—from now until the hour she couldn't suffer any more. The funeral mass for Jack would begin at St. Clement's in less than five hours. But it was no good. She couldn't calm herself down.

COULDN'T YOU BE SOMEBODY ELSE?

Ellie Shea, too, not just quietly disappearing, but instead taking her husband's class—for what purposes of continuing torture?

So at last, and no matter where her life was right now, with the funeral mass coming in the morning, not five more hours, she let herself go...gave herself silent leave...in a way that was now well familiar to her. She closed her eyes to the red glow on the wall and whispered in her mind, Separate yourself—separate.... She breathed...slowly... and then let it begin—with a kiss, warm and long, and then another, and then, her arms thrown softly around his neck, with a resting of her cheek on his chest, and then with his taking his fingers, the way he did that first time, to the fastenings of her dress, as her heart pounded with utter passion, her passion, her own, come from the deepest part of her own true self. She felt it now. Oh, sweet God, the relief of it, from this sorrow and anger, and, again, from every lie, every trap of her trapped life, from her forced marriage on to every forced emotion through all the years of forced devotedness, until she moved, freely, with her own choice of a love. To have loved in this life, truly, before she died, and left the world forever—the difference between having loved and never having known what that meant—what value real love had...to have known this before dying. She said his name, *Richard Olen, Richard Olen, Richard Olen,* in a slow mental chant that gave warm joy to her body. She loved his name. And then she relived it again, his taking down of her dress and his laying her down on his bed, and their kisses, so intense she could have settled for them, never having known a deeper pleasure than those kisses, but then her letting of herself go further, and further, and their making complete passionate love. She chanted his name again, over and over—and then, *My passion. Mine. Mine.*

A loud clumsy sound from below now broke into her reverie—the back door opening with a harsh bang. "FUCK! Fuckin' whore!" The door was kicked again. "And all you motherfuckers, I hate all a ya forever! But now *HE!—HE* knows the value of life! And *HE* has lived to tell about it! The chickenshit!" The door now was slammed closed, hard enough so that its window glass might shatter. How in God's name could Tom sleep through this—for there he was, sleeping! And now a banging into the kitchen table—and no doubt *him* falling to the floor, Connor, clearly drunk out of his mind, the night of his brother's wake— which he just disappeared from, with no explanation. As if he were the only one suffering! He has his life! Jack is gone! Not five hours until Jack's funeral and he's drunk out of his mind! This is too much! And

I do not need it! Almost asleep, almost there...I was on my way *there*.
She rose, put on her robe, and started toward the stairs.

"Officer Rudkus! Fancy seeing you here! And who's with you, Fudkus
Rudkus, fucking Dudkus, cocksucking motherfucker! And, excuse me,
but is that a pistol you have beneath your tasteful jacket? Did you know,
Dudkus, that people can get born with a single shshshshOTT from a
gun! Conceived in a single shot and dedicated to the proposition that
all men are CREATED EQUAL!! And God bless Ameri-caaa....! Home
of the gun. Land of the dead."

"Get up from that floor!" She had made her way through the dining room and stood now in the passage leading into the kitchen. She
looked hard at her son, who sat on the floor, head down. He had one
hand lifted to the kitchen table, but he didn't look up when she spoke
—rather seemed ready to fall to the floor and pass out. Her anger grew
still more intense. Never had she looked at him like this. "I said get
up! NOW!"

Still managing to sit, with his hand reached up to the table, Connor
shook his head—then raised it. He shook his head again, then looked
to see his mother standing under the lintel. "Oh, Jesus! A ghost!" he
said. "Mom, Mommother! Don't cry. I've never seen you cry, Jackie.
Never seen that. And what's the matter? Do you need a change? a
change of life? a change of sceeeeeeene—*Jackie?*"

"What are you talking about?! This is disgusting, Connor! First you
just leave your own brother's wake, with *no* explanation. And then
what? You go out and get blind drunk when you have an absolute
duty to fulfill. Maybe the most sacred duty you'll ever have—to honor
your own brother's *life.* And you just leave. The *disrespect!* And the way
you've now spoken to me! How dare you use such a tone! *Jackie!* How
dare you? And exactly where are we, Connor, with this complete loss
of respect—for everything and everyone, your brother, your mother,
yourself! I don't know if I've ever been so angry! And you have another
duty, mister, every bit as sacred—and that's to put on your fullest dignity, or to *find* it, for your brother's burial! And there you sit drunk out
of your mind! So drunk you might still stumble from it and stink of
it when you'll be a pallbearer—in less than five hours! I am so angry!
And so disgusted!"

"Waaaait...wait wait wait.... Did you say *duty,* Jackiemom? Duty? I
believe I heard you say *duty*—indeed SA-CRED DUTY!—and about
that, I want to say this!" He tried to pull himself up but couldn't. He

COULDN'T YOU BE SOMEBODY ELSE?

almost fell over but managed to get his other hand to the floor and stopped himself. He then got to his knees, regained a purchase on the table top, and raised himself up, placing both hands on the table top to steady himself.

All of it was happening here in an instant. Growing, wildly growing differences, total changes. From both of them—this strange new violence and aggression. And her rage. Truly she had never been where she was now with Connor—and where was this going? It was as if—not just drunk—he was suddenly another person—and she too, becoming another person. And *no*—she did not want to hear what this other person, this stranger who knew none of the respect, the self-restraint, of the son she knew—none of the values they'd shared their whole lives —she didn't want to hear what he had to say, not another word of it. But what did he mean by what he'd said *already?* What might he know? Would he have seen anything? Who would have told him things? She didn't move.

Connor, standing now free from his mother's kitchen table, was not drunk completely—indeed by no means so drunk that he wasn't troubled, somewhere deep in, by his own disrespect. He could feel it, this disrespect—how it was killing something—in himself—and killing things around him. But he wanted to kill things. His mother. Himself. So he spoke—with words meant to kill. "It's a definite concept, mama! A well-defined con-CEPTION—this DUTY, not just some worrrrd!" He stood now straighter, still under the influence—but finding clearly under the influence of alcohol now a full voice, which was connected, an open conduit, to a deep well of words, and thoughts, which would just keep coming, unfiltered. "And what the CONCEPT *is,* dear mother —is that duty, deeee—ooooty, is not the same as plezzzzzzzzure. No, it is not! In FACT, it's gonna be the opposite of pleasure juuuust about half, or no! let's call it three fucking quarters of the time! So Yes! the basic opposite of pleasure. And so when the pleasure-voice inside you says I wanna do what I, the perpendicular pronoun *I,* wanna do, what *me* wants to do—the voice of duty says, Hold up there! If it feels good, do it?—That's *not* the deal here! *That's* what duty sezzzzz. It says you can't just have what *you* want. That it feels good, soooooo-*WHOA* good, doesn't confer on you the *right* to fucking do it! But Wait, you say! What I'll do is keep most of me the same, and I'll just cut off part of me, which won't be the real me, and I'll have that separated *part* of me go off and do what feels so gooood, and have the rest of me, the real

115

me, stay here and stay virtuous—and not really be attached to whatever that part of me, that's not really me, went off and did. But what duty says is THERE IS ONLY ONE YOU! What duty says is this thing called INTEGRITY, Jackie, is more important than plezzzzzzure. Duty doesn't com-part-ment-al-iiiiiiZUH."

"Are you happy? Are you making yourself happy with your drunken irrelevant pretentious tripe? God only knows what you're babbling about—in your little sermons to nowhere. But are you getting the booze out, Connor? I hope you are—because the hour is fast approaching when you'll have to be sober and *decent*. So make yourself happy—if it gets you sober!" So, still standing beneath the lintel, she answered him—and beyond her utter fatigue, and unprecedented anger, she found now that cold determination and fighting spirit that she could muster any day from the beginning of a court case to the end. But this was even more. This was real violence. And if this stranger, who used to be her son, wanted a battle, the stranger in her would give him one.

"Ohhhhhhh HAPPY! That's a good one too, Jackie! Happiness. But there can be a trick, don'tcha know! And that's when—that is *when!*— we don't just *cut out* the little pleasure-part of ourselves and say that what this separated part did wasn't really us (you know, mama, how we just say it was *only sex* and not the real me involved?)—No! What we do now is we take the pleasure part of us and we call *it* the real me! And we say I gotta be me! I've never been ME. I've never listened to my happiness-pleasure voice before, always suppressed it, always fucking tyrannized over it, or let somebody else, not me, tyrannize over it, but now I can hear that feel-good voice, and what it's saying is *change!* Up the Revolution! This isn't just sex but LOVE! And do you need a change, Jackie! Is your happiness voice saying you need a fucking revolution—that you have a god-given right to LOVE! Is it saying that because you were never given your own CHOICE, you now deserve a change! Is that pleasure voice singing I gotta be me! Is that your song now! Did I ever tell ya about the cartoon, *Jackie,* with the guy in the shower singing Sinatra's 'I Gotta Be Me!' And his wife says, in the caption, *Couldn't you be somebody else for a while!* Ha! Great fucking laugh, mama! I love that cartoon. It's my favorite of all time! Couldn't you be somebody else for a while! And let me just ask you, Mrs. Fucking Duty, Mrs. Respect for my brother's *life*—and do not get me started on respect for LIFE!—Let me just ask you: Couldn't you be somebody else for a while?!"

COULDN'T YOU BE SOMEBODY ELSE?

Though still raging, she was now stunned beyond even her own anger. She felt as if some witness she'd put on the stand had now, beyond all decorum, stepped down from the chair and forced *her* up on that chair and then turned on her with unanswerable accusations. Never. She'd never been hit like this. Her first instinct, come from some depth of feeling she'd never known, had been to step over to her son and hit back, hit his mouth with her fist. But she took only some few steps and stopped. She squeezed her fists but kept them pressed against her thighs. At last, then, things came to her, hard, powerful, real as her soul's life. "So you think you know things, do you? You've been told things. Or maybe you've *guessed* things. Or think you've seen things. But I can tell you what you really know—and that is nothing. You think you're funny! Couldn't you be somebody else for a while? I gotta be me—all just some big joke. Trapped in someone else's life, or the life that someone else decided should be yours. You think that's all just a laugh. That you'd be lying on your death bed and that all you could say for yourself was that you did what you were told, that you did what somebody else said was what you were supposed to do—and that you kept doing that and nothing else until you died—you think that's goodness. That never committing the crime of being yourself—that that's goodness. That never hurting anybody ever—that that's goodness. But I can tell you that finding yourself, no joke, no laugh, is the most right and good of all things, that *it* is the ultimate duty in this brief life, and that there is no finding of yourself, none, without hurting somebody else. Two questions you'll have to answer at the end of your life, Connor—Did I choose the right life for myself and did I live that life with the right person? Do I love what I did with my life and do I LOVE the person I lived my life with? And I can tell you right now that if you don't have the right answers to those questions, you have not lived a good life—that your last moments will be filled with feelings of waste and *shame* because you wasted and abused the only life you had."

For a moment he felt for her—and then said to himself, *Tripe,* she calls what I've offered up *tripe*—and listen to her! He took that "somebody else" who would be hurt if she went out and fucking found herself and he made that "somebody" into his father—because that's who it was. And he hated her—more and more as she corroborated every suspicion, every allegation come up against her from the bottom of his heart, until finally he said, "It must be good, huh, Mama? The sex, I mean. The

DIVISION

fucking! It must be good enough so that you actually, maybe, maybe actually believe that it's telling you who the *real you* is. But I have news for the *real you:* take your excitement at this discovery of the *real god-damned you*—and you triple it or quadruple it or run it up exponentially until you scream at the fucking plezzzzure of it, and then you'll just *begin* to get to the goddamned power level of my revulsion at it. Consequences, Jackie! Sex has consequences: what a fucking bummer! So much *fun* runs smack into so much *reality!* Shit! You thought its bullshit orgazzmo thrills were taking you straight to the real you! But what your thrill ride was really all about was breaking my father's heart and breaking my faith in everything on the fucking earth. And all it really is, this thrill ride of yours, is you getting laid and you getting yourself ready to be soon enough bored to shit by your new lover boy and then wondering fast enough who in the fuck the real you is now! Consequences. Hurting, wounding people, no matter how good the sex might feel to you! And what happens, Mama, when it doesn't just take *hurting* somebody for you to get freeeeee—but it takes *killing* somebody? Wait! I know! You'd pay for it! Because you wanted to! Gotta be free! Gotta be me! FUCK the real you!—who would have aborted the brother whose life you tell me I don't respect! That's right, Jacko told me the whole shitload before he died. He saw you with your lover man in the park—saw you drive off with him. He overheard you on the phone. God damn you! The last things we talked about—before Jack died!—were his and Ellie's making of the *choice* and your helping them, because you wanted to, and your needing a fucking change in your life because so much had been forced upon you, like my father, and like me—your fucking SACRED DUTIES. And your job in this brief life, as you term it, *JACKIE,* was to find your joy *in them*—in my father! in me!"

Wounded, spiritually devastated, knowing how many things in her life were now, beyond all resurrection, *dying*—she still had been maintaining some deepest mental poise as her now one remaining son, this child of religion, of merciless Jehovah, had been going violently on against her. And she had determined, as she kept listening to his case, that in her soul, somewhere, she would find the strength—to turn away the momentum of this terrible violence, to fight fire with real fire;—for it was her *life* she would be fighting for, already half over, with the clock mercilessly ticking! For so long now she had known that it would be against some kind of last temptation—the temptation to succumb to

COULDN'T YOU BE SOMEBODY ELSE?

the kind of guilt that this boy was now laying upon her life—the temptation to give up her life to this guilt, to make herself a sacrifice on the altar of his need and her husband's need—to criminalize and capitally punish her own desires—to listen to and *heed* the ice-cold voice that, forever, and as deep as the voice of your desire, says that your every argument for your freedom is a falsehood, a selfish, criminal rationalization—the temptation to give up, capitulate, and think that *because* the kinds of things that this boy, her religious son, was saying were in part real—that there must be no deeper reality, that truth must belong entirely to these ones who wouldn't hesitate to end your life on the altar of their neediness. Acceptance! And resignation! Forever she had tried. Make the best of what is, for better or for worse, as you vowed to do, no matter what you might really feel. And for this do not call me hypocrite! she now shouted in her mind, as her son kept on attacking her—I am NO hypocrite for trying to be Catholic, for mouthing all the right words, for all those years. Damn you, she was thinking as he went on! I was *not* lying. I was trying. But always, from the very start of my marriage, there was the germ of my desire, un-killable—the potential in me for real, not forced love and for real fulfillment—for true love and fullness, instead of the half life and the falsehoods. And, *yes,* she thought now, yes, *back then,* at the start of my pregnancy—if I'd been a woman of the new time, yes, and not still old-school Catholic—even, by GOD, if they brought me in and made me listen to the heartbeat— of Jack!—YES!—I would have set against that heartbeat the heartbeat of my own potential, heartbeat to heartbeat, my *real* life against the undeveloped life of an unknown. Yes, I would have! It is not that you end a life; it is *when* you end a life. It is when! When is everything!

"That's right! When we were in the car—the car you drove off with him in, from that fucking park! That's when it was!" Connor said now again, "When we were in your car, that night, Jacko told me everything. And me sitting right where he sat, your new friend. Shit!"

As she heard him again, clearly heard his words, words strangely re-iterated, and now the things he said about her car, she thought, in a flash, that if he, Connor, hadn't kept Jack in her car, hadn't held him there with his moralizing arguments, his religion, her Jack might still be alive—that it wasn't for any other reason, perhaps, that that conjunction in that alley happened. And now, as this thought formed itself harder and more clearly in her, she just turned her back to him, this second son, who got to keep his life, though he was maybe already dead

DIVISION

to her—and she moved off toward the dining room, saying nothing. But under the lintel she turned a last time, and did say to his face, this one who looked so exactly like her, "If you think, Connor Riordan, that I would ever ask you for forgiveness, you are as mistaken as you will ever be."

And with all the hatred that he had for her in his broken heart, the utter disrespect, still trying to kill anything and everything he could, he answered her: "And if you think that I ever *would* forgive you, you are just as mistaken."

WHEN TO OPEN
AND WHEN TO CLOSE

Robert Teague had been five days home on Calumet when Jack Riordan was laid to rest. Fifty hours he'd been kept in lockup at Violent Crimes before he made his call to home and family. "You lawyer up, Robert," Detective John Touhy had said to him, in interrogation, "and you lose me as your friend. And the only person between you and the State's Attorney's Office—the only one who can have any effect right now on what the charges you'll face will be—is me. You don't want to lose my friendship, Robert—because you do *not* want, son—to be brought up on a charge of capital murder. You're brought up on a murder charge, Robert, and your life is over, win or lose. Nobody ever thinks of you the same way again. If you get off, they think you got away with that murder. Somewhere in the back of their minds they think he aided or abetted. And you never feel about *yourself* the same way, either. Just human nature. You'll feel it all over you—the filth and stink of every word that gets said about you, true or not. It's like a new kind of racism, Robert. You won't be able to close yourself off from the image they paint of you. The accounts in the papers. They'll be your mirror. The life you've lived—and the life you want to live—*all* of it, past, present, and future—it's never the same. And that's if you're acquitted, son, which in a case like this—people out for blood—is by no means guaranteed. Violent black on white homicide. You, a young black man, there with a known violent gangster. And naturally people wondering why it went down at the house of somebody this Robert Teague knew—not either of the other two, just Robert Teague. No coincidence. And that that gangbanger was armed—what chance that they'll think you didn't know that? And if they think you knew it, Robert, they *will* find you guilty of murder. They'll have to. It's the law. But cooperate with me—and things change. You're my friend. And I'm yours. I can say to them that Robert Teague was there by accident. And that he didn't know about any gun. And if I do, your life has a chance to be what it used to be, and what it should be, in your future, which now you'd have back again."

The signed statement John Touhy got from Robert Teague was nine pages long. Just a few more hours, then, after he'd put his name to it, and Robert was released to his father, Maurice Teague having heard from his son that the police—who'd said at Maurice's door two nights before, when they'd come looking for Robert, that they just had a few questions for Robert about an identification—were now finished with their questions. Robert Teague's statement, attributing all exclusively to Watt, was detailed to the minute; though things were left out that Robert himself had talked about, or been involved in talking about. And endlessly in his cell, over all those hours, he thought back on those things—redistribution, black revolution, chattel slavery, economic slavery, a person not being a person, and how it'll take another *war* to end the new slavery, and a gun to the head. And Watt's black magic power—unafraid to die, or kill. But always, too, about the nightmare horror of violence, Watt's violence. What's strong enough to stand up to Watt, who'd long gone across the soul's dividing line to the rock-hard side, no looking back? What could bring ten thousand fallen angels back up from hell?

"Nothin'," Robert had said, when John Touhy asked him what they had talked about, as they wandered over Lincoln Park way, and then moved across that wealthy white neighborhood. "Nothin' much—mostly all about this lady friend of Watt's, this 'entertainer,' that Marcus knew too. She lives in west Old Town, so we were just headed that way, just to get to her place. Watt had called her up on his cell. We were

WHEN TO OPEN AND WHEN TO CLOSE

crazy excited, about going to see this lady, Sara Lee. She works at this club, Marcus and Watt said, V.I.P.'s. They said she looked like Halle Barry. They talked about how beautiful she was, her face, her body, her style, and about what all she'd do for a man. I'll be honest, sir—I was crazy excited to go see her. You can call her, Detective Touhy. Just call Sara Lee and ask if it's true that Watt called her. She works at V.I.P.'s. Ask her what time it was that Watt called, and if he set it up so we'd be seeing her, just like I say."

"He never slept," John Touhy said in private conference with veteran Karen Johansen, who'd spent nearly half her fifty years as an assistant State's Attorney, and had been a friend of Touhy's for fifteen, "and for me, KJ, that's still the sign. The ones who can sleep like babies—they're the ones who kill. Things the surviving boy said, too, Connor Riordan—about Teague's behavior at the scene—about the way Teague spoke to him, telling him, before he ran, that he was sorry, which I'm pretty sure, at least now, wasn't a *sorry* that said, yes, I was involved and I now regret it, but rather a *sorry* that this terrible thing *happened*. Teague's version of his own actions and words matched with Riordan's, too. And Riordan was insistent that Teague had nothing to do with it. Passionate about that. I went and spoke, too, to a fair maiden goes by the name of Sara Lee, beautiful, bright, the kind that makes you wonder how in hell she...." Detective Touhy bowed his head slightly, shook it, looked up again. "Anyhow, very honest seeming young lady, straightforward—and she confirms Teague's claim that he and Sabbs were at the time headed her way for a little get-together and that she would have expected them right about the time the shooting took place. We don't have Sabbs yet, and we're gonna need Sabbs to confirm that it was by accident that he and his cousin ran into each other—and by accident that they ended up behind the house of a kid Teague knew. And that part still troubles me, I've got to say. And I'm sure there are things he's leaving out. Maybe incidental. Maybe not. But right now I can't see puttin' this kid on the six A.M. to County. Ignatius kid, DePaul University student, honors grades, good family, moneyed family, no drug use, no record, all good history with the Riordan boys, and no discernible motive. Also cooperative from the start. Kind of kid I talk to in a whole different way, KJ. Kind you can scare with just the threat of shame, or with the possible loss of his future."

Karen Johansen nodded her head, then shook it.

"Yeah," John Touhy said, "a very rare bird indeed. And start to finish,

123

he at least tells me no outright lies. And we know damn well that before
he even got his little Branch 66 moment, the GD's in County World
hear he's got the word on Watt and they convince him he says that
word to a soul and his tongue's cut out, just before his throat's slit."

Johansen had already zipped her valise. She had a court date at 26th
and Cal in forty minutes. "Don't need to tell you, John...it's not gonna
be any prettier when the projects all go down. Gangbang gospel's just
gonna spread all round the city, and get taken up by a thousand little clusters. Don't we damn well know it—since it's already started."
Like a brain tumor you can't close off, she'd often now put it to herself, thinking of herself as one of a team of excising surgeons, ever just
making things worse, and worse. You cut out the main part—Cabrini
goes down, Robert Taylor goes down, they all go down—and the GD's
go down and all the big organizations—but then the little fragments
you never can get, they migrate now unstoppably through the brain
and start their malignant colonial life and growth. All the displaced
people, thousands infected by life in these hellacious places, and now
they're heading into neighborhoods everywhere, bringin' that sweet
gospel of killing and dying. She bowed her head slightly now, took a
breath, then looked up at Touhy. "But if we can keep this kid alive and
if he has the guts to give us Watt—then at least one damned dangerous
missionary of the gospel of hell won't ever start his mission. It's something. So no—no booking. Cut him loose to his father."

She stopped, shook her head again, sniffed a laugh, then turned to
the door. His father.... How many times, she thought, have we been
able to say that, with black kids in trouble? I'm the broken white record
—but what percentage? And this father, Mr. Teague?—if God ever listened to my prayers, which God does not, we'd be seeing thousands
of Mr. Teagues heading out into every neighborhood in the city, and
not seeing what the Section-8 shuffleboard of Daley's Great Transformation's gonna bring. And what we would get, with thousands of Mr.
Teagues heading out into neighborhood after neighborhood, would be
an entire new world. But how do we ever get *that* little transformation
started? And who would the missionary be who could make it happen?

In Maurice Teague's third-floor, turret-room library, on the second
evening after Jack Riordan's burial, Robert Teague sat with his father.
It was from this room, now two weeks past, that Robert, pointing out
to the Confederate battle flag, flying at half-staff in the Teague Funeral
Home parking lot, had stormed out, calling his father "the house nig-

WHEN TO OPEN AND WHEN TO CLOSE

ger's house nigger!" "Who would blame somebody from this neighborhood," he'd shouted, "if he threatened our lives because of this Uncle Tom craziness! But I know when you'll take it down! When you start to lose business! And isn't it time you ask yourself what self-respecting black man or woman would, or *should* ever let his or her deceased loved one be waked in the shadow of that red devil's rag—that sign that Satan is alive and well in this American world! Jesus-lovin' religion gone sick! Damned pathetic loss of respect for your own self—that's what I see. The kind of submissiveness they preached into us to keep us tame, to make us domestic animals. You want God? I say God gave us resentment, as a spiritual force. He gave us anger, as a necessary gift. He gave us the desire for revenge—in order to keep the world *just*—to see that justice was *done!*"

I won't, Maurice had thought as his son railed on at him in fury, tell him about the stone—won't add fuel to this terrible fire. But I will have the stone, and when that flag is lowered for the last time, I'll place the stone, with every name of the six thousand inscribed upon it, exactly where that flag now flies. And Maurice did not say a word to his angry son about the commemorative stone. Rather he said, "There are places, Robert Teague, that need to be marked—not treated the same as others. The truths of eternity are known when they come out in real places. Without the places, we don't know the truths, or can't feel them, which is much the same thing. So we go to Gettysburg or to the 16th St. in Birmingham, or to the Garden of Gethsemane, as pilgrims, or maybe to a place by a creek at home, or in the woods, where we know something took place. 'Took place,' we say. *Took place.* And when we set *this* place apart from *that,* in remembrance and honor of the truths of eternity that were revealed there—we can come so alive in that special place that we just might feel what it really means, Robert, to get past our limits, and feel the eternal. Just like love. You know what love means when you have real people bring it to life in you, or, best of all, when you find that one person who most truly brings it to life in your soul. Love sleeps until then, unrevealed. It doesn't take place."

Maurice had stopped when he said this, had touched then a forefinger and thumb round his chin, and smiled. But then he turned his mouth down, and took down his hand. "Wrongs, Robert," he'd said then, "are of eternity, too. Places where wrong was done—places of grief and terrible grievance—they can make God's loving truth real for us, too—because opposites call each other up in the human soul,

125

DIVISION

where they live side by side, light alongside darkness. Terrible wrongs were done to those six thousand. And the greatest wrong done them was that it was forgotten that they were sons of God, so I do my small part to remember this, in the place where the forgetting was done."

He had stopped again, then, and looked closely at his son. "I bring people to graves. It is what I do. And I do it so that their hearts by the gravesite, when concentrated on that memorial place, might feel so much love that they can hear the songs of the angels, songs that remain forever unheard by the unforgiving."

Robert, when his father had come to take him home from Violent Crimes, had told Maurice how he'd been arrested, and where—where *that* took place, and how. And he'd told his father everything he'd told the police—about Marcus, about Watt, about Sara Lee. Maurice, for the last five days, had been regularly in contact with his sister Dosey, calling her again and again to see if she'd heard from Marcus, encouraging her throughout to tell Marcus to turn himself in, should she hear anything from him, and assuring her that he would get Marcus the best defense he possibly could. And now, some two weeks (which seemed a lifetime) since Robert left home, just over ten days past the murder of Jack Riordan, father and son again sat up in Maurice's library—in the same chairs they'd sat in when Robert had raged against his father's "insane and downright dangerous turn-the-other-cheek and love-your-enemy nonsense" and his "Uncle Tom disgraces that *shame us!*—and that'll also make us *deserving* targets in our own backyard!" Nor could Robert Teague make anything like a full concession, even now, to his father's "forgiveness insanity."

But over the last hour he had expanded his story—had come clean, gradually...telling his father more and more—finally indeed telling him every last thing he could remember, about what he'd said to Marcus and Watt that night, and about the magnetic attraction, which pulled him toward the gangster Watt: "I was bonding with him, and he with me. It was strong, and real. It didn't matter that I grew up privileged—I felt myself, in a deeper black anger, turning from all you'd done for me." He confessed this to his father—and confessed that he was afraid, too, "that in some real way" he had, for his part, moved Watt to do what he did. "I can't get free of it, no matter where I run in my head. What made Jacko Riordan do what he did, pushing Watt to pull that trigger—that was another thing—the white thing, the property and ownership thing: the *get your hands off what doesn't belong to you, nigger,*

126

WHEN TO OPEN AND WHEN TO CLOSE

thing, and the *don't blame me for your miserable life* thing. It was insane, the way Riordan confronted Watt—like he *wanted* to be shot in the head. But I fear I put the black thing, the *time for confiscation* thing, the *time to pull the trigger* thing even harder into Watt's mind than it would have been that night, no matter how fierce the man is on his own or how much he thinks on his own about the system that keeps on killing black men—and the man is a thinker, as powerful a thinker as he is strong in his body. I don't know if I'll ever get away from the sick feeling that but for me Jack Riordan might still be alive." Robert, stopping, now took off his wire-rimmed glasses and with the back of his hand he wiped his eyes.

Maurice Teague, sixty-five years of black-American experience written on his face, strong, no fleshiness, a trim moustache like his son's, his gray hair cut short, his body still firm, six feet, his strength observable especially in his forearms and veined hands, folded those strong hands now before his chest as he set his elbows on the arms of his armchair. "For all things under heaven, Robert Teague," he said, "there is a time. When to start and when to stop, when to open and when to close—God put judgment in our souls, and our judgment knows the times for each. Where has Watt come from, and what? What *all* went into his raising of that gun against the Riordan boy? To understand all is to forgive all. You know how deeply your father believes this. But the law, Robert, will never do this, never open itself up to an understanding of all, and never forgive. It will always in its shallow practicality close off Watt from his past and his poverty and from every abuse of body and soul he's been subjected to—from all the influences that have made him what he is—*except* now those named Robert Teague."

His fingers still folded, Maurice bobbed his hands a second and looked at his son, without smiling. *"You,"* he said, "the law might well now want to include. It opens itself up to the possibility of you as an influence. It welcomes it—because there is a lust in the law, in our country a capital-punishment lust—to convict and to kill. And better to convict two than one, better three than two. Like a lustful man out after a multitude of women, the law wants notches on its gun."

Maurice now lowered his folded hands and set each on a knee and leaned forward toward his son. "But, Robert, you have *not* implicated Marcus. Better two than three is what you say. And yet you do not say better one than two. *Yourself* you do implicate. You take the position of the law with respect to yourself, closing off Watt's life from the dark

DIVISION

influences that the law won't recognize but opening it to the influence of Robert Teague." The father now gripped his knees more tightly as still he leaned forward. "It's never one thing or another, Robert, never simply close or open. And I want you please to hear me: Be the mercy-giving opposite of the law. *Do* close yourself off from Watt, and do *not* implicate yourself, just as you have closed off Marcus from Watt, and not implicated Marcus. But at the same time, yes, un-close your mind, open it up all the way back to animalized men in fetal crouches in the hellhole belly of slave ships on the Middle Passage to understand all that Watt is. But, Robert, it would be a lust to convict yourself and to capitally punish yourself—a *lust* that got you to convince yourself that you're to blame for what Watt did. You spoke to him only as you have spoken to the world—not to incite a riot, or to load a gun for murder—but to make the world focus on that revolution, as you've said to me, that would take the world past all division."

Again folding his hands, Maurice bowed his head and then raised it. "We are cursed with original sin, Robert," he said, "but blessed with a desire to get beyond it—to stand up and *deny* that we are enslaved by original sin, *deny* that we are hopelessly and forever flawed—and to believe that by our actions we *can* make the world a better place, even a perfect place. And it is in this belief, not in any spirit of homicide, that you have cried out for revolution."

Maurice was now rocking his folded hands up and down—in a gesture of yet stronger pleading. "Close yourself off from Watt, Robert" he said. "Use your God-given judgment, son, to see that the murder he committed started not with your words in the park but with his seeing that car and with the Riordan boy's angry resistance. Guilt starts where?—use your judgment to know when to open and when to close. And even as your God-given judgment says that guilt starts as far back as the fall of man and includes every moment of abuse and violence in the history of man—and that all this led to that shooting in the alley —even as your judgment says open things up to include *everything,* in order that you feel a profoundest mercy in your heart toward Watt, who is the end result of it all—even as it says forgive this man as a son of God full worthy of salvation—also forgive yourself. Listen to your truest judgment when in mercy it says close things off and let the punishable guilt of that murder, and the responsibility for it, start and end with Watt."

Robert Teague again took his wire-rimmed glasses from his eyes and

WHEN TO OPEN AND WHEN TO CLOSE

squeezed his eyes tight, once more then wiping them with the back of his hand. "I've tried," he said, "every escape route you've just suggested. Every one." He wiped his eyes once more and put his glasses back on. "But I don't know if I'll ever stop seeing in my mind what I saw, or stop thinking, no matter how I might try to divide myself from it, that I was part of that violence—and that I'll remain forever in part to blame for it. Black man to be hanged, in his own mind. Justice delivered on himself! Guilt doing its job like the Furies! But then when I think—How did it *all* happen—from the start?" Robert now wiped his cheeks and mouth hard with the back of his hand and then kept his hand raised in a fist. "When I turn round in anger at all of it, from the beginning of the beginning, the way you say, I think of what Watt said about being willing not just to die but to kill, and in my mind truly I become the man's disciple, because I not only feel Watt's anger and want to build the damned anti-world to the white, Mercedes world I'm locked out of, I believe that it truly takes that kind of unforgiving anger to change the world for the better—that to be a real force for change, I'd have to close my heart to the horror I saw, even if it had been Connor Riordan, not his brother, who died, and go as cold to that violence as Watt is—either that or I'll *die* looking out at the exact same world I was born into. Armed revolution is Fourth-of-July glorious if it's white—but what about a black shot heard round the world!"

Maurice raised himself up from his chair, and he stepped now over to the library's curved turret window. He looked out toward King Drive and the Teague Funeral home. His first child—whose compassion, whose guilt Maurice loved, whose anger he loved, even as he wanted to suppress it to death, whose human passions he loved, whose wonderful God-given mind, so beautiful all his life, from that first smile after he was born...his *son*—sat still behind him. Maurice waited silent a time. At last then, "The cotton fields, Robert Teague...back in Artesia, over the years...all got turned into pasture. Years now it's been cattle grazing where we picked the cotton."

Maurice took several slow, deep breaths. "Your granddaddy's half-acre pig farm—it's long gone. The board and tin shack we lived in—all long buried under honeysuckle and gone but for some sheets of rust and some rotted wall, which over the years the hay-cutters would keep on passing by, so thorn trees and bodock grew up around the ruin. And this was twenty years ago, when I went back for Auntie Tee's services. But no matter—every inch of it I will always know."

129

DIVISION

Once more looking out toward his funeral home and the flag, Maurice gripped his hands hard on themselves. Then at last, in a quieter voice, "So many things, Robert Teague, I never told you. I wanted never to fill your soul with anger. Things I've never told even your mother, or Dosey." He stopped once more, and breathed deep. Then, "1951—seventeen years old—I went back to that place. First time since we'd left it, four and a half years earlier. Took the train alone, with money I earned digging graves for old Mr. Williams. City of New Orleans. Switched with all the black folk to the all-black cars at the Kentucky line." He tilted his head back, then lowered it. "Told your grandparents I was going to look at Tougaloo, in Jackson—but got off the train in Winona and rode the bus, back of the bus, behind a rope with a click, from the Winona station on through Starkville east down 82 to old Highway 45—then walked south the six miles to Artesia. It was all still cotton then, 1951. Old Mr. Randall's plantation. I came to it. Twenty-one hundred acres. Run by his son—Mac Randall. Both father and son were still alive and well. Saw the old one still out on the tractor. And the son, he passed me in his truck when I was out on a back road on the east side of the plantation, walking where I would come to this old wooden bridge over Browning Creek. The son didn't know me when he passed me fast on that gravel road, spinning out here and there in his truck, stirring up a hundred yards of dust behind him—but I knew him."

Robert Teague, having listened to his usually strong-voiced father speak in what were now strange low tones, had risen from his chair and come up behind him. He stood close with his father now in that window which gave them a view of the Teague Funeral Home.

"I spoke of places to you, Robert," Maurice said, still in that strange low voice, and now still more slowly, "places sometimes...where great wrongs were done.... Places to be marked and remembered...because the angels might sing to us there...if only we could get past the curse of our hatred...of our violence...." Maurice closed his eyes a long moment. Then, "I mentioned, son, a creek. I believe I did. And Browning Creek...it runs under Stallings Rd. When I was a boy...I'd walk the creek bed there, when it was dry, down among the big, snakelike vines.... I'd walk down there for quiet, and for thinking. And in 1951... after Mac Randall had sped by me like a soul touched by hell's own fire, I came back again, out of his truck's dust...to the bridge...where an entry path runs over a grassy slope down into the creek bed."

130

WHEN TO OPEN AND WHEN TO CLOSE

Maurice's voice had descended nearly to a whisper. He was struggling to say anything more at all. And Robert now put his arm over his father's shoulder to comfort him. Maurice whispered, "Down in that creek bed, Robert Teague, some few hundred yards...ah come.... I...*came*...." He stopped. His shoulders began to heave. He was weeping. And he could manage, as he wept, at last to say only, "Oh, Robert Teague—Robert Jesse...son.... Let's not ask now for any more. Please let's not ask me now...for any more." And Robert, as he put both his arms around his father's shoulders and held him, said lovingly, softly against his father's rough cheek, "I won't ask you for more, Maurice Teague. I won't ask you for any more."

SHE BRINGS IT ALL TOGETHA

It was the smell of his being dead a week that had gotten the neighbors around the fourth shack down from Lusco's restaurant on Avenue G in Greenwood, Mississippi, to do what they never wanted to do—call the Greenwood police. The chain of the door-chain lock still had dangling from it the latch plate which had been forcibly ripped from the door frame, all four screws virtually exploding splinters of the wood, when the victim, Mr. Eugene Sykes, had come to the door and opened it a crack to see who was there. The violence of the attack (Mr. Sykes had received straight to his heart a powerful, deep knife thrust, nearly reaching the skin of his back, which the medical examiner said ended his life immediately, but had also had his throat slit to a depth that nearly severed his head) had the police thinking there could have been a history between perpetrator and victim. But the motive for the murder was categorized still as robbery; for Mr. Sykes's empty wallet was found sitting in the center of the dried pool of blood he lay in; and every drawer in the place lay open, with things strewn everywhere, including a gray metal lockbox, which had been forced, the police were certain, by the same knife that

132

SHE BRINGS IT ALL TOGETHA

killed Sykes, as blood was found on both box and lid. "He all cash," a young neighbor lady said. "Don't use no credit card nor no check neitha. And ah believe he keep his money all in a ol' *box* a his. Quite sure he do." "Dope-sellin' money," the man next door said to the chief investigator, who kept nodding as he took notes, "so t'ain't no surprise it come to this."

Who you? In the two and a half weeks since he'd left behind Greenwood and Avenue G, Watt had made a regularly recurring refrain of that question: *Who you?* He'd headed, when he lit out from Greenwood, not north for Chicago, but south for New Orleans, having decided finally that Chi Town would still be too hot for him—and having also staked himself to an added twenty-two hundred out of the wallet and lockbox of Mr. Eugene Sykes, aka the Gasoline Man, his father. *Who you?* Murderin' motherfucker put his devil face in that shithouse door crack, peekin' out that door, before I bust that fucker wide open. *Who you?*—he asks me, 'cause he don't know me from shit. But before I answer, before I say "Your *son!* You murderin' motherfucker!" so he can gotdamn *hear* it and take those words with him down to his dog-hole fuckin' grave, he's dead, takin' all that steel in his chest, so all I see is his mouth and his eyes stuck open, and him deaf as he is dead-departed. *Who you?* Does no good when I say "My mama's son—she called me Leonardo *SYKES*"—when I did him exactly how he did her, right crost the throat. *Who you?* Gotdamn child-beatin', rapin', murderin' motherfucker—don't even know who it was executed you, servin' you the justice a the law.

Watt remained in his dead father's house, cleaned himself there, cleaned his leather coat, washed and dried his blood-covered pants and shirt, and ate a lunch and dinner there—and when dark came round, he walked over to Greenwood's white side of the tracks to the Alluvian Hotel and spent the night, catching the southbound 9:10 the next morning. In New Orleans' Ninth Ward, down below sea level, Watt looked up some Joliet brothas, Folkin' boys, who he knew were there, and they put him up for those two and a half weeks in which he'd been repeating in his mind the Gasoline Man's final words—*Who you?*—till he said, "Fuck this shit and this shit-moldy place means nothing t' me. Two things to do before I pass, and I checked off one, Mama, with that murderin' thug motherfucker lyin' cut and dead in his blood—shoulda lit 'im up with gasoline, for all he did to you and me—and the other is to make my own history and build that Chi-Town kingdom, only

DIVISION

a witness or two or three in my way. *Who you?* No mystery about that
when I'm finished. And won't find me on some Miss'ippi shithouse
floor when I'm gone."

Straight back the way he'd come two and a half weeks before, Watt,
when he stepped out from Chicago's Union Station, headed east to the
Red Line and took the "L" back north to Clark and Division (with my
inheritance not all spent yet, he thought, sniffing a bitter laugh). But
he wouldn't walk on home down Division, west, to the Whites, and
5-3-4. No Jube now…and maybe never again. Rather he'd cut up Clybourn to Mohawk, to Sara Lee's place, where, just as he'd holed up in
the past when things got too hot for him in the Greens, he'd hole up
now for a time. But, seeing for once no CPD's, he stopped at that Starbucks just north of the Clybourn corner. He couldn't make out now,
through the window glass, if that same chick was in there, the sassy
bitch with the purple-black hair and the metal in her tongue, and those
sweet titties pressin' out against her coffee-girl apron. "Don't blame
me," she says; but I say, "We do."

Carrying still now his gym bag, Watt could see, reflected in the
door's window glass, the silk-shine of his dark blue bandana, again
tight round his skull, and his face and brow, and the light shining on
his black leather coat—as he pushed against the suck of the insulated
door. And he liked his look—gotdamn if he didn't. But when he let
the glass door swing closed behind him and raised his eyes to look to
the counter, he didn't find her—just two young black ladies, one at the
counter, the other with pastry tongs picking up a sweet roll, for—not
a cop—just some young white man, who held his coffee in his bicycle-
gloved left hand as he kept tucked under his left elbow his teardrop-
shaped helmet. He was wearing a yellow and black, long-sleeved bicycle jersey and black spandex bicycle shorts, yellow sports anklets and
black cycling shoes with triple Velcro straps. Watt, as he walked up
behind the cyclist, gripped hard the handles of his gym bag, in which
were his weapons—the still fully loaded 19 and the 30-plus mag and
the again sheathed nine-inch blade.

His grandmama—she says it all started with the gangbangers and
the drugs and violence. Blame it on y'all fools, she says: the final end
a the Greens and all the peoples bein' shipped all the fuck out Cabrini.
But what it goes back to for real, no urban legend, is this motherfucker
here and wherever he comes from, which'd be some long line a white
boys start up things with chains and guns and killin' the ones they

don't buy nor sell, and takin' it all, *all* the money, *all* the land, no apologies, no regrets, which they're doin' again now in the Greens, since the land turned out to be big-ass fuckin' dollas, and settin' up laws and then cops and then ten thousand jails for America's black folk, jus' like the ol' chains, no different, so they can hella sure keep it all—pri-vate-ly *own* the entire motherfuckah—sure as God's a white man. Same's I shot that white boy's what they did, hundreds a thousand times over; only they say it's nothin' to kill a nigga, 'cause a nigga ain't human, so don't lose sleep over it—and, for the final touch, makin' it so I'll never say the same about killin' that white boy. And I don't sleep as well over that's I do over killin' my own father. Slavery—shit goes down into a nigga's brains, not finished for generations and generations. Knowledge. Think it *all* through, deepest fuckin' start to deepest finish.

Outside the window—Watt could see—the white cyclist, having tucked his paper-wrapped croissant in his jersey's pouch, set his sleeved Starbucks cup on the sidewalk as he knelt to work the combination of his high-tech bike lock, which, to secure his sleek road bike, light, highest-quality, he'd wound round the post of a twenty-minutes-only parking sign. The biker took then, when it came free, the tight-coiling cable lock and wrapped it round his bike's saddle-post, then grabbed up his coffee, mounted his bike, and took off down Clybourn. And Watt imagined reaching down now into his gym bag and, under cover of his clothes, smacking up the thirty-plus into the butt of his 19—and then raising up the gun and blowing down everything in this white-folks' Starbucks, human and non-human, including finally himself! Go all violent. Can't build a thing here with them ownin' all the *property* till the end a fuckin' time. But blow down what they build up all the fuck around me, so I don't have t'look at it. Makes me feel like devil-shit, lookin' at it all surroundin' me. So blow it down. And then it's just me standin' smack middle a the motherfuckin' smokin' wreck of it—where I can't look at myself much more either. So bring it *all* to an end before I drop my gun for good. *All*. Or *nothin'*.

He had ordered a black coffee, grande, and the girl who poured it— Ayisha, he'd heard the other girl call her—had it ready now. "A dollar eighty-five," she said, as she slid the cup over the counter, looking, he could tell, at his neck, and reading, he was sure, the X-crossed pitchforks. So he smiled at her, as he paid her, and then, picking up his cup, he said, tipping the cup toward her and smiling another smile, "We're in this togetha, Ayisha." But as he lifted his gym bag and then turned with his coffee for the door, he could hear her say behind him, "Don't know 'bout no *we,* Mistah Whoevah."

Still no CPD patrol car had parked alongside the Starbucks, but as Watt headed now up Clybourn, he caught sight of a blue-and-white about a block up, coming slowly his way—so he turned into a store-front alcove and pretended, 'til he saw the reflection of the patrol car's passing in the recess's window, to be examining the white-folks' merchandise, high-priced leather carrying bags, there on display. Back out on Clybourn then, he headed again toward Mohawk. But as he came up toward Goethe, out of the corner of his eye, all for hella sure he caught her, heading westward right toward him—that sassy-funky white chick, with her black hair still touched up with that crazy-ass purple. But got to say she's lookin' fine in those tight huggin' jeans and that boy shirt all open on that t-shirt, soft pink like her lipstick—suits her good. And right there he thought how different his life might be if he'd said, two and a half weeks back, maybe in white talk, all po-lite—"Yes, I would, I'd like very much to leave room for the cream." But that's gone, he thought, long past the point a no return. Fuckin' Gasoline Man. And he recollected himself into a hard anger. No point, brotha, in some soft-shit fuckin' stupidity over some sweet thing'd turn sour on a dime and say, all sassy, Don't blame me.

But he slowed coming toward Goethe—and when he got there, he stopped. And she had now turned up her head and seen him—and recognized him. She slowed then, too, and stopped, some twenty yards from the corner, where he stood. They looked at each other. And in a silent instant, the feelings they had, faster than language or thought, spoke their lives and their worlds. The sex—they both wanted it: to cross all the lines between them and find in passion a release from every restraint that kept them apart, the heat of this, of his power and her rich feminine body, her beauty, the powerful badness of him, his gang-ster strength, which made her heart pound, and the remoteness of her from his world, the strength of her sharp-cutting mind, which thrilled him in the loins, the battle it would be with her, and the deep, good fucking, he could see it all, feeling her pierced tongue run along his pitch-forked neck and all down his chest, across the face of the devil, and she could see it all, the two of them smashing to dust the walls that divided their worlds and then building them again with raging resentment and distrust as large as race in America, and then smashing those walls down again in wild fucking so good it would lead straight

136

SHE BRINGS IT ALL TOGETHA

to love—for weeks, months, years—until the beast of race and anger led one of them even to try to kill the other, the two of them forever, somewhere down deep, on edge, on the watch, afraid, insecure, angry, one black and one white, and never blind to this curse, yet knowing as no other two in the world the unbounded ecstasy of being blind to all color, all difference and division, knowing, beyond all curses, the return to paradise in sex and love more beautiful and deep than the fallen world. But not. For we are *in* the fallen world, as far as our eyes can see.

And just that fast it disappeared. Damn *shit,* he thought, as he saw her now turn back toward her home. Sheeeeit if she doesn't go all phony on me. Look me in th'eye, look me smack in the eye, like she's got somethin' to say for real—and now she turns away, 'stead a comin' on. Acts like she forgot somethin' back home, checkin' her purse. Why not snap her fingers and shake her head?! Work it up real good. Say Aw shucks or some such. Won't fuck with that phony shit. Won't fuck with it.

So he turned back up Clybourn, quick walking toward Mohawk, not looking back to see if maybe she'd looked back herself, over her shoulder, the way she had before. Leave room for the cream. No way I look back for what she won't give. And no way she doesn't cell phone the police if I follow her, and come up close on her, 'cause she's thinkin' I aim t' jus' take what she won't give a black man. No way she don't call the law down, when it's said and done.

And she *was* scared—even to death. So she'd turned. And if she heard his footsteps now she might run. But she didn't hear his footsteps. And she wanted to hear them—and not to run. The beauty, the power of him, the intensity. *We do,* he had said—and her woman's soul wanted to make passionate, healing love with him, to fuck him so sweet, 'til they both were blind. Was he still at the corner? She wanted to turn. She hated herself for not turning, for not saying *yes,* please come with me. But she was relieved, as she kept walking, that she heard no footsteps. And she was too scared to turn and look. Yet she hated herself—felt even that she was doing something that could turn the entire rest of her life in the wrong direction—as she kept walking and not looking back.

Don't know about no we, Mistah Whoevah. As he turned now up Mohawk and walked north, Watt, collected back into himself after his little moment with the white girl—whole history a shit right there, he thought —and glad, after all, that he hadn't given an inch to that skittish bitch (gon' jus' go home and take that metal out her tongue)—couldn't now shake out of his head those words that that Ayisha had said. She thinks

137

she's one of'em—gon' blend all in, she says Welcome to Starbucks, and she smiles, all civilized. She gon' work h'way in and then work h'way up jus' sayin' Welcome to Starbucks, motherfucker." Watt laughed and took a sip of his coffee, but then saw a trash can and walked over and dumped his half-full cup inside. And he thought again, as he switched it to the hand he'd held his coffee in, of what he had inside his gym bag, and of taking it all to the white world, and then to himself. Ain't no fuckin' *we*—anywhere.

But there now was 1441 Mohawk. A fine, old-school, two-story graystone, which with its bay entry with a parapet, looked like a mini-castle. Won't be long, Watt thought, 'til white folks own it again. Looks too good still, this old-money place they built up for themselves way back. He looked down Mohawk for cops. Then he lifted the creaky, heavy iron knocker, knocked, and listened. It wasn't yet eleven, so a late-night girl might not be up. But someone inside was coming up now to the old heavy door—and pulling it back. And there she was, sweet Sara Lee, his best lady, now just her morning self, no makeup, no evening clothes, just blue jeans and a sleeveless pullover blouse, and her golden-brown hair, not yet fully dry after a shower, pulled back in a ponytail. All natural. Beautiful as Halle Berry, plus those blue eyes. So beautiful... but not yet welcoming him in. She put her head out and looked both ways, then stepped back inside. "Does anybody know you're back from wherever you went?"

"Who says I left?"

She stepped aside, then hurried him in. Then, in the foyer, "A cop came, Watt—a detective—a couple of weeks ago—and again a few days ago. The first time to ask if I'd received a call from you about my entertaining Tumbler and his cousin Robert. And the other day to ask if I'd heard from you lately, if I knew where you were. He has a way—I don't know—it seemed like he might have wanted to stay—and make it a date. But then he turned hard, asking me to tell him where you *were!* So what's this all about?"

Watt, in the very instant when Cousin Teague shouted out to that white boy by name, was sure it would happen—and now he knew it to a certainty: the white boy gave them Robert Teague, who broke, no doubt, soon as they brought him in, and named not just his cousin but his cousin's friend Watt. And no doubt Cousin Teague put it all on Watt and nothin' on himself or his cousin Tumbler, two innocent bystanders. "Bullshit," he said out loud. Then to Sara Lee, "Nothin' but

SHE BRINGS IT ALL TOGETHA

some bullshit, girl, blow over in a day or two. Cops on a witch hunt. Need a few days here, though, 'til I look around and get orientated." But while he said this, what he thought was: Jus' like I knew. Once it starts, can't stop it 'til it's done. It's me or the cousins; and likely that white boy's got to go, too. Can't quit it 'til it's *all* done. Then, "You tell that detective I called you t'fix up Tumbler and his cousin?" But before Sara Lee could answer this first question, Watt asked a second: "He say somethin' like he's jus' checkin' if Cousin Teague's lyin' 'bout that date?"

Sara Lee, nee Sandra Leyland, was the bright and deeply beautiful but lost daughter of two New Jersey professors; her mother, white, taught at Rutgers, her father, black, at Princeton. They'd split with a brutal ferocity when she was seventeen—a fact explaining the brief note that she'd set on her bedspread before she left forever: "What God has joined, let none divide." Sara/Sandra used sometimes her lines of white powder to keep afloat for work and play, and her reefer to sink into sweet dazes, and sometimes a little H just to be dangerous. But she'd never gotten hooked, and hadn't yet hurt her beauty, either of mind or body, in any noticeable way. She knew nothing of the bloodshed that took place in the alley; but she knew that no matter what he said, Watt was in something deep. And she was scared, but told no lies. "No," she said, "he never said he was checking to see if Tumbler's cousin lied. But I did tell him you called to set up a date for Tumbler and his cousin."

Watt stood still, said nothing, then suddenly he reached up and took Sara Lee's cheeks in his hand, hard. She couldn't tell what he would do—would he bash and bruise her face? or clamp down his hand so hard that the inside of her mouth would bleed against her teeth?

But suddenly now Watt eased his grip, which had pinched up her mouth and made a tortured mask of her face, but then kept his hand, warm now and soft, just touched gently against the side of her face, letting her beauty come back—in a way that now pulsed with all her deep power of sex, as still the look of pain lingered in her expression—in her eyes, and in her parted lips, moist, swollen, as if she'd been crying, though she'd kept silent as he'd hurt her. Watt slipped his hand now warmly under her hair, behind her neck and, with an intense look into her strange blue eyes, took her to him and kissed her. And when again, then, he looked at her, Sara—caught up in his power and beauty, and thinking, too, of the times, three, four, when, as if out of the sky, he'd come down like the god of anger on those who'd hurt or threatened

139

DIVISION

her—whispered to him, "I'd never turn away from you. I'd never call the law on you. I'd never lie to you."

They parted—and standing apart...after a time...smiled at each other. She laughed and said, "Breakfast?" And he gave her a wry smile, fun, lascivious. And, yes, he was hungry, and she made him waffles and crisp bacon. Delightful. And not outside, not now—though the day was beautiful—instead all indoors—but they would spend all this day in what for Sara Lee, Sandra Leyland, was a strange perfection of fore-play, never honestly known to her before, and so different from the me-chanical games she could so well please her clients with, which games she enjoyed too, not to lie—but not like this—this slow, all-day-long approach, the kisses, the touching.

And when Louise and Regina, her roommates, and also Watt's ladies, came home, she and Watt, after sharing with them a glass of wine, re-treated alone to Sara's bedroom, where they continued their games, until at last Watt took in his two hands, one at each of the bends of Sara's hips, the bottom hem of her un-tucked pullover. And as he began to lift up the shirt, she raised her arms to help him, as happy to be seen as Watt was eager to see her. Slowly, then, as if it were the first time they'd ever seen each other, the one helped the other undress until they stood before each other naked. And as they lay beside each other in bed, still just gently touching, and kissing, the killer in Watt, again fast as his feelings, saw in the beauty of Sara Lee everything he was not. And he wanted it—wanted to forget himself in this woman he'd just *been* with all day. Wanted to fall through a sweet dark hole with this woman, way she was now, not bought or sold. Never seen more beautiful than this, and won't again. Makes me forget it all awhile, everything I've done and all's I'll do. Forget it all—violent fool daddy, murderin' motherfucker, cut dead on the floor, just like my beautiful young mama, so sharp in her mind—people say she's where I come from. And now it's an eye for an eye, exact, *no excuses* for that devil man, right crost his throat. But forget that here, and that white boy, too, in the car. Forget everything stands between me and what I want—those schoolboy cousins, and that other white boy—forget him too—same's all the white things in Sara and all the black things forgot what they were when they come together and make her like this. She brings it *all* togetha. He remembered he'd said this—to his homeboy Tumbler and Cousin Teague, just before they come up on those white boys in the alley.

140

COMMUNICATION

Connor Riordan, as he had numerous times in the seven weeks since the murder of his brother—had come over Cortland and stopped at the rundown Leopard Lounge, just past Ashland. He'd thrown back a double of Jameson, and then another, and then smoothed things out with some beers...before heading out and walking west a block to Honore...then north to her condo, six addresses south of Armitage. She lived on the second floor of a new beige-bricked duplex that had this black steel window framing, set sharp and dark against the light-colored brick, and three limestone string courses that made this unexpected rhythm on the façade, cool, thoughtful—not dead dreary like the shit-on-an-asphalt-shingle look on those early 1900s teardowns you still could find here—and who's gonna miss these sagging, weedy dumps when the last one's gone? And, fuck you—if she's what gentrification means, then this is one lucky city. Inner city and poverty! There's a fine combination. Talk about a perfect formula for violence. Affordable housing. And low-income. As if there were still union-strong factory jobs here instead of just burger-flippin' bullshit. Either no job at all, or hairnet, minimum-wage slave shit that oughta

DIVISION

make any self-respecting human person just happy enough to shoot somebody. Make the housing hard as hell to afford and you make the city safe—from murder rates blowin' through the roof. Simple as that. Bloody fucking high-density killings—how many a day, Chicago? So drive up the housing prices. Walk west then down a new Division St. without fearing for your life. Nothing more determinative than the impersonal power of money—zero soul, *brother.* My brother. He's dead. Just after I told him I wanted to kill him. *Post hoc, ergo propter hoc.*

He hadn't gone back to Berkeley, and his father had had to do the work to get him officially withdrawn. Three times he'd forgotten to make the calls his dad had told him he had to make—to get the forms, to talk to the Dean. Officially withdrawn. He was already officially fucking withdrawn!—from idiots asking how he felt. How do I *feel?!* What if I said I don't feel a fucking thing—that for days and days I've felt nothing—that my feelings fell into a bottomless hole and that for a while maybe when I looked down I could see them falling and catch glimpses of them getting smaller and smaller. But now when I look down that black hole—deeper than all resurrection—I don't see shit except the hole. Fact is—REAL FACT: I've forgotten what I was look-ing for in the first place. You'd say I was drunk! Drunk for days on end, sleep-in-the-alley drunk, and that I'm just not myself. Myself! Did you ever feel your*self* get so blown apart—dismembered—that you don't remember who you were? Continuous personality! Proof of the soul! Shit! I've got drooling-at-the-mouth emotional Alzheimer's. Blank-stare dementia. Not even remembering who your brother—this red body with its face blown off—who he *was!* even though I'll be walking anywhere now and there he *is!*—'til I cry like a baby and then sweat enough and he's gone again, buried out of sight in his grave. Or maybe looking at your own mother and wondering who *that* is?—and why she lives here? So yeah I'm drunk—because a double shot of J doesn't mope around wondering what it's supposed to do. It just does it.

He never rang the bell. To avoid notice, or arrest, he just walked all around—up to Armitage, then over to Damen, then back to Cortland, then always back again to Honore and up to her place, but never to ring the bell, especially not on nights when he could see—as once again, right now, he could see, framed in that fucking front window—that Officer Rudkus was up paying a visit. He didn't drive here, Rudkus. He walked—from just around the corner, right across from the Leopard. Connor knew, because once he'd followed Rudkus, after he'd left her

142

COMMUNICATION

place. Maybe twice—truth be told—he'd followed him—and then each time had headed back himself into the Leopard.

Maybe it was an accident of proximity—the two of them just running into each other in the neighborhood and saying Yeah, I'd like to go for a drink, and then just sort of keeping it up because it was convenient. Or maybe they were meant for each other—and all was sealed by fate forever.

He saw *her* now, too, Ellie, framed in the window—and he turned and walked away, north toward Armitage. Once before, he'd seen them dancing in that window, her taking a slow jitterbug twirl under his arm, and then the two of them holding each other and George Rudkus kissing her hair, the dark red, as she held her face against his chest.

On Armitage he walked west toward Damen, and he thought about never-ness: never recovering, never having feelings again, never being free of sulfur smells, like stinking matches, or of red flashbacks—never wanting to be near people again with their sorry attempts to console! or *advise!*—never being able to sleep without nightmares and sweats— never not needing to drink his brains into oblivion—never connecting again with his mother, whoever she fucking was—and she was fucking, *Fucking!* And forever-ness: of Ellie Shea and George Rudkus forever— forever together, dancing in the window, kissing and fucking. Forever, his mother and her lover, gone to some unreachable place that had nothing of him in it. And his father, the moment he knows what he doesn't yet know—about his mother's betrayals, including the abortion, for Christ's sake!

He turned north on Damen and would walk on and on then, through the evening into the night, stopping sometimes at benches, burying his head in his hands. He came finally to the wall of Rosehill Cemetery—and then headed east to Ashland, and then came back south, walking miles, miles. And feeling, if he saw black people—whenever he saw *blacks* on the street—call them triggers—that the one emotion that was rising, rather than sinking into that hole—that was unkillable —was anger—at so many things, and people, particular people, his mother and her fucking joy ride—and hard racial anger. Feelings dead everywhere—but not racial anger, which was goddamned alive and well, living and growing like sin—which had to mean that he was in hell. Vengeance Hell. An eye for an eye. Revenge. Constantly feeling, with this risen-up anger, that blacks, who talk about their pain and never about the pain they inflict, the cost, the fucking cost—that they

143

must think they get to go *forever* to the past, ante-fucking-bellum, and endlessly find wounds to suck on, when in the post-bellum present they're the ones shedding the blood, blood in the alleys, my brother's blood! They lynched Jacko! Because he got uppity? That black man poured a whole people's hatred into my brother's head. And don't talk to me about your grandfather's past and your great grandmother down in Mississippi! What about the here and the now that is *all* you're gonna get! When does the sucking on past wounds stop and the real life start! And who's it up to, to get it started? White people?! Are you fucking kidding?! Economics can go fuck itself, too. Fuck poverty. Personal responsibility is everything. But then as he came finally back to Cortland and turned west, again, under the expressway, after all those hours and hours, he wondered who it was up to, to get *his own* life started again out of death? Who are you to talk, white nigger? he said to himself. Who are you? Personal *fucking* responsibility. Start with yourself!

Rudkus. George Rudkus, the lover cop—there he was! Connor, passing out from the darkness of the Kennedy underpass and heading up again toward the lights of the Leopard, saw Officer George Rudkus, dressed still as he was in the window, coming down Cortland toward his apartment. Right there. And now he was looking up, directly at Connor. The two of them stared at each other a moment, much as they had when the officer was on the phone that night, at the Riordan kitchen table… talking to his girlfriend.

"Connor? Connor Riordan, is that you?"

Connor said nothing. He was sober—after all the hours of walking. But he looked as if Rudkus's question puzzled him—or as if he'd been mistaken for someone he'd never heard of—and as if he'd never seen the person who was asking him if he was Connor Riordan. And he was not entirely falsifying; indeed, his every look and gesture just came to him, immediately, as if he were in fact not Connor Riordan and he did not know who asked him "is that you?" But George Rudkus kept moving closer; and after a moment, Connor found a voice he might call his own. He said, "I know you. I didn't, but…I do. You're the policeman…at our house."

"George Rudkus. Are you all right, Connor? You look…. What brings you here? You come this way often? I mean, it's funny. I was just talking to my girlfriend—you know Ellie—Ellie Shea, from St. Ignatius. She was talking about you—just now." He paused a moment. Then,

144

COMMUNICATION

"And not just tonight. She's wanted to call you, to talk to you...about what happened, to see how you're doing. And how *are* you doing? You look...tired."

"Tired? I don't know. I've been walking." But as he said this, Connor was trying to take in what Rudkus had said about Ellie's talking about him, more than once, and her wanting to call him—and yet he wouldn't let himself think that the voice in his mind saying *This has meaning* spoke more truly than the one saying *No it doesn't*. If Rudkus's words had real meaning, he wouldn't be saying them. Would he be generous like that, letting another man know that Ellie cared for him—if she did?

"You walked here? From Lincoln Park West?"

"Yeah. Yes. And all around. Up Damen past Foster and back around on Ashland."

"Christ, that's what? A dozen miles? You wanna step into the Leopard —let me buy ya a beer? We can talk about things, if you want. And then— and I think you should let me, Connor—I'll give those pilgrim feet of yours a lift home. Half way around the damned city you've walked."

Another adviser, another consoler, Ellie's boyfriend, her lover. Fuck. But Connor needed a drink—though not any ride home. He hated Rudkus's kindness, his thoughtfulness, his handsomeness. Handsome, thoughtful, kind—shit—and obviously intelligent. Pilgrim feet. No wonder Ellie liked this guy, cop or not. A good face. Strong. A good man. A kind voice. Connor indeed now, in a flash counter-movement in his mind, or heart, found himself understanding why Ellie liked, maybe even loved this man—and suddenly also, out of nowhere, against his anger, forgiving this in her—or rather understanding that it didn't need forgiveness. He felt an instant change in his heart. And yet did Rudkus's words about Ellie's wanting to call him have meaning? He wouldn't think. Couldn't. Yet he felt, too, a pulse of gratitude for what he wanted now, suddenly, to think of as a generosity, Rudkus's telling him she talked about him, wanted to call him. "A beer? Yeah, I could use a beer."

To call her professor's house, ever—you just do not do this—and it's after eleven. But while the momentum was there, so strong, after talking with Georgie, good Georgie, again tonight, and thinking for days now about Connor but doing nothing, always saying it was the wrong time to call, and so not calling—but now with the number right there on the phonebook page? But if Jackie Riordan answered? Anything but that. When I just hung up, which I would, what would she

145

DIVISION

think? Someone bad calling? Some woman? Me? Her son's killer, trying to terrify the family? Moments of real tension now calling Carolyn
Teague, whom she'd called two, three times a week since their first week
together at Ignatius—ever since Mrs. Teague told her she was glad to
hear *her* voice...and not someone else's.

Ellie Shea kept her hand on the phonebook page, her finger touched
to the name, Riordan, Thomas John, and she breathed, more slowly as
the moments passed, and let herself think of how much she would love
to be lying warm in her bed, talking on the phone to Connor Riordan
in his, whispering to him, everything, all night long. So she imagined...
even as she felt now, too, closing the phone book, her anger again at
his never having given her the time of day. And why did he leave the
wake, when he saw me coming? If he knows everything about me and
Jack? How could he not? He must. So I am punished.

"Not remembering things too well these days. Days of the week. But it
must have been a different day—that last time I saw you, at our house...
when you were on the phone—because tonight is obviously your night
off. But I'm not sure what day today is. I don't know the day of the
week it was when my brother...."

Having the eye of a good street cop, George Rudkus knew that Connor
had seen him at the wake as well—seen him there with Ellie, looked at
them, and that not long after, he had left and not come back. But he
had no desire to play cop now or to say something like "At the wake,
too, I was there"—just to let Connor know he suspected him of disin-
genuousness. Although it seemed unlikely, this guy might truly have
forgotten seeing him at the wake. And about his forgetfulness now—
he wasn't lying. He really didn't know the days. So should I be glad?
Help him get drunk, clearly not for the first time lately—and then walk
him over to Ellie's so she could have a good look? This is the guy you
care about? Fucking charity case. And isn't it just ever so likely that
he's in this neighborhood by accident—that he's walked around the
whole north side and circled back here just because he happened to.

But pride, George Rudkus. Pride, pride, pride—as you've told yourself—how many times now? The pretty boy's got something, clearly,
beyond the pretty face. And it's what she wants. No need to be a cop
to see the obvious. And you she just likes, Good Georgie, which hasn't
changed yet, not a day, over five months, and won't *be* changing. And
you know it. And you ask yourself, one more time, what would it be
but an exercise in self-humiliation to try to make that different? And is

146

COMMUNICATION

this the moment at last—to pass the torch? to this traumatized drunk? Tell him she cares about *him*—because you know, too, how grateful she would be if you let him know? And maybe *better,* yes…for Christ's sake…yes…it has got to be better even to put a generosity gun to my brains than hammer them forever against a wall of loving and never being loved back, just liked. He now did go cop. "You're not here by accident, are ya, Connor? I mean the Leopard wouldn't be the first thought for a Lincoln Park guy, when he's feeling the thirst—and yet the bartender nods to him as an old familiar."

Gratitude, that pulse of it, lost as fast as it came. Connor now wondered if he'd been "made" by this cop as some kind of stalker—or peeping Tom—and if Officer Rudkus was gonna say to him something like, I see you snoopin' around anymore, asshole, and I'm gonna take out your front teeth—or something like, Do you know that Ellie is concerned, Riordan, mostly about your sanity and her own personal safety —that it's this that we've talked about, a lot? "I've been here…," Connor said, trying suddenly not to lie, trying maybe to dispel the notion that he was dangerous by just being honest, by openly confessing things to George Rudkus. And honest confession might feel good, too, like gratitude, not like the shit of hell. "I've been over this way. Truth is I…. Ellie…. She knew my brother. And I've thought of going to see her, to talk. But I've been a fucking mess, George. I've had trouble with people…being around people. I've been drinking. I'm embarrassed. I don't want to be seen drunk. So I walk, a lot. Here. Anywhere. And at Ellie's…I've seen you were there. I didn't want to spoil anybody's evening. Forgive me. Christ. I have been a complete fucking mess."

George Rudkus thought, God, yes, you have. And I'd be doing Ellie one big damn favor, forever, if I just kept you clear of her. Charity case. The greatest of these is—shit. If she loved me, I'd never yield an inch. But it's not gonna change. She *doesn't.* She loves this. So I'll take my bow and go? Because, also—truth—I'd be no cop worth a damn if I didn't feel for the victims of homicide. Why else be a cop? And this is murder. I'm lookin' at it. Not just a life lost, but *lives* shattered. Families. Christ, I took his mother's clothes to the alley. He should be at Berkeley, studying, not here at the Leopard fucking Lounge, which he's no doubt patronized more than a few times. But right here and now for… what? integrity? charity?…he's gonna come to know things I can tell him. "A lot, Ellie thinks about you, Connor—that night when I was on the phone with her, and now too…a lot." He stopped a moment,

147

thinking of that night on the phone. Then, "And Jack. She told me, yeah, she knew Jack—that a time back, there was even a brief thing."

Again, that kindness, telling him how he was on Ellie's mind, and not just the night Jack was killed, but now, "a lot"—this kindness, from this cop. But Connor could see that Rudkus, that George, didn't know about the abortion—and instantly, in a sudden strong, good warmth... of some kind...he determined he would suffer torture before he ever breathed a word of it to George—for George's sake, as well as for Ellie's. Respect for privacy, a sacred thing. It's love that keeps secrets. What's the deepest truth? It's what happens when life gets to proceed and to keep on growing without being wounded, crippled, by vicious revelations of shit-ugly truths that just wound, and fester. Keep secrets— because the shit-truth is a lie. Real truth is beauty. Ellie Shea. "It was, yeah, very brief. Nothing serious."

George Rudkus, again now struggling, resisting a capitulation, wanting again maybe even to get this guy drunk and drag him over to Ellie's, but still, feeling a sudden new sympathy with something in his manner, his voice, said back to him—slow—and thoughtful—for he would...yes...continue now to move things toward an end, "It's not as serious with me...either...as I would have hoped." He tipped back his glass now, and took a full swallow. Then, "Boyfriend...girl-friend. You could give us those names. But when you know, you know." He bobbed the glass back and forth with his forefingers and thumbs, "It's not me she's thinking of when she's thinking for real. Never will be, either."

Never. Connor could see Ellie again as he did that first time at Ignatius—and he felt the fear he'd always felt when it came to her—the fear that if he were ever to make some overture to her and be denied, his life would never be the same—that he'd be sucking on the wound of rejection all his days. And now a sudden new fear that George Rudkus could, possibly, move off its course this old fear that he'd for so long, he knew, taken a sick comfort in—because it helped him to keep on doing nothing.

"Let me take you home," George now said—and nodded, in a way that made his heart sink—as when he needed his gun in a darkened building. He nodded again—and now by uplifting a finger, then point-ing it down at Connor, he let him know. *He* was the one Ellie thought of, when she thought for real. And, pressing down his thumb over his

COMMUNICATION

finger, like a gun's hammer, he said, "It's you, Connor, she's thinking
of. It's you."

In the dead nothing he had become—Connor could make out a feeling of now deepest gratitude, could feel it quickening in the empty hole
of himself—the feeling of gratefulness, which was also still much confused with fear, with crippling notions of forever, and never. Rudkus,
George, had said he was sure Ellie would never change toward him.
He had had the guts to say this, the generous dignity, and to tell me
she thinks of me. He meant this? Christ. Connor nodded back, half-
smiling. He shook his head then slightly, and lowered his eyes. Then
he put his half-drunk beer on the bar, and, as George now nodded and
rose, he rose with him and headed together with him to his car.

As they drove off, Connor said nothing—and he would not—not now
—bring up Ellie's name. Not now. For George's sake. No. But then
loud, laughing, he heard, saw—as they walked the bridge now over
the North Branch—a group of teen blacks, boys, girls, maybe seven or
eight—and feeling an immediate powerful conflict with his own sick-
ening anger, with his desire for vengeance (and the times, sleeping and
waking, that he'd pictured his wresting the gun out of that black guy's
hands, his brother's murderer, and screaming in his face, We'll fucking
see who's going to kill and who's going to be killed!—and seen himself,
then, after making that black filth squeal for mercy, putting a bullet in
his brains anyhow—the number of times—obsessed, sick, awake and in
dreams), he would ask someone who'd been there, in the trenches, a
police officer, how he felt, how he would act. "Cabrini, you've worked
it? Dealt with the gangs?"

Wanting still to speak of Ellie, but more glad not to, George said,
"Four years in the Eighteenth, so yeah, countless times I've been on
calls to Cabrini."

And with his palms again sweating, fighting back the birth of a panic-
aura, Connor said, "Can I ask you—about anger—racial anger? I mean
yours, not theirs. Is it hard or even impossible not to feel it, as a white
cop? Does it take over your mind? Or can you find ways to get above
it?—when you have to deal with the gangs and their violence day after
day? Maybe in life-threatening confrontations? So there's the *fear* that
you'd resent like hell too?—and couldn't divide from the race of the
ones making you afraid? Shit! Welcome to fucking America and its
goddamned anger. One of the sick things, George, I've found so hard

149

DIVISION

to deal with since my brother was murdered is this anger. And every time I see a black person, it's this trigger for anger—sometimes for flashbacks to the alley."

The light at Clybourn turned red. As he came to a stop, George Rudkus, keeping his eyes ahead, not turning to Connor, said, "You need to call her. You need to talk to someone you care for and who cares for you. And do *this,* all right?—do *this:* forgive her every time she says something that sounds like a stupid cliché. She'll say the right things often enough. But what gets said won't matter as much as the time spent. You go to her, all right?"

The light turned, and George turned toward North Ave. He said, still looking ahead, changing back the subject, "When it comes to me, I have my duty. It's not feelings. You *know,* because of your duty, what the right thing is. And you do it. And fuck feelings." He heard his own voice—heard now all that he'd said tonight. Then returning to Ellie, knowing, every moment more clearly now, that with just a few more words he would bring to a last nothing his relationship with someone he could never have all of, he said, "But *you*—you're gonna need a friend. So you call her, and you go. Do me a favor, though." He turned east on North Ave. Then, still looking straight ahead, "Tell her I sent you."

Connor, pressing his hands together, moist, hot, still couldn't believe it—this goodness. He wanted, in his gratitude, and also fear, still fear, to say to George Rudkus I am not going to her—not calling her—not getting anything started with her—because you're the one who deserves her—not me. But he knew that of all the advice he had ever received, this that he got now was the best, most needed. Go to Ellie. And to a certainty, should he go, he would say that George Rudkus had sent him. The police officer at the kitchen table.

George waited out on Lincoln Park West until he saw that Connor had made his way into the house, for with his cop's eye he'd just now made out someone on Menomonee. A black man, wearing a black leather coat, who might or might not fit the description of the one they called Watt. From his glove compartment, George took his Smith and Wesson, and he pulled up to the elbow alley just south of Wisconsin Ave. and then down into that alley between Lincoln Park West and N. Orleans, driving slow toward the back of the Riordan home, his gun on his thigh.

COMMUNICATION

Fuck feelings and just do the right thing. When he came into the dark of his family's home, Connor did not turn on the front-room light. He thought of what George Rudkus, when asked about working Cabrini, against the most dangerous black gangs in America, had said about duty and doing the right thing, no matter your feelings—or lusts. And not able then to walk up past his mother and father's bedroom, he went out in the dark through the kitchen, where he'd seen George, talking on the phone, turning his father's book. He went out then into the garden and walked the lighted gravel path back to the latch gate, against which he would sit until he couldn't anymore.

CCDOC:
DIVISION ONE

On the top floor of an un-reclaimed three-story on the 1100 block of N. Mozart, at the south edge of Humboldt Park, the Tumbler had been staying, hiding, with two old track-team friends from Wells High, Anthony and Rolando Trivett, good friends, but not known as such—and not likely to be thought of as offering him his hiding place. The Trivetts lived with their five siblings and their mother, Renee Bean. And for more than eight weeks, sleeping on the closed-in back porch, which overlooked the back alley, Tumbler had indeed kept his whereabouts unknown to his mother, to the police—and to Watt. In a whisper that made its way along the Humboldt Park grapevine, Rolando Trivett had heard that Watt was lookin' for Tumbler, all right, and lookin' hard, wantin' a little talk with his homeboy—but that Watt was now gone off to the South Side, 'cause a heat all up and down Division.

But some forty hours back now, Tumbler had seen, from his perch three stories up, two patrol cars coming at once, one from each end of the alley, and converging at the back gate of the old three-story, where they stopped. He ran to the front of the apartment to look out on

152

CCDOC: DIVISION ONE

Mozart, where he saw three more patrol cars, now converging on the apartment. Then, just like that, it was six cops, five in uniform wearing bullet vests, and with long guns, and one in an overcoat, carrying a pistol—all breaking for the apartment's front door. It would be the same at the back, Tumbler knew. Renee Bean, who'd been sitting in the front room, had come forward with Tumbler to look out the window. Tumbler was wearing his track-team jacket, with its eagle-winged W. His Sox cap was still on the back porch, where he would leave it. He touched the shoulder of the woman who'd been so good to him these last two months. "Miss Renee," he said, "I can't bring any more trouble on you or your family. I thank you and Rolando and Anthony. And I won't forget what y'all have done for me. I've got to go down quick, ma'am, or they'll be breakin' down your door. But do me this one last favor, Miss Renee?" She wore the look of the sorrow of all black mothers in America for all their million sons pursued by the law of a divided nation—but she nodded, yes, of course she would do this good boy any favor. Marcus took quickly from his wallet a business card and gave it to her. "He's my uncle, Maurice Teague, my mother's brother. He will call her. And he will help me."

But it wasn't until the evening of the following day that Renee Bean was able to contact Maurice Teague, gone to a morticians' convention in Kalamazoo, Michigan, while Mary Tate, Robert and Carolyn were in Benton Harbor visiting Mary's mother—and by that time, the Tumbler had been fully processed and deposited deep into the bowels of the ten-thousand-souled prison city at 26th and California, "County," where customers "Get Served with a Smile."

During a lawyer-less day and night at Violent Crimes, he'd been made to admit that, yes, he'd known Watt for a good time, and that, yes, he was affiliated with the Gangster Disciples, yes, yes, and that, yes, he'd planned to be with Watt that night, but No! NO!—Robert Teague had not been part of any plan and it was nothing but coincidence that they ran into him, and, no, he didn't know that Robert had named him, but he'd thought that Robert might *have* to name him if he was taken in—but No! he hadn't talked with Watt about getting a car—it was just about business they were going to talk. *What business?!* *—GANG BUSINESS?!* Yes, or no, he didn't know what business, Watt never said, not exactly, and no, he didn't think Watt had a gun, or yes, all right, yes, maybe, maybe yes, but they were just going to see this lady, that's all, he and Robert Teague, not Watt. *I thought you said Teague was*

153

DIVISION

not part of any plan! No, he wasn't! That just came up, later, the going
to see Sara. It was after they'd met by accident that they thought of it.
And NO! he didn't think anything when they saw that car in the alley,
and when Watt went up to it, NO!, or yes, and that's why he ran and
said, NO! We don't want this! Yes, "this" meant stealing a car, yes, or
using a gun, yes! But NO, I said We don't want this! Ask that white
boy! He heard me. He saw me run! But, yes, he'd been in hiding two
months, yes, yes, from the police, yes. But he was scared. Just scared.
He didn't know what to do, didn't want his mama to see him taken
away. She'd seen enough trouble. Her children. It might kill her to
see the last taken away. And no, he didn't think, ever, that if he didn't
call the police he would be charged as an accessory to murder. *And it's
NO fucking matter that you RAN, ya dumb fuck, 'cause you suddenly went
CHICKENSHIT or started cryin' about whatever it was that you didn't fuckin'
WANT anymore!* NO! Please believe—he didn't know he had to call the
police! He never heard of that! No! He didn't know that! *Well you sure
as fuck know it now, DON'TCHYA!* Yes, he knew it now! *YES, YOU DO, YA
FUCKIN' GANGBANGIN' ANIMAL! YOU AND YOUR FRIEND WATT!
GODDAMN SUB-HUMAN CABRINI BASTARDS!*

Handcuffed to a dreadlocked hulk, maybe forty, stunk like brand-
new shit, whom he'd shared the staple-bench with all night at Violent
Crimes, the Tumbler got loaded onto the early morning pickup wagon,
a converted school bus with a mesh cage protecting the deputy at the
wheel, which made a half-dozen more stops at cop-station lockups before pulling down into the basement docks at 26th and Cal. "Human
garbage truck for human garbage! You have arrived at the CCDOC!"
So the white, bullnecked host at the dock greeted the twenty-man
chain of them, seventeen black, two Hispanic, one maybe white, maybe Hispanic, before he and other DOC officers (six white, two black
might as well have been white) herded them into the basement holding pens, cinder-block and concrete-floor cages with steel-wire caging.
And they would wait here, with their watches already taken, and no
clocks or any markers of the time, not even hunger; for it is was too
strange in these pens for something normal like hunger. Wait—until
when? And for what?

Two things the Tumbler could tell in this cage, meant for thirty, must
have held sixty: that the best space would be up front, where you might
get some air at the steel-wire caging, but that if you tried to work your
way up there, as every square inch in here, my brotha, was private

154

property, you might get hurt bad. Gangsters were here. He wished Watt was here. You know what you are, little brotha, and you know what you're not. Six, no love for Five. You know what it means. Steel benches were set along the walls and bolted to the floor. He found a space on the bench along the back wall—but could see why there were open seats there as the shitter was set against the back wall too. Some dope-sick motherfucker was sittin' on the shit-stained commode, groanin', wavin' his head back and forth, shittin' out his brains—to the disgust of those who if they'd been able to stand going near that wasted motherfucker might have just laid the boot on him. Just baloney on white bread last night in the lockup—but the coffee—Tumbler feared that black mud—that it might trigger the skitters and in front of a hundred eyes he'd have to set himself down where that hype was now groaning out his guts. But he knew that no matter, as long as he was cooped in this animal hole, he'd never shit in private again, never have personal freedom again or be able to control the first thing in his life. Personal everything—gone. He wished Watt was here.

Last night at the lockup, after they fingerprinted and mugshot him, they took his belt, his shoelaces, his comb and wallet and watch, and put them in a property bag. Nothing had been returned. And now came a loud rattling of some club or stick along the wires of the cage— and from some voice, white, roaring, it was, "Gentlemen! You will remove all coats and jackets, and deposit them at the center of the floor, NOW!" Tumbler was quick enough so that his Wells jacket got buried out of sight beneath the refuse that covered the backs, and showed the pathetic means, of this neither happy nor proud population. The pile made him think of a Camp Ball parking-lot bonfire. Then it was, "NOW, gentlemen, you will take off your shoes, all already without laces, as we do our best to protect you from suicide, and you will kneel down and beat the openings of those boots against the floor until every rock of crack or other sorry sign of your sorry existence falls to the floor. I said, NOW! Start that pounding! Let me hear it!" Tumbler knelt as he was told and beat his lace-less Airs against the concrete floor, hard as he was told—and amidst that sixty-man thumping of boots and shoes, wild, like some kind of poor-man's war drums, he thought of Robert Teague's saying it will take another war to end the second slavery, economic slavery, bad as chattel. War! Shot heard round the world! "All right now, gentleman, get yourselves up and get those boots back on and you MOVE OUT to the walls! And you face those walls! And you put your hands up against them! Grab some wall, gentlemen! NOW!"

After a moment, then, as they all stood leaning on their hands against the walls, a key turned in the cage lock, and four COs moved in and started, each one at a corner of the cage, a threat-filled pat down of every soul in there, including the dope-sick hype, who was getting straightened up now by the hair, his face pressed against the wall. And what would the bull who was making his way toward Tumbler, now just one detainee away, put in his ear? No worse than what he said to any other. But now here he was. And right *now*—Jesus, his hands on his ankles, coming up his legs, patting all up between his legs, up to his balls, around his stomach, up his chest. And now his mouth was at Marcus's ear as his hands kept patting his chest: "Don't worry, sweet cheeks, this ain't the day of your butt-fuck baptism. But trust this: in due time you'll get your little ass perverted-converted." Fuckin' Jesus, Mama—this would be hell I'm in.

The pat-down at last over, they were allowed to retrieve their coats; but now they all had the insides of their forearms black-markered with numbers that matched the numbers on their property bags—plastic sacks, size of a kitchen garbage bag, that for enough of these sorry motherfuckers, Tumbler thought, held about all they owned. Money, Watt said—so you can make something happen. Make self-respect happen. Money, property—ain't just about what you *need*. "You will now SIT, gentlemen. That's right, on the floor, SIT, and NOW! And you'll keep with the FLOOR PLAN, gentlemen, until you are told otherwise." The CCDOC "floor plan" was a separative arrangement devised to keep from moving into bloody confrontations GD's and VL's as well as other mutually hostile forces who had, when it came to violent, even murderous eruptions, very well-known histories in these tight-as-hell spaces. But, mum on explanations, that white bull's voice, in the unbroken, same shout, said only, "Any of you rise without permission, no matter who you are, you get dropped."

A group of white suits, Tumbler could see from where he sat, had gathered outside the cage. Four men and a lady. And now a CO unlocked the door, and let them in. "PDs," an older black said, "gon' ax you you got priors 'n' outstandin' warrants 'n' bond-skippins', 'n' a job, o' if't you's a churchgoin' type, o' if't you's just a real 'n' true nigga an' aint' got shit." The man laughed. Then, "Won't take but a second. Get you reddih f' bond court comin' up. Courtroom 100. Walk you to it down the ol' Boulevahhd. Hands behint yo' back, mothahfuckah. Then bing, bang—call yo' numbah—and through the do' you go. Then it be I-bond if you's new to the worl', letchya go on y'own cogizance, but money bond if you's a normal nigga, which mean you cain't pay it, so you be comin' back this way fo' you know it. Verih smooth oppa-ration. Bam. Bam. Thank yuh, Uncle Sam." The man laughed again.

The suits clicked open their pens and read out names from cards. Hands went up. And conversations took place, quick as the older man had said. Movement then from one detainee to the next, just that fast. But the lady, who'd remained near the door, studying a report of some kind, had not called a name—until now: "Marcus Sabbs?" She was a white lady, so Marcus, who now raised his hand, couldn't tell her age. But not too old. She had blond hair, not gray. She stepped nearer, coming through and around the seated men. She seemed pretty. And, in her suit, still to be not cold, maybe kind. "Marcus?" He nodded. And she came up and, even dressed as she was, squatted down beside him. She studied his face. "How'd you sleep last night?" "I didn't," he said. She smiled. "I didn't think so."

She folded the sheets of her report, keeping it in her left hand. "My name, Marcus," she said, "is Christa Reese. I'm from the Office of the Cook County Public Defender. I'm on its Homicide Task Force. The head of our office, Michael Morrison, has assigned me to your case. He has placed, Marcus, a highest priority on it. Does anyone know you're here? Any family? Anyone? Your mother?"

His mama. Never before had he come so fast to feel the difference between being treated like an animal, and being treated like a human being. If it ever came to it, he would die fighting to be treated as a human being. "I gave my uncle's name to a friend," he said. "My mother's brother. He will call her...." He couldn't finish his sentence. He buried his head between his knees, then whispered, fighting tears, "I couldn't call her myself. My sisters.... My brother. Streets took 'em all. All's she's got is me." He felt the hand of Christa Reese on his shoulder—and he thought about if you were dyin', and someone touched you, or no one did, the difference between those two things...as you died. He folded his hands into fists and swiped quickly at his eyes. He looked up and nodded to this person who treated him like a person. He thought she might be around forty, maybe. And he was glad that the one he got was the lady.

"Marcus," she said, looking like a teacher who wanted to teach him something he needed to know, "in a few minutes, the men here will be

DIVISION

led off to bond court. You won't be going to the same place. Here's what will happen, all right?" She patted his shoulder, gently. Still crouched beside him, she looked then with kindness into his eyes. "You'll be taken to an elevator, all right? and then up to a small detention room. There will be benches there and some other detainees, and you will be placed again in manacles, and be secured to one of those benches. I want you to know this. And I won't be there with you, in this detention room. But in time your number will be called and you will be brought to one of the courtrooms for Branch 66, which is the branch that takes violence cases. You will still be manacled, both your hands and your ankles. But I will be there then, in the courtroom, when you stand before the judge. But Marcus, the judge will grant no bond. After he explains why and asks you if you have secured counsel, you will be taken to the jail and you will be held there until your hearing, which should come in about a week. I want you to know this. It is so much better to know what to expect, even if it's bad, than to be left in the dark. The hearing will be to determine whether the charge against you, which is accessory to murder, is justified. We will do our best to get this charge dismissed, though I want you to understand that the charges are almost always regarded by the judge as justified. So most likely, Marcus, your case will go to trial. And that will mean more time here, as you await your trial."

Christa Reese still looked Marcus in the eye. "I want you to be strong for that, all right? Strong for your mother. And for yourself, all right?" But Marcus now felt as she touched his shoulder, that someone's touch might *not* help when you died, that you might just go off into death alone, no matter that last touch of a hand, which could make no difference. But he nodded. He would be strong. He would try.

"All right," she said. But now, "Your case, Marcus, you need to know this: You're in a difficult spot. The prosecutors aren't going to let it go. You need to know this. But I want you to believe, and to know, too, as I say, that we'll do everything we can. We know your cousin Robert was with you—and you should know that Robert has said you are innocent, that you did nothing wrong. And, Marcus, the brother of the boy who died has also said you did nothing wrong. We'll do everything we can, working with their statements." Marcus was hit with fear, with hope, was torn by strongest emotions, as this lady, Christa, said to him all that she now said. He looked at her now hoping, afraid—even though nothing she said about Robert Teague and that white boy was

158

CCDOC: DIVISION ONE

not something he'd thought of countless times during his two months of hiding. "If Connor Riordan, the brother," she now said, looking again with kindness and encouragement into his eyes, "if he comes out strong for us—if he simply stays true to his own statements—your case, Marcus, will be strong. It will be clear that you had no part in the killing of Jack Riordan, Connor's brother."

It all went down the way Christa said. He was moved and shackled and moved again—to the Branch 66 Court, Violence Court, where she was there, the way she said—and he was asked, the way she said, whether he had retained counsel, to which he nodded yes, and then pointed to her, and said "Christa," which all was recorded—but also the judge said just what she said he would say about bond—that there would be none—and that he would be "remanded" to the CCDOC Correctional Facility—to Division 1—whatever that was, until the time of his preliminary hearing, scheduled, the way she said it most likely would be, for one week from today. Division 1—he didn't know what that was. She hadn't said anything about that—but he was scared now, because the prosecutor talking to the judge mentioned "known gang affiliation" just before the judge said "Division 1."

And there was something else Christa hadn't told him about. At the opposite end of the courtroom from where the judge sat, there was a glass wall—and on the other side of it, a room with two sections of chairs, one section empty, the other with three people in it, a white lady and a white man and a white boy. It was that white boy from the alley, the brother, who'd said, like Robert Teague, that he had no part in the killing of that other white boy. Chained before the judge, but now looking over his shoulder into that glass-walled room, and at that white boy, there with his mother and father, the dead boy's mother and father, Marcus was trying to read Connor's face, for some sign of hope in it for him—but he saw only a blank, unsmiling face, the face of someone who'd seen his brother shot dead by a black man, too many times for just plain killing. Had Miss Renee not called? Where was Uncle Maurice? And Mama? Where was she? Would Christa call her? He wished Watt could be with him in Division One. But he thought how different his life would be if he'd never met Watt, who killed that boy sitting in that car. And suddenly now he wanted to say he was Mr. Jesse White's main boy. He was the one, the Tumbler, when they went to the NFL games and the NBA, who the people always wanted to see —even in Tokyo, Japan.

159

MORE LOVING
THAN LOVED

The 14th of July, 1999, Bastille Day, his forty-third birthday, Professor Tom Riordan, not teaching this summer, had walked the mile and a half to and then back from the De-Paul library. It was beautiful out, balmy, a day to take a break from worrying and grieving—or to try, at least for some few hours. So he hadn't spent as much time reading as he'd said he would; instead he would get home, take Jackie out for lunch, to some place with great sidewalk seating, say the hell with it and start his birthday celebration not later but now—maybe with a glass of champagne. But when he got home, he had not gone up to his bedroom, though he knew that Jackie, working at home today, was up there—he had heard her on the phone...talking...to someone. Rather he had stopped at the foot of the stairs, listening, fully half a minute, and then had retreated quietly as he'd come in, back into the kitchen, where he now sat at the table, thinking—for what? maybe the ten thousandth time in the twenty-three years since he'd first met Jackie Connaughton?—about the difference between being the one in a relationship who is more loved and the one who loves more.

MORE LOVING THAN LOVED

Never in the twenty-three years had she loved him as much as he loved her, and never had he not known it. And not been *grateful* for it—not contemptibly, pathetically, but deeply, honestly grateful. For the fact that he loved her more than she loved him made him ache with love and need for her, always made him want her, so brilliant, beautiful —made him every day feel the passion, and the desire to please her heart, to make her happy. And he wouldn't trade the pain of his unceasing love, and need, the vital life that was in the insecurity of it—not for all the confidence in the world. But he had never debased himself either, been some contemptible slave, or been *needy* or weak.

If he could never escape altogether his feelings, or the echoes of his thoughts, regarding Connor's fragmented ramblings on the night that Jack was murdered, Tom, with a deep sense that he shouldn't press things in this dark, hard time, had not followed up, either—hadn't, not now, talked to Con in any specific way about the things that Con had said that night, working instead just to bring his son back to life, to get him to come out of his room during the day, to come home at night, to talk about his feelings, his anger, his desire for vengeance, his survivor guilt, to unwrap him from his now frightening withdrawal and to slow down his equally frightening, nightly drinking. God knew he couldn't lose another son.

Or lose his wife. He hadn't said a word to Jackie, either, about what was hinted, strongly enough possibly, in Connor's ramblings, because he'd so much more strongly felt the pleasure of watching a distance between Jackie and him, which before this terrible time had for some unknown reason been growing, now shrinking as they came together in their grief. But not in their lovemaking. Still, he felt, she was elsewhere when they made love, which only fired his desire for her, brought together pain and pleasure in powerful intensity every time as at night he kissed her and came into her with all his need—his need to possess her, a need which had maybe never once been satisfied. But in their mornings now and their days, there was the sharing of their grief over Jack, and this grief was so deeply, equally shared, and for both of them so equally powerful, that it seemed to show her yielding up whatever resentment she might have been holding onto in the silences of her heart, all the years of their marriage, over the fact that life, Jack's first coming into life, had forced her into choices she might not otherwise have made (and in the deepest privacies of his own heart, Tom had more than once confessed that he could not regret the elimination of

DIVISION

her options). But on the telephone, up in their bedroom, to someone, he couldn't tell who it was, she had said, "So many years. And now, my beloved boy, his death, it could mean more years, for the grieving. Because how would what we've talked about look now? And feel? But years. I can't give away any more! We are given so few. They pass so fast. And we are gone before we really live—unless we do something about it. I could tell this only to you. You know who I am. You show me who I am. You know what I need. And God how I thank you. You know how I feel about what you've done for me, for my soul."

So he was thinking, too, this Bastille Day, up la Revolution Francaise! —of heads on pikes, of the heads of priests and aristocrats on pikes in the streets of Paris, of summary executions at the lamppost—and of his forty-third birthday as maybe the last day of his twenty-three-year marriage to Jackie. Contract broken. He so loved her that he thought his own soul's death, if it were for her freedom, might be for a good cause. But God damn her to deepest hell for whatever her goddamn *needs* might be! Who was that on the phone?! But now he looked up.

"I didn't know you were here, Tom! I never heard you come in. I thought you said you'd be all day at the library."

She'd come through the dining room without his hearing her either —he'd been that abstracted in his thought—and she was now standing in the lintel entry into the kitchen. She took away her eyeglasses and set a hand against the dark-wooden column. She was wearing home clothes, a black t-shirt and jeans, and just socks, pale blue, which had kept her footsteps quiet. She'd not pulled her hair back, just let it fall. It was some bad dream, an unreality that he'd been in, and now she was there, the real Jackie, his wife. "How long have you been here?" she asked him, and then moved toward the table to take a seat beside him.

"I don't know," he said, "maybe twenty minutes."

"You've just been sitting here in the kitchen the whole time?"

He looked at her face. No makeup. All natural, and more beautiful than when she was twenty-one, her hair no less soft for her having kept it golden. He lied, "Yeah, just sitting here, the whole time." Then, "It was so nice out, I thought I'd come get you for lunch, take us to some outdoor place, get a start on a birthday celebration. But when I came in...." He looked again at her face, her beauty, which was an agony to him. He said, "I heard...." He watched her face change, saw it tighten. He looked through her. He could see through her. He said, "Anger, Jackie, I feel such fucking anger. I could hear it all."

162

MORE LOVING THAN LOVED

"Hear all of what?" She sat straighter. She folded her glasses closed, and in her two hands, now set on the table, she held the glasses, and turned them. She looked down at her hands.

He looked at her—still right through her. He could hear every word he'd heard her saying—to someone. Thank you, to someone. Thank you for showing her who she was, after all the years. What? Years of *not* knowing who she was, what her soul was? Years she would sacrifice no more of! And the sacrifices were all hers! But he said, "That shouting, Jackie...in the alley. I could hear it all again. I could hear that murderer's hand slamming on the roof of your car, and his voice shouting at Jacko. And then the gunfire. I could hear it all, and couldn't move. I just sat here. With the anger. Beautiful day. My birthday. I wanted to come home to take you out, and I ran into this wall of rage, and sorrow, and couldn't move."

She raised her eyes. She looked at her husband, the father of their sons, one now lost forever, the man with whom she'd spent half her life. They'd shared now such an unbearable, life-changing sorrow. No one could know the grief they shared except another who'd suffered the same. Only Bree could understand what she and Tom were going through. Her husband. Jack's father.... But she'd been again now with Richard Olen, her lover. Twice this week. More than twice, in truth, as it had been phone love with him just this morning, not an hour ago, in the bed she shared with her husband. What had he heard? When really had he come in? Her courtroom sense was that he was lying about having gone no farther than the kitchen.

"Someone once said that without anger, without our innate desire for retaliation, there would never be justice. The hunger for vengeance, it's been called a *gift* to us because it assures that there will be justice, with teeth." He wondered, as he spoke, what kind of man would kill a woman because she betrayed him. What measure of insecurity—of a sense of threat to the self's core—would it take to make such a thing seem just? And if she were beautiful, would it be her beauty that really drove him to it? Would he hate her most *because* of her beauty, which beauty would make him at other times want to lose himself completely, to lose all selfish interest in a self-abandonment better than the best thing self-interest ever could provide. He wanted to expose Jackie right now, to kill her with words, to bring her to her knees and then walk out the door forever—but never, at the same time, had he wanted more to kiss her, to share with her a kiss deep as life. One plus one

163

in human relations, he would tell his students, does not equal two. It equals meaning—the feeling of rightness in the self—which feeling of rightness and meaning changes the world for us. Concordance, love with another—one plus one—is everything. Separation, fracture, isolation—one minus one—is worse than nothing. This is what the heart knows—that it's love, or nothingness. This is what moves the heart—to seek love, or, if rejected, divided from it, to fall into anger, jealousy, murder. We're driven by that simple arithmetic of life or death. "But you can be damn sure," he said, "that whoever said that about our so-called 'gift' of anger never knew vengeful anger as a fatal disease—as *the* thing that ends all hope of continuing relations."

She looked up at him again, then pushed away her glasses on the table. "We're so far in it now, Tom. We're living it—the sickness I see in the courts every day. Especially now with our seeing of that so-called person at Branch 66. The sickness of hatred—we just want it, no matter how self-degrading it is." She looked down at her hands again. "How I hate to say this—but maybe there just *never* is any escape…before we die. Maybe it will always be there, the sorrow, and the anger, for all our days just be there, as this *thing* we have to deal with. Murder kills with anger the ones who remain. And ours is just to bear it now, like the living dead, 'til the end of our days." She closed her eyes. "Memory makes us who we are. But sometimes I don't want to know who I am." She opened her eyes, lowered them. "Sometimes I just pray to forget, even when I know it would be the worst possible wrong to Jack—to what his life was. I sometimes wish I'd never known him…never had him." Tears came to her eyes, as they would now. She raised her hands to her face, pressed her fingertips against her eyes—then, after a moment, took her hands away again, and showed a face of full maternal grief and anguish.

And his heart went out. He couldn't see Jackie cry—as he did now, nearly every day, and had never before, over all the years—couldn't see this and not be moved. But she said now that sometimes *she didn't want to remember who she was*—and he wished *he* could forget, erase from his own memory his having heard her, on the phone in their bedroom, thank someone—How I thank you!—some unknown *you*—*not* for helping her forget who she was but for *showing* it to her, whatever it was that she thought she now was. "Maybe not, Mr. Tennyson," he said, looking at her face, wanting to touch her cheek, wanting to push

that cheek away, but also not, rather wanting to touch it so softly—
"maybe better *not* to have loved and lost than never to have loved at
all—maybe better never to have known the person who will break your
heart in the end."

She looked up at him, and he at her, whoever she was now. He shook
his head. "But truly to have had him, Jackie, for the twenty-one years
we did...." And he thought now of the ironies—of her grieving over,
loving and missing the son who was the reason she was forced into a
marriage and whom, to prevent anyone's suffering what she had suffered by having him, she helped get free from the consequences respecting an unwanted pregnancy as she helped him get an abortion for
Ellie Shea, thus stopping another like him whom she so deeply loved
from coming into the world (if his inferences from Connor's broken
phrases were right enough, as far down in his heart he felt dead certain
they were). And now her saying that she wished sometimes she'd never
had Jack. Was there somewhere in this—mixed, confused with it—an
admission? an assertion? that when she carried him, had the times allowed it, she might have sought an abortion for *herself?* And essentially
the same, the irony in this—because, now, it is not that Jack was the reason she was forced into marriage that she says she wished she hadn't
had him, rather she says this because the depth to which she came to
love this son, whom she did bring into the world, has taken her heart to
levels of loving grief she cannot bear, now that he is in the world no longer. "The love, Jackie...so much better to have known this—so much
better knowing this love and feeling this sorrow than never having seen
our son come into the world. I know you know this, Jackie. I know you
do. The same..." he said, looking at her in a sorrow and pain mixing
yet more with anger, "as I do. We share it—so deeply now—the *knowing* that, no matter the sorrow—the agony—of losing it—it's better to
have had something—something that brought our souls to life—truly
brought us to life—before we died. Something that showed who we
are at our best. So much better to have had this—to have had something that, when it's gone, our sorrow proves the value of. And so many
good years, Jackie—we had so many good years."

She pressed her nails into her palms. Had he really stopped at the
kitchen? When really had he gotten home? When he spoke of something his sorrow showed the value of—something they'd lost, after so
many good years, something that showed them who they were, what

DIVISION

their souls were—what likelihood that he was talking only about the loss of their son? And the way he was saying all this now. What had he heard—of what she'd said to Richard?

""Forgiveness," he said, "it's the same as *forgetting*. If you just damned forget or forgive something—what does that say about the meaning or the damned injustice of the injury?—or about the value of the life that ended, or of the life of the injured party—or of the love, of the *years* of love? Our sorrow—and our anger, Jackie, our unforgiving anger and our grief—they *are* signs, god-given signs—I swear—of the *value* to us of what we've lost." He looked at her again, sensing that she was reading into every word he was saying. "And I want to keep my sorrow, and my anger—to nourish them, cultivate them, stay forever damned *married* to them so that something will actually happen—because there's this fear that if I let go and I forgive, then justice won't be goddamned served." He turned down his mouth hard now as he looked at her.

"But we also are given a desire to forgive," she said. And she knew that, if he was, she too was turning the conversation in double directions, using double meanings—saying and un-saying things, arguing now for justice, now for forgiveness—as the heart needed. The lawyer in her could detect the varying suggestions in all he said and every contradiction, or change in course. And she knew herself now not just to be speaking of forgiveness for the gunman who'd injured them but to be pleading, arguing—for her life, *her* life. Asking to be forgiven for it. Did it take killing to get it, killing Tom, to win freedom, and life? "We *want* to forgive," she said, silently at the same time pleading for him just in some immeasurable kindness to grant her her freedom. "Right there with the anger, which, yes, we maybe do have to live with all our lives, is the desire to forgive, also god-given—and it says to us if you want to live, and not be sick to death, you'll follow me. Come and follow me."

He looked at her with a sad smile, and with anger. "If only, dear Jesus," he said, "that desire to forgive had sufficient power—if it were really in control and could subdue our desire to retaliate exactly as we willed it to—just to the point that neither justice nor mercy was lost. And that is what it is, isn't it—true forgiveness?—not a condoning or exoneration that insults justice but rather recognizes every horrible dimension of the crime, and doesn't stand in the way of a just fucking punishment...."—he tilted back his head, closed his eyes, and half-smiled, sniffed a laugh—"...but at the same time, for life, for the future, for growth, friendship, love, vital relations, for healing..."—he again

166

opened his eyes, lowered his head and looked at her, with his heart breaking, torn between anger, and love—"...real forgiveness...it lets go of all the sick resentment. As you say, Jackie, it breaks life out of the *prison* of rage, which liberation is also the best thing this side of the grave for the angry one, for the person suffering the deep grievance." He looked at her, and, again, half-smiled. Would she read this half-smile as a sign of an equally unbearable love and pain? He knew that she knew his words had far more than the plainest meaning.

She said nothing. Tears were in her eyes. She put her head down and buried her face in her arms. For a long time neither of them said anything. At last she took a deeper breath and squeezed the crook of her arm against her eyes—and raised her head. She looked now vaguely toward the back door. She bobbed her head slightly and moaned. "Leonardo Sykes," she said. "I've let myself a hundred times since Touhy told us his name think how ridiculous and grotesque, the way they give themselves names—as if he knew who or what Leonardo was. This is hell," she said, now with tears again falling, "hell to live in hatred like this and discrimination and divisive contempt. What grace of God might get us free? I need to know—because I cannot get myself free! I see him standing over our Jack and pouring death into him with that gun, as if Jack were a thing, not a human being...not my son! I'm in such hell! I can't bear it, Tom! Please tell me I won't have to live with this forever! Please tell me I won't!" She reached for him and now buried her head on his shoulder and sobbed in utter grief and pain as she held him.

Seventy times seven. He could forgive her. Forgive her forever and never love her less than he loved her now, which was as much as he had ever loved her. He put kisses on her soft hair, the beautiful gold, and took the fragrance of her body deep into his heart. He felt the warm, rich beauty of her body, now pressed against him. He cupped his hand gently round the back of her head as she wept on his shoulder —as if he could protect in this way her mind, and her soul, holding her as one would a just-born child, afraid that any mistake in the way he held her could endanger the life of a miracle. In the for-him vital inequality of their love, he revered her. And to look up to her like this— to love her with such intense power because he so revered her—was the greatest joy he could know in this life. He had had this, before death— for years had had this intensity in his love, which he never would have had if she had loved him as much as he loved her.

167

DIVISION

But now, even as he wanted to lift Jackie's face and passionately to kiss her mouth, to take her to their bedroom and make all-afternoon, passionate love to her, Tom heard his son's words—those broken words Con had said. Equal, equal, equal. If you say it's equal, what then? If you say it isn't, what then? Killing is killing. Murder. And he said he wanted to kill Jack for what he did with Ellie Shea. And Mom paid for it, he said, because she wanted to. She wanted a change in her life. That someone on the phone, in her life. Whom she thanked for showing her who she was. And who would her husband be to tell her that she'd supported the taking of a *life* in an abortion if he took *her* life from *her*—never let her be who she is. What is *life?* The right to life? What is killing? What is murder? What would it mean to be Jackie— the one more loved than loving? Even the smallest difference would be life-altering, as he knew from being the one more loving than loved. Her *life.* He had altered it, maybe from its one true course.

But Connor's words. Not you, Dad. Mom. Because she wanted to. So afraid of losing her, of destroying his family, Tom had said not a first word, either, about the fact that Jackie and Con had been coldly distant, *ice,* to each other now for weeks, even with Con so clearly suffering, traumatized, and in need of help and love. Not wanting his marriage to be one more that failed to make it through a tragic loss, he'd said nothing about this ice-cold distance. But he had thought that Connor might have confronted her—come at his mother not with his words garbled but hammered into hard shape. He had not taught *Adam Bede*. And, so complicated and *strange*—but the one moment in which he'd seen Con relieved from his pain was when he'd told him he was thinking about calling Ellie Shea. Sober, or not fully drunk, he'd come in a few nights back and said that Ellie's boyfriend had told him, some time ago, that she didn't love him and that he was moving on—and that she wanted to talk with Con and that Con should call her, go to her. And just as complicated and strange—Ellie's boyfriend was that Sgt. Rudkus, who was here the night of the murder, who stayed on guard—and who...took out Jackie's clothes. With even greater care now and tenderness, Tom held the back of Jackie's head in the palm of his hand. But the betrayals—with that someone, and of those moral values she knew he'd espoused at the deepest levels of his life. Because she wanted to. She killed his life with this, and with her other life-ending betrayal, with that someone—all because she wanted to. Never a god-

MORE LOVING THAN LOVED

damned slave, not an hour, he now said the words that he was certain would start the end, "Ellie Shea."

Immediately Jackie pulled away some and began to divide herself from him. She lifted her head and, putting herself out at arm's length, looked at him. "Who?"

He looked at her and knew from the look on her face, not an honest look, a false puzzlement, another lie—that he was right about what it was that she did, what it was she paid for, because she wanted to. And so dead once, he took out the gun to kill himself twice. It was his birthday. He wanted to kiss his beautiful wife a last time, place his hand gently on her cheek, under her golden hair and take her to him, but instead he closed his eyes and asked, "Who was it on the phone?"

THE REAL GIRL

Richard Olen, Richard FUCKING
Olen—as he sat at the Leopard bar, Connor Riordan, in order to work
up toward violence his detestation, repeated the name of the man his
mother had left his father for—fucking Richard Olen, the one who
fucks my mother, gives her a pleasure that she calls *happ*-i-ness.... It's
a warm gun, Mama. Maybe he'll knock her up and give her a wanted
child, a boy, maybe—Richard Olen, Jr.—my never seen or known half-
brother. Nor would I ever want to see or know him, or it. Or see that
bitch, his/its/my mother.

Connor had ordered a second shot of Jameson and now slapped down
the empty shot glass on top of a ten-dollar bill and headed out. He'd
seen George Rudkus here one time, maybe a month and a half after that
time George had driven him home, and he didn't want to see him again
and have to say once more, with maybe another two weeks now having passed, that still he hadn't seen or called Ellie (though he might—
when?—have thrown it in his mother's face that he was going to...).

Marcus Sabbs, 921 Cambridge, and Leonardo Sykes, *Watt,* 534 W.
Division, his grandmother's—"up sixteen flights of hell on earth!"

THE REAL GIRL

George had let it out where they'd come from—the one who, before he ran, said We don't want this!—Marcus Sabbs—whom Touhy had told them about, too, before that bond hearing, where they saw him. And the killer. Watt. Leonardo Sykes. The two Cabrini locations, north of Division and south, and the names, Marcus Sabbs and Watt, were now indelible in Connor's mind, where nearly all good things were clouded. Berkeley. He had to stop and think about what his roommate's name was.

He hadn't shaved in several days, or showered. When he'd left the house, he'd tripped over a shoelace he hadn't tied—and he'd found himself staring then a long time, as he knelt on the sidewalk, at the dirt under his fingernails. How long since he'd left the house? Since he'd left his father there trying to read the books he couldn't read? Will his love for that woman, like his son's, turn to pure detestation? Hatred and anger for love—one piss-poor exchange. Will his father's love intensify into insanity? As he walked toward Honore, Connor saw, indelible, that picture of her in her gray suit and her cream-colored blouse and her braided gold necklace, all of which would minutes later be covered in blood. Her eyeliner having run—the killer lawyer about to cry, standing there holding the column with her diamond-ringed hand, her engagement ring, shining beside the gold of her wedding ring, symbols of forever, or in her case just a life of acceptance, which, in *time* she would no longer accept.

Just like the terror images of that black nigger (a word he'd given himself the right to use in the silences of his mind) bandana-ed, with his black gun, this image of his mother would come to him in his sleep. What sleep? He hadn't slept in weeks. Or he knew he'd had some fitful moments of sleep because of the nightmares—which showed him he was still imprisoned in his same self because they would always leave him in the same pool of sweat. And that ghost image of his mother would say to him, too, in his dreams, that he was a chickenshit who knew the value of life, not like his brother, who stood up for what was his, his property! his self and life! which no trespassing fetus, no zygote jellyfish, had a right to invade and occupy! Your brother, who was always, from the day he was born, better than you, religious boy—you who got to live. Could his hatred for this gold-necklaced bitch ever in a million years turn back into love? Or is the human soul nothing, after all, but a one-way street—with no reverses? Is that what it wants to be, forever—a one-way street headed into a pure dead end? There was pleasure in his hatred for his mother—and, addicted, he could suck on it like a poisoned breast until fucking doomsday. Did he tell her he was going to see Ellie Shea—use Ellie just to punish her? Did he...?

It was still light. Had it become August yet? He didn't know. He'd reheated that pasta—but had he eaten anything else today? He'd lost his ability to keep track of things, to measure. The time, the day. So much dead and gone—except rage. He came up now to Honore and by force of habit, mechanical, irresistible, turned toward her place—again. He looked at his fingernails, as he walked, tripping now on a sidewalk crack, clumsy though not drunk—just those two shots of J. He licked his lips and teeth for the whiskey taste and thought about prayer—which was just a pure waiting for grace, not some verbalized begging—Gimme a Mercedes, Jesus, or a fucking blow job—every clear word of a verbalized petition showing how stupid and small you are. And about death, maybe the last, best grace, the perfect answer to the deepest possible prayer, the one you pray when your soul has become nothing but a sickbed of hatred and rage. My mother and that nigger, night after night, and like a cloud by day, the inescapable shit stink of matches, the fire-cracking gunfire, which any loud noise now could bring back! All this shit had fucking raped him and put its alien seed, and life, inside him. So let it come, Lord, death, the only good thing left, when life's last pleasure is a sucking on poison. Only the dead can be forgiven.

Fuck! She was standing in the window, looking. Too liquor-dulled and stupid to wait until dark—that's what he was! Had she seen him? God damn me for a fool. Shit. He wanted to run, but...to be thought insane on top of looking like a peeping tom. Maybe she'd seen but hadn't recognized him. The face scruff, how many days? And the hair barely combed—fingered back. The dirt. Shit. How did his mouth smell? His body? The dirt. This t-shirt—how many days? He couldn't remember. What did he weigh now? So many days—with no appetite. If he looked in the mirror, what would he see?

"Connor Riordan? Connor—is that you?"

He could pretend he didn't hear—but some trace of something, shame? dread of looking insane? made him stop—before he turned the corner at Armitage. But how to make it seem as if he had no expectation that he would find her here—no idea that she lived here? Maybe even of who she was? But why lie? Why? He turned her way. Did he look tired to death of evasion or sick introversion, withdrawal,

THE REAL GIRL

or whatever the cowardly reluctance was that crippled him, always, when it came to her? Or like someone grateful to be stopped—by the one he'd always run from? "Ellie Shea," he said, and, listening to his own voice, he thought he'd uttered some kind of superstitious talisman in a dark place. He feared that when he looked up she'd be gone.

She had hurried to catch him. But now she'd caught her breath. She took some steps towards him...saw him there before her...not himself... not what he was.... George had told her...if you want to see what murder is...look at him and you'll see what it is. She heard herself say, as if they'd spoken many times, though they never had, "Connor, I've been meaning to call you...to ask you how you are...for so long.... I thought...well...I don't know what I thought. I should have called."

He raised his head. Five years since that first time he saw her. All those years, looking away, yet still looking. He looked at her now, his mind focusing. Sandals, cutoff Levi's. Her skin summer colored. A white t-shirt, feminine, with an embroidered neck, floral, green and pink—the shirt loose-hanging and graceful. He could see her taking it from the rack in a store and holding it against herself, happy. Cloud-streaked now, the red sun sent a softened dusk light, west to east down Armitage. At the wake, she'd come out past the flower-filled vases, the light shining on her dark red hair. And now this evening light. Mechanical—he'd thought again and again as he'd taken this same corner, of never and forever. Never his, forever someone else's. "George," he said, "George told me that you'd.... He told me you'd talked about me."

"Yes. George told me he'd seen you. That he'd run into you.... Connor, I live right down the street here."

He closed his eyes and tilted his head back some. He sniffed a laugh. "I know." He kept his eyes closed, breathed deeply, then looked. She was still there.

She was smiling, kindly—and as if, as George had said, a caring, a feeling for him, that maybe somehow had made and was making this moment happen—and that was in that smile? "Come on over to my place, okay? We can talk."

A chrome banister, a wire-spindled balustrade. He ran his hand along the spindles as he walked up the stairway—then thought about the dirt on his hands. He saw it then, from the inside, the space he'd looked up at so many times from the outside. Kitchen, dining, living all one, the wood floor shining gold blonde, the south wall exposed brick, burnished red, with large watercolor paintings, chrome framed, two on that south wall and, he could see, as he came fully up into the room, another on the north, just as large, and all three by the same artist—the two were of birds, a swan with wings widespread, a standing ostrich with its neck extended, legs crossed, and the one alone, of museum statuary, figurines set in glass cases, Field Museum display cases, the reflections in the glass as strong as the objects reflected, and the statuary Chinese, beautiful. And the colors of all three paintings remarkable, the samenesses, the changes, like species, species of color.

He saw speakers on the floor. They'd danced here. But now he was here, not George. He looked to the kitchen, stainless steel stove, refrigerator, dishwasher. The overhead light, soft, shaded, hanging over an island counter. He was in her home, and she was there. Not a dream—the real place, the real girl. Will the heart sink in disappointment, when the real finally replaces the imagined? He shouldn't be here—so disgusting, filthy, stinking now like a street person. He could taste again the whiskey in his mouth. And smell himself. He hid his hands and sat, not on the couch against the south wall, beige leather, soft, where she could sit beside him, but on one of two single chairs, Barcelona, dark-brown leather, set beneath the painting of the figurines. And he looked at the beautiful birds, the ostrich, and the swan with high upraised wings, white, but suffused with striking iridescent color, on the wall across.

She came in and set a glass of beer for him on a low glass coffee table that divided couch and chairs, and then a glass on the other side for herself, as she took a seat on the couch. She hesitated to say—she thought, was it too much?—but she said, "It's Stella. I've seen you.... I think you like Stella."

He looked at her there, smiling, sitting before him, in her home, her shirt, white, with the floral embroidery, loose at her shoulders, at her neck, beautiful. And there was a trace in the room of her fragrance. He nodded and kept his hands back. She took a sip from her glass.

To have been caught, stopped, finally—and to be here, with her. Those impulses that do want to dig until they dig up and bring to life disappointment whenever the real comes, they just stopped now, and breathed. And to what tomb in the soul does a feeling like gratitude, again gratitude, as with George, go for its three days of death before showing it wasn't dead after all? He made sure to say again that George had told him she had talked about him—and now, too, that George had said he should call her. Go to her. Forgive her every cliché. Forgive her. She'll say the right things often enough. "So you're not the

THE REAL GIRL

only one who didn't call—and who meant to call, wanted to call. I
wanted to call *you.*"

She sat now with her calves pulled under her thighs. Beauty and the
Beast, Christ—he kept his hands back still. But he looked at her—at her
face, her lips, her hazel eyes, her hair cut still round her face as at the
wake. He knew her hair's changes. Knew it also long and flowing, the
dark red. And never wrong—somehow never wrong. A woman who is
an artist of her own graces—he loved this. His mother. Beauty doesn't
just come on its own. Always, from when he was young...he loved to
see a woman make it happen—then give the gift of it to everyone.

They talked, then; and as the time passed, talked more comfortably,
about their not calling and about George and what a good man he
was. Yet Ellie thought again, and more than once, as she looked at
him seeming like a veteran of the violence of some faraway meaningless war—that this was, as George said, murder, right before her. And
it would take more than a magic kiss to bring him back. And her, too...
more than a kiss. The touch of those lips. Don't you wish this was
you...little brother? And so she was punished. Punished. Come to a
city she'd forever wanted to come to and now seeing it at last, but in
ruins, and knowing she'd been involved in its devastation, which he
must know. He must. They talked about Ignatius, and Ignatius teach-
ers. And he thought of her classroom voice, the way it would seem, all
those times, almost to come and touch him—but this now was different...the actual reach of it.... And could desire be brought back from
the dead? Often enough...she will say the right things. Give her time.
Carolyn Teague came up. Ellie's best Ignatius friend. And so now, by
means of the strange connectedness, Robert Teague, the alley, Carolyn, Ellie, which in both their minds seemed some webwork woven in
dreams, it would come at last to Jack—to the unspeakable horror, and
the grief—though only for a brief moment, as if the dark thing could
be approached only by slowest degrees. She spoke of the hundreds
and hundreds who'd come to pay their respects. The Riordans are so
loved, she said—and your brother, Jack, was so loved.

He went quiet, withdrawing back into himself. He hadn't once
reached out for his beer.

More empty, silent moments passed—until finally, again hearing her
own voice, and wanting to hear it break this silence, to hear it deliver
things now from any repressed unspokenness—she said, "I took your
father's class this last semester. It was incredible."

175

Only after Jack died had his father mentioned she was in his class—
because of what she'd said at the wake: Tell Connor I'm so very sorry,
please tell him. So much in that moment. Jack. Ellie and Jack. His
mother, listening. His father, not knowing...anything. He himself gone
from the line—to get drunk. She'd done extremely well, most memorably, his father would say. Unsurprising, utterly, to Connor, knowing
her, hearing her as he had, in class after class. No listening, or understanding...like love's.... Love is blind. *Not* loving is blind! Stone fucking blind.... On your deathbed...never to have known this. But strange
that she was there, in his father's class. Or not strange. Sometime since
that second time he saw George, he'd told his father he was thinking of
calling her. Good, his father had said. Good. Good. But had he told
his mother also, just to punish her? He did. He did that. He kept his
hands back still. Carolyn and Robert's. She could have known from
that party there, that he liked Stella Artois. Or was it from that night
at Butch's, when she left with Jack? He reached out finally with his
dirty hand for his glass. He took a long drink. Then, "Maybe ten days
ago my mother left him for another man."

"Oh my God," she said. "I'm so incredibly sorry. I had no idea. That's
so painful—on top of everything, so painful for you, and your father,
my God."

His mother's infidelity, and her final abandoning of his father. So
painful for you and your father—but he couldn't stop a sudden thought
now of those other things that would destroy his Catholic father's life.
He looked at Ellie—and took another drink. All those thousand miles
of distance from her all those years—always, the farther he'd run, the
closer his heart took him to her. And this actual closeness now, what
place was it taking him to? Did his father know now about Ellie Shea—
whom his son for years loved so much he was afraid to say it or think it?
He told Jack he wanted to kill him. If Jack hadn't been killed, would
his brother be here now? Or ever be here? "I have tried," he said, in a
low voice, "over the past several days, to think about ways that I might
come not to hate her forever." He took another deep drink. "But don't
get me wrong. It's for my *own* sake," he said, unable to say clearly how
much he wanted to escape the burning hell of anger he found himself
in almost every waking minute. "It would be for therapy that I would
stop raging over her. That makes it selfish and morally bullshit—not
that I care. And I have no plans, *none,* for seeing her again."

Ellie had listened intensely to every word, but had looked away, as

THE REAL GIRL

it had been so heart-rending to hear what he said about his mother—
and because, too, in a silent place in her mind, not silent, she feared
that Connor Riordan, who *must* know things, he has to, associated *her*
with his mother, a woman toward whom she herself had conflicting
feelings, the darker side of which she was not proud. And now to hear
him determining so brutally hard upon anger—and for him to be here
now, but seeming like the ghost of someone who, the night his brother
died, died with him.

She turned his way but still waited, a long moment, thinking she
shouldn't say what she was thinking—but not knowing if she would
ever see Connor Riordan again (yet she couldn't be so punished—not
the one who, better, she believed it, *better* than anyone else in this world,
knew the beautiful person who had lived before and then passed into
this ghost), thinking she ought surely now to say it. "It won't happen
—I don't think it *can* happen—that you can just say, 'Let's solely for
health's sake lose the anger'." She stopped, waited, then, "Please know
that I know that something like this takes time. Anger time. You're a
human being. You'll need your rage time, but I think the healing, the
therapy, comes only if you work yourself out from the anger in some
larger, deeper way." And who was it she was pleading for now?—she
knew—"I mean you can't separate the healing…you can't just divide
it…from some real discovery of how to see her…your mother…differ-
ently from the way you now do. But that *will* take time. So give yourself
time…." She looked at him, smiled a soft smile that suddenly now came
to her warm from her heart, as she said, "some good time…in hell."

Find the person in her, he thought, made in the image of God, its
beauty deeper always than the crime. Condemn the sin, not the sinner. And that nigger. Let him who is without sin. But *un*equal, not
strong, rather slave-shit *nothing:* It's what he made me when he called
me chickenshit and slaughtered my brother as if Jack, too, were nothing—turned him to pure running blood, flowing, too, over her clothes,
her jewelry. The black man got his sweet revenge and made the white
boy feel so much fucking less than a real person—not even a two-thirds
person, Massah! You fuckin' own me! Equality—gone! The white boy
a slave now, chained to his low self-esteem—his self-detestation. And
so I want that black gun to settle the score—to restore the equal sign,
with bullets to his face. And what has my mother, as she finds her fucking passion with Richard Olen, made my father feel about himself?
How many hours out of every twenty-four does he feel half a man?—

177

DIVISION

while, unrepentant, she fucks Olen. The greatest sin, she said, was to kill your true self with a false goodness. You'll have to answer for it on your deathbed—the crime of killing your own soul's true growth, its true flourishing. And not for killing my father?! And who would *I* be to forgive her for what she's done to *him,* with all her betrayals—of everything he is and believes? No one in his Catholic family ever divorced, either. He'd be the first, because of her. Divide her from her sin. Fuck that shit—and that unrepentant murdering nigger too. No need to see repentance if you have deep faith in the personhood of the offender...the real girl, the fragrance of her, the paintings on the wall, the glasses of beer. Stella Artois.

Yes. No. Yes, she would. *Would she?*—think it worth it to work on bringing him back—if it took a lifetime? His lost eyes were as beautiful as ever, even more beautiful in their lostness. And his remarkable mind and soul—she knew they were in there, past the trauma and rage, the beautiful person beyond the street person. But what if all he has now, in truth, is anger?—rage, too, at her?—and as deep as her own sorrow over all that happened with his brother. He went silent exactly when I said how Jack was loved. Would, could he feel compassion if he knew about the voices I hear, in the innermost recesses of my womanhood, and life—those that tell me I've forfeited my right to pray, unless to the goddess of self-interest, because for myself I stopped a life that had started inside me? Would I have died if I'd let that life live? Could I plead self-defense....

And how to begin, here and now, with this boy so lost to his wrath— this boy who I *know* is my choice, no one else, ever...God help me.... But I cannot start with lies. "I wonder, if I were to say to you that your mother is a soulless, faithless bitch—what you would say to me? I think you'd be angry as shit and that you'd say that while *you* might have a right to go after your mother, *I* don't. And if I really pushed hard and said but she *is,* she *is* a horrid, soulless bitch, I think you'd fire right past my protest and say, You don't know my mother! You don't know a thing about her! Who are you to talk about my mother! And maybe you'd go back to memories of love that really for you define who she is."

"Divide," he said, "the sinner from the sin. So forgiveness begins. It's hatred that identifies the person entirely with the offense. Sees nothing in the criminal but the crime." He stopped. He closed his eyes again. Words can kill. Words could reach into the growing life of this moment, with Ellie Shea. We so hunger for life in the flesh, even an hour of it,

178

with the real girl. But words could kill this moment before it began. Yet it had to be all the way *real*—this coming at last to be with her.

He opened his eyes. Words came. "The night," he said, "of Jack's wake, I saw you. But before you got to me in the line, I left. I went out and got drunk, and never came back—to Jack's wake! I got drunk as shit, as on so many nights now, since Jack died. And when I stumbled through our back door around three in the morning and fell drunk into the kitchen, my mother came down." He looked across at Ellie. Was she afraid now of how words can kill? "The night he died, Jack told me—so many things...about my mother. He told me she'd felt forced into marriage." He looked still at Ellie. Did her look say that she feared where this was going, as he'd known, once, where things Jack said were going—and that Jack took there, all the way there, for what purposes? Not truth but fucking secrets are beauty.... "He told me she wanted change in her life, wanted to find her *own* life, not the one she'd been forced into, because when she and my dad were young...they had to get married. I'd never known any of this—but for some reason, Jack knew everything. For some reason he'd come to share in my mother's secrets...and he told me...that night...."

Was Ellie's face honest? Was she bleeding inside, fearing where things could be going? Did she fear they'd come out? Want them to come out? I wanted them to come out, with Jack. Wanted them *born*. Her face looked troubled, no doubt troubled. She held her hands together, tight. "Change! I was shouting at him. I said was she *fucking* someone who is not my father! And Jack told me, *Yes,* there was a man—however it was he knew! And that night in the kitchen, I said to my mother—that that's what *she* had done—divided herself from her crime, betrayal, sin—said to herself things like the woman who went out for the pleasure of *fucking* wasn't the real Jackie Riordan. The real Jackie Riordan was still fine and good. I told her she divided herself up, compartmentalized herself, for moral convenience, rather than live a life of integrity, undivided. And how many people who do wrong, maybe *all* who do wrong, do it exactly that way—by separating themselves from their wrongdoing, from their actions! Forgiveness of others, forgiveness of *self,* every kind of forgiveness uses the same fallacious, bullshit-convenient separating operation that unethical people, people who lie to themselves, use to comfort themselves as they keep on doing the wrong things, un-fucking-repentant."

Her face, he could see, Ellie's beautiful face, was pained. She had

DIVISION

moved her calves out from under her thighs. And had lowered her feet to the floor. And now she rose and stood. Her lips were trembling. She was looking toward him in her pain, starting to cry. But still he said more words, words that could kill this moment before it started. "Jack! He told me so many things that night. More and more things—that infuriated me! About things he'd done, too, against what we'd always believed, things that he knew would kill me! And I told him I wanted to kill him! The last thing I said before that animal came up and *murdered* Jack was that I wanted to kill him!"

She had bowed her head. She stood there now crying. "You know it all," she said. "I knew, Connor, that you knew it all. Jack and me."

Now he rose and came to her, stepping round the table. He had shed himself of all the lies and his hidden angry feelings, but immediately was sick-ashamed of himself for having so wounded her. He thought this first close moment with her would also be the last. He thought he'd *set out* to kill it—to kill everything, his life, *her*.... And to hurt his mother.... He was in agony, for he could see nothing in Ellie but what he loved. And now her voice, here...for him.... Never had he loved her, loved anyone, like this, and wouldn't again. This will not come twice, not in a lifetime. He felt the filth of himself, who couldn't even walk the streets he stumbled down. The now months of drunkenness and disgust. In his hatred of himself and shame, having hurt her like this, he said, "I am so sorry. I will regret this... I will so deeply regret this. I'd better just go."

She looked up. She said nothing, but knew and could feel the passion in his heart—what he'd said, the anger, the rage at his brother, at her, there was love in it, that went deeper—and in his apology. She'd sensed the affection of his heart in the street, in the way he turned and looked at her and said her name—and had known of it maybe forever ...whose fault? That night with his brother—she knew. Little brother. *Why* had she done what she did? All for such foolish, weak-angry reasons, but love in those reasons—why ever hurt someone like that who didn't haunt your heart, own and haunt it? She had done it to Connor... the way Jack did.... With tears falling, tears in her eyes, she reached out and took his face in her hands. She looked into his eyes as she held his face tenderly in her hands, the lost Connor Riordan, and all his anger —at life, at her—and then brought his face to hers and softly kissed his lips. Would it take a lifetime? she wondered again, as tenderly, a second time, she kissed him, his beautiful face, looking so lost...a veteran ...of betrayal...and of murder.

180

LOVEMAKING

Her second glass of pinot grigio half-empty in her hand, Jackie Riordan let her mind relax away from any effort to talk to Richard Olen, as she sat facing him in his living room, seventy-two stories up in the Hancock. Richard's chair was turned toward the city; Jackie's toward the lake—though she looked now neither out to that great dark blank, broken at night only by the red blinking light of the water intake crib more than two miles offshore, nor at Richard in his chair, as he sat there, still in his dress shirt, his tie loosened, between her and the lake window. Rather, she let her eyes run over those things of his she could see from where she sat—the decoupaged sideboard on which the open bottle of pinot sat green-golden before the shelves of glassware, one shelf for all the paper-thin smoked crystal like that of the wineglass she held, which wore, faintly, the kiss print of her rose Dior touched over with her gloss—the striking six-panel hanging of Wright-style windows, imitations of the architect's arrow-feather designs delineated by thin lead mullions—the silver throw pillows set evenly on the gray Lily sofa beneath the Wright-style hanging —the matched candlesticks, each with three upreaching tongues of bronze to enfold the candles, placed at equal distances from the two ends of the top of the sideboard—the hanging lamps, dropped to varying heights from the ceiling, their tubular fixtures various in color, all reflected in the window glass.

None of it was hers. She recalled an afternoon when, after having made love with Richard, she asked him who did his interior work, so that she might have him or her come look at her own home on Lincoln Park West. And now she thought—this is how the mind works: it knows your choices, your commitments and what side you've gone over to, and instantly it rouses voices from the other side to challenge, cast doubt upon, deride those choices and commitments to which you have altogether given yourself. The mind will never just let you be separated, divided—either all one thing or another. This is something you've got to expect—and then fight. You've said you had to find your own right life and your own right love before you die. And the moment you concentrate your intention into an action, the damned mind, in perverse reflex action mocks at you by saying that the place you've chosen, as *yours,* will never really be yours and that the relationship you've chosen, seeking to find your one truest soul mate, will be with a stranger.

She raised her wineglass and, placing her lips upon her own faint kiss print, sipped once more from his gray-smoked crystal the Villa Russiz that Richard knew she loved. She then looked at him, as in after-work fatigue he dozed lightly in his chair. Physically not Tom, not an athlete; five feet nine, not six feet one; his gray-brown hair at fifty thinned and receded; his face not handsome like Tom's—rather sharp lined, thin browed, pitted under the cheek bones, and intense with an intellect razor keened in courtroom battle, the face of the only man in her office she was glad she would never have to oppose and who, ever challenging, at times outright intimidating her, could thrill her as Tom, with his poetry, could never. But Richard never knew Jack—and so there could be with him no intimacy in grief, none that was real. More than once she'd put her finger to her lips when he'd begun to speak of her lost son, even though he'd never mentioned Jack's name without making clear his respect for his mother's feelings and for Jack's life. Nor when she slammed her hand down on her desk and cursed Connor—"God *damn* him! He grants himself the right to be his own mother's personal Fury!"—was Richard unwise enough to join in any way in her imprecations or to encourage her even slightly in her bitterness. Richard never had or wanted children, not with either Helen or

LOVEMAKING

Janine, but he knew how to keep his mouth closed to a mother of two. He knew, too, though, that he had license to say the exactly right sharp thing about Tom—the thing that could make her laugh the wicked laugh and that could warm her between her thighs, and that one time, memorably, had the deepest magic power when he whispered it to her in his bed. His bed, the bed of a stranger—so, across the hard dividing line of her choices, her mind, from that other side, the old side, now whispered its taunts again as she looked still at Richard Olen, dozing, and lifted the pinot to her lips.

"Distant. Beautiful...and distant. I like it." His eyes still closed as he started to speak but now opening, Richard suddenly pulled himself up and forward in his chair. Maybe he'd never been asleep. He set his elbows on his thighs, and then his chin on his folded hands. He looked at her with a roguish-cunning turn of his mouth, not quite a smile. "Uncomfortable. Not sure, maybe, you've done the right thing. Or how I feel about you. Or how we feel about each other." He lifted his head, tilted it slightly back, and looked at her with a wry grin. "Promises," he said, "to be an interesting evening." He picked his own glass up from the circular coffee table that separated the two of them—the marble-topped table, Baccarat, its bronze legs the roman numerals for 12, 3, 6 and 9, set clocklike around the table. "I like it very much," he said, as he lifted his glass of the Villa Russiz and took a sip.

She lowered her eyes and smiled. She felt the sex immediately—felt herself signaling it, too, with her smile and with the way she lowered her eyes, and now crossed her legs, warm against each other. He liked it very much, the vibration; and she liked it—the real threat of danger in their new...brand-new living relationship—the threat of an emptiness in it as blank as that out the 72nd-story lake window. An interesting evening—with this man who could read her mind, here, and in his bed. She wanted him, right now, this mind reader, brilliant, powerful— who shook her self-confidence—worried it into a keenness of vigilance while at the same time firing her desire. But she hated the look of any kind of desperate rush—hated how it made her choice of Richard Olen, her life choice, look somehow desperate. She spoke of what she'd just been thinking: "It's the way our minds work. You make a change. A choice—of one thing—or the other. And voices coming from the side you didn't choose, or the side you left behind, begin to accuse you of everything from abandonment to outright murder." She took her glass to her mouth, not sipping it, rather just looking over it. "But a

long time ago," she said, her voice softening, sexual, "I learned that
guilt is the real killer."

Richard set his glass on the table. He touched an index finger to his
lips, as if to hold in waiting whatever he had to say. But now he lowered his hands together and folded them, sliding his fingers slowly up
into each other. "So many times he looked at you. Over twenty years
he looked at the way your lips would touch a glass, at the way your
fingers held it, at your eyes—looking back into his. So much history.
Shared history. So what right have I to come in and end it, compara-
tively speaking, in no time at all?" Richard leaned forward and looked
up into the eyes of the woman who, just over two weeks back, had, for
him, left her husband—left her home, her surviving son burning with
anger, and come here to live. Did he even love her? If he did, would
he still when her beauty, this startling beauty, now at its richest, no
longer thrilled him? When things changed for her, as they would before too many more years passed, would he even be there to change
with her? All he knew was that he'd never known anyone like Jackie
or known any feeling like that he had for her. Many women he'd made
love with, but none, ever, like this—never before had he seen or felt
such depth of passion, such hunger, for everything. He took up his
glass again and turned it round slowly by its stem, with his forefinger
and thumb. "Rights," he said, "the *right.*" He looked up at her, focused,
intense. "I've said to myself that I'd have the *right* to kill for you—all history with anyone else be damned. Every year and day of it." He took a
sip of the wine, then lowered the glass and looked at her again—with
a look that searched her—searched for more of her than he yet had
found and that invited her, with her deep-disturbing, beautiful desire,
to uncover in him even more than she had yet uncovered. "The god-
given right to kill for you, Jacqueline Connaughton... And I promise
you, I would. I would kill for you."

She said nothing, though she'd come instantly to a place far, far out.
What he said, every word, took her out farther and farther. She held
her wineglass in one hand—now away from her face, so he could read
her face, read the signs of a need she couldn't describe, even to herself. He would kill for her. Not just words. Not a shred of doubt. He
would do it. Still she said nothing, but now with her free hand she unfastened the top button of her blouse, and bringing to her eyes, her
mouth, every sign of a need like none she'd ever known, unfastened for
him, for him only, never any other man like this—the second button,

the third, all, for him only. Now she put down her glass and, slowly, no rush, no desperation, reached behind herself, and, for his eyes, Richard's, unfastened her bra, softly let it half fall, and then, closing her eyes, let the deep pleasure come. She raised a forefinger to her tongue, wetted it and then ran it slowly, wet, across a breast and down now to the nipple, and round it. Then again wetting her finger—and then touching, massaging herself again. Only for him, she searched, her eyes closed—for her deepest self. Down through her dark, beautiful pleasure, oncoming, she searched for herself—did this for Richard only, who would kill for her, this powerful, un-intimidated, un-cowed man, to whom she would give now, with indescribable need—her truest, deepest self—all of it to him, because without him she never would have found it. And he had come to her now. His hand was in her hair, his fingers twisting, tightening themselves in her hair—and then turning, forcing up her face for the kiss.

Tom Riordan, his son gone out, God knew where, sat alone in his study, steps away from his vacant bedroom. Weeks—and not a word from her, not a fucking syllable. She sent her bitch-sister, Celeste, with a list of things to be retrieved, Bree having refused. And no driving by, either, to walk up and confront them—not with the two of them sky-high in the goddamned Hancock! No breaking his door down, no pointing a gun through his window, whoever the fuck he is and whatever he looks like! He thinks he can come into my life—come into my home and steal my life from me. Not a continuous hour now of concentration. I haven't read five pages, not two, without stopping and raging. To get so inside me and take my mind from me—for how long?—the rest of my days? To force into my mind all the images of her fucking him, her giving herself to him, taking him into her mouth, between her legs, cumming for him again and again—to ram these things into my head so that they haunt me non-stop, day and night—to turn my soul's life into a porn film starring my moaning wife and *make me watch it* for days on end, for years, so I can't work or think, ever. What diabolic life force gives them the power—and the right to send me into hell when they're the ones doing the betraying, the thieving. Just like that godforsaken demon who slaughtered Jack! Who in God almighty's name is he to come and drag me down into hell's darkness, when *he's* the murderer! And he's out walking the streets! And the two of them, who keep cramming me down into hell's blackness, are off in bed moaning in the porn film that runs non-stop in the fucking center of my head. And for how long? When do I fall out of love with her? And if I ever do before I leave this world, won't that be another theft accomplished—the robbery of my love for her? the best thing I ever knew, the deepest, by far, my soul ever goddamned felt, or ever will!

And what's worse—her giving her heart and body to someone not me and so making me *nothing,* for some Richard Who the Fuck is He Olen—THAT, or her *deliberate* assault on the deepest values I live by, her going straight like a smart bomb to the dead-on rape of the things I most deeply believe in—and that for years she *said* she believed in, in ways that appeared to confirm that she had no regrets about our so-called mistake, or about our marriage, and no problems anywhere in her soul about forgiving me, herself, us. Values we appeared to share—completely! And now, Christ!—that look on her face when she came out and screamed it right in my face that she'd paid for that abortion, because she wanted to! *Never,* she as much as said with this, would I have married you if I'd been able to free myself of that child inside me. Never! No matter what she might have said over all the years of our marriage—about life, the right to life. Jack's life!—the gift it was to us! And sanctioning Jack in the abortion, giving it her imprimatur, so that of course he went right ahead with it, she's stolen Jack from me, too—taken him out of my heart with a goddamn Metzenbaum scissors and suction catheter—torn open the skull and sucked out the *contents!*

I need to picture it—*all* of this horrid shit. I've got to!—so I can fall out of love with her. If I don't fall out of love with her—all the way—I'll die. So how, in all fucking truth, could I, or *should I* forgive her, if forgiveness would keep my love for her alive? If I don't kill my love dead, I'm the one who dies. So let me think it—put it right before my eyes: Jackie, right now, as I sit here, gone from me and fucking another man! And what makes the fucking so deadly important? Just guy rage? Control-freak rage? Ownership rage? Fuck all materialist morons. It's the deepest giving and receiving—that's what sex can be, and was, at least for me. When you gave yourself to me, Jackie, in our sex, you *made* me with that gift, and gave me, at the deepest level, the power to give my own self back to you. And with my giving of my own self back to you, I made you. Sex—what it is, is Come into my house, and then you invite me to yours—Take the secret I give to you and by means of this secret *be* the strong you and, so empowered, give your secret to me, so I can be the fully strong me. The pride of the receiving, the ecstasy of the giving, the beautiful, powerful making and un-making of

LOVEMAKING

ourselves, of you and me, at the deepest level of the soul's hospitality
—or so it was for me, our sex. And that's what it *is* for me—right at the
heart of it all, the joy of it, and now the murderous anger and pain of
it—of sex, sex with you. The only woman I ever made love with! God-
damn you! *Lovemaking*—I knew its diamond value in the fullness of my
passion with you, and I know it even more now in this jealous agony
—seeing the movie of the giving and the receiving hour after hour, because you're magnificent in that movie, Jackie, at last you really are,
but with somebody else, magnificent giving yourself to this man I've
never seen, taking him inside you, welcoming him, warm and deep.
Loving, choosing him. And killing me—as you claim your right to
choose. And God damn *life* how I despise you!—so much I can't even
breathe, thinking of how much—and yet maybe never enough to stop
loving you.

Tom Riordan now folded his arms on his desk and buried his face
inside them. His eyes tearing, he pressed them into his shirtsleeves.
For a long time, he didn't move. Then at last, while still in pain, not
only in his mind but in a tightened throat and back, in a pounding in
his head, and now in his fingers as he had for some time pressed them
white hard on the backs of his arms, with his *life* still in pain, he began,
nonetheless, to relax some, to loosen his fingers, and to take deeper,
slower breaths. His head still down, his eyes raw, still pressed against
his folded arms, his sleeves now wetted by his eyes and mouth—he
managed still to ask himself... But if I kept her, from the very start of
our marriage, which, yes, would be the exact moment of Jack's con-
ception (and was it, in those early days, just sex for her, never love?)—
if in all truth I *kept* her from coming ever to know the kind of love she
brought out in me—then to what degree would I have to answer for
that in eternity? She was the one I loved more than any other woman
in the world, but I was not the man she loved. And if I kept her from
finding the miracle she gave me...?

He lifted his head from his arms and sat up. He turned off the desk
lamp. He breathed still slowly—and let his body now compose itself,
relax away from pain, as he looked out his back window in the dark—
toward the alley. One's own body, or mind. The division between inside and outside—who would I be to say to her that the location of
the presence of another, of an alien life *inside* you, matters not, when I
feel so invaded by the penetration into the inside of me, into my bordered self, by him, by images of him and her, by imagined pictures of

DIVISION

that alien black man—that *Watt*—who turned Jack's face into a pool of blood? If there were a way to kill them all, to scrape out these alien presences inside my borders, I would do it! And who am I to say that Ellie Shea can't have a bordered self, a body, her body freed of alien presences, divided off, safe and separate—or that my Jackie, my love, can't have a self, *her* self, free of me? A right to control what happens in her own body, or her own soul.

But it's always kill, kill, kill, Jackie, to get that control over your own soul's or body's space, over its property lines, every inch of which are drawn beneath the Tree of the Knowledge of Good and Evil—in its dark shadow, which is death. It is always kill to control your own body.... Until maybe it isn't. Resignation. Acceptance. All right, I will let the child be in me. I will get married. But that's not enough, that resignation. What stops the killing, the murderous protection of the interests of the bordered self—is not just acceptance, but forgiveness—is the letting down of all the borders of the self, the body—is the body crucified, the nails and blood, past all pain, all bordering, all self-protective, defensive pain signals, red stop signs of blood all taken down, and a letting of the nails come inside me!—so that he can come in, Richard Olen, and Jackie come in beside him, with him, in love at last, fresh from sex, from lovemaking, with Richard Olen, her real and true love—and Watt, that unknown alien, that horror, that WHAT, can come into me—because I am an all-forgiving purest nothing, with no borders, no divisions, no race, no property that can be robbed, no *body* that I have a right to kill for, no inside or outside—all that's left of me being the un-bordered meek one, who shall inherit the undivided earth. Forgiveness is a duty. But far more deeply it is blessedness. It is Christ Jesus.

He rose and walked to his window, not hearing his son, Connor, coming in at the back door, or coming up the stairs, or now, behind him, standing in the study's open door—as he said, prayed out loud, now to some force that could give him the strength, "I have to become nothing. There's no life, unless I'm nothing. Let me be nothing. Let me get out of this hell of murderous anger, and be nothing."

"Dad—Dad, it's me. It's Con. I'm here."

Tom Riordan turned to see his son, disheveled, clearly drunk again. Even having seen Ellie Shea...at least that once.... Still so lost, the smell of alcohol all over him. Three days, God help us. So, so discouraging. He couldn't lose him. If he lost this boy...it would be the end.

Connor came forward, clumsily, and embraced his father, held him tight—then desperately tighter. "She is such a fucking cunt!" he said, "such a fucking, fucking, *fucking* cunt!"

"Please God no!" Tom said, holding his son back tight, loving him, desperately, "Please God don't ever say such a thing, Con. Don't ever say it. You will be lost. You'll be lost. I know this." Then, as he pressed his son's head tenderly against him, holding him still tight with his other arm, "I know we'll both be lost."

It's already settled, Richard Olen had said; it's an embarrassment now for people with brains to say they're pro-life. In thinking circles, just to utter that empty buzz word "personhood" is simply to court contempt. The term's as tabooed as the c-word (he thought to throw in n-word, but didn't, despite his utter contempt for the confidence that some pro-lifers have that the era of abortion will be looked back upon by history as an even greater darkness than the era of slavery or the Holocaust). What was a guilt, he said, is now a virtue—and what was a virtue is now a guilt. It wasn't easy, but the cultural work is done. Personhood is out, choice is in. And that he's against abortion is a thing he keeps secret, you can bet, even from close colleagues.

Long before coming to live with him, Jackie had told Richard all about Jack and Ellie Shea—but had only some forty-five minutes or so ago mentioned to him that Connor, in a manner odd, distracted— but also bitter, aggressive? intended to wound? to punish?—that he had said to her, a few days before her final battle with Tom and her departure from Lincoln Park West for good, that *he* intended to go to Ellie Shea, himself, and to see and talk to her again and again as time passed, because Ellie Shea meant more than everything to him. And so now she and Richard, lying naked together after beautiful, long sex, had turned to talking about *issues*—discussing things, going over them, for the last three quarters of an hour.

As Richard spoke now, Jackie closed her eyes to all the things belonging to his bedroom, his things, which, as they'd talked, she'd been scanning now and again in self-flagellating compulsion. To stop with this, she shut her eyes—but now her mind brought vividly before her that picture of herself that was her son, the one who looked just like her but who thought like his father, the one who was always her, and not her. He stood there in her kitchen. Her living son, whom she felt such a fierce anger toward and who returned that anger to her, who was her, in his face his mother's son, hers—and whom she was deciding never to see again, as he was, she knew, choosing never to see her...

DIVISION

this one who no doubt informed his father about the abortion and so lit the fuse for his father's whispering of the girl's name in her ear, on that last day...which might not...have come so soon. Connor...he was her son...oh God help me....

As her eyes began to fill with tears, she shut them harder—and held them shut...some good time...till the tears were dry and gone. But still now so sensitized from her long sex with Richard, and finding that she needed only to touch herself lightly to feel warm echoes of orgasm, she did so, again and again—until at last she turned toward Richard, who'd for a time now gone silent, and whispered to him, softly, "Will you do something for me?" He looked at her questioningly. "Would you," she asked, "do me a favor, right now?" "A favor?" he asked. She reached her hand then beneath the sheet and touched him, leaving her warm hand on him. Then, caressing him with her hand, she whispered in his ear, "Would you fuck me so sweet I'll never cry again?"

SHE SAY YOU COULDA BEEN A PREACHER MAN

Lifeless Levolor blinds, dust-covered, cracked and skewed, darkened the second-story street windows of the rundown two-flat on the 7000 block of South Rhodes that Watt had settled into six weeks back, with Markeeta T—a girl he knew from back at Tha Jube. Sleepy-sexy, and long and lean like a runway model—but still the same bitch she's always been. Still treats all the world like nasty shit. And like to call a man a fuckin' piece a dirt all the time she's beggin' him come tie up her wrists to the bedposts. Watt could feel the just-right texture of the silky scarves he used last night to shackle her down. Schooled real good in that shit, ahright, when I'm a child. And won't it steel-rod a man's dick when he sees a she-devil go all soft and subdued, ready to cum all night, too, 'cause she's lovin' him masterin' her—she the slave. Fun and games, motherfucker. Not like that sweet stuff back with Sara, just me and her, no whip 'n' chains, just two plain people— till I recollect I'm past the point a that.

The lots adjacent to the now lone two-flat at 7029 S. Rhodes Ave. were vacant rubble fields, each fenced at the street by chain link sagging from tilting fence poles. And what deep-buried city records showed

DIVISION

who owned these dead-empty parcels of urban decay?—not likely the properties of the last ones to play rat-dodge in the now long-gone, moldy two-flats that once stood, or slouched upon them. Not enough substance to those departed souls even to be ghosts. But now out of the second-story side windows of 7029, Watt saw cars coming in from the back alley, and could hear them crunching slow over the rubble of both the abandoned lots. His new homeboys, like to count the number, pullin' up side by side, all in formation, let the world know some shit's goin' down around here now.

"Keeta T! Get your sorry ass down there and let those boys in! Told you to be lookin'!"

"I *be* lookin', mistah! No need f'you t'be barkin' no orders at me! Ah can fuckin' see they heah!"

"Bitch—your uppity, back-sassin' shit gon' cost you some day, roll-a-dimes pussy or no," he said to himself, as he watched her head down the back stairwell to let in the boys, as ordered. "Gon' bend that hard-ass pretty-woman shit to my will. Bend it till it breaks."

No black leather or blue-black bandana, his skull shaved clean, a tight-trimmed mustache and goatee, and a pair of wire-rimmed glasses, and, for the street, turtlenecks to cover the pitchforks on his throat—Watt could walk up and down 71st St. now and even take a turn up Cottage Grove and stroll along the graveyard wall there and stare right into the windows of the District 3 station—any time. Fuckin' Lonnie D tells me how I commit suicide pullin' that trigga brought the shut-mouth to that crazy white boy, spoutin' out his thousand-year-old white-boy shit. Suicide?—lest, *what?*—I head down to Miss'ippi and hide out all my days in some sorry-ass nigga shack nigga side the Yazoo? Reparation. Redistribution. Revolution. Revenge. Build that 4-R's kingdom, Mama, before I die. Name's still Watt, no matter what I look like.

In the front parlor—some on the sofa; some in arm chairs; some in fold-up chairs that back in the kitchen Keeta T, with her cigarette hand, had pointed to while with her other she flipped the pages of a fashion magazine; and some sitting hunched on the parlor floor; and one perched in the front window seat before the bent and yellowed blinds—all of them waited in quiet for Watt to call their meeting to order, anticipating that the man intended to make happen something different from what they'd been accustomed to. Rasheed, Kermit, John T, Hosea, Walter, Newsome, Jamal, Isaiah, Calvin, Preston, Tarik, and Brandon: Twelve. When he finished the count, Watt nodded, smiled,

192

liking his number—the Disciples of Jesus. But now, his count done, he waited, creating just the silence he wanted as he stood before them—tall, ripped hard as ever, in just a dark blue t-shirt, his tight-bearded face a concentrated image of all his command power.

"'Heah be the dividin' line,'" Watt finally said—but then he stopped, with now a dark look on his face, and turned his head slowly to look in the eyes of each of his twelve, one by one. At last, then, looking up over their heads, past them, thoughtful, "'Us over heah; y'all over theah. All be for peace. All be for the common good, dividin' it all up equal like this. We don't cross; y'all don't cross. Everbody be happy. Plenty to go 'round. No need for no greed.' That's what he says to me last night, Mr. Benjamin Lloyd, Mr. Bennie Twin Bill. He says, 'We got all we need, and y'all got all y'all need—each of us inside our separate territories. Don't neither of us need no more. All the trouble start when somebody start thinkin' different.'" Watt now turned his head slowly once more, moving his look from face to face. "Sound good to you? Peace? The common good? Equality? Inside our separate territories plenty enough to go around so we all can be happy? No need to cross the dividin' line. No need to start trouble. Neither of us needs more." He stopped, waited. Then, looking across the collection of faces, "I'm askin', doesn't that sound good? You can feel it, can't ya, right here and now? The good, good peace comin' over you? Feel it comin' soft? Feel it comin' like sugar-sweet sleep? Like all your worries are gone? Enough to go 'round, the man says. Enough for everybody. No killin', no dyin' necessary. You can feel it right now as I'm sayin' it, can't ya? —that sweet peace tuckin' you into bed like your sweet mama—kissin' your forehead? And doesn't it feel good? Yes, suh. Does it not?" He waited again a moment. Then, "I'm *askin'* you!"

They looked, all of them, as if their answer, just the saying something out loud, might lead them right here and now to some lasting change, deeper even than any they had expected—and so they didn't answer.

A slight smile came to Watt's face, then disappeared. "Can't be killin' it," he said, "'fore it comes to life." He started slowly now to pace in front of them, this way and back, and back again. Then he stopped...and looked at them, his power concentrated in his eyes. "There's somethin' inside you, and you can't be killin' it 'fore it comes to life. Don't need more than what you got inside your separate territory. Don't need to cross the dividin' line, startin' up trouble." He intensified his look yet more. Now he raised his voice. "Hell. Fuckin' *hell,* my brothas! Talk about need!" But then he stopped, waited, and said again, more quietly, "Hell fuckin' hell." He turned down his mouth and then pointed at them, bobbing his hand. "Nobody tells you how much you *need*. Nobody preaches to you sweet Jesus sermons on the common good, or the public gotdamn interest." He closed his fist and turned his mouth down harder. "That somethin' you got deep inside you—it ain't about equality! It's 'bout what you gon' find, my brothas, the other side that sweet sleep a peace—what you gon' find once you get past that sweet, sleepy, trappin'-you-down bullshit! You gon' love that sweet peace so much you let it kill dead the best thing you got?! Down inside you it is, like when you're a little baby inside your mama's belly, floatin' your little ass in all that warm bath water inside her until you feel what you really need—message a God sayin' get me the fuck out—gon' step out this sweet sleepy bath water—don't care what it gon' cost my mama in pain, don't care if she's bleedin', don't care if I come out cryin'—won't gotdamn abortion myself down in heah and never be born, jus' stay sleepin', never knowin' the light a day."

He closed his eyes—and waited. Then, "What is it, my brothas, we're talkin' about? What?" He opened his eyes and looked at them hard. "Not peace. Not the common good. Not dividin' lines you don't need t'cross. Not gotdamn equality. Tell you what it is. Take it right out the white man's dictionary and tell you exactly what it is. It's *superiority*. It's gotdamn *supremacy*. It's sayin' what you *need* is everything you can see, fuckin' gotdamn all of it. And can you feel it, mah brothas? Can you feel this badass gangsta fuckin' thing inside you, other side sweet sleep, other side sweet peace, this thing sweet peace wants to kill off in you, this thing you got says, Don't you abortion me with sugar and spice and everything shit nice, sayin' to me no killin' and no dyin' jus' equality and sweet, soft democracy and equal fuckin' rights and lines a division ah ain't supposed to cross. Shit tryin' to kill you 'fore you ever live, mah brothas. Shit tryin' to keep you from ever knowin' 'fore you die what you got inside you. And you *look*—you look at all them out there got it all. How they get there? How they get it all? Tell you *what*—they listen to that message a God say you come out and be born no matter what you do to your mama's belly and guts. Message a God says I put somethin' inside you *long* 'fore I put in any sweet shit about equality. Message a God says it's slaves and masters and the slaves gon' lay down and be fucked and like it. Message a God says which one you gon' be?"

SHE SAY YOU COULDA BEEN A PREACHER MAN

Watt could see that he was awakening not just that Greater Grand Crossing local operator inside his men, not just that four-block ghetto hood they saw every time they looked in the mirror—but that deep gangster they'd never seen but knew when they did that he'd been waiting inside them since the day they were born. "Line a pride," he now said, as he once more looked above them, now touching together his closed fists, tapping them. "Line a pride. You come the fuck alive and you move out past that dividin' line you're never supposed to cross and you *take* some a that territory that that sleep-shit killer called sleepy peace says isn't yours, and you *make* it yours, and you draw that line a pride out further than what you had before, and you never give up that new line a pride, feelin' the possibilities you never felt before 'cause you been floatin' so easy down in yo mama's belly—and feelin' all the new *life* you got, now that you *started* somethin', you go on and draw another new line a pride out even further, 'cause you took some more territory, and then a new line a pride after that 'cause you took some more, and then a new line a pride and a new line a pride, 'cause you're takin' more and more—'til you know, my brothas, that it's a different way a doin' things than what your preacher was sellin' you. You seein' now that that good old way's been killin' you and makin' things sweet for somebody else. And what you come to see is that what they call evil and what they call good's all jus' a game works for them who's already got what's worth gettin' and aim to keep it—tellin' people who got nothin' that it's motherfuckin' *evil* for them to cross the dividin' line and come on after somethin'." He stopped, raised his head, took a deep breath, then looked down at them. "Got to change the *world,* my brothas, got to turn it upside down and call what they call good, *evil,* and what they call evil, *good.* 'Cause what they call evil, it's that best thing you got, that gangsta man a power that I'm callin' to here and now—that gotdamn man a supremacy."

He pressed together his fists, and again looked across his twelve, the men he wanted to build his kingdom with, his nation with, his new nation, after Fort's, and Barksdale's, and Hoover's all now were gone to little block-by-block fragments a shit. He waited still—then finally, with a quiet intensity meant to move them to the last stages of conversion, he said, "Lest, my brothas, you're afraid to die. Can't *be* afraid to die, and ever find that deep gangsta of power inside you. Can't *live,* not a day, if you're afraid to die. And that's the real sleepy-shit motherfucker, the one keepin' you from knowin' what you got—fear a dyin'—

DIVISION

makes you good in their way, evil in ours, 'stead of evil in their way, good in ours. Message a God don't belong to them, lest you let it. You be the ones who say what that message a God is. You be the ones make the laws—'til the jails are all for them 'stead a you—'til obey the laws means keep their hands off your property—'til this shithole street full a shacks is where they're livin'."

He waited—until at last he heard one of them say "Amen," and then another and another, until they all had said "Amen," and had nodded their heads, and closed their right-hand fists and pumped them as a statement of commitment, a confession of faith. And when it became quiet again, Watt looked across them all once more and said, "There was a time, y'all—when this world all got started—this world where we're over here and they're over there, where they got it all and we got nothin'. And that startin' time came when some white boy said Gon' take what I need, and what I need's got no *enough* to it, no sleepy fuckin' limit to it, no dividin' line to it except line a pride after line a pride 'til I got the whole gotdamn thing. And then, after he took it all, that white boy he brought in sweet Jesus, and then the preacher man, and he told that preacher man to say this world, with its one big white *property line,* it's the good world God wants, and all y'all nobodies out there, you got to accept this world in the name a God, and obey the rules protects it in the name a God, lest you don't want God lovin' you, lest you don't care if you spend forever in the fire a hell 'stead a that sweet place a peace God gon' give you you keep your mouth shut and you do what you're told. And then some dumb fuckin' nigga he sings a spiritual. And then every dumb fuckin' nigga in America, land a the white man, he joins on in with tears comin' out his eyes. And th'only thing better for killin' dead that gangsta gon' change the gotdamn word—the only thing better than their jails—is their Jesus, sweet man a peace."

Watt stepped toward them, his twelve—extending out his closed right fist, inviting them to stand and to touch their fists together with his—which they did, every one. And as they all now held their right fists touched together, he said to them, "And who is it speakin' Jesus-peace now, and equality, and obey the soft fuckin' sleepy rules and I'll give you heaven—who's workin' on your fear a dyin', fear a bein' the gangsta you're born to be, the one thinks you're gon' lay down on your belly and roll up your backside for a fuckin', is that chickenshit nigga calls himself Bennie Twin Bill. Time for peace, my brothas—and

196

SHE SAY YOU COULDA BEEN A PREACHER MAN

time for war. And you lift your hands together with me if you understand what time it is now."

Thus it began. And after he'd given all his twelve, one by one, sets of specific instructions on how to make headway here, and here, and *here* into the territories of Benny Twin Bill, every inch of which was drawn up clear and exact on the military map in his mind, Watt, as he sent them out to start their new lives, as a last gauntlet, told them with a quiet ferocity how much it would mean to do some *thing* that confirmed them in their new lives forever, so there could be no coming back, not this side the grave.

When they had gone, he told Keeta T, as he watched the cars crunch back out across the abandoned rubble-lots, to fetch him his jacket. As she brought him his Guess brown lightweight, Keeta could feel the heft of his gun in the side zipper pocket. "Gon' pay you a second visit to the Twin Bill?" she asked him, soft-voiced. He didn't answer, just took the jacket in one hand and then her cheeks round her mouth in the other—tight between his forefinger and thumb. "You ask me a question like that again," he said, squeezing up her mouth to the point of pain, "it's gon' cost you." He turned from her then, and went out—zipping the jacket's collar up around his neck as he descended the stairs. "Same motherfuckin' animal you always was," Keeta T said, as she listened to the door shut behind him. "Animal since you's a ten-year-old chil', though you gramma she say you coulda been a preacher man. Make me laugh."

Watt, having put his message into his men, starting things irrevocably toward a street war like those he knew on bloody Division—would walk now to reflect on things he'd have to do himself, and hadn't done yet. Do, and do soon. No stoppin' half way over the river a blood. Got to go all the way. Sara Lee, she sensed it that there's trouble gon' find those cousins—college boy and the Tumbler—says it's got to be another way to get what you need and not harm those boys. "I don't know Robert Teague," she says, "but I know Marcus. How bright that boy is. How beautiful. How gentle. And I know that his cousin Robert has come from a better world and so he might have all the beauty and brightness of Marcus even raised up, by his mother, and his father, who Marcus told me is the best man he's ever known." And Sara looked at him—and she said, "So don't you bring any harm to those beautiful boys just to help yourself. There is always another way. Always."

DIVISION

Watt turned onto Cottage Grove, and, as he liked to do, bringing things to the point of absolute all or nothing, walked up to the District 3 station and stood there looking in. He waited, a long moment—then continued north down Cottage. He thought about how none of his twelve had the brains of those schoolboy cousins. None. But Sara doesn't know about that alley...though it's known. And if it wasn't known where he was...it was known. He always knew it would all be known, before he ever came back from N'Orleans, where he could never stay. So it's same now as ever...same do or die.... Since he's a kid... never different. He saw their faces, heard, as he walked on now, Robert Teague making his college-boy speeches, and saw Tumbler spittin' on his hands and flyin' on down that alley to put a smile on the face a ol' Jesse White wouldn't come off. But nothin' else to say about it. And that white boy saw me too. So time'll come, time's here, when I signal to the homeys in County that it's got to be some jailhouse dust-up takes mah boy Tumbler's life. And white boy out stumblin' around shit drunk on the streets. Sorry-ass motherfucker. Gon' follow him for good now and find a good dark spot for a killin' accident I hit and run from. People got t'think the fool's just drunk-stumble one time too many. And the revolution boy, black college boy. River a blood—and on the otha side, a kingdom. No different from any kingdom ever was. Ask any king how it was he got there. All the same. There's those that cross, and those that don't.

He had come to the end of the long west wall of Oak Woods Cemetery. Oak Woods, where Robert Teague had said they threw all in one big hole the scattered, washed-up bones of the six thousand Confederate war prisoners who died at the notorious Camp Douglas, Chicago's dark secret. Fuck that shit, Watt thought, as he looked east a block down 67th and saw the closed iron bars of the cemetery's gate. I'd a been in charge, those slave-masterin' motherfuckers woulda been thrown out the December lake and their bull-whippin' asses all frozen out there till their white fuckin' bones washed up on those beaches niggas got killed f'wantin' to swim at—back in the day.

198

CONFIDING

Mary Tate Teague placed a glass-globe vase on her dining-room table and began to arrange the dozen white roses it held. Each of the whites had bloomed well open and yet was still unfolding; all were gorgeous and right when set under the softened chandelier light, against the glowing dark cherry of her table. For thirty years she had lived at 3314 S. Calumet with Maurice Teague, who purchased the house in 1965, thirty-four years ago, when nearly all its best things were boarded up, broken or defaced, and who spent then four years working to bring it back, room by room, to its origins. Just twenty years past the Civil War, 1885, the house was built—by the same construction company that built Olivet, right down the way on Martin Luther King, Mary Tate's and Maurice's church for all their Chicago lives, and to which, all their married years, they'd walked together, every Sunday, rain or shine. But changes were coming. Robert had begun his fourth year at DePaul and Carolyn her third. Her children would be moving on into their own lives, and the nest would empty, and would come perhaps to seem too big, too vacant, too lonely. But it was so hard for Mary Tate to imagine leaving 3314, every inch

DIVISION

of which she had made hers, Maurice his. Every object, every picture, every piece of furniture in every room had for each of them its personal history. And that her home would someday just pass into the hands of a stranger....

"Every evening I spoke to ghosts here," Maurice had said to her, when recently they talked about the day they might leave. "As the darkness would come on, when I was alone here working—ghosts of the craftsmen who first put together what I was bringing back, and who I was sure couldn't trust a black man; of the architect; of the wealthy white first owners...angry, territorial ghosts disturbed by my presence here, as owner; and ghosts of the first-wave southern blacks who huddled here, early as 1910, in the tight slum-rental partitions when the whites fled because of their coming; ghosts of my own migrant Mississippi family, who came here—December of '47, in the second great wave; the ghost of my mother, sweet Early Dawn; of my strong, good father, Aaron Robert, who took us to Chicago, after Jesse's disappearance, to lift us up from what he'd been mired in from the day of his Mississippi birth, back before the turn of the century—extreme, uneducated poverty—violent, murderous apartheid; and ghosts of the dangerous, frightening people we were penned in here with; and of the frightened; and of the slum lords who never looked in or cared who was here but whose names were on the deed, which I made mine. Ownership, Mary Tate—every innocent, color-blind board and nail whispered to me in my nights by myself here that it's got to be both a hard, caring, loving holding on, when you make a place yours, and in the end a smooth letting go, each one, the possession and the handing over, right and good as the other, if you want to lay old ghosts and leave none behind."

She sat in a chair that faced a front window and could see the glow from their funeral home's parking-lot light, which shone on that flag, red, with its starred, blue X-cross. And soon would come the stone, permanent, with the six thousand names, each one of a child of God, Maurice would say. How much persecution would they suffer for his righteousness' sake? Epithets out of the windows of cars; threatening remarks; people spitting as she passed; friends shunning her at Olivet. And now she'd seen Maurice pick something up off their front steps, a bullet, she was sure, set upright and that Maurice—who had never lied to her—said was "nothing, just a little twig." She couldn't drive her only too human heart beyond divisions. She wasn't so good at forgiving so-called sons of God. And what if she had to forgive Maurice

CONFIDING

because of something that happened because of something he did, for his righteousness' sake? Please, Lord, let it go to the final end, she prayed. From the very start, over thirty years ago, and every hour since, she had loved Maurice Teague with all her heart. And the greatest of all her fears was that she would ever come to love him any less. To the final end, Lord, she prayed—let me love him as I always have.

But she couldn't stop fearing for her son, Robert, either. Far more for Robert than ever for her own personal safety she was afraid, for the evil was still out there. The beast called Watt. Or stop fearing for Marcus, sweetest boy all his life, best boy ever raised in the middle of hell, and now imprisoned even deeper in hell. The Cook County Jail. Dear, dearest Dosey, who'd suffered so much, having tried so hard with her children.... What would that white boy at trial say Marcus didn't do or did? And please, Lord God, never let Robert Teague be charged —or be hurt, all because he happened to be where he happened to be that night...not wanting to come home...because of that flag.... If only Maurice had called Robert sooner.... Lord, I beg you, never let me suffer such a grief as to see my son in any way lost to me. And I'm told that both of them were here—that white boy and his brother, the poor child—no mercy shown him, none, by that Watt. St. Ignatius boys, just like Robert. Perhaps in this very room. So many things brought so close together in my life—in my mind. And the only result of the closeness is fear.

"It's so real, Car. So beyond choice—beyond anything you can just tell to *stop*—I mean the way he might just break into a sweat—or might just go off in his anger—maybe at blacks—maybe at you if he saw you— some terrible burst out of nowhere—and you don't know when it will come. But I've brought up Robert to him—even though I was afraid to. And he's still there—the real Connor—the one who with his last breath will defend Robert's innocence and Marcus's too. And the real Connor *will* be there for Marcus, when the time comes. I don't need to—but I promise you I'll keep on helping with this. But the real healing.... If I could go into where he's hurt—and dig out the malignancy inside him—if I could do it, it would be the thing in this life that made me happiest. But I just don't know. Six weeks since he first was here. And still the drinking...not always but.... He'll come by every three or four days. Sometimes sober...sometimes not. And still...anger... sudden explosions, which half the time he doesn't remember. I don't know if I have the answer."

201

DIVISION

Carolyn Teague, lying on her bed, on the phone with her best friend, Ellie Shea, could hear, even as she was on the phone, her father and brother upstairs in the library, and she knew what they were talking about, even though she couldn't make out their words. If her mother weren't downstairs, she would be involved as well. The one house with its three stories, all the Teagues enduring one pain together, but her mother, downstairs, suffering her separate resentment for what her father had done and was doing; and her father up in his study, alone in that distant determination of his, now trying to explain it, again, to Robert, who still struggles...and Robert's sister, that father's daughter, and that mother's...in her bedroom, separate and alone in her own way.... Carolyn was glad she'd be spending next semester in Italy—for every hour here now, this common pain but also lonely suffering was inescapable. And six months ago, this house knew none of it.

There had been silence on the other end—a long moment. Carolyn began to think she and Ellie got disconnected. But at last then, Ellie, in a voice Carolyn strained to hear, "There's something I've never told you." Again silence. Carolyn heard her father and brother. At last, then, "There was this night...about a year ago. Jeanie Bessette and Molly Joyce and I stopped into Butch McGuire's. And Connor and Jack Riordan were there. You know this. You know I've always had feelings for Connor. And it's more than you know—way more—more than I had ever wanted to talk about. Intense, painful—even though there'd never been a single thing in the way of words spoken between us— which was always the problem. But that night it had been some time since I'd seen him, so my heart just started pounding when I saw him." Ellie again went silent a moment—then, "But when he saw me, after looking right *at* me, eye to eye, he just turned away. Turned his back, and before I got to where he was, he'd walked off to join this other group of guys and girls at the other end of the bar. And this would be s.o.p. with him for *ever.*"

"Did it ever occur to you, girl, that that can be a good sign?" In an instinct of her friendship with Ellie, Carolyn had tried to say this in a light, teasing way. But she had sensed, as well, that there'd be no easy bringing things back to normal.

Yet now Ellie did say, "It actually was...a good sign. He's told me that he was just feeling too much—that he'd always been afraid of his own feelings—for me. And I told him that I knew exactly what he meant— because I'd always been afraid of my feelings for him. It's so crazy.

202

CONFIDING

You're afraid to communicate, and when you do, you don't know if
your words are real or unreal. We didn't know whether to laugh or
cry when we confessed all this to each other—about how we'd felt, all
the way back to the beginning of things, at Ignatius. But right then,
we should just have stopped wondering about things and made love."

"You haven't yet?"

"No. And I don't know. There's so much trouble there now. But that
night at Butch's. If we'd known each other's feelings. So much might
be different now.... Might be so different...."

Carolyn's mind was beginning to extend filaments, readying itself
to weave things—as she listened.

"But I just got really angry," Ellie said. "My heart, even after years
of nothing from him, had just started beating hard—again—when I
saw him. But then I tried to make myself ice, when he turned away.
I said, *That's it. I'm done. No more hope or expectation along that line—ever.*
And there was Jack, his brother." She stopped again. She was stifling a
moan of pain, Carolyn could tell. Then, "Oh my God, I wish you were
with me now. I need your shoulder—as much as you've ever needed
mine, with all that's happened to your family."

Carolyn felt things coming yet closer. She could hear her mother on
the stairs. Jack Riordan. Ellie said his name. God knew what all was
coming. But let things come, Carolyn thought—'til they were all as
close and personal as possible. "Tell it to me, Ell," she said, "whatever
it is. Jack Riordan."

"There's just so much. But.... At Butch's—that night—try as I might
to forget he was there, all I was thinking of was Connor. I knew, without looking, exactly what he was doing. He's told me it was the same
for him—with me. But somehow—or I know damn well how—after
two hours of this, his never looking over, never coming over, even to
see his brother—I ended up leaving. With his brother. We all left with
Jack, for the Standard on Milwaukee, Jeanie and Molly and I. But it
was such a different thing for me—this Jacko Riordan night—than it
was for them—because of Connor. And then at about two-thirty in the
morning, we went back to Jeanie's. And I'm still having the feeling
of walking out that door at Butch's. I can still feel Connor over my
shoulder—feel him looking at me, even if he wasn't—and feel like I
was slapping him in his face as I walked out with his brother. And I
don't know—is that when you know the feelings you have for someone are the real thing?—when there's so much anger right there ready

203

DIVISION

to happen? Anger and self-protective pride and rash spite, the shittiest of feelings...but which you wouldn't be feeling if you weren't in love? And the way Jack talked about Connor that night. It was all mixed up with brotherly affection, but I could feel this sort of serious rivalry. Cain and Abel. And it was like we were in a conspiracy—Cain and I."

Again she stopped, sighing now audibly. Carolyn could hear her hand tapping—hard—on some surface. At last, then, "At the end of the night...we ended up alone, in this room at Jeanie's, Jack Riordan and I. And this is so hard to say. Not because of the what but because of the *why*. We had sex. God, I still can't believe it. Jack Riordan and I had sex that night. And Connor was the motive. For both of us. *That* was the desire. That was what kept pushing things till four in the morning, or whatever hour it was going to take. And when we were in bed, Jack said something. Or really just whispered to the wall—but definitely so I could hear—that he was sure that Connor, or 'little brother,' wished he were the one who was here, with me. And his saying this suddenly shocked me into this intense hope. I had become dead certain that night—and this is what really explains my anger—that Connor Riordan and I were *never* to be—because of his...I didn't know...his always turning away from me. But if Jack's saying what he said about *little brother* wishing he were the one in bed with me did give me that shock of hope, it worked too...like dirty pillow talk—and it 'moved' us both. God. Jesus. How this has made me wonder who I am. And I don't *ever* want to be who I was that night, especially because of the pathetic *why* of it all. I can't stand it. I.... There's so much I wish had never happened...."

Carolyn immediately in an impulse of friendship deeper even than her curiosity—"Sex will take us places that don't have anything to do with who we really are—false places that let us know that we are *not* the sum of our actions—that we are not what we *did,* even if we were all on fire when we did it. You talk about the real Connor. I know him, too. I know, even though he saw his brother murdered in cold blood by a black man, that his race anger isn't the real Connor Riordan. I've had race anger that isn't the real me. I have it every day. And, Ellie, I know the real you. And I *know* that sex can take us to false places. I've been to false places, not just with race, but with sex." Truly Carolyn would let Ellie know that beyond all those simple and unjust courts of so-called justice that ask only what you *did*—that she was understood, and forgiven. She had spoken to Ellie now too in the way of a kind, caring

204

CONFIDING

preparation; for she was certain that her friend had more to confess.

"I love you, Carolyn Teague," Ellie said, "my truest confidante."

Ellie stopped again. And Carolyn waited. She was certain not only that her friend had more to say but that she was quietly pleading for help to get free of burdens. "There's more, isn't there. And you want to let it all go. So let it go."

"Oh, my sweet friend," Ellie said, her voice trembling, "you know there's more. And...the stupidity...the irony...as if some twisted god were in charge of my life. Not just did we have no real feelings for each other, none, but we both...Jack and I...were in some kind of thing that just *proves* how stupid-sick sex can be...how the sickness heats up the sex...in this witch's brew of sick stupidity."

Carolyn heard anger in her friend's voice, but also still the quavering that said she was on the verge of tears.

"And of course—oh my God—of *course* I got pregnant."

"Oh, Ellie...."

"I got *pregnant*. And when I found out, I cried so hard I ended up laughing like some hysterical insane woman. I was out of my mind. Ten hours one day...just sobbing...thinking how all I wanted was Connor and I had Jack—inside me. And where do you run, from something *inside* you. But we *are* what we do. I mean, you can't divide yourself from it—by some *choice*. That is a total joke, believe me. Or at least for somebody like me. But I couldn't make a sacrifice of my entire life for the random biological stupidity of it all. And the fact that it wasn't even *me* who had that sex. So all the arguments for abortion became so hopeful for me now. Those familiar arguments...became my personal litany of saints: my body, my privacy, my inside, my health, my future, my ownership of myself, my right *not* to be a good Samaritan to this alien Jack inside me, who was *not* a person. *Not*. Not yet viable. Not conscious. Not sensible of pleasure or pain. Not capable of desire. Not *anything*, just potential, which is nothing actual."

She stopped. She breathed now in shorter, quicker breaths. And Carolyn, with a ready contempt in her mind cutting off all the platitudes, said nothing, rather waited for the rest to come.

"But for somebody like me...good lapsed-Catholic girl, but still Catholic to the bone...what all this does is set off the opposite argument, which you hear then non-stop: how if I didn't take aggressive action against it—if I didn't actively intervene, because this isn't about not doing something, simply opting *not* to be a good Samaritan to

205

what's inside you, it's about walking over to the other side of the road, *actively,* with a knife, and ending something that's living and growing —if I didn't do that, then this nothing inside me would be capable of a full human future. So it all falls apart, and those saints don't intervene for you with any god...if there were any who would listen. But you just can't sacrifice your own real potential and real life to something so undeveloped, so *invisible,* unknown, alien, and *unwanted.* And now arguments for actual self-defense start coming to you, because you feel like, or maybe let yourself feel like your life is in danger, the actual *life* of the mother, as if what was inside you were a cancer about to metastasize, and not a growing person. But then you say to yourself, *You're just rationalizing!* And it all goes back—to the opposite. It's not a disease but a child—and not just his, but yours."

Carolyn, even as with full compassion she listened, had already moved ahead—to the conclusion—because there had been no child. And because she was thinking also immediately of the murder, and of her brother, and her cousin...because it was Jack Riordan, the victim, who'd gotten Ellie pregnant, she asked, "When you told him, did he help you, Jack Riordan?"

"He did. He was good to me. Never ran. Never asked a question. But it gets so much more confusing. His mother found out. She heard Jack once on the phone. And she insisted on helping, on paying for it...even though I was in no need of money. And I thought it was good to let Jack help me...good for him. But what I think now is that maybe she wanted just to confirm a change in her life...to make some no-going-back kind of statement. It turns out she'd gotten pregnant when she was young and that that's why she got married to Professor Riordan. I would never let this out—but it's out already. She's told the world. But it's all so complicated. He's totally pro-life, Professor Riordan, passionately pro-life. And so is Connor. And...I don't know where to run from all this in my own mind, because I don't know how I feel myself, I truly don't. But we just so needed, Jack and I, to separate ourselves from what was never us in the first place. But now I'm so tangled with it...."

She was crying. Carolyn waited until she stopped. "Right now," Carolyn said, "I hear you working this out. And don't stop. You're with *me.* You know there's nothing you need to hide."

Ellie took a slow, deep breath. And another. Then, "Connor, with me...blaming himself for things.... But I've asked things, too.... I don't know why we want to know. But we have to know.... We can't

CONFIDING

not know." She stopped, then, slowly, began again. "On the night he died, Jack...got in this argument...with his father...not about me...but about abortion. So it *was* about me. And when he stormed out of the house, he got Connor to go with him. But as they sat in the car...in the alley...they started to fight—about abortion, because Connor had asked Jack what had gone on between his father and him. And Connor, suspicious about why his own brother, a Riordan, had suddenly turned pro-choice, got out of Jack all that we'd done. And it all came out about his mother's involvement, too. But it came out specifically about Jack and me, I think, because Connor's mind was driven to questions by his memory of that night at Butch's.... And that's exactly when it happened.... As they were sitting in the alley fighting about what Jack and I had done, and about their mother—that's when Robert and Marcus and the murderer came down the alley.... And Jack was all worked up and angry...and so he got defiant with the murderer. Oh, dearest God, I can't... I cannot get free of thinking I'm part of the reason.... That if it weren't for me.... And his *mother*.... And she's now left Professor Riordan for someone else, saying she'd been forced into a marriage she never wanted and had now to get her life back. And before she left, Connor had brutal confrontations with her, in the aftermath of Jack's death, all about her seeking *her* life. And he's so infested now with all these snakes of rage—about Jack, about his mother. And I'm *not* insane—I know I'm not truly the cause of it all.... But I feel like I *am* at the center of all this pain. And I just want to make *something* better.... It all comes at me in my dreams. And it carries into when I'm awake. I see Jack's casket, closed because of the violence of his death. He wouldn't be recognizable—because of the horrible way he was killed. And he seems ten million miles away from anyone I ever knew. And that saddens me...so terribly. We didn't have love, not even affection. But I can't bear that he's so utterly alien—and gone. And he was killed...he died...and is gone forever—all because of an overwrought moment. And I was carrying his child, which is just another alien thing for my mind—and it, too, gone where? The nothingness. My not being able to reach or touch anyone or anything—or do anything—it's so painful. And his mother and father standing there, at the wake. It was incredibly hard. I swear she hates me, Jackie Riordan, when you'd think it might be sympathy—but no, the total opposite. And Connor. I so want him. I want him so bad I'm bleeding with it. But he's so lost. And is he supposed to forget that his brother and I did

207

DIVISION

what we did? Just forget? And forgive! Just press delete on all images of it. What about the images in *his* dreams? And all *he* believes in? And Marcus is in so much trouble. And Robert has this agony in his life, and you and your mother and father. I know I'm just putting things together, constructing them, all to torture myself, and that it isn't fair to myself to think that none of it would have happened if Jack and Connor weren't there fighting about me—and if Jack had never fought with his father because of me. And if there'd never been that night at Butch's. But I've even dreamed I was Watt's companion—dreamed I'm the smiling whore under his arm as he raises his gun. And pro-life placards, saying *Stop Abortion Now* and *MURDER*—shaken in my face. All this in my dreams. And I can't ever help anybody. I'm in the middle of all this pain and I can't do a thing. I so want just to take Connor *into* me, make love to him and heal all that pain. But I feel so helpless. I can't make Connor better, or anyone. I don't know where to begin."

Carolyn had sat up on her bed, and now, still sitting, she turned and set her feet on the floor. She bent down her head. "Here's where you begin," she said. "You say we are what we have done. We can't divide ourselves from it. We have to take responsibility for it. I say we are not what we have done and that responsibility is one thing and who we really are is another. And I see you, by the way, as responsible for none of the things you blame yourself for—and I *blame* you for none. But because you blame yourself for everything, you also have this desire to fix everything and help everyone. And what I see is the real Ellie Shea, right now and for her life, making *use* of her feelings of helplessness and guilt to inspire herself. To do what? Maybe to love the whole damned world and care for it 'til the day she's gone from it. You had an abortion. You chose. And it didn't come easy. You say you can never *choose* to make the difficulties go away. But all of what you've done and thought or dreamed you've done—your conscience regarding it, and the wisdom that's in your pain—all of it is making the real you, not casually divide yourself from your past actions, but caringly, wisely divide yourself from them, and *just enough,* Ellie, so that what you've done is going always to be there beside you, inspiring you towards kindness and caring but never to be on top of you so damned much that you end up crippled by self-hatred. The sinner is and is not the sin—that's your life, my sweet, good friend, and your life will be beautiful because you are and you are not what you have done. I'd say you start with knowing that. I'd say you already know it. I could hear it in every word you said."

Ellie, softly now, and as if she were closing her eyes in a prayer of gratitude, said, "If you only knew, Carolyn Teague, how much I love you."

"Simple rule of life," Carolyn said. "If you love a friend, as I do you, the love'll be returned. So I do know."

For over an hour, in his library, Maurice Teague and his son, Robert, had been discussing Marcus Sabbs's situation—his legal counsel, the dangers Marcus faced in County, the likelihood that amongst the gangsters at County there might be henchmen of Watt—and then, once more, how Watt came to be Watt, with both father and son, now in a partnership of thought, measuring the weight of blame that might be placed here or here or here—in racial history; in social injustice; in poverty; in slavery, chattel and economic; or in the independent character of Watt himself; or in the original sin in the Garden. No antagonism, father and son discussed these questions regarding the man Watt. But the flag was flying still at the Teague Funeral Home, and Robert, who now had risen from his chair and moved to the window, looked out upon it. Then with a suddenness that, rather than come as a surprise, seemed to bring things at once to the point to which they'd all along been tending, he turned to his father: "You spoke to me of Artesia, of a bridge over a creek, of a white man who sped by you in his truck, of a creek bed that you would walk down for thinking. But then you asked me not to ask you for anything more. Yet you told everything to me in such a way that I would have to ask sometime for what it was you couldn't say."

Maurice now rose, and moved slowly across the room to stand beside his son. As he had for days now, with the terrible recent bloodshed and trouble—and as he had for years—he was thinking of the secrecy that long ago Early Dawn had sworn him to; for his mother had feared that if his father ever knew what had been done to Jesse, and by whom, he would take to murderous retaliation—and then to a certainty, in the cycle of violence, be slain himself by the whites in revenge for the revenge he'd taken. And so, because he never would be told, Aaron Robert Teague, never took the law into his own hands—and in the end channeled his sorrow over his son's disappearance, and his vague, suspecting fear, into a hard determination to leave the South forever. And more than half a century ago, he did take his family from Mississippi

DIVISION

to Chicago—to the city's Douglas neighborhood, which even then had long been called Bronzeville, in the center of Chicago's own Black Belt, and to this very house—where Maurice now stood with his own son, whose asking for what he asked, Maurice most certainly had made inevitable.

Maurice now placed his hand on Robert's arm. "You and Carolyn, Robert—you're what I will give.... You're the future...." He for a moment closed his eyes. Then, as he looked again into his son's face, "But our past, Robert Teague, I mean not the whole of black history but that personal past, our family history, from which I've come, and you've come.... It has dark hidden things...secrets personal to us, which— because my mother made me swear to keep them, I have kept virtually all my life. I know the value of secrets. I know that secrets save lives. They saved my father's life. And because my father would go to his grave not knowing something terrible that I, his son, knew, I promise you—this only multiplied immeasurably my compassion for him as he lay dying; and still in my memory of him, all is multiplied, my love, my respect for him, all my feelings of honor for him—because of those secret things he never knew. And for my beautiful mother I bore the secrets deep in my heart, because I believed and still believe she was inspired by the Lord when she swore me to secrecy. I was not yet twelve years old."

For fifty-four years, Maurice had kept inside himself the dark truths about Jesse's death, which, no more than his father should have known them, should his children; for these truths must educate Carolyn and Robert into the soul-killing curse of racial bitterness and anger—and could involve them even in that cycle of violence from which, above all else, he wanted to free them. Always he had believed that the vow he swore had committed him to nothing less than a taking of those truths with him to the grave. But Aaron Robert Teague was now gone these forty-one years, and Early Dawn more than thirty; and in deepest truth the thing that finally brought Maurice's soul through the hell of anger and beyond it, past all divisions into the oneness of his God, was nothing other than the dark obscenity of Jesse's death. The agony, the torturing guilt of leaving Jesse un-mourned, un-buried. The desecration of his mutilation. Only an extreme of darkness can produce the extreme of light that is true salvation. And in his most kind and courageous brother's sacred blood, Maurice's soul at last had been washed

CONFIDING

clean. All persons are equal children of God before they are children of men. To come to understand this deepest truth in the freedom and undivided oneness of God takes nothing less than the blood of tragedy. And by the violence and suffering, the terror and pity, that his own eyes had now seen, Robert, Maurice was sure, was ready to find that ultimate light of truth which shines only in the full truth of darkness. Maurice looked out at the billowing flag, which he would replace with the stone; and standing at his library's window with his son, he would now finish what he'd started: "He's long ago gone to his Maker, Robert, but Mac Randall was the white man's name...."

HEART OF
DARKNESS

Undecided, Connor Riordan had crossed Division and wandered awhile among the bars on Rush, a couple of hours, until he thought, "Fuck it. This is the day." His beer and whiskey buzz made his walk a little heavy. But he wasn't stumbling. He wiped his hand across his mouth. He liked the feel of his high. Then back up at Division—he turned west, which put Cabrini immediately upon his horizon. He passed Butch's without looking, though he was thinking he could bury himself there, but good. He'd called her, told her he was from the *Trib,* Annabelle Lester, the grandmother—and it seemed she'd bought it. He resolved to see her.

George had given him her name. How many times now had he seen George Rudkus? Three? Four? He'd given Connor his cell number, and Connor then put it in his contacts because, yeah, George no doubt knew what was up when he put it to him hard that *Watt was out there*— and that nobody was ever more than seven feet from a spider. "Pull a drive-by in broad daylight. It wouldn't be his first. So you learn to look, and to take cover if you see something rolling toward you strange. Or a car window suddenly coming down. And call me if you need me."

HEART OF DARKNESS

By a gun, a person's life could be blown away faster than the sound would come. And maybe today would be his day to be rejoined with Jacko. My brother...he'd stop anybody who tried to hurt me. And because of this grandmother's grandson.... Fucking Satan. Shit stink of sulfur. Jacko.... He didn't hear my pleas. He wouldn't listen. Because I'd made him crazy! I guilted him into rash anger and defiance, and it....

Connor shook his head, stopped, breathed slowly. He wiped his mouth, then started again westward along Division. George said this grandmother was an activist. Lived in the Whites since they went up in '62—thirty-seven years. And before that, from the time she was twelve, it was the Rows. A Cabrini lifer. Half a century. And now an activist. Part of the tenant group, George said, that won the consent agreement for one-for-one replacements for demolished public housing units. Had joined the fight for a right of return for displaced Cabrini residents forced to move by the wrecking ball and given not units in the neighborhood—rather only Section-8s, which the court deemed sufficient for the satisfaction of the one-for-one replacement agreement. So the Great Transformation was begun. "And between us and the wall and the relieved white population," George put it finally, "they've got as much chance of coming back to Division St. as the Palestinians to Tel Aviv."

Ahead of Connor now on Division, Cabrini began more and more to rise up as a shadow-casting wall. And Christ Jesus—the Jane-Jacobs-I-told-you-so *mistake* of these "projects"—these "developments." The grim modernist tower-world of the vertical ghetto. Send 'em up higher and higher so they'll never spread out a single inch wider, toward our world. Richard J wanted concentration camps. And he fucking got 'em. But not the great wall-face it was—rather now the massing punctured by the power of the ball and crane. 16,000 people, George said, now down to 6,000, but maybe another 5,000 squatters come out lately from under who knew what rock to squat in the unfilled vacancies alongside the gangbangers, who use the abandoned units for gun armories, whore houses, crack dens, and maybe discipline and interrogation rooms. "Power vacuums everywhere, with the old main gangs breaking up—and gangsters, with their old home buildings taken down, now feeling the need for new fortresses. Power grabs. Every little tribe for itself. Word was, Watt, smelling his opportunity, had moved to the building they call Camp Ball on Sedgwick from his old

213

building on Division, 534, where he'd lived near the grandmother—building they call Tha Jube."

"What does it mean, Tha Jube?" Connor had asked. "It means," George had said, "everything the black world knows and the white world and the police force will never find out."

But as he came up to Wells, the street to the west of which, not that long ago, you'd never leave your car, Connor saw no changes to black, no fading away of the white world, rather a continuing line of upscale shops and offices—and white people all around: white pedestrians, white cyclists, white women. He kept on, and felt, so far, un-threatened...un-triggered. And as he approached Orleans, still it was half white at least. He looked under the "L" tracks for Carson Field, site of the movie *Hardball,* site of the old Cooley High, but the ball field was as gone as the school, and what no doubt were high-priced condos stood where the field had been. And just this side of the tracks, a library, looking very new and very nice. And lots of white people, still, some walking even south toward, and right on into, Seward Park, where no white person would ever venture, even maybe half a year ago.

Concentrated poverty and intransigent goalless and hopeless dependency combined with highest-density urban dwelling, and in those high-rise prison cages. Look at those balconies all steel-wire shut, so nobody could drop down a bowling ball nineteen stories on someone's skull or throw a living person screaming over the railings. The whole fucking shithole the most perfect formula for disaster and bloodshed. Mothers fifteen stories up, high on crack, screwin' for another dope score, and their pre-teen kids sellin' the shit down on the shell-casing dump of a so-called playground—in the ultimate perfection of un-supervision. Only a complete ass-wipe idiot wouldn't want these pieces of shit torn down. And only the same moron weeps a tear over the city's gentrification, rather than celebrates it, which in truth every white person does, no matter what he or she might say in the public white voice. Right now I'm walking where not long back I would have had my throat slit. And what do my wandering eyes behold but a Starbucks!

A white girl in her Starbucks apron out talking to a cop in his patrol car, leaning over with her hands on the roof. Pretty face. Funky hair, purple, black. Sweet, sweet body. Bet that boy in blue would like to protect and serve her, all right. Let her wear his cop cap when she rode his night stick. What? Did I pipe that bullshit out loud? She'd turned her head and was now looking over at him, maybe having felt his eyes

HEART OF DARKNESS

on her. Could she read my mind? Or what the hell? But now she smiled, as if to say, maybe, isn't it nice not to be afraid anymore to come down here? Don't we white people love it? And Connor, while he kept walking along Division, the Walk signal being lit at Clybourn, smiled back as if to say, yes, we do.

But it wasn't three minutes farther west before it seemed as if that girl's smile had marked the frontier border of the civilized world. Chicago—with borderlines and boundaries ever and always on its postlapsarian brain. South Side. North Side. And all the other lines and cuts that mark hard racial divisions—train tracks—expressways—major streets—park boundaries. Not welcome to Englewood. Not welcome to Lawndale. Not welcome to Bronzeville. Not welcome to Beverly. Not welcome to Bridgeport. Not welcome to Humboldt Park. Not welcome to Marquette Park. Not welcome to Edison Park. Not welcome to Greater Grand Crossing. And on and on, the most segregated city in the goddamned world splits and cracks. But maybe nowhere the way it does here on Division, with the Cabrini Reds on the south and the equally notorious, shithole Whites on the north—black on black crime's world-infamous Mason-Dixon. Gang versus gang. Vice Lords. Disciples. Walk the wrong path, and you're dust. "The Castle" torn down ten years back because it was the most dangerous place in America. And here he was, lone white boy—and nowhere near shitfaced enough. Blacks everywhere now. Only blacks. And seeming hard cases. And the rank stupidity of his so-called plan—to say he was a reporter from the *Trib,* needing an interview with the activist grandmother. "Tell those young men in the lobby you're looking for 'Mother Lester'," she had said on the phone. Safer maybe to play a heroin junkie ready to Jones.

"Hey, brotherrrrrrrrrrrrrr." He heard a mocking voice behind him on the Division St. sidewalk. Should he turn? He heard steps behind him, coming closer. He didn't run—rather did turn—to see four blacks, none in black leather, none with a dark-silk bandana. Or with a gun? Ball caps. Two had White Sox caps, black, brims angled to the right— but no school jackets with a W. They were young, maybe just fifteen or sixteen. One wore a basketball headband, dark blue, one a hoodie with his hood up. Connor said fast, "You guys know Mother Lester? I'm looking for 534 Division, where she lives. I'm from the newspaper."

"Whatchoo want her for?" one of the ones with a White Sox cap asked.

215

"I've come to interview her about her fight to keep Cabrini residents from getting screwed by the City."

"She too late," the one with the headband said—and they all laughed.

The other boy with a Sox cap now asked—was it with real belligerence?—"Got you a *press pass?*" He was big. He made the others laugh, but he didn't laugh. "No press pass, mistah, can't let you go, one way or anotha."

"Just wanted to talk to her," Connor said, feeling the sweat pooling in the palms of his hands—but also readying to break into some kind of wild show of rage, not caring what it would cost. If he had a gun....

"Ain't got no press pass, man," the big one said now, turning his mouth down in a determined scowl—or was he just playing him?— "we might just have to...."

But now there came the weird electrified *whoop* of a police siren, and a blue and white CPD patrol car that had just been passing them on Division suddenly pulled a U-turn back across traffic, and came up with a screech to the sidewalk where Connor suddenly found himself alone, the four young blacks having beaten a retreat, fast-walking and then trotting away into the canyons of the projects, immediately as the siren had sounded.

The driver-seat window of the patrol car came down. A full-faced, red-moustached white cop, sitting next to a black partner, looked at Connor with his mouth turned down. "Narcotics, ya dumb fuck, 'll get ya dead six ways from Sunday. Learn the value of life—and get your white ass back the hell east. Get home to your goddamned family. And get some help." He put up the window, then pulled off fast, with his car set still against traffic for a hundred yards, turning then hard and bouncing up into the projects, with the blue lights of the patrol car flashing.

Connor remained where he was until the flashing blue lights were gone out of sight. Just three minutes east and he'd be back again over the border—into Starbucks territory. The value of life.... The chicken-shit knows. Just turn back towards Starbucks, three minutes. But he must by now be in the 500s West, with Larabee, 600, not far ahead. And that building now only a little farther west down Division, set back behind its parking lot, must be 534. No number was visible as he walked into the near-empty parking lot, crossing toward the building's dark hole of an open-recess entry, but there it was, black spray-painted on the wall: *Tha Jube.*

He counted the high-rise's stories, following up from the tenth a black soot stain that began with a flame shape at a boarded-up window and then ran up to the building's top—the sixteenth floor. 1619. She lived at the very top. He began to step toward the entry but saw now a silver-gray Mercedes S pulling into the lot and then, getting out, this white guy in a business suit, tie undone, around thirty, big Irish-lookin' guy, the ghost of Jacko future, no doubt some trader, and clearly on course to wreck his life. He was stepping quick toward the entry but then saw Connor and stopped. He smiled. "You're lookin' lost, white man. First time at the store?" Connor was thinking of what to say, when the guy said, "Come on with me. I'll get you past the little 'S' fucks up to the bomb squad, which would be, my friend, the very best on the North Side. Rock to biscuit, highest quality pharmacopeia." Connor now followed the guy, who said no more, just walked on quick up to the open entry, past the spray-painted "Tha Jube" that had next to it, Connor could see now, a six-pointed star with the letters BOS inscribed across it and next to that the words "Niggas Gon Die."

Inside, in a foul-smelling semi-darkness, there was a broken turnstile at what had once been some kind of checkpoint, and past that a guardhouse that had in it not a guard but two bandana-ed teenagers, one with his feet up on the window counter, the other with his back turned, who, when he heard people approaching, looked over his shoulder and, while he didn't come out to stop or question, kept his face dead stone expressionless when Connor's guide nodded and gave him, cautiously subdued, a slight fist pump. The one with his feet up never moved, just peered expressionless and hard at Connor, from under the right-turned brim of a Raider's cap. The smell of weed, Connor caught now in a mix with that stench of what had to be urine. And he thought, when he saw now two entire walls of them, of what George had said about the broken-open, dangling latch-doors of the mailboxes in these buildings, where no postman has dared come for years: "When all it ever was, was welfare checks in those boxes, then maybe that's all it would ever come to in the end: every one of these people robbed at some time by some-damned-body else from right amongst 'em. No resources, no hope, not a shred of mutual respect or trust left—the definition of hell on earth."

The building's elevator had no doors, and the cage must have been grounded in the basement or was stuck hanging up above, for the shaft at lobby level was an open darkness, empty of everything but fetid stink. Every wall around was scrawled over with graffiti—crazy, pre-conceptual signs, it seemed to Connor, of a no-language for which there would be no corresponding script in any known tongue. It seemed every light fixture had been vandalized, none repaired. So what would this place become, when, next hour, the sun went down? He followed the white guy up stairs that ascended beside the elevator. The stink was everywhere in the concrete and cinderblock stairwell. "They'll have the little kids piss where they want to keep the hookers away," the guy said. "Doesn't work. But just a hop, skip and a jump now. Grocery's on three." On the second landing, however, there were two skull-capped, weight-pumped dudes, one tallish, long-necked, the other built low and thick-set like a running back, both in dark-blue t-shirts, maybe Connor's age, twenty, with walkie-talkies. The tall one was on his; the other dropped his down and said, breaking into a smile, "Gerry C, my man. Whaddup? And what you got witchyou?" The white guy said, "Rennie, s'up. Got a new customer for ya. Name is...?" "Connor." "Corner," the guy said. "I like it. Corner. Friend a Gerry C's a friend a mine." And he stepped aside to let the two whites pass. But Connor saw this thick-set running back for no-team lose the smile and pick up his walkie-talkie again the second they'd gone by.

When the white man, Gerry C, opened the third-floor door, it was onto a scene of numerous sundry sellers and hard-core-looking buy-ers, men, women, gathered in the corridor, mostly round a door some thirty feet down the hall. But one guy, young, not gangsta, nicely dressed, was sitting on the floor right near them, his back against the wall, smoking a glass pipe that sent up a smell like burning plastic or the inside of a Bic pen cap. And Gerry C, maybe drawn hard now by the chemic scent, stepped quickly ahead into this dark bazaar with-out ever looking back, even letting the metal door close behind him right on Connor—who, suddenly now brought back, without think-ing, to his original purpose, didn't push the door back open, rather let it click, and fix closed, upon him.

Alone now on the landing, Connor peered over the railing, looking down to see if he was watched by the walkie-talkie men below. Slowly, then, he began to sidestep up the next half-flight of stairs—and then, turning his face forward, to walk the rest of the flight straight up, at first still slowly—but then, having turned up onto the next flight, climbing more quickly—and at last two steps at a time up through the foul stair-well, now lighted by a window, but then, without a single light fixture

HEART OF DARKNESS

un-vandalized, getting dark and darker, until another window let in light again, and everywhere the walls spray-painted—here, there, and there again, recurringly, with six-pointed crowns—or three-pronged pitchforks—or the letters BOS, or VLK, inscribed sometimes inside the six-pointed Star of David. An indecipherable hard-fucking-gangsta lyric that Connor, as he saw the words painted on the wall again, in his mind named "Niggas Gon Die." Equal, equal, equal. He recalled saying these words to his father the night Jack was killed—*murdered!* His blood everywhere! Bullet after bullet—in Jack's face! What did Marlow, that piece of shit, amid his incomprehensible, his impenetrable darkness know about *that* kind of horror?

He stopped, breathed deeply, bowed his head. At Gibson's bar today, he'd talked to the bartender about Berkeley. *Heart of Darkness*—the guy's all-time favorite book. At Berkeley Connor had written a paper—said the worst horror in that book of so-called horrors, the real heart of darkness, was Marlow's fucked-up racist vision. As he went up that river, or up this fucking staircase, where there were no devils, he saw devils—his white mind conjuring them up out of its terror to the beat of drums that his white brains could no more read than he could the hieroglyphics on this wall. If he opened that metal door here, now eleven, twelve stories up in this nightmare—*what* would he see? More correspondences between myth and reality? More hints and warnings corroborated? Preconceptions confirmed? Would there actually *be,* right there, dope-head mamas fucking for another packet of dust while their kids are down on the street in right-turned Sox caps ready to kill somebody just for walking down the Division St. sidewalk? Why do stereotypes last and spread? Because there's persistent correspondence between the type and the real—that's why! Because all of it—it is *all* this real, actual stairwell to hell. And why am I here? How did it all come to this shithole? Who started it all—this shit? And *where* did it start—this shithole America? The sinkhole of sin and pain and *murder* and racial anger. What are the origins of this stinking stairwell of fucking shit? Time to goddamn start over! Are there persons here? Are there not? Persons! Equal. Up in this dark fallopian fucking tube of never-born life. No lights—all broken. Christ. Five words. *All men are created equal.* But in the dark they are killed before born. Ellie. Such beauty... and kindness. There is nothing that I, I, fucking *I* know better than that she is my life!—*nothing,* except that there are devils I see when I sweat in terror hearing the incomprehensible dark drums in my brain.

DIVISION

He wiped the sweat from his neck. He shook his head—then breathed deeply. He began again then to step, and climb—but now he heard above him steps descending. Not many. Maybe just one person—he prayed, just one person—with no gun. There was light breaking in again above, and as he turned a corner around and up to another flight he could see a man—*alone*—yes—standing above him at the next landing with the window light behind him. And he wasn't young. Connor was yet more relieved—the man wasn't at all young. So he continued now, slowly, to step up toward him; and the man, maybe late-sixties, maybe more, now continued to step down. As they neared each other, Connor smiled at the man, who wasn't smiling. But as he came nearer, Connor asked him, "Do you do this every day?"

The man, still descending, said nothing, just, with his face tensed, looked at Connor...and kept looking. But then, as they stood nearly side by side, the gray-headed man, dressed in his poverty—ragged flannel shirt, ill-fitting pants with one leg torn at the knee—said, "Sixteen stories, twice't ever single day." He stopped then, and Connor nodded. Remaining there, the man said now, "Two year since CHA fix a firs' thing round here. Elevator's no good for more'n a six month stretch, now and again, long's I remember. But the children knows me and leaves me alone." "You carry up your food?" "They don't rob me. Don't huht me." Connor nodded. Then the man said, "You ain't police." Now he smiled, warmly. "Jus' took you a little wrong turn somewheah?" And Connor smiled back, nodding his head, feeling an even deeper relief, which touched closed, for the moment, the hell-gates of his fear and anger. "Mother Lester," he said now. "I'm looking for Mother Lester." The man nodded. "Top flo', first place on the lef'.Live nex' t'Annabelle near foty year." Then, pausing in thought, he asked, "Newspaper?" Connor nodded. The man, now turning, and stepping again down the stairs into the dark, not looking, said, "Mebbee she 'spectin' you."

220

I AM HERE WITH YOU

Connor no longer felt high, though he knew he must still smell of booze. And he disliked the thin fraud. Newspaper man. But what apologies did *he* need to make! And he wouldn't stop now, not 'til he got what he wanted—which was to come to the start of it all. 1619. When he pushed open the metal door onto the sixteenth-floor corridor, what was there was...a Cabrini kids' high-rise playground! A tot on a squeaking tricycle, who, when he saw a white face, turned in fear and tore down the corridor toward—his mother? grandmother?—a woman in slacks, heavy, unkempt hair, Bulls jersey, cigarette between her fingers—and toward the light she'd made for him by keeping open her apartment's door. For there was no light working in the corridor here, either. "Git on in heah nah! Don' make me say it twice" So she ushered the child in—and then shut the door behind them, leaving Connor in the dark.

But he'd seen it, the first door on the left. And now he stepped over to it, and knocked.

Waiting in the darkness, he heard steps approaching and then, for some moments, locks being turned. At last, to the length of a lock chain, the door cracked open; and in the light, a face stared out over the chain. Female. Dark black. Sixty something. "Who you?"

"I'm from the *Tribune*. I think we talked on the phone."

The face, un-smiling, continued to peer out for some time over the chain. At last, then, after the door was again shut, bringing back the darkness, the chain was freed from the slot, and the door was opened. And by the woman, whose face made him wonder—was it like that face? Watt's?—Connor was shown into a living room, hot—the heat pipes, exposed, clanking—the walls, dull-white-painted cinderblock, one filled with photographs. Was one of him there? Among the photos was a picture of Jesus, with the shoulder-length hair, short beard, soft-white robe—Jesus as he has appeared to millions. And on the radio, coming from the kitchen, gospel music. Black. She asked him to sit on a sagging cloth-upholstered couch, faded green, the arms worn to the undercloth, as she went into the kitchen to turn off the radio. She was slow-moving, obese; she labored to breathe. When she returned, she seated herself under the photographs on a broad square ottoman, its flower-print cover cheap, torn—and she folded her hands. "Used to be scared to climb down them stairs 'cause them gangbangin' fools say I ain't paid no taxes to 'em. Think they the IRS. But ain't gone down 'em now these five months n'more cause I'm 'fraid I cain't get back up. You don't move, and don't move, then ya git mah way. Jus' the way it is. And the elevator never gon' be fix agin. Not part a they plan."

Connor, feeling only still his fierce anger and contempt, was wondering if it would ever be possible for him again to be drawn in his heart to black poverty. He had felt gratitude to the old man on the stairs. Love your enemy. Would there be any readiness for this love in a not wholly dead human soul? This obese black woman. This inactive fucking activist. Watt's grandmother. She was his enemy. It started here, with this black woman fucking some no-doubt deadbeat brute and then her spawning someone who with some other deadbeat brute spawned Watt. And she'll blame whites for it all—every bit of rot in this place—this death place, birthplace of murderers. But he wanted more from her, so he asked in a voice meant to keep her talking, "What plan? Whose plan?"

She set her hands on her knees, which were draped over by the skirt of a wide, beltless, pale blue gown that came down not half past her calves, which, thick, leading to no ankle, were covered to the point to which her gown fell by stockings that she'd not pulled up but had

I AM HERE WITH YOU

rolled up in bands just below her knees. Her shoes, worn at the heel, style-less, orthopedic, perhaps to ease nerve pain. "They grand plan," she said, "to fix nothin'; plan to make it so's they ain't two niggas left who ain't miserable enough not to leave; plan to make sure nobody ain't credit proofed and drug tested gon' get to stay; plan to make it so's everone get to stay ain't got no reckit, so it ain't none stayin'; plan to let Section-8s be valit no more'n a year, so's them's takin' 'em best be gettin' out soon; plan to make it so's the right a return gon' be wore out t'nothin' by the passin' a time with nothin' bein' done, no places built to return to; plan to take back they gold mine, which we don't own, for all we livin' heah half a sentry."

Connor had said nothing. But with mixed feelings now of self-contempt and contempt still for her, he'd been thinking to himself, asking—which set of urban legends, myths—which bullshit—was sorrier bullshit—the white? or the black? Would he hear next that whites had started the spread of AIDS in the black community? But blacks—take a look at the reality of it, you white fuck—had equal power of mind—and here it was, in this obese black woman, a match for you any day. As he listened to her, he found he could re-clothe her poverty, re-body it, re-language it. He could think of buying her new shoes, as a kindness, or a kick in her fat ass—his enemy—who sat here beneath her family photographs—and whose face.... He asked her, "What will you do?"

She looked at him; it seemed still with suspicion, still with that face that had peered over the lock chain. But now she closed her eyes, tilted back her head. Then she looked back down again. "Use t'be," she said, "ah had hope. Gon' *stop* they changin' mah life without me havin' control—over wheh ah live, wheh ah die. But ain't got no mo hope nah than them gangbangin' fools jus' say—*Evihbody got to die sometime.* Ain't got no sense a no future, them boys with they drugs and they guns. It jus' be sayin' you cain't think up nothin': it's what violence is. You cain't build nothin', so all you gon' do's tear down and kill whatevah you lookin' at—hatin' yosef 'cause you's *nothin',* but don't want t'hear nothin' 'bout that from nobody else. But sittin' here all the time nah alone, them wreckin' balls comin', ain't got no sense a any future mahsef. They's gon' tear *all* this place down—clear as day. Viability. They study say ain't none of it nowheh round heah. But it been mah home near all mah life. Which ain't nothin' to them's jus' casual declarin' *ain't viable*— like they ain't no human bein's livin' in it. And ahm one a them ain't got no credit, ain't got no clean reckit. Don't know about even a Section-8 f' me. So wheh's ah gon' go? And wheh's ah gon' stay? You know what ahm sayin'? Do you? You even a newspaper man, mistah?"

She looked at him now directly, rocking her folded hands at him, leaning toward him. Then, "Ah ax you that 'cause you jus' sittin' theah ain't takin no notes, don't come with no camera team, way meedya do, and you comin' to me ain't done nothin' s'long they ain't no one gon' remember me—and you smellin' bad a whiskey and not lookin' like no newspaper man a'tall. So ah been axin' mahsef *who you really be?*"

Connor, before he could say a word, felt an overwhelming sense of his own foolishness. This pitiful ruse. No point in lying further. And the darkness, he had seen now, was coming on. He felt the room was filling with it. How would he get out of here? He felt the warm aura of a flashback—the now-familiar warning in the brain. He took a breath. He shook his head. It seemed gone—no pictures, maybe, now, of ripped flesh would flash across his brain. Satan's film fest. "Who am I really?" he said. "That…is a good question."

"That ain't no answer," she said, her face concentrating now in anger.

"You're right," he said. But the anger in her face only intensified—and this angered him. Was he the one who had to explain, to apologize? His fear and his own anger compounding, he, again shaking his head, managed nonetheless to say in a restrained manner, "I'm sorry. I've intruded into your home. I should go." And now he rose.

"You sit back down, mistah, and answer me. You cain't jus come into mah home pretendin' t' be somethin' you ain't and git all mysterious when ah ax you who you are. You answer me."

He didn't sit. He felt a new full rush of contempt for her and hatred. Who was she to tell him anything? And fuck her *home*. Fuck her wall of pictures and gospel-music bullshit. And her dime-store Jesus. "I came here," he said, his eyes now fixed on her face, his mouth tensed in anger, "to find out where it started."

"Wheh *what* started?" She was looking up at him—but then turned her eyes to the couch and jerked her head toward it, directing him to sit.

And because now he was determining, all darkness be damned, to have it out with this woman to the end, he took his seat again. "My brother's murder," he said, in a manner meant to let her know he yielded nothing to her peremptoriness, let it be her house or any place on earth.

"What I got to do with yo brotha, whoevah you be? And you gon' tell me? Or I have to put it all together?"

"Don't play dumb with me, *ma'am*. Watt! He's *your* grandson. He

I AM HERE WITH YOU

murdered my brother in cold blood. And you know exactly who I am."

Clearly now deliberating with herself, she waited before she spoke. She pursed her lips tight. Then, "So you sittin' theah, mistah no-newspaper man, thinkin' you come t' the startin' place. You found it f'good! Starts rightcheah! With this exact ol' nigga lady you lookin' at. An' y'all done give her soooo much. Give her this place she done fuck up beyond all repaiah. And she lay down up heah f'some dumb fuckin' animal and then some othah dumb fuckin' animal and on and on till she put out a whole worl' a dumb fuckin' animals ain't wuth thinkin' about, say nothin' a payin' f' *them* too. Jus' look up t' that wall behint me and see all the shit you payin' fo, 'cept the four of 'em dead fo' they's twenty-five. An' you know yo' brotha's dyin' come right down them stairs you come up to find *me*—right straight down them stairs out from me and right down out the street t' wheh you livin' and end of it all be your brotha dead. An' you gon' examine me nah, and you gon' get settle in yo' head what you already settle fo' you come up heah. And ah'm wonderin' is you satisfied, jus' the way you's satisfied fo' you started?"

"Oh fucking yes," Connor said now, and he would vent a fury that had been building all the while she'd been trying to complicate what was goddamn fucking simple, "you just couldn't get out. All the years you've been here, for your whole fucking life, every door in the world has been closed, so you couldn't ever get out. Couldn't get educated. Couldn't say no to whoever the baby-daddy it was who knocked you up when you got made a baby-mother, just like your goddamn baby-mother before you and your baby-daughter after you. Fuck you! You could never escape the weight of the world, the weight of history, and just be you! The independent you! The personally responsible god-damned you—who determined to get out and make her world and her children's world better! And now you sit here sixteen stories up in this stinking shithole and eat and fucking eat 'til you can't goddamn move and that's somebody else's fault. Fuck you to death! You didn't act. You just let it all happen—all the shit of your life, as if some white slave master were chaining you down—telling you what you can do and what you can't and where you're going to live and where you're going to die, as if you were never free to choose a thing. Fuck you! It's all lies! No matter how true they all may be, how deep the truth in your bullshit may be—it's all lies in the end! And the end result of all your lies *is* my brother dead! And your grandson is *not* a fucking animal. He's a re-sponsible person who freely shot my brother in the face. And shot him

225

DIVISION

again, and again, till my brother, a human person with incalculable value was nothing but blood! I was there! And fuck you and your do-nothing self-pity! Sitting here in this shithole without moving. It does start here—with you!—up here eating yourself to death, paralyzing yourself, burying yourself in this death place, which you won't leave, because of *what?* You name it, *what?*"

The heat in the room, suffocating, and his ranting anger, his life now of deep-seated anger and fear, brought the sweat to his hands, his neck, his back. He was trembling. The heat pipes clanked. And it was still darker now. How would he get out of here? Down sixteen flights in the dark! She had said nothing, as he'd raged on. Said nothing, done nothing, not moved. Her face, *his* face, Watt's; in the darkness, it all became one. All black faces. He wanted a gun. Who wouldn't need a gun to get out of this place! She hadn't moved—all the time he'd gone on. But now, not changing her stolid face, she rose and stepped over to a tassel-shaded floor lamp that stood along the wall she sat against, and she pulled the chain. Light. Electricity—somehow electrons found their magic way up the wiring of Tha Jube, to this single lamp high up in this decayed tower of darkness—maybe six months from the five-ton wrecking ball, maybe less, if there is a God. Hope fucking Six, now past all hope. And that it would come to this—could have been seen from the start.

She sat again on the ottoman, the hem of her beltless gown again resting at the folded-up bands of stockings pulled not to her knees. She caught her breath. At last then, in a steady, deeper voice, "Thought you might be you. Ah know 'bout you." She stopped. Then looked Connor in the eye. "And you think ah cain't hold you heah? You think ah cain't call him? You think you git out this building ah don't let you? No, you don't think it. Ain't thought it once. Come heah 'cause you one crazy white motherfucker. Crazy white boy...all fitna die."

She tilted her head, nodded—then leaned toward him. "You tell me I's all immobilize, all paralyze. Why ah cain't get out on m'own? Why ah cain't get out the life ah been livin' since I's born? Why ah cain't keep mah children off the streets, the drugs, the killin' game they dyin' in? Why ah have them childrens in the first place with mens don't mean t' be they fathers. And all the answers ah give mahsef, you say, no matter how much truth be tol' in 'em, gon' be lies in the end, lies ah tell mahsef so's ah don't have t' take the bull by the horn. An' heah you are fitna die but still tellin' me what all's wrong with me and how

226

I AM HERE WITH YOU

everthing start with me. And the drinkin' you done today ain't the only drinkin' you lately be doin'. You's plain drunk on the phone, time you call me. Think ah don' know drunks when ah hear 'em? And now you's tellin' me bout yo' brotha dyin'. And how's ah gon' know you ain't somewheh glad he be kilt by a black man 'cause that gon' prove what you all along be thinkin' bout niggas and it make you glad t' know you's right all along? And how ah know the one kilt yo' brotha ain't thinkin' in his mind he an instrument a justice when he pull that trigga? Wheh you comin' from? Wheh he comin' from? Wheh any of us comin' from? But it all start rightcheah with me when it come to yo' brotha's dyin. 'Cause a ah cain't get out a what ah'm in. And what's gon' get you outa what you in? Say ah gon' eat mahsef to death jus' fo' you drink yosef to death. Why ah cain't change, you say. Same as you, mistah. And it ain't jus' yo' drinkin'—be yo' hatin' and wrathful ways an' yo' wantin' to die 'cause yo' brotha be dead, his blood comin' up fo' yo' eyes so bad you cain't live on with it. And why you cain't get outa all them feelins and all yo' drunk ways? You up heah with me, mistah, 'cause *you up heah with me.* And ah got as much blood a kin fo' mah eyes as you evah got. But that be black on black killin', you say. Don't start nowheh else but with black peoples. And you brotha's dyin' don't start but in a black man. And when mah grandson he walkin' in his mama's blood when he's ten year old and he found her up heah on the flo' all cut crost her throat it ain't nothin' but anotha nigga done it. Though he a miracle a brightness, he gone all to the gangbangin' darkness 'cause he jus' a nigga by nature. Good Book say ever one of us done eat the fruit a the tree's forbidden. All equal. But one gon' be startin' in Lincoln Park with a rich mama and daddy, and anotha gon' be startin' heah. So it ain't all equal. 'Cept now for you. You's with me nah—a nigga all shut up in injurih, all shut up in skin's all scar tissha, all shut up in hundreds a years a histrah press all at once togetha in the barrel a that gun kilt yo' brotha. And ahm glad you ain't carryin' no gun a justice, 'cause you don't care 'bout nothin' 'cept it's a nigga kill him and they all the same. Same's ah feel 'bout white peoples. You think ah's sittin' up heah jus' too dumb evah to hear the words *collective guilt,* and don't know what they mean even ah do hear 'em, or the words *social justice.* Thinkin' yo' brotha don't say no words to that nigga who kill him, or that nigga he don't understand whatevah yo' brotha do say, he jus' kill yo' brotha f'nothin'."

All the while that this Mother Lester spoke, Connor could hear his

227

DIVISION

father, and himself, expressing disgust for the endlessly re-echoed term *closure,* which for them both was never more than a euphemizing of the violent demands of the vengeful Furies. But as he listened to her, he wanted it—and yet still despised it—fucking closure, which is an impossibility at best, and at worst a cloak over a poisoned dagger. But he wanted to close her mouth—shut up this grandmother, who clearly had been in contact with her murdering grandson. Stop her and him, too, in full fucking closure. Forever. And if closure is a lie, it's no worse a lie than the endlessly un-closed echo chamber of Mother Lester's moral equivalencies. It's all equal, in the big, ever-open picture—all the same—what Watt did with his gun and what Jack did with his words. Every word of Jack's nothing less than a bullet in Watt's face. NOT! No moral or immoral calculus can ever make equal what is *not* fucking equal, no matter if infinite worlds with all their histories get poured into the understanding of Jack's action and Watt's action. And Watt, her grandson, is still out walking while my brother is shut up and buried in a coffin that was closed at his wake! As he listened to her, Connor was thinking these things—and as he would look to see how dark it had gotten.

But in the growing darkness, with her lamp the only light—as he listened to her—against himself, despite himself, and while hating her—he respected this person—for all the deep truth she was telling, if mixed with lies—for things she was saying that he'd somewhere, every hour, thought himself, and believed, since Jack died. Things about himself, his mind. And things, yes, about the endless big picture. Social justice. Collective guilt. Endlessly un-closed; everyone implicated. If untrue, also true. And this woman's power of experience, of mind. She'd earned his respect. And it must be a start—a beginning of something, a pure, honest *respect* for someone. Love your enemy—not just the beautiful ones but this older woman, obese, this woman of anger and suffering —but *not* lies, somewhere not lies at all. His grandmother. Love her as you love yourself. Fucking impossible, to the death. But you do it, if you can.

She was breathing hard. But she had brought her speaking to a close. Her head was bowed, and she was slowing her breathing, deepening it. At last she caught again her natural rhythm. But still her head was bowed. Connor wanted no more to harangue her, fight her—never again, though he knew he could fight her, 'til they both were *finished.* He let himself receive the feeling of her home—and of the misery of every-

I AM HERE WITH YOU

thing gone. Shattered walls, dangling rebar, and then dust, shoveled off, gone, as if they'd never lived here. He felt sympathy now, truly. But in this darkness, he was afraid. How would he get out? He could think of no way out. He looked at her and let come from out his soul something that seemed to be coming already on its own. "Annabelle," he said. He said her name. And she looked up. She said nothing, but looked at him in a way that said he had touched her. He said again, "Annabelle." And then, "I'm afraid. I'm so afraid. It starts there, all of it, with the fear. All that's in my head.... All that I've said to you. You said I'm here with you. Yes. I am. And I'm so goddamned afraid. How do I get home?"

Still she said nothing. But after a time, she rose—and made her slow way to her kitchen, where, in the dim light, she reached for something in a drawer. He felt a new fear. But...it was a light—a long, silver-metal flashlight. She held it up—and then waved it toward herself. "Come ohn," she said. Then, as she stepped toward the door, she tapped the flashlight three times on the kitchen wall.

Connor rose from the couch and, while afraid of whatever dark journey lay before him, went to the door and stood beside her.

She looked at him with a look that made him want to trust it—to think it was kind, forgiving, engendering of forgiveness. She said, as she handed him the light, and pressed her hand now over his to help him hold it, "He don't know yo' heah. And ah ain't nevah gon' tell him you come. Take that with me to the grave. But you keep yuh eyes open f'him. You keep yosef safe from him. Don't take no mo' crazy chances. Don't you act no mo' like you's wantin' t'die." With her hand still on his, she looked at him—with that look that he would trust—would believe was for reconciliation, lasting.... Then she turned—and unlocked first the chain lock, and then the latch lock, and last the dead bolt— and then opened the door. With a light of his own, the old man whom Connor had met in the stairwell was standing out in the corridor waiting, ready to guide Connor down the sixteen stories of Tha Jube.

And, as Connor would turn to go with the old man, feeling in his heart now a profound, an immeasurable gratitude, Annabelle Lester, standing still in the open door, with her mouth pursed up in what seemed a smile, said to him, "You keep that light, mistah newspaper man. You keep it in memrih a me."

229

PERSONHOOD

"A flashlight?" Ellie Shea asked. There was nothing unusual about Connor Riordan's just showing up, never having called, but he seemed even weirdly absent, distant, as he remained deaf to her question. He smelled of alcohol, again, though he appeared sober, and the scent was only faint. Nor were there any signs now of the angry edge. But suddenly she found herself asking, as it were, terminating questions: Does he have no explanation for the light? Does he even know he's carrying the thing? And if he's reached some point of no return, would I be free, in good conscience?—no duty now to anything, no point in any more trouble or effort? Her queries gave her a sudden rushing sense of liberty, as might a hand on a weapon. But also they stopped her breath, like a shock of pain.

He sat on the couch beneath her two beautiful bird paintings, the ostrich, the swan. Hooded brass accent lights atop the frame of each brought to the living room a warm, soft light. The granite top of the kitchen island glowed under the overhanging, softly dimmed lamp. Beneath the lamp, on the granite, twin red roses stood together in a tapered glass vase. As she came over to sit next to him, he placed on

230

PERSONHOOD

the coffee table before him the flashlight, fifteen inches, hefty, the grip
along its silver-metal battery shaft showing a full history of use. Before
leaning up again, he touched the light several times. "She gave it to
me," he said. "His grandmother, Annabelle Lester."

"Whose grandmother? Who is Annabelle Lester? And where did this
happen?"

"Tha Jube. 1619."

"What?"

"I went to see where he came from."

"Who?"

"Leonardo Sykes. Watt. I went to see his grandmother. Annabelle.
534 Division. Apartment 1619."

"You went to Cabrini alone? To see his grandmother?"

"She gave me the flashlight, to get back home. She sent me with
Isai, her old friend, so I could get back down the sixteen flights in the
dark." He paused a moment…. "Cabrini. Moments when it was quiet—
if always so fucking foul and dark. Then you'd hear shouting, anger,
violence, maybe, about to break out, on the corridors. Three separate
times, on different landings, we got asked if we wanted sex, even Isai,
seventy-one years old. Some of the women not much more than girls,
hooking there in the dark. Addicts, broken women, lost. Ready to suck,
ten dollars, or fuck, thirty straight, fifty anal. No fucking doubt AIDS
was there. Just step into their 'place' and catch your death. A moment
of pleasure, sex, drugs, what's it worth? In Tha Jube—apparently it's
worth dying for."

He stopped, was agitated. He let out, like pained breaths, several
quick, short groans. Then, "There was this group of gangbangers,
teens, maybe a dozen, rushing up toward us in that stinking-shit tube
of darkness. 'Land of no fathers,' Isai said. One of them, maybe, I'd
seen earlier on the street, big, dangerous, I think, maybe—asked me,
out on Division, when I said I was from the newspaper, if I had a
press pass; said if I didn't, he couldn't let me go, one way or another.
Isai pulled my light down, hid me behind him. One said, 'It be the ol'
man.' And by some miracle, unfathomable, I swear, as fucking God,
they respected Isai."

He closed his eyes. He breathed several quick, short breaths. Then,
his eyes still closed, "Fitna die. Crazy white boy fitna die. Annabelle
knew why I went there. If I'd heard the sound of a gun in that stinking
sixteen-story tomb…. Just the thought of that, on the way over here

231

now, made me put my hands over my ears as I was walking down the street. You know what prayer is when you can't walk down the street without putting your hands over your ears." He opened his eyes now but bowed his head. "And you *keep* praying, when his own grand-mother has told you—'You look out for him, you keep yourself safe from him'—and when you can feel him over your shoulder, smell the sulfur of gunpowder, in your mind. And when you know something of the black hell he's come from." He lifted his head, bobbed, rocked it—then tightened his fists. "By flashlight-light—insane graffiti every-where. All sound and fury, signifying hopeless violence. Niggas gon' die. He crawled through his own mother's blood, when he was ten. He found her dead on the floor with her throat slit—in Tha Jube. Watt. And who would have killed her? Most likely someone he knew."

Connor felt Ellie's hand on his brow, her fingers running across his hot, moist forehead and then through his hair, her palm then touching his cheek. He looked—saw her face, her hair, dark red, cut round the pale skin of her face, and the light glowing on her dark red hair, and her hazel eyes, her lips, neither smiling nor turned down in sorrow, rather, maybe, expressing the same need as his—to close all distance between them....

And now she did, gently, bring his face to hers and kissed him. But he thought now again where do true, pure feelings go, un-shat-upon feel-ings, un-frozen? He kissed her. Kisses—to find his feelings again. He'd loved her from the first. But this was just a thing now that he *knew*. He wanted the feeling, not the godforsaken knowledge. Was it guilt that stopped his heart? And all, too, that he knew about her—how to get *rid* of that? How to get rid of all he knew about himself, the one who felt all the racial rage of America? History, the godforsaken crippling shit of it. Never to be moved out of the way—divided off, hard—so you could live and breathe again. Was it good, at least, that he *hated* that he couldn't get rid of the shit stain of his history, collective, fucking white-American, and personal, the blood everywhere, *murder,* and his mother? Was it good?—his *hatred* of the fact that he couldn't get rid of the memory and anger, the shame? Was a *hatred* of indelible human stains a gift from God? It was an emotion, at least.

He pulled his face from her face—but only to look into her eyes. He waited, and thought—then he said, "But there were moments...up with Annabelle, in 1619—when...I didn't despise her. When I got past my contempt—for her black everything, for her separate, black fucking

232

PERSONHOOD

language, her clothing, her obesity, for her never having left Cabrini, her failing to get her family out, her having no husband, for her family's all failing to get out of poverty and fatherlessness and crime, for her blaming whites—for *everything* that every white person ever hated, or felt contempt for about impoverished black people—for the *time,* the century and a half without change, without improvement, for the fucking expense—and for the fact that her grandson murdered my brother in utter ice violence. For some incredible moments, I was free of *all* of it, all of my white fucking shit, my anger and contempt and blind stupidity, which was there silent beneath my verbiage all my fraudulent liberal years, un-blessed years. So *un*-blessed."

He closed his eyes, a long moment, then closed his hand tight. He pressed the forefinger of his fisted hand against his mouth. At last, then, he lowered his hand and opened his eyes. "I raged on, telling her all my feelings, spewing anger, up there in her place. And she met me with her mind at every point of my raging. Person to person. She answered me. When I'd gone up there to trace everything shit right back to her, Jack's death, and all the shit of Cabrini, the gangster darkness, the violence. And I'd begun to feel...for these moments...this freedom of pure respect, un-fucking-stained by the goddamned death shadow of *me*. White *me* was gone. And I said her name.... 'Annabelle.' Her name. It just came to me to say it. She knew I was as trapped as she was. She knew me. And she felt with me. She told me I was a nigga now. We both were.... Up there in Tha Jube. She knew it. And it just came to me—to say her name, with pure respect, which she sensed. I am sure she did. Then I told her I was afraid—so fucking afraid. That it was terror that made me so lost, and angry. I said I didn't know how I would get home. I told her I wanted to get home, and that I was afraid. She said nothing to me then. But she knew it all. She stood up and went to her kitchen. She signaled through the wall, for Isai to come...and be my guide. And then she gave me her light."

He leaned forward and picked up the flashlight from the table. He held it over his knees and looked at it. "She gave me this—in that hell hole where every light has been vandalized. Nothing repaired. All fucking dark. And she told me not to act anymore like I wanted to die. Love your enemies. Love. Affection. I felt it. And this release—like I'd died to all the shit of me and been freed—for a moment—from all unloving disrespect for another person." He put the light back on the glass table, touching it once, twice. He turned his face to Ellie's. "Is it all

233

we'll ever get? Moments here and there of freedom? All the rest of the time, remaining just what we've been made by the past, the scars, the shit we live in? The scared *self* we live in—that pathetic fragment—fixed in it, locked inside our godforsaken, fear-driven, race-driven definitions of so-called worth. Self-protective fucking walls of fear. She told me to keep it, the flashlight...to remember her by."

Ellie touched Connor's hand. Then, feeling a pang still from the shock she'd given her soul when for a moment she thought she could in conscience give up on him, "She was right. You've gotta stop. I beg you, with her, to stop acting as if you want to die. Curiosity is good, until it isn't. Good when it drives us toward the truth...in your case, about his world. The Cabrini of Watt. And understanding, getting back to the beginnings, the causes—it's good. But curiosity reaches a point when it's suicidal. Suddenly we *want* to uncover some final truth that will kill us, that will get us to hate ourselves, to death.... Or, like you, in order to satisfy our angry, hateful sense that we were right all along about the horror of the place we sought out, we crazily *want* to be killed there—as she said you did."

She paused, her face showing deep concern. She had him listening —not now to his own thoughts. She waited, another moment. Then, "Freedom. You wonder about freedom—from ourselves—from what we've been made by life—freedom for more than just a moment. I don't know...I don't. Truly. Maybe *time* will be the answer. It brings in so many afflictions, time, so many, as you say, scarring afflictions; but it keeps working, maybe, to undo, or modify, to lessen the pain of what it has done. Maybe, in some true healing way, time, like a miracle, will take the dark things that have been done to us, and that we've done, and not wholly obliterate them but put them at safe distances—right measures of distance—so that the things done to us, and that we've done, will both be there and not be there, continuing through our memory to give us wisdom but never anymore overwhelming us, as they all in time will have faded away just enough. I was talking to Carolyn about this...."

Ellie paused, looking away. Then, "You have prayer.... And I know that for you prayer is no ridiculous verbalized conventionality offered to some even more ridiculous conventionalized deity. God. People say the word 'God' like they knew him, her, it. God would want us to.... God has a sense of humor. God is laughing. God is shaking his head. I want to put my hands over my ears against *that,* I promise you." She

PERSONHOOD

looked at Connor again. "But for you...prayer...it's just this open-ing of your heart...so that some silent force might have space to come inside you and start doing things like make time actually heal you. It's a creating of this space inside you, your prayer—so that the force that can understand your silent pleas can come in and start to place things at safe distances in your soul. Or place barriers, good strong walls to keep you from trying to die in some dark tower in Cabrini. And why wouldn't we call this a personal force? A force we can pray to. Who's the one who just calls it *source...?* Ridiculous, too, if you hear that word even *once* too often. *Source.* But still so much better than 'God'...."

She looked away now, blankly, toward the coffee table. "I haven't prayed," she said, "not in a long time. I haven't been able to think that I'm not found out, even in the most secret places inside me. Guilt's insane. It hurts people like you, who've done nothing—who've only been done to. Guilt doesn't care. It builds self-blame, non-stop. It takes elements from everywhere and non-stop *constructs* self-blame, with no concern for justice. And when you *do* do something, it redoubles its poison efforts...until you really know what they mean when they say that the one hardest to forgive, the one you can not forgive, is yourself." She stopped a moment—but still looked blankly before her. Then, as if she'd thought this now many times, "It divides you in two, guilt or shame does, and one side of you is made into a hanging judge by it, and, relentless, un-forgiving, the hanging judge cannot stop looking at the other side of you, the shamed part of you, and hating and curs-ing it for shaming the real you and, worst of all, even when it's been violently ostracized, for still never going away...for it never goes away, this shamed part of you."

Ellie still just looked ahead, but her face now showed she was fight-ing back tears. "And when truly you can't manage this," she said, "can't stop it, can't endure it, this not forgiving of yourself, one side of you against the other, the judge against the convict—and at the same time you have no capacity to pray for help—it's not a good place to be."

She turned to Connor, barely holding back her tears, which had begun to gather in her eyes. His dulled mind had never been able to associate Ellie Shea with real sorrow, though they'd talked now, so many times. And his own compassion, so fucking dead—where was it? He could feel affection for his enemy—some moments. And not for the person he loved more than he loved himself? But this sorrow on her face. Never seen before. It changed her beauty. Always her beauty

235

was more to him than some *object,* some *thing.* But still her sorrow now changed it, made it even deeper for him than it had ever been. His mother divided things off. Not Ellie, she won't separate herself from herself. Haunted by the part she can't run from, she faces the hanging judge.

He'd said 'Annabelle.' And feeling Ellie's sorrow, seeing it in her beauty, Connor said, "I love all of you, Ellie Shea. All of you. And this changes everything—all the rules—all the lines—gone. No judge. No convict. And you need to love yourself, *all* of yourself, the way I love everything about you." He touched her pale cheek a moment—letting his finger trace, gently, the corner of her mouth. "There are things that can't be helped. I think about you and Jacko. I think about all of it." He looked into her eyes. "But I love all that is you. And this brings everything together...and leaves nothing unforgiven." And yet now, even as he spoke, and told no lies, he wondered what prayer is best for the resurrection of lost, bullet-after-bullet gunned-down feeling? How do you recall it truly to life? And what life without it?

She took his hand. She pressed it. She raised and kissed it, then held it against her cheek. At last she lowered his hand and held it warm in her lap. "Things you've said to me," she said, "things about you and Jack, about Jack...and me, about your mother—all that you've said and that we've talked about, getting it all out—it's all brought such life to my guilt. I need to say this, Connor. I have to."

She looked at him, now pleading for understanding. "It's made it so I can't forgive myself," she said. "I need to say this. I wanted to change the culture of myself, the way the culture all around is changing. It's finished—abortion guilt. The whole culture of abortion guilt—who can't see this? And I would have gotten to the new guiltless world. Some ups and downs, some really bad downs, but I would have gotten there. I would have done all the work in my mind that's getting done every minute in our culture, making what was a guilt and a shame into something wholly permissible, and making our old not-permitting of abortion on deepest moral grounds into the new deepest embarrassment, and shame. I think—because I have felt it going on in me—of all the extraordinary, deep work it takes to effect a change like this—all the internal shouting down of voices; the down-below-the-nerves torture and imprisonment of dissent; the culture building; culture reversing; the spreading of the new virtue and the new shame into every last corner of our world; Foucault's work, only now it's the work of making it

236

PERSONHOOD

a punishable obscenity to say a word like 'personhood.' All of it was going on in my head, the re-wiring of my soul, to fit it with the new world. And maybe I would have found even some new source to pray to, because really it's a religion-building that's going on. But you're your father's son. The two of you the last Catholics. And now, because of you, and my feelings for you, I'm the last guilty Catholic girl."

She pressed his hand against herself. Tears were in her eyes again. "And that fight Jack had with your father. And then the fight you had with Jack...just as they were coming down the alley. And your mother being gone now.... And your brother gone forever. That fight...about me...that it kept you there...as they were coming...." Her lips now were trembling. She was crying, now hard. She didn't wipe her tears, rather pressed Connor's hand and held it harder against her lap as her tears fell over her face. "It's not a good place to be," she said, crying, "where I am now." She closed her eyes on her tears, still letting them run on her face. "But I swear...I'd rather start here, in this hard place, with nothing hidden, nothing repressed. Everything understood between you and me. I'd so much rather start with this, and with you...even if I never pray again."

He held her hand as she was holding his, pressed on her lap. And with his other hand he reached out to her and took her to him, held her now with his arm around her. On his neck he felt the wet of her tears. He kissed her hair, moved his mouth with kisses to her face, kissed her tears, brought his wetted lips to her mouth. He felt her press his hand now between her thighs. She held him tight to her and they pressed their joined hands warm against her, caressed her, both of them moved by her need, as they kissed now with that passion that is a blessed blind-ness and forgetting. The kisses, deep, long, and the way they touched her together, caressed her, shared in the need between her thighs, then touched, explored each other, until they at last lifted their hands each one to undress the other—all of their passion sent every dark, haunt-ing thing in their lives away, to some good distant place. After years of desire, this sex now was blind, and good. And their young bodies— each found the other's even more beautiful than either had envisioned. But now she whispered softly to him, "Not here. I want us in my bed. I want every night to go to bed with the memory of you having made love to me there. If you're not with me, I want you to be with me, in my bed, inside me, holding me, every night." They rose then together. But now she stopped and smiled. She reached to the table for the flash-

237

DIVISION

light, and, laughing, she touched on the beam and pointed it to her room. She smiled at him then in a way that did—for that moment—make him at least believe that the life in his heart might be reborn... out of the nowhere and death, the darkness of murder, into which it had disappeared. Smiling still then, beautiful in her human beauty, changed, she took his hand and said to him softly, "Follow me."

CCDOC: DIVISION ONE TO DIVISION NINE

"Man don't plead—he gon' pay they 'trial tax.' Hundred day f'that; hundred mo' he ax for a continuance, which he gon' do when he up f'violence. Average time 'n the Shank Factory, man ain't pleadin'?—be two hundred fifty day fo' he gon' go t'trial."

On the third-floor tier in Block Four of Division One of The Cook County Jail, the largest single-site prison in America—a city of ten thousand men, eight thousand black—Marcus Sabbs had for the last six of his now one hundred and fifty-four days behind bars shared a cell with Quentin Reavis, 'Q,' a GD out of the Greens, twenty-eight years old with a fifteen-year voluminous sheet, and a man of serious violent street repute. Back in Cabrini, Marcus hadn't known 'Q'—but every waking hour now, it came back to him the way Watt, who knew the man well, had said that when it came to enforcing the law of the Folk, capital punishment, torture, "You can believe—'Q' gon' get it done." And not three days in, the five-foot ten-inch, pudgy-powerful, ruthless-fisted 'Q' as he looked at him with a dead look, held out for Marcus, in the palms of his large, thick-fingered hands, his 'piece a

239

candy,' a cloth-hafted, seven-inch steel shank knife he'd received as a welcoming gift from respectful admirers.

There were GD leaders all over County. And within hours of his arrival, the kites, coded gang missives, started coming into the cell 'Q' shared with the Tumbler. The drums were beating, Tumbler was sure, for some kind of show of force, either some VLK'n, or some bloody settling up between one splinter of the GD's and another; for in the man-crammed-hard-against-man, massive overcrowding in County, even more than on the street, it was all about division of turf. The CI's, Criminal Intelligence, had been visiting again, and again, over the last three days. They knew blood was in the water. Police dogs had been in every cell, sniffing for contraband—also, loosely leashed, just barking in anger, snapping at flesh. Three times the ERT's, the Emergency Response Team, had rushed the tiers—forty strong, white bulls with batons, and black bulls right with 'em, might as well be white, every bit as full a hate and anger. But all this place was, was hate and anger. And noise. No hope for peace, not an hour. Just this morning some crazy motherfucker set his cell on fire, just so he could get a CO, any CO in there so he could beat the fucker to death—though he managed only to bite one of 'em's neck and spit bloody spit in his face. And last night all four tiers of toilets, flushing down not shit but who knows what kites and contraband, or just noise to create up-fuckin' chaos for the ERT's, half a them motherfuckers sadists crazier than the inmates. 'Q,' who flushed his kites, still kept his shank well hidden, the blade up a bed leg and the cloth handle in a sock.

"Yo lawya, she gon' tell you what she gon' tell you. She say she doin' somethin' special for ya. Workin' day n' night for ya. Average time gon' be average time, no mattah what she say."

Marcus, sitting up on the upper bunk, above 'Q,' now, by way of answer, lay back and set his hands behind his head. Christa Reese, his lawyer still (and had he stayed with the PD just because she was kind to him when he was scared to death?—stuck with the white lady slavishly, out of some death wish? even though Uncle Maurice had said he'd pay for the city's best?)—she'd said nothing about any trial tax. Was she jivin' about why it's takin' all this time? More'n five months in this violent shithole—make the 'jects seem like paradise. Who the fuck wouldn't think about doin' himself here? All boredom or bloodshed. Bologna and gas-station white bread and yellow plastic-wrapped cheese and sugar drinks 'til you can't shit for days. And when the shit

240

finally comes, the stains of it in the open toilets out to ruin the repu-
tation of stainless steel. The majesty of the law. Stick your head in it
and smell it, motherfucker.

Was there a trial tax? Price to pay if you don't plead out? Got a right
to a speedy trial—unless you want a fuckin' trial. But Christa—seemed
she'd always tried to let him know what's comin', make him feel less
helpless, less a slave in chains. And what she'd said was that the white
boy, Connor Riordan, was unstable now. His father said his son was
having a hard time. And we need him to be stable, Christa said, but
right now he isn't. We need him to confirm in good, strong language
what he told the police. We need him to stand up to the prosecution,
who will know he could get confused, could maybe even turn all around
and in anger accuse you. They could try to trigger an anger in him
as they recall in graphic detail his brother's murder and get him to put
everyone who was there in the alley in the same category—to see everybody black as equally guilty. Robert will be strong, Marcus. But Robert
won't be enough. That's why we've asked for time, to let Riordan gain
his strength. He's our most important witness. And I know he wants
to help you. But he needs to find himself and be himself. They'll ask
him if he knows what *We don't want this* means—and we need to be
sure he does. We'll need him to get its meaning all closed down tight,
so that it means exactly to him what it meant to you when you said it.

Christa cared. Seemed to care. She'd come to talk to him, personally,
every ten days or so. Keep him human, keep him alive, over five-plus
months. Touch me—show me a human face—before I die. Steal 'Q's'
shank out the bed leg. Just bury it in myself. Got to lie to Mama. Tell
her I'm all right. I'm gonna make it. And then bury 'Q's' shank right
in my heart. Put my finger on it now—and mark the spot. Press it *hard*.
NO. No, I can't do it to her, not after all our family's gone—either to the
street or to the grave, or to wherever my father went. Can't remember
his face. But can't give up on livin'. Got to make Uncle Maurice proud.
Mama proud. Robert, too. But what the fuck I'm doin' in here and
Robert's not? Rich boy's out free. Cabrini boy's facin' life. How'd it
come to that? Can't trust a single soul. Justice. Just ice. And this fuckin'
'Q'—never smiles, never says nothin' it ain't makin' things hopeless
or like there's not a single worth-a-shit human being in the whole universe. Fuckin' sociopath. Best believe, he gon' get it done, Watt said.
And minimum two phone calls a day—from who? his loved ones? All
this new hot trouble, like a world war's comin' on, when exactly'd this

DIVISION

shit start? Started right when this motherfucker showed up. If I didn't
see myself dyin' of crazy in one of those Protective Custody cages over
in Nine, I'd ask for PC. Twenty-three hours a day of solitary, nothin'
but a slit in the door to peek your eyes out—I'd tell 'em I got to have
it to save my life, though I might die of crazy in that hole. Wild Man
from fuckin' Borneo, all caged up. Could Christa get him safe-caged?
Or was the white lady good for nothin' but talk?

When he'd been taken away that first day, after his blink of an eye
in Branch 66, it was into a steel-wire cage where he was kept until that
cage was packed tight with others being processed, five hundred in a
single daily County shift, and then out from that cage into a line and
then on to another cage until that was packed, and then into another
line, and then on to another cage, and then another line as each time
they called out the numbers marked on their forearms like they were in
a concentration camp for not Jews but Chicago-American niggers. And
then it was a shuffling from booth to booth to get your picture taken
and your prints rolled and x-rays taken for TB and to tell 'em did you
have AIDS, or were you a hype or a drunk about to go shit crazy, and,
lastly, were you in any kind a mood to kill yourself? And then, after
bein' stamped as processed, it was strip down again to your bare black
ass and now grab your sack and bend over and spread those cheeks so
we can see you got contraband wedged up your asshole—see that's a
ball a shit or a rock a crack—up there in the blackness. And then move
on again like not people but cattle 'til you get your state soap and your
plastic-smellin' bedroll and your uniform DOC's—though not before
they one last time stick their white noses way up your negro ass-crack
just to let you know you got no private place in this world. No control
over your life, just leg chains and bars—it's what it all started with and
it's what these motherfuckers bring the American nigger back to. And
what's gonna die in this *processin'* is every human thing but, maybe, the
human gangster. If I could be him, I'd be Watt, even if it meant I'd
have to kill me. Go ahead, kill me 'cause I ain't worth nothin'. Either/
or, motherfucker. Either Watt, or nothin'. Only way to show you're a
human person in this white man's prison world: it's *be* Watt.

In the day room, the exercise room, the yard, the mess hall—it was all
the way Watt said: GD's here, VL's there, each gang trying to push out
the dividing line. And inside the razor wire you came to know the Book
of the Six, just like Watt said. No love for Five. Marcus had always
meant to keep his body pure—no tattoos. But he had now a set of

242

crudely hot-penned X-crossed pitchforks, one each at the top of his right and his left arm. Unity, loyalty, the sense of belonging—they're gonna take on a whole new meaning when it's a matter of life and death. Not twelve hours passed without a serious outbreak—somebody bleeding, somebody shedding blood. Two nights back, some VL who'd used a toothpaste cap to stop the lock of his cell door ambushed a brother, grabbed him by the dreads and busted open his head against the bars, mashing his face 'til both eye sockets were full of blood. Woulda killed the brother if his cellmate didn't nearly bite the motherfucker's hand off.

But no real trust, even between brothers. No loyalty. GD's—one minute they're all for one, one for all—and the next it's brother against brother. Internecine war. War everywhere, especially since the comin' in a this motherfucker below me—personal friend a Watt's. And who's he talkin' to, ten dollars a call for your fifteen minutes? Who's payin' that ten? Not 'Q.' Sleep with one eye open, sharin' a cell with this animal, and Watt wantin' me dead even more than I want it myself.

In the day room, in the yard, in the dining room, in the weight room, where they lifted water-filled plastic bags, all the equipment having been broken or stolen and weaponized, made into shanks; in any free space—Marcus would hear it from the GD's: Who you think put you in heah, ma brotha? Cops don't be talkin' to Watt. Be talkin' to yo cousin. Ain't gon' get nothin' from the white boy don't know you f'shit. All niggas the same to white boys. So it's comin' from you rich-boy cousin. Sold you up way Watt never would. You countin' on that cousin? You hopin' that white boy come 'round f'you? Sheeeeee-it, ma brotha, you don't plead against Watt, then he take care a you. You do plead against Watt, then he gon' take care a you a whole different way. Take care a yo' family, too. But you stay by him, he gon' stay by you. Take care a them's can huht you, 'cause they's the same ones gon' huht him. You stick by him, he gon' stick by you. Brothers of the Struggle, my man. And Watt, he ain't afraid t' die fo' he give up a brotha. But he ain't afraid to kill, neitha, if a brotha give him up.

Can't be a neutron. Can't go back to St. Joseph's. No soap's gonna take off the tattoos. Gonna need the GD's to the end. Can't quit a gang, once you start. And no blamin' the affiliation for gettin' me in this place. Or no point to it. Won't change things. So keep on the road you started on with Watt. Or pray the white boy doesn't send you up for life. All he has to do is say the word—and you're in for *life*. Rather be dead, sometimes, than depend on his findin' himself, or on what he's

DIVISION

gonna say, whether t'kill me or let me live. Wants to save me. Maybe
rather burn in hell than have to hang on his white self for my salvation.
Unstable motherfucker.

Nothin' unstable about Watt. So maybe the white boy won't be
around to testify. And maybe Robert Teague.... Can't think about that.
Can't let myself get converted to that way a murderous thinkin'...GD's
tellin' me Robert's my enemy. Got to be a line you don't cross. But
best not to think. Just wish to live. Don't wish Robert dead. Would
you kill a person to free yourself? How about when it's, if you don't
kill, then you die? Call it self-defense. Better just to close your eyes
and let it happen—and when you wake up, trouble's gone. Thank you,
Dr. Watt. Or would you let *yourself* be killed, just so's not to kill somebody else? But what's the reward for that?

But fuck if all this shit's not just playin' in my mind. Watt's gonna
do what he's gonna do. All away from me. All in the dark. So I don't
have to see. And nothin' I can do about it.

But...I can't be pretendin', neither...that I don't know what's goin'
on.... Be a phony if I do. Like Watt said to me. And knowin' what I
do know.... Best keep my eyes open for what this motherfucker below
me's up to. Keep myself alive with my own eyes. And Christa—she's still
talkin' to Connor Riordan's daddy. Says she *knows* Connor Riordan
wants to help me. And Uncle Maurice. Feel like the man can see right
into my mind, whenever he comes and talks to me. And Mama—she'd
say the Lord can see everything. Maybe he can. So best never be caught
dreamin' about if somebody's out the way. Pay a price for dreamin'
that way, somewhere in this world or the next.

In the exercise yard of Division I, under the watchtowers, there were
several basketball courts—"Only city courts," a cafeteria friend said,
"where they ain't took down the rims t' stop bangers congregatin'—
or where the real game goin' down, with the for-real *play*-uzzz—ain't
talkin' about basketball." But it wasn't that often that Division I detainees were let out to the yard. So when at lunch that day the word
went out that there'd be yard time in the mid-afternoon, Marcus's
attention was keened, for he knew that there were those who'd see in
this the perfect opportunity to start up whatever in hell it was they'd
been readyin', three, four days now, to get started. And he saw that
the 'Q,' when the word goes out, he lets his lunch sit and heads off
to make a call, bow-leg animal motherfucker not just gettin' calls but
havin' somehow, too, that out-call account lets him make, himself, to

244

who-the-fuck-ever, one a those ten-dollar calls. And as he set down his own sandwich on his plastic plate, the Tumbler, thinking too of protective custody and of safe solitary confinement for whatever weeks, months, were necessary, imagined the conversation between 'Q' and whomever—and, exact particulars aside, in terms not in essence different from those of the actual conversation that at the phone shelf in the day room, was just then taking place.

"Motherfucker out the Five give us reason. Fucked with the lock and then come down and grab a brotha by the hair and start bangin' his face up agin' the bars 'til he near kilt the brotha. CO let me know, too, they's gon' be yard time this afternoon, and they ain't gon' look too hard we put the boot on VL skulls 'cause one them motherfuckers took a bite out the neck of a CO. Been workin' it good near a week and got near twenty brothas ready. And, brotha Watt, ain't no time like the present, 'cause the ac-ro-bat gon' want some fresh air. Motherfucker's been cooped up long enough it's got to his mind."

"Good place t' be, my brotha—where things jus' got to be done, no questions asked. Good place. All kinda surprising things gon' open up when you're in that place seems all closed down except one last door—and you got to bust through that motherfucker, or die. Take a life, or be taken. Do, or be done. Place a war. And always good for me when it's someone with me understands this. You ain't a man a questions, Q. You're a man's gon' do things. And you get this thing done, my brotha, it's gon' make all the difference, once you're out. Fifteen months worst case. And fair chance you gon' walk clean. Benny Twin Bill—the man's been laid to rest. And his sheep are mine now. And all that motherfucker's pastures. Buildin' a kingdom where we make our own justice, which you gon' be in the mood for once you're out again past the white man's. Check out one more time his might-make-right thing. Look good and close. Take a lesson from his book. And understand, you get this work done, you gon' be my chief a police. Law of advancement. You trust my gratitude. You trust me."

That afternoon in the yard, Marcus saw that no shotguns stood up in the watchtowers overlooking the main exercise area, which, behind its twenty-foot-high chain-link fences, everywhere topped with glistening razor wire, comprises four full-length basketball courts. The GD's, maybe forty strong, were grouped under the north-end basket of the second court. The VL's, all on the fourth court, were ten of them playing in, while the rest, maybe twenty, were watching a game they had

going. But now Marcus noticed that as a huddle around Q had broken, a movement was beginning forward from where it had gathered—
toward the third court, the one that separated the GD's and VL's. And
quickly now Marcus, aware he had to watch out, maybe for his life,
still found himself being forced by this momentum into the third court.
Those regathering around Q, Marcus, amid the push, still could tell
put themselves in place to keep him moving forward toward the fourth
court, where the VL's had suddenly now stopped their game and begun
to gather into a formation facing what was now a clear GD advance.

"Which one you cunt motherfuckers grab Gee Gee's face an' pull it
into them bars!?"

So the gauntlet was thrown down by one from those re-huddled
around Q. And by now both gangs had moved well into the third court
and, in their main bodies, stood facing each other not more than ten
feet apart. No spoken answer to the challenge came from the Vice
Lords. But then out of the silence—for whatever those reasons are that
that first gunshot which starts a battle is fired (a mix, maybe, of death
wish, rash honor, dread of shame, aroused suddenly against all inertia,
and which takes a young man up into its violent determination)—a
VL who had the ball under his arm slipped it down to his throwing
hand and hurled it with violent speed too quick to deflect right into
the face of a GD who in the continuing forward push of things was
now just a body length in front of him. And as with this the battle began in a mad rush of bodies into bodies, with violence deadening fear
and, on both sides, gangster honor fixing souls into hard ruthlessness,
the intent behind the blows, everywhere, moved swiftly to the borders
of murder. And Marcus, impelled into the vanguard by the phalanx
around Q but at the same time driven by them toward the battle's left
flank, found himself confronted by a VL before him—but also feeling
behind him a gathering threat from Q and his men, maybe fifteen, who
seemed to want to force him forward but also to separate him off to
the left for something *else*.

The Tumbler, quick in his extraordinary athletic gift, ducked the
VL's first swing and, from his crouch, sprung a powerful uppercut that
knocked the VL back—but then had to turn just as quick to face the
GD's—and Q.

War within war. Loyalties, in this violent place, were all to nothing
and to no one. And there it was—confirmed as expected—the seven-
inch shank with the cloth haft—his piece a candy, which Q once more

246

now dandled in the palm of his hand. And the Tumbler knew what he had known from the start—that all of this dead-staring animal's calls in the day room were to, or from, Watt. The men with Q now created a nearly closed ring, which left within it only the Q and the Tumbler, while beyond them all the larger battle raged on. And now, not caring to offer a first syllable of explanation, the Q began to come on, waving the shank slowly before him back and forth, stepping toward the Tumbler. And the unarmed Tumbler stepped now back and away, back and away—until he could sense the double posts of the basket behind him and see above him its backboard, rim, and net.

He had nowhere to run. He could see that the powerful, murderous Q, the law of the Folk, was ready to come in for the kill. He waited for the Q's lunge and then, in a desperate surprise move, he leapt up from a dead jump to grab the basketball net and evaded the slash of the knife by, with sheer acrobatic miracle, pulling his entire body, legs tucked, up above the onrushing Q, who, slashing and missing, clumsily fell forward to the ground. But the Tumbler, hemmed in by Q's men, still had nowhere to run. And now the enraged Q was picking himself up from the ground. The Tumbler, still holding himself up on the net, now brought both his hands up to the basket's rim and began to swing his body back and forth in a pendulous movement that rapidly took him high and strong so that he might, he thought, even vault himself in the air past the enclosure of Q's men and make a run, maybe toward the VL's.

But now the Q, having risen, was coming again, and the Tumbler could think of nothing but to swing still higher in his pendulum, to make himself at least a more elusive target. But then, as the Q came at him, knife raised, the Tumbler saw a different, new chance and brought his full pendulum force right down toward the unguarded face of his enemy; and in his powerful downswing he hit the Q so flush and hard, with both his feet square to the Q's head, that he knocked Q's two hundred and fifteen pounds to his back, having completely stunned him, though not before the Q had cut his calf with a last wild slash of the shank. But while cut and bleeding, the Tumbler, as Q's men tightened round him, still was able to chin himself up over the rim and with a powerful last hoist to bring his elbows up onto it. Then with remarkable speed, which made his enemies now for a moment just stand and watch him, he raised himself up on his elbows and then hands, and then with a pushup lifting his torso high on his hands, he swung his

247

DIVISION

hip up onto the rim and then grabbed the top of the backboard and
took himself entirely up onto the ten-foot high rim, where he stood
now safe above them all—yet still from there, in a kind of mad athletic
brilliance he climbed even higher onto the top two of the four armatures that supported the backboard and, legs spread, one foot on each
of the armatures, stood balanced there overlooking all, his feet a dozen
and his eyes nearly eighteen feet in the air. And as right then, too, from
his high perch, he saw shotguns charging into the yard in full force, he
roared out suddenly, from deep in his soul: "I'VE BEEN TO TOKYO
JAPAN, YOU MURDERIN' MOTHERFUCKERS! I'VE BEEN TO
TOKYO JAPAN!"

His wound wasn't deep. They bandaged it in the infirmary and then,
from there, never returning him to Division One, took him to Protective Custody in Division Nine. Behind the iron door, in solitary, with
only a single window-slit letting in light, he thought of his mother, and
of his uncle Maurice, and of Mr. Jesse White. And as he fought back
tears he repeated to himself, "I told those murderin' motherfuckers
where I've been. I told 'em. I TOLD 'EM I GOT OUT."

DUTY

Always another way, Sara says. Can't be comin' at the expense of the two cousins. Marcus so bright and good, and Robert Teague, same thing—but top a that, Cousin Teague's got his life raised up higher yet by his Jesus-lovin' family—the gravedigger and his lady. As he took yet another dare-it-all walk past the District 3 station, pausing right in front and staring in from the sidewalk on Cottage Grove, Watt, cold furious for days at that gotdamn Q (for whom he'd have no more use) and his failin' to get done what had to get done (and, Miss Sara Lee, there's no other way but at the expense a those cousins), smiled now despite himself as he pictured that crazy high-tumblin' nigga standin' up top the basketball backboard yellin' out Fuck y'all, he's been to Tokyo! And *fuck me,* he said, as he crossed Cottage and began to walk along the cemetery wall toward 67th—jus' *fuck* me if out a either a those two I couldn't a got more in a day than I get out a thug motherfucker like Q in a lifetime. Human over animal, every time—and I was all future-invested the right way. Had the Tumbler and about had the reparation-revolution boy. But a man come t' the river that white boy takes him to, sayin' right up in his face, back

249

side a his white-boy mansion home, sittin' in his rich-boy Mercedes, *You take your nigga hand off my property, and you blame nobody but your nigga self for your fucked-up life*—then man's got to do what he's got to do, even when there's no comin' back from it. But like t' stiffen' a man's dick when he knows he's comin' up past that point a no return. Somethin' about it, dark and true—hits a man crazy-like in the pleasure spot. So jus' pull that trigga. Pure and simple, too, once the line gets crossed—the way it ends the thinkin' and starts the action. But that white boy—struck me now a thousand times—why in *the* fuck's he comin' at me all uppity like that? Crazy motherfucker jus' beggin' to die. White man's dividin' line 'gainst a black man gon' run deep as hate can go—and back atch'ya, my brother. Knowledge. But still— what came over him, death starin' in his face? Not like that otha one— chickenshit drunk-ass bitch who, by some snake-eye throw, he *knows* Teague and can separate Teague out when it every time's gon' be one big equal nigga in a white boy's mind.

We *do*. Fuckin' right we do. And when it comes to makin' ah own law and justice, right out ah own mind, WE DO. And when it comes to us or the cousins or that white boy, we do what we need to do. Been long enough wastin' time with this shit. Let the kingdom come. Barksdale. Hoover. Motherfuckin' Fort, Black P Stones Black Prince—take that trip from Aberdeen, Miss'ippi to Florence, Colorado, by way of Chi Town, MY TOWN. And send a Rocky Mountain fuck yo-self to King Larry Hoover. Let the dead bury their dead.

So Watt would continue to put it to himself as he kept walking along the cemetery wall down to 67th, where he turned east—to see that while it was getting on in the afternoon, the gate to the graveyard was not yet closed. And when he came up to it, he turned and passed under the *Oak Woods* sign into the wide-spreading cemetery, silent as endless eternity, and would take as much of a look-see as he could before closing time.

Meanwhile on the 1400 block of N. Mohawk, a blackwall-tired municipal vehicle, monotone forest-green Chevrolet Lumina, with the police spotlight atop the driver's-side side-view mirror, had pulled up in front of 1441—the so-far un-rehabbed graystone, quaint-beautiful, with its parapet-ed entry bay—the home of Miss Sara Lee and her two roommates, Monica and Kai-Kai, who danced with Sara at the V.I.P. gentlemen's club.

Detective John Touhy had showered and shaved, scrubbed his teeth, mouthwashed and put on a clean shirt and a fresh-pressed suit in the locker room at the 18th District Station house. This would be his sixth time coming to see Miss Sara Lee, Sandra Leyland, whom he now called Sandra and who called him John, as he had asked her to. Build trust. Faith. And maybe you could get somewhere you'd never otherwise get. Make it personal. But never go too far—even though part of you, John Touhy, wants to go too far—wants *her* more than you've ever known yourself to want anyone—truth be told.

Every day between every visit, he'd thought of her, now over six months. The more he thought of his marriage to Jean, which he'd never betrayed, and his police duty, which he'd never betrayed, the more warmly he thought of Sara Lee, Sandra. And as he shut now the door of his car, he felt, as he'd felt every time he'd come back after his first seeing her, a sweet difference in his heartbeat and a rush of bewildering pleasure, both because he was overcome by her beauty but also—and up 'til now he'd divided himself from the thought of this by building a wall against it in his mind—because he was in love with her.

She had spoken of her and Watt having been lovers. And John Touhy also found it confusing that this, too, would be so deeply true—that when he thought of Sandra's loving Watt, and to that point of unshakeable loyalty which she had so far shown—when he thought of them not just having sex but making real love—that this would for him transform Watt into someone he could no longer despise—into a human being with all the human complexities. It put him, personally, vicariously, into Watt's life and soul as he imagined Watt going into that beautiful place where you found the real Sandra and she found you; where you gave yourself to her and she gave herself, all her beauty and soul, to you. But as he walked now toward the door at 1441, he thought that the new things he had to tell Sandra—that the Fugitive Apprehension Unit of the U. S. Marshall's Office had come to Chicago as a result of the investigation of the violent murder, in Greenwood, Mississippi, of one Eugene Sykes, who turned out to be Watt's father—and that the Marshalls were here, warrant in hand, because there was every reason to suspect that the son was involved in this murder—that these new things might at last turn her against him and get her to say where Watt was.

He'd never seen Sara Lee at the gentlemen's club, but as the door's knocker sounded against the plate, he suddenly imagined her in glistening sex-beauty warming the loins of numbers of crude-laughing men and some silent, gazing men—and he felt the heat himself. But another

DIVISION

moment, then, and the door opened, and it was Sandra, in need of no glitter, nor of anything other than her pure beauty—to touch a man far down in his heart.

"You're back again," she said, smiling, showing only her face—those startling blue eyes, her golden skin—beyond the cover of the door—but then stepping back and taking the old, heavy door slowly along with her, opening it wide upon herself, welcoming him in. "And how funny," she said, still smiling, softly, as she stood now in the small foyer, "but just today I was thinking of you."

He knew she knew. He could see himself now with her eyes, in his fresh-pressed suit, clean shaven, groomed. All given away. So, with it come this far, he might as well say it, just as he felt it. He closed his eyes, smiled, and with a feeling that he was sailing down from some high place, soft and slow, with pleasure, he said, "And I've been thinking of you...not just today."

He opened his eyes to see her smiling, still. A sweet awkwardness was there now, for both of them. And it gave him a warm joy to see on her face just that touch of embarrassment, human, natural—and to feel that what he'd said about his thinking of her, not just today, had started something new and different—which the instant he'd said it, he'd prayed it would.

She smiled, still self-consciously, but now reached forward and—such sweet happiness for him—she took his hand in hers—and she led him, not into the dining room, where they'd talked every time before, but into the parlor opposite, and now to the couch, where she sat, and then placed the palm of her hand on the cushion, tapping it softly to invite him to sit next to her. She was at ease now. And she had relaxed things for them both—acknowledging, indeed now leading the moment. And he let himself be led, sitting down beside her, feeling a breathless new pleasure. Just to be this close with her—and she not Sara Lee but herself, wearing jeans and a cotton, beige-buttoned blouse, soft white, plain and simple, her hair soft brown touched with gold, her skin, flawlessly beautiful, her lips, untouched, soft and rich, her blue eyes, ever striking under her dark brows and against her golden skin, and her fragrance—was it just a scented soap she'd washed her skin with? or a touch of perfume?—no matter, it was her fragrance. And he knew, as he'd known from long before he'd left the station, that John Touhy was bringing John Touhy this evening to a turning point in his life. And now, with all the warm promise of the choices he

252

was making coming true, there was this whole new pleasure, moving through him like a drug.

But if he died here, in sex, and was found—the disgrace. His mind couldn't escape division, conflict—a pain mixing with the pleasure. And the lies he'd need to tell Jean, her face growing older, but still Jean, more Jean than ever, so fiercely bright, always ahead of him, and good, such a true, good woman—one never to lie to. His only woman, ever in his life. He'd never lied to her. But so easy to think of lies now. Where were you today? What was your day? So easy to come up with answers, all of which would work because she'd never not trusted him. And more than his entire life, his marriage, more than all his own good history, all that he'd made of himself, he wanted the kiss that would spell the beginning of the end of it all. He wanted the self-annihilating caress, with this young woman, more movingly beautiful than any other he'd ever known—who, with just the warm, moist touch of her lips, could save him from the feeling of a living death. He was a police officer—in pursuit of a murderer. He wanted the kiss to come, with Sandra, and the passion. He wanted nothing to stop the moment that she'd now helped him to lead on, tapping the couch softly with her hand, to invite him. It was begun. Please, God, don't stop it.

But rather than reach out to touch her face, to take her to him for the kiss, he took her hand—to his lips, and kissed it softly, with warm love—but then let his hand fall, still holding hers. He said, looking at her still with love, close beside her, "We've been contacted…by the U.S. Marshalls' Office. They've come to Chicago with a warrant, resulting from the investigation of a murder, in Greenwood, Mississippi. A man named Eugene Sykes was murdered, brutally, in his Greenwood home. And this Eugene Sykes, it turns out, is Watt's father, formerly from here but for the past eleven years living in Greenwood, where he was born. Witnesses at a Greenwood hotel and here at the Union Station and from AMTRAK have given accounts that make it clear that Watt was in Greenwood at the time of the murder. They have a warrant—and no other suspects, nor reason to believe there will be any other."

Watt had never spoken to her about the death of the Lincoln Park white boy—and, after their initial discussion on the day he'd come to stay with her on Mohawk, she'd never asked again about why it was the police were looking for him—though one time inferring from questions he'd asked that Marcus Sabbs and Robert Teague had information that might damage him, and that he might desire their silence more

253

than their safety, she'd said to him that their personal safety, their lives, were of such a value that this must force him to discover and to choose, to the end, alternatives to his own convenience. There *had* to be other ways, she'd said. Once, though, too, after they'd made love, while he disclosed nothing in specific, he had explained his needing to keep hidden with her, by saying, with reference to his being wanted by the police...that something had happened that *had* to happen—and that his reasons for making it happen were as deep as any he'd ever had— even as any he'd had for protecting her with a strong arm. And for that, she knew, there had been reasons deep enough even for extreme measures. She owed her life to him, she knew.

And she knew now about the white boy—Jack Riordan. John Touhy had told her about him. And he'd told her about Marcus's arrest and about Robert Teague. And she'd remained ever consistent with John, insisting always that the things that Marcus had said and those that Robert had said were all true—that they were coming over to see her, on the night in question—that they were on their way, at the hour in question—that there was no mention of business to be conducted between the time of the call and that of the arranged date, the span between these times exactly right for a walk from Lincoln Park to Mohawk. And *yes* she most certainly would testify to that in court. But she would never say where Watt was now, insisting always that she had no idea— though she'd known since the day he left here, where over his days with her, he'd grown his beard, and shaved his head, leaving at last with new things she'd gotten him, clothes, eyeglasses—that he was hiding in plain sight on the South Side.

But suddenly, with the noose tightening, forces closing in, the CPD, the U.S. Marshalls, with the warrant, and with no other suspects, Sandra feared that Watt might need a wholly different kind of protection. She withdrew her hand from John's, Detective Touhy's. But she kept close to him on the couch. She lowered her eyes, then half-looked up, and, thoughtful, soft-voiced, after a pause, began, "How is it, John, that we become what we become? I was one thing, and then, after things happened to me, I was another. I was in one place, and after those things happened, I was in another. Now I'm here. And where will I be? I'm never sure, now, what I have to do with who or where or what I am."

She turned her head a moment, and paused, silent. John Touhy, the conflict in him now between his desire, which had been forced into

DUTY

abeyance, and his care, respect, sympathy, all now mounting, saying to him *listen*—readied himself to keep listening.

Sandra, her mind moving now from her own experiences to what she imagined of Watt's, began again, as if addressing not just John Touhy but some highest court where determinations must take into account everything that makes us what we are: "When he was ten years old, he walked into his apartment, in Cabrini, and found his mother dead on the floor, her throat slit. He stood in his mother's blood, at ten years old. He's told me that not a day goes by without his mind returning to that moment when he found her." She looked up. She saw that John Touhy was listening, it seemed truly as a man, not a mere officer of that law which considers only the thing done—and nothing of what was done to the one who did it. "And *what,*" she said, "even before that, did he start from? Beatings and abuse. His mother, too, beaten and abused. Condemned to drugs and to selling herself for drugs. I know this. Sixteen. I was no older, not really. And she was sixteen when she had Watt. That could have been me. And condemned—to killing her conscience over and over with every trick and john until her conscience was gone. But never utterly gone, never any final freedom from shame."

John Touhy—never having seen this side of her, Sandra having always with him, for him, divided herself off from her past and her pain, keeping things light (as if for a Sara customer)—felt now painfully ashamed of himself. He couldn't believe he would participate in such slavery—that he would be part of the capitalizing on Sandra's personal history of pain and hardship—on what had been done to her. That he would rationalize, discover lie after lie, as needed, so he could be part of this exploitation—without being caught, either by his wife or his own conscience. The deceiving, self-deceiving officer of the law. John the john. Husband and trick. But even as he felt torn by guilt and shame, he wanted her. The pleasure he felt sitting close with her was nearly overwhelming. Her fragrance. Her face, her eyes. And now the human feeling she had for Watt. And Watt's human life, his pain and suffering. And her pain, which in his shame he came to see—to feel. The depth of the injustices. He let his passion take on now the dignity of compassion—for he could feel that a deepening personal connection with this beautiful woman was giving now a new pleasure and strength to his desire for her.

"The Gasoline Man," she said. "Watt's father was called the Gasoline Man. He was the one who enslaved his mother, sold her into drugs and prostitution, kept her chained. He brutalized her and brutalized Watt, for years, beat them bloody against the wall if either tried to improve, to learn more than he knew, because this might mean he couldn't control their every motion and that his pimp money would dry up, or that they'd embarrass him with a power he didn't possess. He was a savage—one of the most feared, Watt said, of all the OG's. And he was the one who slit her throat. Watt knew. It's what he lived with, every day from that point on, when he was ten—the image of his mother, lying in a pool of her own blood, and the knowledge that the murderer was his father—who never once acknowledged him as his son. So if Watt, or if the person, or the instrument of justice that Watt was made by what was done to him, killed that man, John Touhy, it was an eye for an eye, which is the only law and only justice that blacks in white America ever really count on. They don't have the law, John, that you represent. They don't have the police. So how can they bring about a just punishment, or find closure?"

But he was not a policeman now. In his guilt and shame and compassion and pleasure, in his desire, he could feel himself rising beyond all the simplicities of his life of commitments—every narrow, confining duty. And the transcendence of it all worked like a drug. The pleasure of his rising beyond himself, beyond the cop, beyond all crude, stupid divisions was a drug, which maybe he would feel running all through him still when he made love with this beautiful young woman —all through the time, un-conflicted, feeling a pure sincerity, feeling an undivided love for her and for all things—past all the crude simplicities and closed-mindedness of a lifetime in *law enforcement*. And was the time come now for the kiss?—to start the night? Surely yes. But as he let himself feel this, and let himself go—and *because* he was letting himself go—his self, his life, came back—extremes, opposites, meeting again in his divided but not divided soul. The cop—came back. His voice came to him. As if ready to take a statement, he asked her, as he looked close into her eyes, "Why was he called the Gasoline Man?"

As she had tried to explain and defend Watt by bringing things back to the origin, his father, she'd felt running through her mind as an undercurrent the thought of her own father, Jonah Leyland, who left her when she was sobbing—shook her from his knee as she'd clung, falling, begging—and also images of her mother, Frances Priester Leyland, tearless, raging at her husband, cursing him in homicidally violent language—the two of them all the more awful, for years, because of their

DUTY

intelligence and sophistication, their capacities for inventing insults that would undermine even the most basic affection for life and self-respect—those two who'd overcome all racial divisions in their good days, her half-black father and her white mother, saviors of America, of the Union, and let none divide what God has joined. She'd never forgiven them—instead she just *left,* forever, never looking back, or calling. And when she'd been with married men, she'd in a not altogether unconscious vengefulness indulged retaliatory feelings against marriage, licensing a secret destructive desire, an invisible and yet never wholly undetectable violence toward marital happiness and faith, which destructive desire she found would add a warm power of wickedness to her seductions and would enhance the pleasure of the sex not just for her client, to whom in a soft, kitten voice she would whisper wicked things, but, also noticeably, enhance it for herself. But this man, John Touhy, a john—and *not.* Handsome father figure. Human being—who had kissed her hand. He'd asked how it was that the Gasoline Man got his name.

He had let her hand go, and she touched her two hands together, fingertips to fingertips, and now pressed the tips of her forefingers to her lips. Then, lowering her hands, "What all was he feeling," she said, "the man who gunned down Martin Luther King? Just before he pulled that trigger? What did he feel in his mind and hot between his devil's legs about what all he might be starting—the history-making of it all? And what made it so that the ones who didn't just come from Mississippi but were the most miserable—the utterly penniless downtrodden sharecroppers, wholly uneducated, un-skilled, destitute—that these would be the ones who'd end up in the very worst, most miserable conditions when they came north? Hopelessness followed by hopelessness. He was living in the darkest dens of the West Side, Watt's father, at the time King was killed. Come from the Mississippi Delta to another complete segregation and more poverty and now gangster life. And it was during the MLK riots that he got his name, the Gasoline Man— because he'd lit on fire more buildings than anybody else. And that's what it is—violence—you light on fire your own neighborhood because, after endless disappointments and deceptions, you want everything even possibly good or hopeful to be burned to the goddamned ground. And when there was nowhere for the burned-out West Siders to live, they started to move them into Cabrini, first forcing and then, with the cascading influx, scaring out of the project what would come in the

DIVISION

end to literally thousands of people from working families, who ran away hard as white folks, and turning Cabrini thoroughly into a vertical slum, with no more paying tenants, no more community, no more anything but countless fatherless babies living down on the street. Lost kids—an endless fund of gangster recruits, defacing every wall and vandalizing every light, when they weren't in school, which was day after day. And that's how it started for Watt—when, after the West Side riots, the furious Gasoline Man came into Cabrini, in time noticing Watt's mother and then, when she was fifteen, getting her pregnant and making a slave of her."

She bowed her head some—and then, looking up at John Touhy, fresh dressed, handsome, she reached with both hands for his hand and took it and held it in her hands. "But listen to me, John," she said, "blaming and then exonerating, and then blaming again, and then not. *Not* blaming Watt but then turning around and *blaming* his father and then *not* blaming his father but turning around and *blaming* James Earl Ray and then wondering what all explained *him*—and what made me into me, whoever I now am." Softly now she pressed John Touhy's hand in her hands. And with her striking blue eyes, whose power she knew, she looked closely at him. And she told him, "But the ones I never stop blaming, John Touhy, the ones I never forgive, are my father and mother. When I was a girl, I used to think that when I chose a man, it wouldn't be because he was white or black—because I was at the same time perfectly both and neither—so that when I chose, it would be entirely for love. And I loved my parents for giving me this perfect freedom and a perfect self-esteem. I loved them. They gave me so much. But it wasn't the same perfect mix for them as it was in me, and they started to split apart and hate each other, for only God knows what reasons—and as only brilliant people can hate and tear each other apart. And my heaven became hell, so I had to get out from it, and I've never looked back since the day I left and I cannot, cannot forgive, even after all this time. I blame them. I hold them responsible. And my unforgiving anger is always with me, even though I don't feel like the same person I was. I can't remember her. I just remember her anger."

She still held John Touhy's hand in her hands, with a truth of affection he could feel; but now she looked away and closed her eyes. Then, as she looked at him again, "And when I'm with a married man..." she said.... "Please let me confess and be honest with you...John...." She looked at him, now curiously, with a slight smile. "Let me confess....

258

DUTY

I take my revenge," she said, still with that slight, curious smile. She now took his hand in her hands and set it on her thigh and covered his hand with her two warm hands. "Let me confess," she said again, in a softer voice, "...to satisfy my anger...against marriage...I whisper to the married man I'm with that he deserves to be free from the prison of it...the lie of it." She let his hand free now, to rest against her thigh, and then she reached her hand to his face and touched her palm against his cheek, and then lifted her hand to touch and softly trace his lips with a finger as she said...in a whisper..."I tell him he's lived with the lie too long. He's been a prisoner of the lie...too long...far too long."

Overwhelmed with desire, John Touhy pressed his hand against her thigh, where she'd set it. He moved closer to her, on fire for her. He loved her voice. He loved what she was saying. Such deep pleasure he took in what she was saying. Such pleasure in her beauty. And all of it now, all the passion and the heartfelt compassion, all of his desire, all his need just to bring to an end all that he ever was and had made of himself with narrowing lies, all of it, all his desire and his need was now coming together. And her fragrance, the beauty of her eyes, her skin, the softness of her voice, and all that she was saying—the pleasure of hearing what she was saying, that his life was a prison and a lie.

"Let yourself feel it," she whispered, as she moved her hand to his shoulder and began to take him to her, while at the same time he reached for her, to take her to him, close for the kiss. "Let it happen. No more lies."

And it was all that he'd ever hoped. And beyond anything he'd ever known. The kiss. In the beautiful darkness, in the abandon, he still could feel, or think without thinking—that to have known this before he died was to have known at least one moment of a life complete. Her lips, with hunger and the need of all his life, he kissed them again, knowing, before he passed out of this life, the pleasure of this taste. And between their kisses now she began again to whisper, saying, with her cheek warm against his cheek, her lips to his ear, "You don't need the lie. You don't need her. She isn't what you need. She was never what you needed."

And in the darkness, feeling that it mattered not at all now that he would go farther and farther, having gone already too far to turn back, he heard that beautiful voice—She was never what you needed—She was never what you needed. He heard this come from her lips. Then with his cheek against her cheek, Sandra's, Sara Lee's—as now suddenly

259

DIVISION

in a new and different way he took his hands to her shoulders and pressed them hard with his fingers, inflicting hard pain, he whispered in her ear, "Where is he?"

She pulled away her face. And broke apart from him. She looked at him with those eyes, and once more with that slight smile. "I'm sure," she said, no longer in a soft, warm whisper, "that it must be time for you to go on home—and for me to get ready for work."

THE BRAIDED NECKLACE

Ellie Shea and Connor Riordan, seated together now at Jeanette's on Chestnut, a block east of Michigan Ave., had been walking, all the way up and over from Grant Park and the harbor. As they'd made their way, Connor curious, wanting very much now to know details, they had for some time been talking about the class Ellie had taken with his father. And still, with an energy of responsive, probing interest, he was asking her to go on. "So these divisions," she said, "in the soul. For Blake, they're these mental states. Or they're *places* in the mind, or soul, that for him pre-exist there, and, when you're in these places or states of mind, they produce definite and exclusive passions, preoccupations, fixations. You fall into one state of mind and you're all for law and order; you fall into another and you're all for revolution. Here it's all justice and judgment; there it's all mercy and forgiveness."

When she'd been in Tom Riordan's class, everything Ellie had been through with Jack...and, after Jack was killed.... All these things, always, in the silent workings of her understanding, would be moving together with everything the father said, strand intertwining with strand. And every day—that living reminder—in Tom Riordan's, she could see Jack Riordan's face. But it was Connor she had heard in his father's voice, and found in every sensitivity of his father's clear and passionate thought. His father's mind, and soul. His mother's face—the bones of her face, the eyes, the skin, his mother's mouth. That sudden sharp pang of grief—in that moment when, Jack bringing her, she had first met Jackie Riordan...and saw Connor again at Ignatius. His face, when he walked into class, or when she walked into class, and he was there before her. But only one time, in one class, did he respond in a positive way to something she said—and then for days after that, lying in her bed she would imagine intimacies of conversation.... But four years went by—and nothing. That party.... He was there, talking with others. Stella Artois. His lips...moistened...touching the bottle's rim. Could she have made happen, what she wanted to happen? And if so, why did she not? Girls should be cool and wait. Make the boy start things. Was that it?—at first?—when she was fourteen, fifteen? And this child's game—or this outdated damned gender nonsense—it took on some sort of life of its own? and lasted? Maybe, somewhat. Or very simply she stayed behind a wall because someone she loved just didn't care for her? Yes. For sure, that. And the anger, finally, after years, because his never approaching read for her as a deliberate cold repelling. But did she always know he did, or might, care for her? And if somewhere she did know, or feel, maybe, what he felt, or might feel—then for *what,* her own never moving, never making things happen? Pride, still? Sloth? Wrath? Which, or how many of the Seven Deadlies, were moving, silent, invisible, deep down inside...the ordinary life of an ordinary girl, a girl always well provided for, her life uneventful? And then when she did make something...so much...happen...what place *that,* in her soul? Little brother, don't you wish this was you? Could she say she was surprised when she heard this in that dark place (mysterious and dark at the heart even of ordinary girls)—the place where you learn that to *Know Thyself* will take a lifetime? And where sex sometimes carries a gun? Always in her understanding, in its silent mysteries, all these things interwove themselves with what Tom Riordan said as she had listened to him in class. Call it learning. William Blake. Love seeketh not itself to please, and builds, in hell's despair, a heaven. Love seeketh only self to please, and builds in heaven's despair.... A Poison Tree.

THE BRAIDED NECKLACE

But now with so many separative walls broken down, and, on this special night with Connor, at Jeanette's, just the two of them, intimate, and in a new, better world, she went on, with him listening to her as thoughtfully, in his way, as she had listened to his father. "In these states.... I'm not sure you even call them states of mind—because you don't *think* any more in them, you just pull the lever for one party or the other, liberal, conservative, left wing, right—and begin to hate and fear the opposition, as you completely identify your now divided, fragmented self with the party you've chosen." She breathed in, slowly, more deeply—letting things come to her. She touched her forefinger to her thumb—and for a moment pressed them against each other. At last then, "He, *however,* says...he *insists...*Blake...that these states—they are *never* the true you. The *true* human soul—it's never divided. It's always integrated. Coordinated. Your real soul is never so stupid as to be partisan, letting some broken-off division of it, conservative, liberal, become a control-freak usurper of everything. It never in some tribal way sets control altogether over imagination, or imagination altogether over control, conservative over liberal, or vice versa." She stopped... and gave now a warm look to Connor, having let that come to her, too. "Your father, when he talked about these things, was always so clear but so passionate. I so loved the class. Old Testament and New, God the Father and God the Son, all one in the Holy Spirit, the undivided three-person God."

Connor, thinking again now of how when he had heard her in school, his feelings, if he concentrated them, closed himself inside them, were such that it seemed Ellie Shea's words might physically touch him, was recalling once more too (though now beneath the level of thought)... how a beautiful woman *achieved* her beauty.... The *without* inseparable from the *within.* He had always been proud...as a kid...seeing all of her in the beauty of her face....

Ellie, having again paused to take thought, now pursed her lips, then half-relaxed her mouth...into a crooked half-smile. "Of course," she said, tight-raising her cheek now to cock an eye, "your dad would explain that what can come then is the Fall, which, for Blake, is this dark descent into the illusory world presented by the senses. The world of pure *matter.* The world of only what we can see right before us. And when we fall into this world, we don't believe anymore in the invisible, which, however, happens to be the infinite, the creative source of everything new, the fountain of endless creative process, as opposed

to the fixed world we see before us, with our eyes, which we now think
and insist is all there is. And when we fall into or stop with this fixed
materialist error, we start to believe that *we're also* nothing but limited,
finite bodies. And not, anymore, infinitely creative souls. We start to
think, like reactionaries, and often enough like violent reactionaries,
that there's nothing real or valuable beyond what we already know. Or
that we can touch and see. Or that we've already identified ourselves
with. And this original metaphysical error, or Original Sin—as it puts
fear of change and fear of death and consequently rigid self-protection,
Blake calls it 'stony dread,' at the center of every damned thing—starts
up the primal division of the world: One party now fixed against the
other. Or one race, or one creed fixed against all others. It divides the
human soul against its own wholeness. It sets this part or that part
of the soul tribally against the other, or all others. It calls what *we've*
embraced, *good,* and a matter of pride, and everything else, *evil,* and a
matter of shame." She paused again now, tilting her head. She raised a
finger and, slowly, traced it from her temple to her cheek, then closed
it back slowly into her hand, lifting her head again upright. Then nodding slightly three, four times, "Excessive self-consciousness and self-
definition and self-defensiveness—these are at the center of everything
after the Fall, along with fear of change and of the different, of the other.
In your fallen state, you become the entirely partisan politician selling your soul's truth because you're scared to death of not pleasing
your partisan fragment of the electorate. Or you become the chained
dog barking at strangers."

Her tone had become serious. Connor turned his look aside, then
looked back at her again. "If it really were, Ell," he said, his tone now
deepening, serious too, "just a matter of changing your metaphysics—
if you could *choose* your way out of hell, if you could just listen to a great
preacher and go home with your life changed, in possession now of all
the strong faith of a convert, after your William Blake moment—that
would be great. And maybe my dad is that preacher, Catholic-style. I
know that I've never known a better person. And I live with him. And
I know it has killed him, watching me. All the drinking, the getting
hammered, the day-long withdrawals into my room, only coming out
at night to get hammered again." He put his hand over his mouth a
moment, then, rubbing it across his lips, set it down. "But—and I don't
know if Blake ever came to this place—the place where, after something
really *happens* to you, you go into a fixity beyond choices—beyond any-

264

THE BRAIDED NECKLACE

thing you can *do,* except wait and, in wordless silence, pray. *No* words. You called it *time,* the healer you wait for. Patience. I've learned about patience. Just waiting, wordless, with a faith that you need to keep secret, because if the devil, who knows every deep way to prevent every submicroscopic measure of healing, finds out that you're believing in something, he'll get into your brain's electrical system and wire it his way...toward sweating terror. And the healing force that you wait for in silence—you know you better not try to name it—because if there *is* a God, you know that he/she/it *hates* religion, and will toss you to the devil for the first sign of it in you. Try to name God, in the place I've been, and you'll get a lot worse than those mystifications Moses got at the Burning Bush, when he asked for God's name. But the devil—I know this, too—hates communication, conversation, hates confiding in a friend, hates confession. He hates my being with you, because he knows it makes me believe in talking to you."

Ellie had considered it progress, another sign, a start of a new step, when Connor suggested a trip to the Museum of Contemporary Art. He said he was interested to see how a brilliant artist who'd been born into the Great Depression, who'd manned an anti-aircraft gun on the *Enterprise,* been on deck through all the fire and blood, the Kamikaze attacks, seen ships go down carrying hundreds, then had re-upped for Korea and had been through hell again, how he would express himself in sculpture; and so they visited the H. C. Westermann exhibit at the MCA. They both had been struck by the meticulousness and beauty of the artist's woodcraft as it was displayed in his surrealistic combinations. After more than an hour walking the exhibit and then a drink on the MCA terrace, open on an unseasonably mild 2nd of November, they had taken that walk through the park to the lake and then back, timing their stroll to meet their 7pm reservation at Jeanette's. Connor had eaten numerous times with his family at the French bistro a block off the Mag Mile.

Connor sat now with his back to the Chestnut St. window, through which Ellie looked, her face wearing a slight flush still from their walking in the autumn air, which did go chill at last as the night had come on. She was wearing a black cashmere jacket, simple, elegant, and a silver-gray, silken blouse, and a beaded chain with a tasseled-metal and stone pendant. Always different, her look, and beautiful. A flesh-colored lipstick tonight.

She smiled. "I'll whisper it quick," she said, "so the devil can't hear.

265

But that we can talk about the things we're talking about, and go to the museum, talk about art, literature—I'll say it quick—it's progress."

"And, oh shit, does the devil hate progress." Connor laughed a quiet laugh. Then, "You know—and don't tell Satan this either—but I've been able to think lately…about Jack. In ways I haven't. And your talking about things like states, divisions of the soul…it's made me think about Jack that night…. In the way I have, behind the devil's back."

He took a sip of his red wine as the waiter placed on the tablecloth a breadboard with a butter dish on it, and two golden-brown baguettes.

"Property," Connor said. "The place in the mind where the idea of property comes into being—it's one of those Blakean zones, I'd say. The home base of *Meum* and *tuum*. And Jack just fell into the *It's-my-property* zone, in ways that you would never say represented all he was —even though he went half-mad for it in a split second. Got into all the obsessions and fixations, right outa nowhere. But when a mind-zone is timeless, it doesn't take time to get into the passions that go with it. All the feelings of your privacy, or your property being invaded, trespassed against—in one second these feelings can kick in and become complete, which they did with Jack. So outa nowhere, to that Watt, it was *Get your hands off what doesn't belong to you!* But then it was also *Don't blame anybody but your fucked-up self for what you are!* And this is another one of those zones in the soul: the place where you have to be able to say to a person that he is responsible for his own life and to be able to blame and judge that person for things he's done. To state the obvious, if we couldn't hold people responsible for what they've done, the civilized world would fall apart—no law and order or legitimate punishment—or praise either, or attribution of merit. But when someone is in the *zone* of justice and blaming, this idea of the world's order depending upon responsibility becomes so over-simply and *unqualifiedly* true that this person must think that independent responsibility has *got,* also, to be deeply, deeply true, without *any* qualifications or mitigations. And Jacko fell into this eternal zone of over-simple justice and blaming, too—the place where nothing that anyone might have suffered before committing a crime is to be taken into account—and out of this place, he mercilessly spit all the rage and righteous indignation belonging to that place of blame-justice, right into Watt's face— all of that rage born in timeless eternity, but, for all that, *not* a rage representative of the entire Jack—even if he was for the moment entirely in that zone of hard, merciless justice, raging, blaming like hell. Or

THE BRAIDED NECKLACE

he was in both the place where property is born *and* the place where pure, unqualified justice and blaming are born."

Connor turned the stem of his glass. He watched his hand turning the wineglass on the white tablecloth. Then he looked again at Ellie, seeing her there ready to listen to him, waiting. "But where we go now, Ell, here in America, is to the idea that slavery, the calling of human beings unequal and the turning of them into property, especially as this sin lasted here for a quarter of a millennium, was so great a sin that it took the independent responsibility and the culpability right out of the enslaved—made it impossible for them, for centuries and beyond, to be truly free of the curse of their slavery—to be wholly responsible for themselves. And of course we would deny this, even with anger, as Jack denied it—for their sakes as well as ours, because no one wants to be a slave or a mere pitiable animal who can't be held responsible for himself. But if you're Watt and you've come from where he's come from, and you hear this about *OUR* property and *YOUR* responsibility and culpability—*Get your hands off what doesn't belong to you* and *You've got nobody to blame for your fucked-up life but yourself*—and you have a gun—then maybe in the space of an instant, every whip and chain, every hour of the millions of hours of forced labor, every instance of the millions of instances of denied humanity pours into you and through you, and you become the revenge of ages. It actually helps me to think Jack died in this moment that was filled with eternity, with eternal states come together in a conjunction that was about freedom and responsibility and mercy and justice and equality and property and the great primal American ur-sin of slavery—that it was this terrible but beautiful conjunction that had tragic meaning—that it wasn't just some local, sordid, car-jacking absurdity—even though I want to say of both Jack and Watt that they *were not* and *are not* what they came to be when narrowed down by passion into fixed states of the soul, profound as those states are. We are not fixed states of the soul. We are, as you say, infinitely more. And when we pass out of a state that we fell into, no matter how deep, we should be thought of as pure again, as clean of that state, as having been merely visitors there, in a place that is not our true home, which is a pure and undivided everywhere."

He looked at her across the table, again grateful for her beauty, the grace of it, the art—the way it could compose his soul and ready it for loving her, which was the thing he feared most the devil would find out. "All that I've said, Ell, about the way self-deceivers divide themselves

267

up and say that that part of them which did wrong was somebody else, not the real them—the way I've spat at the excuse and surreptitious license of compartmentalization, calling it the starting-ground of immorality—I was wrong. Or I was right but also wrong. The real person —I agree with Carolyn—is not the action performed in a zone of him or herself. The real person is the whole human soul of that person, and when he or she emerges from the partiality and the division he or she lived in when they did wrong, they emerge pure. Forgiveness, Ell—it's realizing this about real persons, and *feeling* it. Forgiveness as a principle, as a duty, that's good, but it's all from the realm of law. Forgiveness as a deep and blessed *feeling* is from the world of grace. But grace isn't chosen. The ego can't just decide it will take some grace, please. Grace comes to those who wait and pray, in ego-less silence—and let time, or the nameless force, do its thing." He smiled at her now. "But then it's amazing," he said, "—and take this from someone who lost his emotions almost entirely to a numb goddamn deadness—amazing how fast deepest feeling comes, and *forgiveness* comes—when you love...."

Words. Never at all adequate—and the idea that she needed forgiveness (and from him!)—which forgiveness, however, he knew she wanted and needed. She wasn't that night of revenge she took against him, with Jack. She wasn't her night with Jack—or any of the things that followed. He picked up one of the baguettes now and broke it and took some butter from the dish on the breadboard, and then, smiling at her, passed the breadboard over. "Best French bread *anywhere*," he said, spreading butter on his piece. "Let it change your life."

She pulled the breadboard toward her and smiled at Connor, letting him know she was glad for what he'd said. But she looked now a moment toward the entrance to the restaurant. Over Connor's shoulder, out the window, she'd seen someone passing—that face, and another. And now, for real, yes, she did—she saw them entering the restaurant, that very face, here, and now, his mother, Jackie Riordan, whom Connor had neither seen nor spoken to once in the three and a half months since she'd left home, and her new man, whom Connor had never seen—it had to be him—Richard Olen. What now was best?—that Connor would see his mother and go over to her and be at least civil, and maybe begin something good, some kind of reconciliation, and say hello civilly to Richard Olen and begin to know him—as a person, not an enemy? But did even she herself wish, at all, to be seen now with Connor by

268

THE BRAIDED NECKLACE

Jackie Riordan? Or to say hello? And what would happen, if Connor did see his mother—with her new man?

"Jesus *fucking* Christ...." Noticing how Ellie had turned, Connor had followed her look and now had seen what she had seen. Immediately he took and lifted his wineglass, still over half full, and drank it down; and as their waiter passed, he reached out and touched him. "How about a Jameson straight up and neat?" Clearly peeved by the tone and abruptness, and the touch, the waiter only nodded—but he made his way to place the order.

"Fucking Christ Jesus."

"Connor, I'd be so happy just to go, if you want.... If you're too angry to be here or to say hello, maybe we should just go."

"Look at that piece of shit, holding her arm—and her letting him. If I had a gun, I'd fucking shoot somebody. I swear to God—and fuck the consequences. If you knew how much detestation I was feeling.... Jesus fucking Christ."

"Connor, please, let's just go."

"Talk about coming into a zone. In a fucking instant. I swear I could kill. Look at her, all gussied. And that bald piece of shit. What is he? Five-six? My father could break that fuck in two. How in living hell could she choose *that* over Tom Riordan. Fucking Christ."

The waiter arrived with the Jameson on a tray, from which Connor took the glass before the waiter could serve it, and shot the whiskey back, placing the glass back on the tray and saying, "Make it another." "Really?" the waiter said, with an effeminate, amused tone—but clearly sensing now some interesting impending drama. "Really," Connor said.

Ellie, now sick with worry, waited, uncertain as to what effect anything she might say would have. Connor wasn't looking at her, rather only at his mother and Richard Olen, who had now taken seats on the other side of the room, clearly not having noticed that Connor and Ellie were there. The waiter returned, and again Connor took the whiskey from the tray. But now he set the glass down on the table before him, though still he looked not at Ellie, rather only at his mother and Richard Olen, who still had not noticed him, even as he glared at them. Connor squeezed the whiskey glass, which, had it been thin, would have broken. He had begun visibly to sweat. Ellie, suffering now again the sinking feeling that it would take that lifetime to bring Connor Riordan back to himself—and yet knowing how much he *had*

269

DIVISION

come back, with her—again ventured her heart. "Connor," she said, "the time will come. I know it. When you can see and talk to her. I know it will. But it's not now. You're not in the right place. So, please, let's just go. No damage has been done."

He took the glass to his mouth—and shot the whiskey down. "This doesn't concern you," he said, still not looking at her.

Her beauty now tortured from its grace, her lips trembling, tears in her eyes, Ellie said, "But it does. It so, so does, Connor. It does concern me."

"No it doesn't," he said—as he squeezed his glass again and then set it on the table—and let it go, spreading his fingers wide a moment before fisting them under his thumb. He rose then from his chair, and without another word to Ellie, began to move across the room to where his mother sat with Richard Olen.

Neither saw him coming, though he'd begun to march toward them in a way that had people looking. His hands were gripped tight into fists, but he said nothing, as he neared their table. His mother had her back to him, and Richard Olen, who now saw him closing in, did not know at first who he was—though immediately he could gather, as Connor at last took a chair, pulled it back and seated himself next to his mother. At first startled, Jackie looked at her son for a moment blankly but quickly then—her mouth turning down, tightening—with an anger matching his.

"You come here for old time sake?" he said to her, "to recapture some of that old family feeling?"

"Good lord," she said, "what are you doing here?"

"Ah, fuckin' A, have we not gone a journey? What am *I* doing here—at Jeanette's? Shouldn't we be asking what are *you* doing here—with...?" Connor turned to Richard and said, "I'm sorry, I don't know who you are. I'm this woman's son. And you would be her—what?"

Richard said nothing but curled his lip ever so slightly—and sniffed a quiet laugh.

"My son has a drinking problem, Richard," Jackie said, with anger and contempt.

But Connor ignored her. "Richard!" he said. "I know who you are! There's absolutely no fucking accounting for tastes—but you're my mother's *choice!*" Connor did not notice that Ellie had now come up and that she was standing nearby behind him.

270

THE BRAIDED NECKLACE

Jackie saw her and again said, "Good lord."

"My mother," Connor said, "has a speech aphasia which makes her repeat her own words. But the woman can fucking choose, *Richard*. She believes in the *right to choose*—and in helping people make ever so difficult choices. And her choice of you, given, you know, what an obvious piece of shit you are, had to be a very confusing choice. I can tell you, it bewilders the *fuck* out of me."

"Connor," Ellie now said, "let's just go. Please, let's just go."

He turned to face her, but as he did, he could see that his mother wore the same braided-gold necklace she wore the night Jack died. And Jackie now said, taking even a sudden hard delight in the fact that her son had just brought up the subject of choice while not knowing who stood behind him, "Won't you introduce your friend to Richard, Connor?" She turned her eyes now directly, coldly, on Ellie. But Connor's eyes had remained on the necklace. "Oh fucking Christ," he said. "Oh goddamn fucking Christ." His hands were hot-sweaty, and his brow, his neck. "Goddamn Jesus *Christ.*"

Stung by Connor's insults to him, Richard Olen now broke his silence, speaking low, through his teeth. "You need to keep it down—and watch the way you talk to your mother."

With that cold look at her, Jackie Riordan had been letting Ellie Shea know that she found Ellie's remaining a living presence in her life, a living reminder of difficult things, which, while they had to be done, were far better hidden and forgotten than not—to be a fact noxious to the peace she damn well deserved for helping to extract the girl, quietly, from all those difficulties. Instead of just disappearing, there she was like a curse attaching her persistent irresponsible presence now to her second son. Unbelievable—the curse of it. But Richard Olen, who never one time had crossed the line and entered the fray of Jackie's hostilities with that second son, now had crossed that line; and the instant he did, Jackie turned her look from the girl to Richard, who seemed now to be fast abandoning all restraint, as Connor, while still looking at his mother only, now asked him, "What did you say?"

"You *heard* me," Richard said, in a bring-it-on, hateful-contemptuous manner to Connor, who, a thousand haunting memories, rages, shames running through his mind as he looked at his mother's braided-gold necklace, *did* still hear the voice of Richard Olen—and with now the unrestrained fearlessness of the survivor who hated his life and was wholly careless of it—turned, his face white, and said to this usurper, this mastermind *lawyer,* "You worthless thief. I know you. I know your kind. You worthless goddamned womanizer—who happened, of late, to his fucking ignorant surprise to find a woman unlike any of the second-rate fools he's suckered in the past into his momentary shallownesses of pseudo-affection."

Curiously now Jackie looked at her son with a wrinkle of a smile, as, in those terms he used, now elevating his voice, he went after someone whose dominance, which she'd never been able once to overcome, had for that reason stirred her.

But Ellie, as Connor raised his voice now to a level that had people looking, fearing that he was losing all that he'd gained, hearing, too, still, what he'd said, unforgivingly, about choice, the right to choose, stepped back a step—expecting some burst of violence. "You dare to say a goddamned word to me about my mother when you stole my father's life. You stole our family's life, as you knew *nothing* of its value. And let me ask you, you worthless sonofabitch, are you tired of her yet? Because I know you, you soulless prick. And I know that you don't have endurance in you. You don't have the real thing in you. You have slick lawyer brains and a slick lawyer's money—and *things.* But you don't have what it takes."

Jackie Riordan had never seen this: Richard Olen rendered speechless. But she'd never seen him rise up, either, in seeming preparation for some violent physical assault. And Richard now had stood up and was looking to come around the table. And Connor was rising to meet him. Ellie Shea, seeing so much returning darkness now in Connor's face, the fury in his eyes, and feeling the loss of every step of progress they had made, backed up still more, heartbroken—and let the waiter who'd brought the whiskeys take her under his arm and move her out and away. Jackie, too, rose and moved back among people nearby, all of whom had now risen. The staff was approaching in numbers. And Connor, before he could be held in check by one of the bartenders, who would come up and grab him as another would come between him and Richard Olen, said to this man who took his mother, "If I had a gun right now, you *shit,* you don't know how hard I'd pull the fucking trigger." Then as he was grabbed by the strong bartender, he turned to his mother and said, "You should have loved my father. You should have loved him." And she looked at her son, with a face now of truest deep sorrow, and said to him, "I couldn't." He heard this. He saw her

272

THE BRAIDED NECKLACE

face. The gold-braided necklace. But then he was pulled away, and he did not hear her as she said, "I am so sorry. So...sorry."

He was taken by both bartenders to the street. One said, as he let him go, that he'd heard the things Connor had said—and that he understood —but that Connor couldn't come back now, or the police would be called. "Are you OK?" the man asked then. And Connor said he was. But as he was left alone and was standing by himself out on Chestnut, he could see down the street the black cashmere jacket bending into a cab—and then the cab pulling away.

DOORWAYS

On the last day of class before Thanksgiving, Professor Thomas Riordan sat in his office three stories up on Kenmore Ave. in the center of the DePaul campus. With his back to his door, he looked out his window—and over the bare trees saw, though with a dead outer eye, the blue of the distant lake. For nearly a month now, he'd kept his door wide open—to let in whatever interruptions might help break him out from the reviewing of mental pictures, unvarying, and from the thoughts, the feelings, also unvarying, fixated, that made a slave of his mind. It had been three weeks since he'd heard from Detective Touhy and also from the public defender, Christa Reese, that a serious, near-miss attempt had been made on the life of Marcus Sabbs, who'd been kept ever since in the Protective Custody unit of the Cook County Jail. They'd tried to stab him to death. No one doubted that Watt was behind the attempt.

Christa Reese had called to press upon him once more the need, now all the more urgent, for Connor's help in saving the life of an innocent young man. But as had Touhy, who'd stressed the need for every kind of caution, she had warned, too, that Watt was as dangerous to Connor

Riordan as he was to Marcus Sabbs or Robert Teague. And so now an irrepressible sick new life in Tom Riordan's pain would manifest itself in images of Watt lurking about, Watt breaking into his house, Watt taking the life of his second son, having taken already the life of his first—which horror in the alley he could again not stop seeing. Watt! goddamn sonofabitching *Watt*—to have him again on, in the mind, a constant, un-killable presence! If images in the mind were destroyable, he would unload as many shots into them as it took to stop these visions of Watt. And he could think it permissible even, *yes,* to take out Watt the living person for the unceasing invasive assault on his life. Kill him for the real and present threat now, to Connor, who sees no one anymore, not Ellie Shea (and so Ellie was safe, at least, Connor had assured him, responding in a lifeless mechanical tone, but insistent), his son who again just hits the bars, walks the streets, courts his own death, night after night, unstoppable short of chains. And kill that malignant animal, *justifiably,* for the *never*-healing wound—the heartless, brutal murder of his first son, lost to the endless silence of the grave. What would he have become? Jack. So much life, energy, power—torn apart, ended. And my good memory of him...because of...so many things... stolen....

And—at the same time now—Tom Riordan's misery and pain were bringing to him pictures of his wife, ever-fresh thoughts, sick, of Jackie gone off with another man, truly in love with him, locked in his arms, passionate with Richard Olen, breathless, finding pleasure in bed with that womanizer in ways she never had with him, and more beautiful than ever. The vital new life in his morbid agony, in all his grief, in his sense of loss, in his sordid-wounded pride, in his anger, was such that he could only rarely now find that still small center of self-annihilate peace which he every hour sought. He'd felt compassion, compunction. He'd said to himself that, yes, he *should* have to answer for it if he prevented Jackie from finding that depth of love in her life which he had found in loving her—which he still felt, every hour, loving her. He'd wanted even to bless her, in whatever place in her life she was now. The word *cunt*—right out of the depths of hell it comes—so hateful. But this Watt, ready to kill and keep on killing his way to the freedom he lusts for—unrepentant. Haunted by this unrepentant, unkillable monstrous evil, Tom Riordan, his mind not his own, wanted to be broken away from his unhealthy meditations.

When after death we are judged, he thought now, let's do hope it's

DIVISION

just "What did you do?" and not "What did you think? or feel?" And, Jesus Christ, *not* "Were you happy?" It would be nice if that invisible soldier in us, conscience—the small, invisible thing that keeps fighting against violent feelings and thoughts and that won't cross over and join them—that won't give up on insisting on at least *doing* the right thing, no matter if happiness ever comes—if conscience the invisible soldier could win a day or two of peace, here on earth. Get a reward in some happiness, here and now—the good not-killer, who never took the easy pleasure that comes with just quitting on salvation, kept the faith that it would never be too late for it, and kept doing the right thing to attain it, even though this was never a pleasure. Conscience, the soldier who'll go to court with Con, my son, who will say and do the right thing, no matter what conflict with his feelings is involved. Where is the reward for conscience?

Suspicion. How could we not be suspicious of this kid Sabbs (a Gangster Disciple, for God's sake), or even of Teague, his cousin and the only one who knew Jack? How are we supposed to be convinced they were there innocently? Beyond a reasonable doubt. Reason—a comrade of conscience. But how can you close off your unreasonable feelings about the murder of your son—about the blood everywhere in that car? Her Mercedes. Justice is just this hard push against dark feeling, against sick un-killable suspicion, against the desire for revenge, against the unreasonable desire *not* to divide this one from that one but instead to lump them all into one indiscriminate capital-punishment slaughter. Justice set against dark, vengeful feelings. A commonplace conflict—until you suffer in that moral conflict with your own dark feelings every minute of every hour....

And when it's your son they killed, *yours, and no one else's.* Your children—they aren't like your nieces or nephews, even little Billy, who was not mine. It goes so deep, when they're yours. All day every day after they die you can think of nothing else, for months and months. And after any hiatus, any relief time, the obsession can come back, because its real life is eternal—not subject to time. And once it's back—then you once again can *not* believe that anyone can be thinking of anything but the death of your child. Or that the sun comes up.

And forgiveness. Conscience the soldier will *do* forgiveness, even when he cannot feel it, will forgive even his own child's murderer, against all dark feeling. Conscience will do the right thing—all for its reward not *here,* where we cannot escape dark feelings or find happi-

276

ness, but in heaven, which can only be a peace that is called no-rewards
—a place beyond all desire, where your children are not yours, where
there are no possessions, and where we shall not know each other as
man and wife. So maybe I would prefer never to goddamn go there.
Fuck heaven. I'll take the love—and the loss—and drag all the agonizing
images with me to the grave and my godforsaken no-reward. Heaven
is no place.

Ellie Shea, on her way to see Professor O'Gorman, had quickened
her step when passing by Professor Riordan's door, relieved, as she
took a quick glance in, that he was looking away, out his window. But
so often, she knew, when you're reluctant to do something, but then
go ahead and do it, because you should—the result is a magic double
pleasure. And so, her appointment with O'Gorman finished, overcoming a thousand complex reluctances, despite the fact that she hadn't
seen or heard from Connor in over three weeks now, and that...with
his other son...with the help of his wife...who'd left him for another,
that other whom she'd seen, the two of them together—feeling that,
despite all this *life* and pain, she should stop, she did...stop by Professor Riordan's office...and tapped lightly on the jamb of the open door.

Bullshit heaven. Goddamned *no* place, he had been thinking, still,
where no one *does* a thing—when he heard the tapping and turned.
"Professor Riordan," she said, standing in his doorway, her hand still
touched to the door's frame. And he thought—in one of those frac-
tions of seconds that remain with us for a lifetime...that she might have
been *sent,* coming as if out of nowhere, standing there in his door, safe,
the girl who in one way or another touched every fragment of his broken life. "Ellie Shea," he said. "Come in. Have a seat. And how are
you these days?"

The things Carolyn had said to her about her actions' being part of
her life and not part of it, those words ran through Ellie's mind as she
took the seat across the desk from Connor Riordan's father, feeling
at the same time anger against Connor for the bitter things he'd said
about *choice* at the restaurant, right after all his words on love and forgiveness—and for his ignoring her desperate pleas to him, as if she
didn't exist, and his relapsing into hard liquor and rage, and his not
calling for now such a long time, and his relapsing no doubt into more
hard liquor and more rage. "I've been better," she said, truthfully—but
actually now surprising herself as she had so quickly opened things
on this personal note, with her professor. She turned her head slightly.

277

DIVISION

Such a face—so beautiful—how could he not have received a lasting imprint of it, even if it had been, with her, only a single class? And those essays that come, maybe once in a half-dozen, ten years—that show that a student is your equal, and more than your equal—that make you think, no, I did not write something like that at that age, nor could I have—her final paper was one of these, one of the ones you always remember. The fate of women in Hardy. Not George Eliot. Not *Adam Bede*. Yet it wasn't literature she was here to discuss. He rose and went to his door, half-closed it for a greater privacy, and came back and sat before her. "I've been better too," he said.

Sensing immediately the difference that his engaging with her so quickly, equally, on a personal level had made—feeling an opening come with his half-closing of his door—a confessional screen—Bless me father—she looked up and said, "For a number of weeks he hasn't called...."

"I know, Ellie. I know.... He's cut himself off. He's in a bad way. And he was doing so much better—with you. But...thank God. He's assured me you're safe...and that he would never expose you, ever...." He went into a deeper concentration, visible in the tightening of his face and mouth.

What had he meant? Her look now suddenly was worried, questioning.

"This is so hard," he said, "so bewildering to hear myself saying such things, coming from the world I come from, and that you come from, where things like this are never heard of—but an attempt, Ellie, a serious attempt was made on Marcus Sabbs's life—and Connor's life is most certainly in danger as well—and Robert Teague's."

Carolyn in Italy, Ellie thought. Of course, she must know...those two missed calls.... And this is all so unreal...and yet so truly terrible.... Connor...my God.

"And out he goes to drink...no matter what I say, or do, and wanders the streets 'til who knows what hour, knowing that that Watt is out there—and that he's already tried to kill one witness. It's as if he is courting his own death. Every night. And why he's taken this new darker turn he will not say. He's not angry at me. He tells me every day he loves me. Tears in his eyes. But he puts me off if I try to get through to him—or even mention therapy—or even if I plead with him that he take care of his own life and safety, with Watt out there—and with Marcus Sabbs nearly stabbed to death. And why this new iron-hard resistance.... I just don't know. But, so deeply I have been glad knowing

278

that you haven't been out there with him. To think that you'd ever be in danger.... Thank God you've been apart.... But please forgive me —I'm trespassing on your privacy."

Ellie met his eyes. And Tom Riordan thought—equal—if it were possible that she and Connor had for each other an equal love, a deep and pure and full mutual respect and love.... This incredible girl—for my lost son. He could be found. A life forever with this girl, safe, thank God...who could...would have been the mother of my grandchild...who carried that child inside her, Jack's, who will never have one now.... God help me, I can't believe that here she is, sent—and in truth nowhere for me to run, or for her, not this side of heaven.... But still the place, here, in our lives, the extraordinary inner place where our cold principles, in the invisible silence of grace, negotiate a God-sent treaty with mercy...where the electrons in the brain become angels and, in miraculous beauty, sew together the birth of forgiveness. Love this girl, Connor. No matter what, love her. But...parents have no part in determining the loves of their children, which have to come from within, as a matter of their own choice.

Where do I go now, Carolyn? Why have I come back into the life of the Riordans? Even for the one I love—why? Jackie Riordan's hard look reproves me. So deep. And now this terrible danger—unimaginable, but real. Marcus. Robert in danger. Death. Real death. And Watt—coming again into the world of the Riordans, with his gun. But she could hear Connor, too, saying that the devil hates communication—which means, she knew in her heart, that goodness must *love* communication, her coming in to talk to Professor Riordan. *God* loves this. God our personal savior. Nonsense that makes the mind scream. She closed her eyes, breathed deeply a moment, then, opening her eyes, "Please forgive *me,* Professor Riordan, please, for telling you this—but I believe...or, let me just say it, I *know* why Connor's been the way he's been, these last weeks...out there, on the streets, no matter the danger."

He looked at her now, eagerly.

She waited another moment, wondering again why she came to this man's office? why she took his class? What right did she have to be involved in any way with his second son? Leave them alone. Love confers only so many rights, even if it's the love of your life. But she had begun an explanation and must finish it. "We went," she now said, "to see this exhibit at the Contemporary. It was a wonderful time. Connor's healing—it was a day you could really see and feel it. But after a walk,

we went for dinner at Jeanette's on Chestnut, which I know you'd all
gone to as a family.... And please do forgive this...."

She looked up at him, feeling now uncertain, reluctant, discomforted
by her own compassion—yet she felt a pleasure, too, despite all her confusion, in breaking down the divisions between student and professor
—in her talking to this man she so deeply respected, person to person,
as equals—and an even deeper joy, suddenly now, too, in breaking
down divisions between her and Jack Riordan's father—this felt so
good, despite everything—this moment that no doubt she'd wanted
when she took Thomas Riordan's class—that her heart had all along
been begging for in the dark. Yet still in a confused discomfort, reluctance, though with a determination, too, to communicate, to keep going, feeling her way in the dark, she said, "...Connor sat with his back
to the window...and across from him, I could look out...and see. It was
your wife. She was with the man. I'm certain it's why Connor is where
he is now."

He felt an immediate loving sorrow, knowing Con had kept this
from him, and anger that Con would suffer so.... Nor could he help
the sudden pain...hearing about even this single one of the realities
of Jackie's new life. But he felt a pleasure now, too, in opening his
shut-down heart...to this girl..... "Our word *angel*—it comes from the
Greek for messenger." He said this in a warm, most kind voice—com-
municating, personally, with Ellie Shea. And there was pleasure, too,
somehow, in hearing of this painful new reality—from *her.* Was it the
pleasure of grace?

Her heart so touched by the word, *angel*—she would always remember that Thomas Riordan had said this to her. She smiled. But immediately feeling impelled, feeling all the difficulties of the moment, yet
still heading on blindly—where?—she said, "He could tell from the
way I looked out the window. He *knew*—before he knew. Somehow,
maybe...I don't know...because we were at Jeanette's...." She stopped
again. And would she go on now only because she was so far in? So
many feelings of uneasiness—this could not possibly be good. Not possible. And such painful things to say—but he knew, this good, kind
man, what his son was going through. She went on. She said, "And
then...Professor Riordan...it was the alcohol. Connor downed a two-
thirds-full glass of wine all at once—and ordered whiskey—and took
a shot down, and then ordered another, and took it down. And it was
like all that he'd been recovering from came back out of a dormancy,

280

like a hidden virus. And it so breaks the heart—to see a relapse—to be there and see it—and not just a relapse into the hard drinking but into the anger.... We'd talked about progress, about time as a healer. But then out of nowhere the pain and anger came right back, as if time had healed nothing. We'd been talking about Blake, and your class. It had been such a beautiful day and evening. And then in a single moment the pain and all the trouble came back."

He let his face fall, thoughtful, sniffed a kind of hopeless laugh, then, "To read Blake, Ellie, intellectually to understand Blake, to teach Blake —is one thing. But to be Blake, even as you know it would change your life—is another. But forgive me, the teacher. I didn't mean to interrupt you—though it is, I'll be honest, painful to hear what you're saying. But, in the same way as you say for Connor, I already know.... I know it all. But please go on. I want to hear it."

Bless me, father.... The devil hates...and so it must be good. But, Carolyn, my friend, where now? What pleasure in the pain? Why am I here? Who *am* I? But now suddenly she felt, sitting with his father, even an impulsive, aggressive sympathy (rash? self-destructive?) with Connor, who'd started to go for Richard Olen's throat, as she said, smiling, nodding, to an equal, this man before her, in pain, so kind and good, Connor's father...and Jack's, "He couldn't even hear me as I said that we could just leave.... He just rose and walked to their table. I followed, but...he didn't see me. He went and sat by your wife —and began to cut the man down. If words could kill, that man would be very, very dead. But to your wife, too...."

But now all at once Ellie felt that her inexplicable aggressive sympathy for Connor in his attack on Richard Olen...and Jackie Riordan... had indeed rushed her to the brink of a precipice, a death—which maybe she'd really always wanted—and still, not knowing where she was going, she went on, saying, tears now welling up in her eyes, "He couldn't see me. He didn't know I was there...right behind him. And he said to her...things...."

She stopped. And now despising herself for having come here, for having taken this man's class, for having pursued Connor Riordan down the street that evening, for inviting him back to her place—and, completely believing secrets now to be better than communication, secrets kept forever—she couldn't go further. She began just to cry. She put her hands over her face, bowed her head and wept.

Tom Riordan couldn't believe he was here—that so much was coming together here—that when she came, was sent here, safe, he'd made a shield of his office door knowing, somehow, that something like this might happen, and that now it was happening. So much in him wanted to pretend, to evade, to act as if she were saying something that he didn't understand...something about herself...and about her and his son...Jack.... He wanted to pretend that her tears were incomprehensible to him—that he had no idea what Connor might have said to Jackie, not knowing that Ellie stood behind him—no idea what would make her break down like this, crying before him. But something else in him knew that if he failed in this moment—if he failed this girl—he would have to answer for it. And Jackie...he should have to answer.... He said to her, with a sense confused, and then not, a sense that most truly it was better not to evade, and yet also that there was no need, ever, to say out loud, to bring out of a secrecy in which they both would share, any of those secret things that they both knew, "Ellie, here's what I know—that to the bottom of your soul you are good, Ellie Shea. You are so very, very good. You are perfect." He softened his voice, then, and said again, "Perfect."

She kept her face buried in her hands, a long time, crying softly. And in purest respect he waited, silent, and would wait in a happiness of utter respect, for however long this beautiful girl might need to recompose herself. At last, she raised her head, her face still in her hands— and then slowly opened the curtain of her hands, wiping dry her eyes with the flats of her fingertips, showing her face at last, with her eyeliner now smeared—and a look of exhaustion, of the kind that comes from living a lifetime in a moment.

He smiled at her and said, "People in the office are going to think you wrote me a really, really bad paper."

She laughed, as tears came again, and she wiped them, her hands shaking.

Softly he said then, feeling the joy, the pleasure of what to his faith was an inflow of grace, "And about that, they'd be as wrong as they have ever been."

On the seventy-second story of the Hancock, standing at the window, looking out on the lake, and now down on its various blues, its greens, and at the white wings of the gulls, hovering, diving, Jackie Riordan felt again in this place, his place—for all its desirability—those pangs of alienation. And as she had often over the last three weeks, she thought of Richard's crossing that line which before then he'd never crossed—

282

into the privacies of her life as the mother of two sons. She wouldn't cry. She would carry inside her now, in silence, her grief over the loss of her son Jack. She would sew together inside her soul a mother's ever-living memory of her son's voice, his smile, his life, his energy, his beauty, his everything, his gorgeous eyes, his beautiful simplicity and laughter. And her son Connor's complexity, his fierce intelligence, in battle like hers, but different, and so clearly beyond hers, and his difference from Jack, so wonderful, the differences between her two different sons— her motherhood, incredible the power, the pride—Connor's taking down of Richard, the pride she couldn't help still feeling in this—yet her continuing deep anger at Connor...and yet her still deeper worry now, about his *life*. Had she ever been for him the mother she should have been? And the difficulty of all relationships. Did Richard Olen have what it took? She looked again down at the gulls, their wings white against the shifting darks of the lake, and, as she heard now the key turning in the front-door lock, she did not look toward the door.

THE SOURCE
OF SELF-RESPECT

Still half-drunk, smelling like every place he'd been in and every drink he'd shot down his throat, Connor Riordan, his back against the wall as he sat on his bathroom floor, held the silver-metal flashlight he'd been given by Annabelle Lester. As the impulse hit him, he would click it on, or click it off and place himself again in the dark. Now with it on, he pointed the light into his face. In his mind, he heard his father: "Do you have any idea what it's like to be awakened at 4 A.M. and then to see a police officer at the door? Do you have any idea what it's like to think that the death now of my second son has come! But no, just goddamn drunk, *again*— brought home by the cops, saved from a trip to County only by the kindness of George Rudkus, who knows him and cares about Connor Riordan, even though Connor Riordan doesn't give a goddamn about his own *life*."

Don't you act like you's wantin' to die. And you keep this in memrih a me. 1619. Annabelle. You think ah cain't call him come on ovah heah? Obese, ankle-less in her orthopedic shoes and rolled-up stockings, sixteen stories up in hell-steaming heat, her place too dangerous

284

for her to move out from, and nowhere for her to go. He clicked off the light, and in the darkness and silence, his eyes now tight shut, he tried to recall how it was that he ended up in the Eighteenth District lockup. He could remember being out on east Division, Butch's, and where else? He couldn't recall, only that somebody said, was it— "Shocker, Connor Riordan drunk again"? Then arms grabbing his arms —he couldn't move—bound—yelling—at whom? Faces. Then put in a car—or pulled out? How long? And then?—thrown in with black guys. Everyone black but him. He had to be afraid. God damn. The aura. Wet blood, everywhere. Sulfur stink. Fucking matches. He was afraid, in that cage. He remembered raging in silence, wanting to say *fuck to death* everyone in here, making it so I have to be afraid! Fuck you! Did he yell? Cabrini blacks. A black-man cage. Christ. He remembered one putting his face, black style, right in his face and saying, "Shut da fuck up, white man, or you gon' be sorrih you didn't." FUCK YOU! Telling me what to do! Did he keep yelling? He was too afraid. So fuck you again, a thousand times, making me afraid! Fucking bossing me, telling me what to do. Putting your face up in my face. I'll fucking kill you.

His head had been spinning in that shithole. He'd sunk to the concrete floor and put his head between his knees. Sick drunk. He held, though, his gullet and gut together, but for that rising taste of vomit, and then fell asleep on the concrete, one knee raised up to stop the whirlies. And then—what time?—it was George, shaking him, raising him, taking his arm. His arm again held tight—but, still drunk, he yelled over his shoulder, back at the blacks, at the top of his lungs, "You killed my brother! You killed my brother!" And one of them saying, "Don't nobody give a fuck about yo brotha!" And another, "You fuckin' kilt *ma* brotha! You kilt *ma* brotha! Honky-ass bitch!"

He clicked off the flashlight—then clicked it on, and then off. To be or not to be. Choose. You're just like them, George said, as he drove him home. Just like the down-and-out Cabrini dopers and drunks in that cage. Only they've been given nothing, and you've been given everything. But you don't choose to make yourself worthy of what you've been given. *Can't want it,* my little sister used to say. *Can't want it.* And that's what it was, for Ellie with me. She couldn't want me. But you she wants. Can't *not* want it. But you—you choose to keep making yourself unworthy of what you've been given.

And his father now, the same. Exactly. She'd stopped by his office. She'd spoken to him about Jeanette's. So his father knew. But not possible that she'd spoken to his father about…what he'd said to his mother…about…*choice*…things Ellie had overheard, standing right behind him. She believes in the *right to choose*—in helping people make ever so difficult *choices*. Can't have happened—that they talked about all he'd said about choice. Not possible. Not. And choose, his father said. And George. You choose to keep making yourself unworthy. And his father—things can be chosen, even by those in pain. "I know," his father said, "how a life can become enslaved. Do you think you're the only one who finds the image of your mother at Jeanette's with *him*—to be painful? Do you think you're the only one trapped by his own thoughts? by pictures in his mind, appearing and reappearing— pictures of Jack, pictures of your mother? Do you think you're the only one who suffers? The only one chained down! But I can tell you—things are going to change between *us!* I've been an enabler. I've thought that I should never treat you as if things were simple—that I *must* respect the complexity and fragility of your feelings—that if I confronted you in plain terms and challenged you and goddamn shamed you that I might lose you. So I stood back, gave you space! Didn't push! And look where we are—because I've not taken sufficient action—because I've too much allowed you not to choose your life over your death. I've let things happen. And you've let things happen! And on top of it, you could lose somebody who you say you love and who loves you back. Your mother didn't love me. She just didn't. Or not enough. Do you know how painful that is for me—and will be until the day I die? But you have someone who *does* love you, for Christ's sake! But you prefer to choose your suicide mission! Drunk on the streets—deadly enough! You could die from it even with him *not* out there! But he *is* out there. Watt! He's out there! Marcus Sabbs—he's in a cage—to keep himself from getting killed! They tried to stab him to death! And here you are out walking the streets, drunk, courting your own death, while Marcus Sabbs—whose life, I needn't remind you, depends on you—is in a cage! For his safety, twenty-three hours a day!"

He clicked the flashlight on again and off again. Then, in the darkness, *I'm in a cage!* that's what I said to him. *I'm in a cage!* I AM IN A GODDAMNED FUCKING CAGE—ALL DAY EVERY DAY! And before he walked off in anger, he said to me, between his teeth, "No you're not."

Existence precedes essence. Responsibility. Choose your life. The simplistic dicta of bullshit philosophy. I will click on this light. *Click.*

THE SOURCE OF SELF-RESPECT

And I will click it off. *Click.* I am determining what is happening. But who am *I?* What am *I? Click. Click.* Who is doing this? I am. *Click. Click.* Bullshit. Bullshit. Who or *what* is flipping the switches in your body's electrons, determining whether you do this, or that—at the absolute start of things? Let there be light. *Click.* And darkness. *Click.* Experiences. The forces, the experiences that make me what I am—those motherfuckers know exactly how to get down into the electrons of my body or soul and alter them, impregnate them with exactly what they want to. Ghostly electricians. So good at what they do. Diabolic electrical engineers, with evil intent giving life to dark deadliness, inside my body, deepest down inside. And the idea that *I,* whoever *I* am, could get down below them, those forces of fate, and by some free act of my will, whatever that is, alter at an even deeper level the electrons of my body-soul and, by free choice, change my life for the better—what is that but some humanistic ideologue's notion of personal fucking liberty, extra-corporeal choice, supra-electric magic. *Click* for the light.

But *click* again for darkness and hear in the blind dark some antihumanistic ideologue's fatal counter-pronouncement: We are all on the train there is no getting off. Pregnant with the Rosemary's Baby of hellish experience. And it will bear what fruit it will—and imprison us in the ghetto of our drunkenness. Alcohol casting effective spells far down in. PTSD casting spells. All those devil voices now chanting effective incantations down inside my body and soul, which they own, down inside the electrons that they bend against my will, that they make drunk and make pregnant with fucking Damien—devil voices chanting until my devil-engineered mind echoes them exactly, saying to me that it's all a terminal disease, your life, all a done deal—so why not just end it—take the gun to your head, you chickenshit guilty survivor—fucking kill yourself, because there's no getting off the train we've put you on. And down at the very start of things inside you, what other voice is left? Down where things begin, could I ever, by some free act, some choice, just summon into my body's electrons angels more powerful than the forces of hell? Or use patience and just wait for those angels —at the fountain. *Source.* Ellie. What is hope? And when it's lost, where does it go? To what place do we send our prayers?

By the time he awoke, already past noon, his father had gone out. Twice to wake up on a floor—in a single twelve-hour stretch! How many hours was it in that goddamn lockup? Fucking drunk tank. A whiskey coating on it, with a tincture of vomit, his mouth smelled, tasted like

287

shit. His throat burned, from the puke, the yelling. He stank all over. Even his hands, dirty, black under the nails, seemed to have a foul-as-shit odor. Heavy as lead, sick, dizzy as he tried to rise—but now he reached for the vanity's bowl and steadied and pulled himself up. Then in the mirror he saw what? Unshaven, greasy-haired street person, homeless lost soul—inside his Lincoln Park home. Throw him out. Kick him to the street. Invasion of not his but somebody else's property.

He went downstairs, threw on his winter coat and took to the streets. North, and then east to the park and then south through the park and then past the Cardinal's mansion and the palaces of North State to Division and then west toward Butch's—NO. His mouth tasted still of last night. Connor Riordan drunk again—shocker. Fucking disgusting. Drunken fool. Spent the night in the tank where he belongs—NO. God damn it. I don't know who or what the fuck I am—but I'm not going in there or into any other fucking antechamber to the goddamn drunken-fool's lockup. How do you summon sufficient disgust and self-loathing? Who or what just says *enough!* I don't know who or what it is, but some goddamn thing is saying it, down in as far at least as the source of nausea, the fundamental puke fountain. I, fucking goddamn I, whoever the fuck that is, is-am not going into any shithole to get fucking shitfaced. Enough! Christ! The shit filth and disgust! My life is this taste in my mouth, which I've turned into a second un-wiped asshole. Pure shit in the mouth. That's my life.

He took a seat on the bench of a bus-stop shelter. Gray, icy-fucking December. Chicago shit. But still the sweats, the toxicity seeping out. But he'd piss his pants before he went into one of those places, his fucking sorry haunts. Uncle Jack Connaughton lighting up a cigarette— he looks around the room at all his friends and sees he's the only one, at fifty-five, still smoking. And he says to himself what kind of an asshole am I? And he stops right then and there, after two packs a day since age sixteen. Never smokes again. Connor Riordan drunk again— shocker. Guy who knew me well, clearly. Guy my age. Peer goddamn pressure. The power of shame. Enabling me rather than just plain confronting me—because I've played the threat-of-suicide card—too worried about losing me to just plain get in my face and shame me—my father. Things will change between us now. He loves me. And I'm killing him. Equal. Fucking *EQUAL!*

He turned sideways on the bus-shelter bench, hunched his knees up and buried his head on them. He let come into his mind whatever would come—and what came was the image of his mother, wearing that gold-braided necklace, at home, then the image of her wearing it at Jeanette's. And then the recurring train of thoughts, thoughts he'd had now a hundred, two hundred times, since he'd seen her at Jeanette's, wearing that thing. His father, if he didn't buy it for her, would have thought she bought it for herself. She bought big things for herself, her car, her kitchen. But Olen would ask. He'd want to know. A man of *things*. Did *he* buy it for her? Was she wearing it right there in our house—something Olen bought her? Or when she went out with my father! Getting some secret wet rush, wearing Olen's gift when she was out with my father. She wouldn't wear it in Olen's place if my father bought it for her—because Olen would notice. He'd ask her where she got it—so it couldn't have been that my father bought it for her. I'd like to fucking choke her with it. But she couldn't. Couldn't love my father. Can't want it. Ellie couldn't love George. Can't want it. Not anyone's fault. But God fucking damn her—if Olen bought her that piece of shit, she *could* choose not to wear it in our house! But maybe she bought it for herself. Then maybe she did *not*. But necklace or god-damn no necklace—fuck the ignorant, blind rages, the recurring pathetic brain rants—I can choose not to head back to those puke-hole bars—with a little help from a rock-bottom feeling of shame and disgust. You think ah don' know drunk motherfuckers when ah hear 'em. Annabelle. Going to click on the light of self-respect, for Christ Almighty's sake. Deepest voice inside me wins, winner take all. I am getting the bleeding *fuck* out!

MOTHER
AND CHILD

At Sammy's Red Hots at Division and Orleans, under the shadow of Cabrini, he ordered a Coke—then standing at the counter-ledge along the window, looking out at whites and blacks street-mingling in the changing neighborhood, he sucked the sugar-sweet carbonation through his teeth and swished it around to clean his mouth. He thought then—the Starbucks at Clybourn. But, as he headed out again onto Division, seeing the brand new library, right next door, he went in there, found the men's room and, avoiding the mirror, washed his hands and face and finger-cleaned his nails and finger-combed his hair.

921 Cambridge St., in the Cabrini Rows. He headed out now from the library. After waiting for the Walk sign, he crossed south over Division, passing first along Seward Park, seeing whites and blacks within the paling, and the field house under renovation, then looking back across Orleans, seeing a large old red-brick building with the words "Divine Providence" inscribed above the door, God's plan for us all, everything happens for a reason, and then, farther south, St. Joseph's School, now with students, black kids, gathering at the front door,

290

MOTHER AND CHILD

ready for dismissal, winter coats—some open on their uniforms—pushing, bursting at the exit, and faculty, white, black, trying to hold back the stampede. But now hovering, looming over Orleans, the high-rises, not the Cabrini Whites but the equally infamous Reds (and he could see at the top floor of the one that now loomed largest a boarded window and then next to it a window broken but not boarded, just gaping —and from both windows, one more time, soot scars in the shape of flames). And then farther ahead, churches, black churches, St. Matthew's United Methodist—was it not from here that MLK marched? For fair housing—in the city the devil named Division. And south across Oak, the MB Union. Missionary Baptist. The United and The Union. And then one more—St. Luke's Church of God in Christ. The third of three. God in Christ—undivided. The Blessed Trinity. My father in his class. And Ellie. Blake's states of the soul. Then at Locust, old St. Dominic's, long empty, boarded up.

At Locust he turned west away from the busy, mixed world on Orleans into the ghetto-black projects of Cabrini, passing under the old deserted Italian church, and, on Locust, crossing Walton and then Sedgwick and then Hudson and then Cleveland and then Mohawk— every one of these street names familiar to him as each of these streets came up into his Lincoln Park neighborhood, where, as the race of its population changed and hence the prices of its addresses changed, each street's name took on an entirely different meaning—the color of money, or rather the money of color, being the prime-ultimate source of meaning in Chicago.

Got you a press pass? Bandana boys. Teens, right there, heading my way. Fucking shit on earth! And what do *I* mean to them? What meaning in my strung-out look of scruff? White boy lookin' to get fixed. Act the part, Mr. No-newspaper man. Say "Say, man." Say "Yeah, man." Look like you know your destination on the death train.

And he said, "Say, man. Yeah, man."

And thereby, without incident, he passed, having whispered the shibboleth—saying exactly enough of the right thing, too, with the filth of his person. He couldn't look, but felt that the bandanas, too, had passed well on, to something, someone else—and fuck you to death for making me afraid, *again*—too god-fucking-damn scared even to look over my shoulder. One more day of sweating fear and I *will* fucking kill somebody. One more day. But now, safe and sound, hardy har har, here we are, Cambridge St., used to be Milton St.—the blind bard

291

of lost Paradise subsumed into his university. Not a soul among the soul brothas knowing the origin of either street name, or the meaning, having gone to Jenner School, where one learns...what? Maybe that this is where the Black Hand dumped the bodies in the Italian days. Lessons learned—in Chicago history. Cycles of poverty. Cycles of violence. Enslaved in cycles of shit forever. God's plan. Ellie, the light on her hair, the first time I saw her. To love and to be loved back. Do you know what you have! You goddamn drunk-again ingrate fool.

He turned south down Cambridge, alley-like...like the backs of the streets up in his neighborhood. The alley. His hands sweating, he looked down the row-house row at the one-step concrete stoops, the stubby black-metal overhangs above the doors, the paint peeled off the black metal of the eaves, the doors all windowless black metal. And at boarded windows, all up and down. And at gang paint, war paint, sprayed on walls and on boarded windows and doors. Six-pointed crowns; Stars of David; X-crossed, three-pronged pitchforks. VLK. He was learning the language, the signs, the furious alphabet of historically disrespected persons. Niggas Gon' Die.

The black experience. Formative. Determinative. Down the Cambridge St. Rows, 927, 925, 923, every pathetic, sad door the same, all the same, the same sad and hopeless poverty. Cycles of poverty, repeating, and of violence, the endless historical inheritance of despair. Who ever gets out? He saw no sign of life at 921, the metal door not unlike the doors, no doubt, of the Protective Custody Unit of the Cook County Jail, just a bullet-size peep hole to provide the weird distorted view of fear and distrust.

He knocked—loud enough? Nothing. But then footsteps. And now again, the working of locks, not just one. And once more then the door cracked open to the length of the latch chain. And again the face of a black woman, not at all as young as he'd assumed she'd be, old as Annabelle—so another grandmother? Grandmothers in this culture....

"You lookin' for drugs, mister," she said, "you come to the wrong place."

Mr. No-newspaperman. No. No bullshit ruses. "Are you," he said, "...the mother...of Marcus Sabbs?"

She peered out from the dark. "Who wants to know?"

Connor felt now—and more and more as he looked at this woman, early sixties, her face worn, sorrow in her eyes—that he held another's life in his hands, her son's—and that, as he had come to find it, the

MOTHER AND CHILD

last truth might be found in Marcus Sabbs' relation with this sad-eyed woman, his mother...not Jacqueline Connaughton Riordan. "The night my brother was killed...Mrs. Sabbs," he said, "...I was there."

Annabelle. The door not slammed—just closed, again—and again the sound of the latch bolt sliding and then clicking out from the latch-plate groove. Then the door of distrust opened. The devil's enemy—communication. And this place—step over the threshold...into a different world. Not the Cabrini white people imagine. Let the door of a city church close behind you and enter the quiet and peace of a different place. Her small sanctum in the center of a hurricane. "My name is Dosey," she said.

She showed him now an armchair and took her seat in another, facing him. "I'm Connor," he said—in this quiet, clean place...next to godliness. An artist, like Ellie, one who cares where everything goes, who makes her home a composition, and her world.... Each piece chosen, not picked off a salvage truck. White assumptions. He looked at her, this sad lady, with a face that surely once was beautiful, was still beautiful. Her dress—what day was it?—was she going to church?—Christ, what day was it?—her dress was of African design, colorful print, a high belt and short bodice, sleeves puffed, with colorful print, care taken with everything in her dress, in her home—her pictures, no representative images, just abstractions, two geometric, one of pure shifting colors, all fine, and each set, not mechanically in a row, rather where she sensed would be best, here, and here, and here. He looked long at her. Then, "How could it be, Dosey, that Marcus came to be with Watt that night, or any night? How did it come to be?"

Damaged goods, Miz' Reese had said. Unstable. And for so long now she'd bitterly resented the fact that her son's life was in the hands of someone, white, who couldn't be trusted to save him, who could, with a word, put him away for life. Looks like he's been out all night, the night before, too, and who knows how long he been this lost rich boy, lookin' so bad, unclean. But his brother was killed before his eyes. And before that happen—before the killin', maybe just a good school boy, mama's pride. My Marcus. And my dreams. Murder—gon' split a life in two—*before* and *after*—I know. Never the same.

With her hands on her lap, and her head turned away slightly, toward nothing, except her own thoughts, she said, "With the Lord Jesus, sir... I have had my quarrels." She closed her eyes a moment. Then, "Had my Johnnie B when I's just sixteen. Come here then with Mr. Sabbs, and he

293

DIVISION

been gone from me since Marcus jus' five years old, more than fifteen year. Never did hear from Mr. Sabbs again. Come up from Arkansas. Maybe he went back. Don't know. Don't have people there. And Johnnie B left this tearful world eight years now—shot down by a gun. Thirty-nine years old. Told me many times he'd lived beyond expectancy. And my girls, all three, long gone from me. Don't call me. Not for years. Lost to the drugs—what they call the game, the life. Ain't no game. Ain't no life."

She took a breath, looked toward her front window. "This place, outside there," she said, now turning back, looking at Connor, "wasn't always like you see. Best place I'd ever been in ma life. Come from Miss'ippi when I's ten. Couldn't live there no more." She looked now directly at Connor, then, after a moment, looked off again. "And then we live here...but it's squalor too...even worse. Danger even worse. And you thinkin' ain't a place for ya on the entiah tearful earth. Worst feeling. *Worst*. But then ah come here, to Cabrini Homes. Nineteen hundred and fifty-three. And people cared for each otha." She looked back again at Connor, now with an earnest look, intense. "So beautiful here, it was. And people looked out for one anotha. And then one day— been here fifteen good years by that time—Dr. King got shot dead by that white man James Earl. And all the riotin' started—and all's like war here. Army mens and tanks and guns. And all the last white peoples gone now for good and all the good black peoples and all the stores and all the carin' anybody had about this place, the beauty, the flowers gone, the swimmin' pools, and everything repaired...no more... just broken glass in them empty pools. And all my children come to get los' to what was left, the gangs and drugs, the vahlence. And Mr. Sabbs, los' to it, too, and him most likely gon' now from this worl', me never knowin' where or when he left it. But not my Marcus. My baby. Place ain't gon' get him."

She stared at the wall. She breathed deeply. Then, "That *Watt*—he's all of it. The end result. And my quarrel with the Lord, sir, it start for good when Marcus start seein' that Watt." She turned her gaze back to Connor and now squeezed her hands tight together. "But in a mama's heart ah know what the devil put togetha, the Lord gon' divide. Ah know ma boy he won't stick with that Watt. And that Watt, he set out gangsta mens to kill my Marcus, over to County, 'cause he know, too, that Marcus don't belong to him. And a mother knows. She knows her chil'."

294

She separated her hands now, put each on a knee, and leaned toward Connor. Then, most earnestly, "And ah know the Lord, night yo brotha pas', before that terrible thing happen, the Lord He divide ma son from the devil, put the sword a goodness twixt 'em. He heard ma prayers at las' and save ma son's soul fore it's too late. Save the las' thing ah got—and that'd be what's down in Marcus Sabbs' soul—the goodness a that boy—it's all's ah got left. And a mother knows—she *know* when the Lord send an answer 'bout her chil'. Stop ma quarellin', ah did. No more quarrellin' with the Lord—'cause ah know He answer me."

She put her hands on the arms of her chair, and saying no more, she stood, and she signaled with her hand for Connor to follow her, which he did, out of the small living room, not into the kitchen (spotless, with copperware, shining clean, hung on the wall in a pattern) but around the corner of a wall, and through a door, into a bedroom—where on the wall Connor saw first a Wells High School pennant with the winged W, and then on shelves track trophies, golden runners with winged heels, and, along both sides of the one window, framed photographs of uniformed boys, in tumbling outfits, the Jesse White Tumblers, Connor knew, and Mr. White himself with his arm around—it had to be Marcus—no Sox cap, no track team jacket, instead the red sweat pants and the red sweatshirt of the Tumblers, red the color of the Vice Lords, and Jesse White negotiated with the blue-wearing Gangster Disciples so that his boys would never be in danger wearing their red team colors. That picture had to be in Japan—the architecture, the wooden bridge over the pond, the lily pods. No doubt Japan. And on a neat desk facing that single window, a computer monitor and keyboard. The hard-drive tower was set below, inside the leg recess of the desk, and its small green light was on, pulsing in silence.

Dosey now turned to him and took his two hands—thank God he'd washed them—in her two hands. She looked into his eyes, with her sad eyes, tightening her grip on his hands. "This is where he belongs," she said. "This is his place." Her voice began to rise. "Not a prison— for the rest of his life. Here—in his home, his place. This is where he started. Here. And from here he'll go into a future. To make a home for him—all his life it's all I've wanted—to get him started right, for a future—to have a future. Not a life in prison."

She still held Connor's hands. A strange, non-threatening ferocity was in her eyes. Connor felt his hands warming in hers. But now she let go. Connor looked again around the room, the quiet nest she'd raised

DIVISION

him in, her son, and then down again into her eyes. "Before, Dosey," he said, "before the firing of the gun, Marcus said, 'We don't want this. Nothing is worth this.' *This*. What does *this* mean?"

Again scanning the room—the photographs, the winged trophies, the neat desk, the single window, the light on the hard drive pulsing—and then once more looking down into this mother's face—"I knew," he said. "I knew what it meant. And then I didn't. Look at me, Dosey. My life has been...I've been drunk. I've been out night after night, even with Watt out there. I smell the gunpowder. I hear the sounds of that night. And I've been drunk. And I've lost my understanding of what Marcus meant that night. I had it. Then I lost it."

He let the images of everything here, and the sounds of Dosey's voice, her words, spread across his mind and sink in. Then looking at this mother who had lost everything but her last son, he said, "But I know it now, Dosey. Marcus...chose not to join Watt. He chose to separate himself—to run the other way." She stared, and in that moment, they truly understood one another, the sad mother fighting her fears and the sad young man fighting his.

Instantly now a thousand doubts about everything in his life rose up in his mind, a thousand rages and regrets, all coming at once, hordes of devils, but he knew he would never betray this woman, this mother. And he would go to see Ellie—straight from here to see her, be with her. Straight. A change had come. Deep, real.

As Dosey stood apart looking up at him, he, with a sudden processing again in his mind of all she'd told him of her life, said, as if out of nowhere, and against now a hard braking in his mind, "Dosey, *please* forgive me—and do *not* answer me if you do not want to—but I have... I feel...this need to know, from *you*—because I've never known anyone for whom this is more real than it is for you.... You were just a young, young girl, when you had your first. Only sixteen. And your life, after that.... Your Johnnie B, your girls, gone from you, and Mr. Sabbs, and you *here*...in this place lost to violence and decay. What, Dosey, if you'd had the choice, back when you were a girl—the way girls have the choice now—not to have your baby and be brought at such a young age into the life of a mother.... Dosey, it would or could have been so different for you. You could have finished school. Really started your life—the way you want Marcus to start his. The way your brother, Mr. Teague, started his and made it what it is, breaking out of

MOTHER AND CHILD

so much.... Have you ever thought what you would do, if you could
have chosen...?"

She looked at him not as he feared she might—as if he were some
rudest invader of her privacy, some violent trespasser who'd gone over
a line he had no right to cross—and was his question racist as well?
What would she think? What made him ask it? What right had he?
None. And that she didn't look at him, right now, in anger—was it because she was still afraid he might betray her? And put her last child
in prison after all?

For whatever reason, she took to his question not, it seemed, with
any resentment. She turned her head slightly, as she had when they
sat in the front room. Then, once more as if she were conversing just
with her own thoughts, "I aim to pray in church this evening—tell the
Lord my quarrel with Him is over. No more to it. Don't never want to
start it up again. Never did quarrel with Him all them years before,
not about ma life, or ma children, or anything that happen. Never felt
ah had to forgive the Lord. But you askin' if ah'd chose, if I'd could
of, not t'have it be the way it was...all them years ago...when ah had
to quit DuSable High, jus' fifteen, and have ma Johnnie B and come
here with Mr. Sabbs."

She hesitated. Then, at first slowly, "Ah aim to ask forgiveness one mo'
time today—for all the times lately ah *have* thought about that, 'cause—
ain't gon lie—I've thought it many times, recent days, and months."
She sighed—took a slow next breath. "But tell you this—if that trial it
frees my Marcus, ah won't never think about that again." She stopped.
Then once again slowly, raising up her eyes, "Jus' be grateful for the
Lord's plan—path He put me on...so long back.... Jus' be grateful."

ROBERT TEAGUE

To respect, his father had said, the individuality of every single, separate one of those whose bones got washed up in that Chicago City Graveyard and then got buried all in that undistinguished heap of a mass grave at Oak Woods—to get the name and the home Confederate state of each one right, of every one his distinct place of origin—was to use the gift of memory for God's highest purpose in giving it—which is to enable in the heart a steady loving concentration upon a nameable, memorable someone, which loving concentration can initiate in our infinite souls an expansion beyond all selfish narrowness, all divisions, all partialities. Opposites produce each other. The universe began with an infinite expansion exploding out from an equally powerful concentration. And our tears, so much wiser than all unforgiving anger, will not flow until names are named and we concentrate our memories upon them and we stand firmly against these names' flowing away. Walls of names. The Viet Nam Memorial. All memorials. Names cut in stone.

"But who even knows these long-dead soldiers?" he had said to his father. "Who will look at their names and be able to recognize a single one?" "All the more heartbreaking," his father answered, "and all the more important when it is just a seemingly futile last striking of a match against the darkness. And right here in our place is where they died—of impersonal disrespect—in the thousands. This is the place. It makes all the difference for the heart. I have been at Gethsemane. I have been at Gettysburg. And at the 16th Street in Birmingham. When the place is the true place, things change for the heart."

But to cut all six thousand of those names into that stone which would rest where the flag still flew now over the Teague Funeral Home parking lot had taken more time than at first was thought. This, however, had in no way deterred Maurice Teague from his intent, which was to fly the flag until the stone was placed.

As through the parted curtains of the home's south viewing room he looked out on the parking lot and the spotlighted flag, which his father now, for the preserving of it, had him take down every night with the nighttime closing of the home—Robert Teague saw a lone, empty car in the shadows of the lot's northwest corner, parked up against the bank of plowed, mid-January snow. No doubt someone, once again, had used the lot because parking spaces on the street all were taken. And now to lock the lot's gate, he would have to wait for the towing company, which could take sometimes a half hour or more.

He had left his cell phone on the settle bench; but now after he'd walked over and gotten it, he just sat with it in his hand and didn't call the towing boys. Rather in the meditative silence of the room, he let his mind wander back into his debate with Maurice Teague—over everything. His loving relationship with his father had been entirely recovered. But even after that night when Maurice finally revealed all that had happened back in Artesia to Jesse, and all that Maurice had said about the absolute moral and spiritual necessity of transcending racial divisions, Robert had returned to his belief that there is no easy separating of such transcending of divisions from abject capitulation.

How do we get past things?—that image of young, strong and courageous Jesse, shot in the chest, close range, with a 12-gauge and, in true white fashion, shotgunned again between his legs! Jesus raging Christ! The sick, murderous insecurity of whites—with all the morbid conventionalities of their bloody violent sex-obsessed psychoses. God forever damn them. But now, from his father, it's Nelson Mandela: *Unless I leave my anger and my desire for revenge behind, I am still in prison.* And from the other side, too, Connor Riordan, Connor. What does he do?

DIVISION

For the rest of *his* life! The white boy, whose brother was murdered by the black Watt, right before his eyes...a gun put to his head.... What does Connor Riordan do to get out of his prison?—his lifelong unjust incarceration? And his parents? His mother? His father? Perform an exercise, an act, Maurice Teague says, to confirm you in your commitment to the sanity of God, which the world deems madness. Act. Take yourself to the river and get baptized beyond the old Adam. With the commitment to action, call into your soul God's saving grace, which will change you down beneath your blood and bones. Place yourself beyond the point of any going back, *commit,* so you won't fall prey to the sloth of the soul, the self-protective do-nothingism of the devil. Find a sacrament, and perform it. Fly the flag. Have the stone cut and place that stone—not under a bushel. Let your light shine before men. Act as if you had faith, and faith will come to you. And never once forget that love your enemies is not a suggestion.

But what of every forgotten slave, every unnamed, lost one, those black lives cut off in the millions, never a one allowed to come into the light of fullest and free life—and the long, fucking *how long!* cultural result of this monstrous, still-living sin! And this flying of this flag, cutting stone memorials for *them!* Why not just mark their graves with a bullwhip! And the shaming his mother has had to endure. And that's it—so far down in—*that's* what never ends—the inner battle with your sense of shame and pride, which say over and over that it is not some sanctified transcendence you arrive at when you let go of all your grievances, all your desire for revenge—and just forgive. *No,* they say, it's death you come to. It's the abandonment of self-respect you come to. It's Uncle Tom's fucking cabin, which is the death of your pride—and your pride is *you.* To erase the boundary between what is you and what is not you, what is inside and what is outside, to come to some borderless place where all is a blessed undivided *one,* with no good, no evil, no black, no white, no race, no gender—it's merely to come to the place of undiversified lifelessness, where everything is all just a meek, flat-lined nothing. And, Maurice Teague, you, a mortician, how can you have a memorial for a nothing? A no one? How can you complain about our lack of respect for the dead, as you do, when you think the way you do? How can you complain that day after day you see an ever-increasing desire to shed the burden of paying respect to persons, living *or* dead? How can you complain about any of this when you want everyone to be an ever-forgiving no one who stands against nothing, and for nothing?

300

What is the point, Maurice Teague, of being *born?* Why not just live forever upon the umbilical feeding tube in the dark of the undivided womb, where you don't know yourself from your mother?

If right now, Maurice Teague, you had any idea what it meant for your son to obey you and go and take down that rag flag and put it safely away, rather than fucking burn it—desecrate the shit out of it, Old Testament style! that X-crossed rag shit of NOT sons of God, rather JUST sons of men, from birth, and before birth, as even their DNA must have been shaped like a swastika—if you had any idea of the battle going on *inside* ME—the war that my pride fights against this death call saying Obey your father—if you could hear the fucking war cry of my pride and my shame shouting out *Fuck obedience,* and GODDAMN REVOLT!

Robert found himself squeezing his cell phone to the near-breaking point—but finally now, after an effort, he stopped. Breathing more deeply in order to relax, he wiped the sweat alternately from one hand and then the other. Then on each hand he blew a cool, drying breath. At last, then, he flipped the phone open and began to scroll down his contacts to the L's and Langland's Towing. But then it occurred to him that he might check and see if the car was still there. He rose, moved to the window and saw through the curtain that, yes, it was—some featureless, dark-toned, American something, faced out toward the plowed, banked snow and the iron fence. No respect for private property—and equally short-sighted with respect to their own convenience, in view of the fact that the Private Property: Vehicles Will be Towed at Owner's Expense sign was as clear as the Teague's enforcement of their policy was consistent, given the effects on insurance costs of not enforcing it. Robert, peeved at now having to wait that half hour to close, put in the call to Langland's. Then he flipped his phone shut and set out to do the dutiful. He walked over and took his coat from the rack at the door and put it on. But, first, as always now, he would cut off the spotlight that shone on the detested flag, to mitigate some at least of his gagging disgust with what for him, and for the entire surrounding neighborhood, was a ceremony of self-abasing shame. Or a plain fucking madness. In the light coming from King Drive he would see enough of what he needed to see.

He reached to the switch panel at the door and cut the parking-lot spotlight. The X-crossed battle flag, limp on a windless night, faded as fast as Robert wished it to, at electric speed, when he pushed down the switch; but the flag was still there, his adjusting eyes could soon see, persistent in the half-light that remained. Under the eaves, before stepping out into the lot and winter chill, Robert let the door closer pull the heavy exit door to a full close, peering over now, as he waited, at that lone car. He had had a feeling, suddenly, that someone might be sitting in the driver's seat—but felt an uneasiness, too, about approaching to make sure. He waited, rather, to see if anything moved in the obscurity. And waited. But it seemed there was nothing. No one. Nor any vapor from the exhaust. Only he marked, and made a mental note of the license-plate number—something he would never ordinarily do —KTK0009.

KTK0009. As he walked in the semi-dark toward the flagpole, he would commit it to memory. KTK0009. And still as he walked across the lot, he several times glanced toward the car to see if he could detect any presence, or motion. Still none he could see. But at the pole, even as the snap hooks holding the flag scraped and clicked with a sudden light touch of breeze against the aluminum pole, he was feeling, uncomfortably, the quiet in the near-empty lot. He was listening, in the near silence and half-dark—for what?

He began his task. He freed the halyard from the pole's cleat and began to work the loosened rope through the creaking pulley block, and to lower the flag. Length after length of the halyard, the feeling of the flag's coming to him—induced what? A begrudging respect, a collapse into acquiescence? The Empire of the Sun, saluting on the one hand the P-51 Mustangs, but also, on the other, the Japanese Zeros, the kamikaze pilots, their white scarves blowing in the wind. Ken Burns. Shelby Foote's honeyed voice speaking of the immeasurable valor shown by both sides in conflict after conflict of the Civil War. A soldier in battle loses all sight of cause and stands alone facing eternity—just a man, no longer in the mere world, standing alone before the God who made him. With the red X-crossed flag and its thirteen white stars now before him, Robert opened and unfastened one snap hook and then the other. Touching the flag. He disliked even touching it. So fucking shameful. And folding it. Ken Burns or not. The honeyed tones of Foote's Southern accent. He'd like to crumple the thing into a desecrating cloddish ball and stuff it in a dumpster. But at least, now, not the triangle-after-triangle reverent fold, no twenty-one-gun salute with the mournful sounding of taps, just a plain bed-sheet folding and then a carrying of this sieg-heil emblem of deper-

302

sonalizing disrespect for human life, black human life, of course not fully human, to the storage closet—better it were a trash incinerator.

The flag now folded, Robert set it over his arm and headed back toward the south door of the Teague Funeral Home, obediently to put the flag away, and then to wait for the towing boys.

But now suddenly as he came in under the eaves and stood before the door, startling him, a figure, a man, black, imposing, thick bodied, emerged at the west corner of the building, coming from the side where the car was parked. Then merely, in a low voice, "Cousin Teague."

Robert's seeing the body in silhouette had been enough. He had known—maybe even when he'd seen the car—maybe all his life. And now that voice. Meaningless the differences that he could perceive emerging now, in the half-light come from Martin Luther King—the eyeglasses not unlike his own, the bearded face, the hairless skull. "You..." Robert Teague said.

A low growl, animal-like, then a short low laugh. "See you doin' like that mortician told you. See you come home to your daddy."

He could talk until they came—the towing boys. Maybe they would come faster tonight. And one time before, he had engaged his attention. It had meant so much to engage it, that night in Lincoln Park, the attention of Watt. He was drawn to Watt. "Yes and no," he said. "Back home and not."

"Back home, and not." Watt's look was fixed—in an unblinking stare. But a smile, cynical, revealed now, in the half-light, the white of his teeth. "Can't be two places at one time, revolution boy. Not possible—f'one man." He lowered his look now and shook his head slowly back and forth. Then, looking up, "Recall you's gon' put a gun t' somebody's head.... Reparations. Redistribution. Revenge. Had me listenin', too—thinkin' maybe you had you a gangsta soul, somewhere deep down that schoolboy self. Saw a future in the kingdom for Cousin Teague. Gon' take this college boy on a real recruitment trip, I's thinkin'—over t' sweet Sara Lee. Grease the boy's wheel f'real." Watt took a step forward, then another...and now stood no more than a body length from Robert. "But then," he said, "jus' like that, comes the moment a truth." He sniffed a laugh, shaking his head. "And Cousin Teague, he finds a line he ain't gon' cross. Line between sayin' and *doin'*. Line between respectin' somebodih else's life, Jesus-like...and respectin' *y'own.*"

Watt took still another step forward—and again he smiled. "But

DIVISION

college boy's never been to no jail. Jus' let the incarceration get done by Cousin Tumbler. Kilt that boy the quiet way—with words. With what he told the po-lice. No way, Cousin Teague, the Tumbler ends up facin' life lest his cousin says his name. Says 'Marcus Sabbs,' lives over t'Cabrini, down Cambridge Street. And then that tumblin' nigga's gang affiliation, connection to likes a me, gon' do him before that jury." Watt took in a deep breath, letting it out slowly, the vapor from it faint but visible. "And which way you gon' go, revolution boy? Which road you gon' choose? The college way, the schoolboy way, the rich boy way—*their* way—like your daddy talks, the gravedigga, sends you to school t'be jus' like them, only nevah gon' be like them, no matta how many schools you go to? Or you gon' go the deep black nigga way, mothafuckin' gangsta way, the road you go down when you gotdamn pull that trigga f'real? You or me, Cousin Teague, future-choice of every Chicago nigga in the world."

He took a last step forward, standing now face to face with a silent, motionless Robert Teague. Then, in Robert's face, "White boy says t'me nobody's t'blame f'my fucked-up life but me—and ah can jus' take my black fuckin' nigga hands off what doesn't belong t'me. Knowledge. Mothafuckin' knowledge. You can't hear *all of it* in that white boy's words? You gon' run off, cryin' to your white-boy friend sayin' you're so sorrih. So sorrih. You gon' start that revolution sayin' you're so sorrih, 'stead a pullin' that trigga? Can't pull that trigga and take a life, you get *nothin'* done. And what you got now hangin' over your arm, all folded up nice and respectful?"

Robert had never answered. Never spoken a word, as he stood under the eaves of the Teague Funeral Home, face to face with Watt in the half-darkness. He had, for a brief moment, hoped that the towing boys would come sooner than ever before. But even as Watt had spoken and he was hearing all that Watt was saying, and then felt the man's approaching steps, coming like death—his mind had been flashing back through his life—over images of his father, Maurice, who always loved him, his hands, strong, warm, his voice, why hadn't he looked that night to see if his father had called? Why? Mama, Mary Tate, always so proud of him, and Carolyn, so beautiful, his sister, and his shining all through school, St. Ignatius, Jack Riordan, that laugh too loud, but had his words to this Watt killed Jack Riordan? a gun put to his head... his words...and Connor, blood all over his shirt...and all those speeches to himself about revolution, his books, he could see himself turning

304

page after page, and hear his fights with his father—about forgiveness, forgiveness, God's sanity a madness in the eyes of the world, and his saying to the police, in that windowless room, Marcus's name, Marcus Sabbs, lives over t'Cambridge St., KTK0009, and his father, Maurice Teague, that mortician, man of God, act, do, let your light shine, the key to the kingdom of heaven is forgiveness, shameless capitulation, house nigger take up a gun, could he call him now? too late to call his father...now? Was there a question? What was that hanging over his arm? A question? Act. Do. Let your light shine. "Find," he said, to no one he could now see, "a sacrament.... Find a sacrament...."

He felt suddenly surrounded, confined—by arms, so powerful. Their power un-opposable. He said no more. He couldn't move, couldn't struggle. Then he felt against the side of his neck the flat of a blade, cold—and then its razor edge, burning hot, and moving, moving deep into his throat and across.... And in his ear a voice....

"Jus' let it go, baby. Don't fight it. Don't fight it now. Got to be me, Cousin Teague. Can't be you. No two ways. Got to be Leonardo Sykes."

Still, for a time, holding the dying body against him, Watt at last stuck his nine-inch blade back under his coat—and slowly then he let the bloody, and at last lifeless body of Robert Teague drop down between his legs...to the pavement.

Covered now himself in blood, Watt wiped his hands on the flag that had fallen beside Robert's body. Robert's glasses, broken, he saw fallen on the pavement. Schoolboy glasses, like the ones he wore now himself. He left them where they lay. And now he unfolded the X-crossed battle flag upon the pavement—and he rolled Robert's body onto the flag, and then folded the body up into it, tucking an end at last over Robert Teague's face, softer than his cousin's. Looking then out to MLK, and seeing no one, he went to the car and then backed it up slowly, stopping it alongside the flag-draped body.

With no key to its trunk, having stolen the car, Watt opened its side rear door. Looking about and seeing no one, he went to the body, lifted it in his arms and then laid it across the back seat. Then, as he sat again at the wheel, "Think some neighborhood nigga killed him. Gon' blame that mortician's foolishness. Coulda had this boy, too, weren't for that crazy motherfucker—coulda had him come my way—human over animal, million times to one...."

As Watt pulled out through the still-open gate of the snow-aproned, iron-fenced parking lot of the Teague Funeral Home and turned south

305

DIVISION

to 33rd St, he could see out on King a tow truck, slowing at 33rd and preparing to make a turn directly toward him. He hurried then his own westward turn on 33rd, though not so much as to make himself noticeable; and on Calumet, a quarter-block west, he made a quick, but not too quick, southbound turn, looking as he did back east to see the tow truck turning north toward the gate of the lot and then signaling with its blinker a turn into the now-empty Teague Funeral Home parking lot—Private Property: Vehicles Will be Towed at Owner's Expense. And against his hard determination to keep on crossing line after line, and never stop, never look back, Watt, as he saw that truck pull in, felt not for the first time the retarding weight of the possibility of his own imminent death.

But then on Calumet, just south of 33rd, he stopped—in front of a stately stone home, three stories, lights lit in its top-floor turret room and in its dining room, and in the kitchen next to the dining room— and now, getting out and then again looking all about him for eyes that might see him, and once more finding none, no one now walking on the dim-lit winter street, he removed from the back seat of the stolen car the burden he had wrapped in the flag that for months now had flown above the Teague Funeral Home. Quickly then on the stone porch, at the front door of the home he'd stopped before, he laid down that burden, and then knocked hard three times fast on the front door and then fled, driving away south on Calumet and then east on 35th and then south and away on Martin Luther King Drive.

In her kitchen, Mary Tate Teague had been startled by the three loud knocks at the front door. Their loud, hard violence worried, disturbed her. She moved to the foot of the stairs and called up to Maurice, who had heard the loud knocking as well and was already on his way down. Together then, they made their way to the now strangely silent door, where, seeing no one, they waited—hesitant, uneasy, afraid. Maurice moved to the dining room window, touched aside the curtain, and looked out. No one. He returned then to the front door and, taking at last its handle, opened it to see what was there.

306

OLIVET

Home to the longest-continuing black Baptist communion in Chicago, dating back to 1851, the Olivet Baptist Church at 3100 S. Martin Luther King Drive rises up high in beautiful rusticated limestone blocks embracing arched, lofty stained-glass windows. The church's cross-peaked steeple to the south and east looks out on what was once the eighty-acre grounds of the infamous Civil War prison, Camp Douglas, the exact northwest corner of which it towers up from now, at the terminal point on a diagonal across from the tomb of Stephen A. Douglas, Abraham Lincoln's silver-tongued anti-abolitionist opponent, for whom the U. S. constitution was exclusively a white document, written by whites and only for whites, and whose property this entire extensive stretch of south Chicago once was—and whose name, Douglas, still is given officially to this district of the city, which, however, for over a hundred years has been called Bronzeville.

Olivet, the place of olives, Gethsemane, the winepress for the tears of Christ the night before he died for humanity's sins—taking its name from this place where Jesus suffered and prayed, OBC, Olivet Baptist,

DIVISION

the black "mother church" of Chicago, in its early days was a crucial station along the perilous Underground Railroad, and then later *the* depot in Chicago for blacks fleeing from the murderous depersonalizing degradation, sorrow and sin of post-bellum southern apartheid, both in the first and the second great migrations. And in the Red Summer of 1919, Olivet Baptist, this historic church, was the best refuge as well for harried blacks in the deadly and prolonged Chicago race riot, the worst in that bloody year's nation-dividing racial violence, said to be caused by the great number of African-American veterans returning home from the First World War, soldiers who had fought to defend what was called their country and who now sought work but were competing for jobs with whites—and who, in all the northern cities they'd left the South for, sought space as well beyond the tight entrenching of them in segregated, notoriously decayed slums. Olivet Baptist had opened its arms today for the funeral services for Robert Jesse Teague, the most promising son of Mary Tate and Maurice Aaron Teague, parishioners at Olivet from the time they were married there, now some thirty and a half years ago, when they began their life together in their beautiful restored home, just walking distance away.

For Robert Teague's funeral, the church was filled, even high up to the last pew of the great overhanging balcony. And noticeable among those gathered were the number of white faces, those of friends of Robert Teague's and of his sister Carolyn's from St. Ignatius High School, some scattered few, and more from DePaul University; and those of the Riordan family, father and son, and of the close friend of both the Riordan boy and of Carolyn Teague, Ellie Shea, who sat with Thomas and Connor Riordan, not far behind her friend Carolyn and the Teague family; and of Mrs. Riordan, Jackie, who, her divorce proceedings at last begun, sat not near her husband and son but, unaccompanied, at a distance behind them and across the aisle, in the section opposite; and of the police detective John Touhy and his wife, Jean, and, next to them, of Detective Touhy's fellow officer George Rudkus, who had become a close friend of the detective's as they worked together on the case, known to every soul black and white at present gathered, of Jack Riordan's murder; and of Christa Reese, the public defender, who was defending in that case Robert Teague's cousin Marcus and who sat also with George Rudkus and the Touhys. And over next to Mrs. Riordan, or not quite next to her, a woman of a fair brown skin and golden-brown hair, strikingly beautiful, neither white nor black,

308

OLIVET

or both at once, named Sandra Leyland, or Sara Lee—both she and
Mrs. Riordan indeed beautiful in ways that would make men, black
or white, hesitant to place themselves too near either of them, as they
sat unaccompanied.

Sitting in the first pew next to her brother, Maurice, who sat between
her and his wife, Mary Tate, Mrs. Dosey Sabbs, her dress black satin,
her face covered by a black veil, was wondering, even in this home
church, her girlhood church, if there was anyplace anywhere in this
tearful world that she could truly call home. Place suppose to be peace-
ful, but jus' make you feel the opposite, way opposite things will come
on all contrary-like when they jus' up and do. The death of her beloved
nephew, whose body lay beside her now in the coffin raised up on its
bier—not just the death, the horrid, violent murder of Robert Teague,
which followed close upon the murderous attempt made on the life of
her own imprisoned son, had made it clear in the depths of her heart
that Dosey Sabbs's quarrel with the Lord her God had never ended.
Got a life to it now as sure as the returnin' seasons. Cain't kill such a
thing. Carry it with me to the grave. But Mary Tate won't hear from me
too loud that Watt's the one took Robert. Won't push her when she's
strugglin' not to think it's somebody else—somebody out to get Maurice for that flag they found Robert all swaddle up in—which would
make Robert's passin' the fault a Maurice—like it all start with what he
took upon himself to do. Won't push her. Jus' quiet-like try to lead her
away from thinkin' that. Duty for my life. But now my heart's all torn
in two again, Maurice explainin' why he fly the flag, to me, to Mary, to
Carolyn, tellin' me how Jesse pass, so long ago, and why he kept that secret all the years. Can see Jesse's face again now, so clear, lost so long to
me—always thought he just disappeared, like Mr. Sabbs, but not anymore. Jesus help me. And beautiful, sweet Robert gone—you hearin'
me, Lord?—ain't got no-*body* now but that white boy to speak for Marcus—in the comin' trial. And Connor Riordan, for all his promises,
which I do believe the boy.... But him bein' here today with gangsters
doin' what they do—comin' to funerals with guns. Drive by with guns
at services, havin' lost all respect for human life—and human death—
includin' their own. Show you what it means when *all* respect is lost.
And yes I do wish there'd been a way to stop them child-mamas from just
havin' and havin' 'em, seein' how they make tension twixt every soul
here in this church, with Connor Riordan's brother killed by the very
same one, murderin' jus' like the one murdered Jesse. No difference.

309

DIVISION

And peoples thinkin' Marcus—but not Robert—was part a that Riordan boy's killin'. Can see by the way they look at me.

Seated on the other side of her parents from her Aunt Dosey, Carolyn Teague, while she was sure her mind should rather be simple and
silent in grief, was thinking of how different her family's feelings were
from the feelings of all those here who'd come to pay their respects
(and because she knew so many of them, she'd noticed especially the
white folks out there)—of how different things are when it's your own
son, your own brother. All those months of it being so close, even
half across the world, in Italy—never leaving, always on the mind—
the death of Jack Riordan, the imprisonment of Marcus, the fact that
Robert was there that night—but none of this now causing anything
like the pain of her own brother's being gone. Murdered. Her brother.
Connor Riordan. His brother. And the Riordans here now. And Ellie.
Both our brothers, Connor, murdered. Most likely by the same man!
Brothers. Brothas. Sistas. Jacko Riordan was not ma brotha. Every
attempt to make us feel the same pain, me for his white brother, him
for my black brother, falls short, always. The sorrow I feel, unbearable. Connor Riordan's sorrow—even as our anger might go toward
the exact same person—if also unbearable, is his, not mine. Is white,
not black. That godforsaken flag and what it stands for—it's what it
all goes back to. Fly it no more than fail to keep the secret of Jesse's
death. Robert Jesse Teague. God help me, please, please help me....
Ellie...the joy we felt becoming friends, the joy we've always felt being friends—it has always been that much more wonderful *because of*
the divisions between us—the feeling of overcoming divisions is a joy
from God. Who knows this better than the two of us? Times I swear
that race was created for the grace we feel in forgetting it. But still it
is what it is—and what I feel mostly right now, when we have such a
shared sorrow, you and Jack, all of us so bound together, Robert, my
brother, and Connor, all the living and the dead, Jack Riordan and
Robert Jesse, white and black—what I feel mostly, right on the verge
of what should be the deepest shared experience, is that my sorrow is
mine and yours yours—that, over my shoulder now, you've all come
strangely from your white neighborhoods, for the first and maybe last
time into my black church, when I'm trying just to grieve in my black
way, for my brother. But mostly now my mind and soul, here, in this
place, should try to silence the noise and find the grace.... No flags,
even in deepest secret.

310

OLIVET

Mary Tate Teague would breathe and then see it again. No exercise of the breath could dispel the image, which she would see again and again when she closed her eyes—of her folding back that blood-stained flag, as she held Robert's dead body, and of her seeing his lifeless face, his mouth covered in blood, red-black blood across his throat, his glasses gone, his eyes still shocked open, as if the terror of his dying would remain with him forever—this image so different from that of her folding back the blanket he was wrapped up in by the nurses at Mercy, the first minutes of his life. These images, the one calling up the other, that of her son's first moment in the world and that of his last—that terrible last moment and that beautiful first—they knew how to work together, in perfectly timed interchanges, to tear apart her heart. Who killed her son? Cut off his life before it could really begin? Such a hot temptation —with her all the time now—to blame her husband, who had told her now about his brother Jesse, and the depths of rage he'd sunk to, telling her how he went back, some years later, to where Jesse lay, and stabbed, as with a murderous knife, a cross of sticks into the ground, neither, he said, respecting Jesse or Christ crucified. But still the urge, all such explanations aside, to go back among those gathered here who had in one way or another let her understand their contempt for what Maurice had been doing with that flag—and join with them now. And there were many. Many out there whose eyes she could feel, who took that satisfaction which comes from seeing one's dark prophecies come true. That bullet on the steps—not a twig—was a warning. And why all that time without calling him? But Robert said he'd shut off his phone, so it wouldn't have helped. But why *that,* too? Why did your son shut off his phone? Not by accident.... And now so bitterly, exactly ironic how the more she'd prayed, these last few days, that she would never love Maurice any less than she always had—how just that particular effort at prayer would start her mind moving fast away from him, in angry doubt, every single time. So silence that prayer before it starts! Close it off! Suffer persecution, with the righteous man, who is your husband. And just to wail, to beat her breast, the way her mama would—just to wail and wail, the way you still could at one of our funerals, black funerals—something these white folks would never understand—that would maybe appall them—black women wailing until they found the pure simplicity of pure grief, not touched by thought, all just pure sorrow and pure love. She would share the simplicity of such a pure grief with Maurice—a grief for all children of God—if she

311

DIVISION

could just wail and silence her temptations into unconsciousness. Beat her breast—'til she found the Lord instead of her anger and shame.

Connor Riordan, recalling how with Ellie, who sat beside him, he had felt a sudden burst of hatred for his brother Jack disappear with a kiss. To hold such a kiss, to feel the release, forever, that he felt making love to Ellie—the release from self, memory, history. We all have a past. A criminal record. A sexual history, both Ellie and I—and everyone else! But the gift of touch, sex, when it's not just sex but lovemaking —can it clean out our history? expunge our record? The trace now of her perfume, of her cleanliness—and her soul's cleanliness going so deep—past the reach of flashbacks and sweats, past traces of the touch of others on her, my brother, and of others on me. The desire to get out of here and go away with her, to laugh, talk, kiss, try to forget— forever—to make love again—as a prayer, in hope. He knew the history of this church. All of America's pain here, black, white. This black church, where you noticed your white self as much as in the stairwells of Cabrini. George is carrying a gun, right into this church, under his jacket. He'll take us to the car exactly as he took us in, his eyes watching the street, the crowd. Good George with his gun under his jacket. If you think the threat isn't deadly serious, George said, just look at Robert Teague's coffin today. Walking the city's streets, any time night or day. Wanting to die. My suicide mission. In the black lockup. Drunk. Lying there in his casket, dead, Robert is me, his throat slit. Both of us in the same one's sights. By the one who's looking for me, Robert was found. Marcus Sabbs was nearly found. Jack was found. Seven bullets in the face taking him to…what…nowhere? Does everyone in this church feel the same fear right now—and because I'm here, feel it even worse? Watt chooses to get what he wants and wouldn't hesitate to cut short the life of anyone in his way. But if Watt burst in now and I turned to see him, would my last thought be of my mother, as when I turned I also saw her, sitting as she is now across the way? Amazing how her being here, her presence, calls up so much that even in an hour like this, even if this *were* the hour of my death, it might be the last thing I thought of before I died. Pray for us in the hour of our death. Her being here in the flesh, it brings up everything—all my life, for better or worse. And my father, what is he thinking now, with her here? And what, before he died, did Robert think of? Of his father, who put up that flag, to the damned city's and world's bewilderment? the man sitting there next to his mother, who shares with my white

312

mother the exact same grief, the two of them having held their sons in their arms, covered in blood. Watt—it must mean *vengeance.* Mr. Teague's name is Maurice. He says we are all children of God before we are children of men. Ellie says he is an amazing man. My father is an amazing man. Black. White. Blessed are they, their sons murdered, who then seek all the harder to find their true human souls. And my mother, and Mrs. Teague...sadder than the Virgin holding the dead body of the word made flesh.

Walk in with *her,* to give pain to Jackie. Revenge. The eyes in the back of Thomas Riordan's head could see his wife and the woman who sat in the pew with her. Beauty. Jackie's beauty. It brings hate if it doesn't bring love. The more beautiful the woman, the more terrible the hatred of her. To triumph over Jackie's beauty with that other woman, hot homewrecker it would seem—would be a satisfaction. Doubts about Robert Teague, and about his cousin Marcus, all settled today in the agony we share as parents, Jackie and I and Mr. and Mrs. Teague and Mrs. Sabbs. Let my anger die, dear God, and let me just grieve, with all of them, Jackie included...brilliant, beautiful woman, my wife, soon never to be my wife again, for a single moment. At least he is not here with her—although what chance he didn't read that letter with her and that they didn't seal it with a kiss. The divorce has now legally started —but truly it began before we were born. So forgive her. Forgive her Olen. Let her find love. If only today she didn't look the way she does, but instead looked like ragged hell—it would be a satisfaction. I cannot say that word.... Cannot in the silence of my mind call my wife...that word.... And even faster than Officer Rudkus I would throw my body before Connor and Ellie Shea—and take Watt's bullet. Dear God, I would. And the last words I *would say* would be that I forgive Jackie— everything. Unbearable. To feel her presence behind me now, the way I do—unbearable—when all I should feel is pure grief, in my oneness with Mr. and Mrs. Teague, and with...my wife...Jack's mother.

Sandra Leyland, Sara Lee, would no longer protect Watt. Seeing across the aisle Mrs. Touhy, the woman she so could have hurt—and feeling still now her power to destroy her, and kill a marriage—and looking at John Touhy—looking, as it were, at her own mother and father, though both these two were white—and the woman, Mrs. Touhy, seemed stronger than her mother, and better—a better woman, *not* a professor, so probably more plain bright. And feeling at the same time the power of Watt, the sex power, personal power, of the man who

DIVISION

did what he needed to do—and whom she had defended, as he had defended her, with his strong arm—the sex-joy of his power, her defender, the getting lost in his strength, the sex, and love. But she would not defend him anymore. Murder is *not* a doing of what you need to do. There is another way, always. And sweet Marcus, nearly killed too. And his own father, no matter how evil, the Gasoline Man. None of it necessary, no matter how Watt was made, used, abused. So John Touhy would find out where he was...not far from right here.... And Mrs. Touhy—to see her now in person—I never see them, the wives. She knows nothing about me—and it will stay that way. And it will be no weakness of hers, not knowing—or in my knowing what she'll never know—none of this makes her weak. John Touhy will bear the secret—and so will I. Is that the Lincoln Park brother, there with the man—his father?—and that girl, beautiful style, beautiful face, gorgeous. So, so different when you actually see them. But where is the wife?—the mother of the Lincoln Park murder victim and of that boy there, his brother? Not hard to find among all these black folks—unless she broke off from family when the trouble came—and kept apart till it was too late to call them anymore—or to be together with them. So she wouldn't come to this. But I know, and feel, where she is. I can see the same face right next to me now as I see on the white boy up over there—the brother who lived—and who now surely is angry at everything, if his mother has left, which clearly she has. Almost six years since I've said a word to my mother or father. And all it does for me if I start to think that it's never too late to call—is make me angrier. Such a desire, a *need,* to think that it *is* too late—and that I'm safe, forever, from having any obligation to call. Too, too late for calling. Good. Thank God. I have made love to the murderer of both these mothers' sons, lost myself in his arms. I have been everywhere—and I am nowhere. What to do? Choose what to do. But if Watt should find out what I did—what would come then? Not his kiss.

Not glad—but glad, glad and relieved that Richard wasn't with her. Enough tension already, Jackie Riordan felt. They look like a family, with her there now taking my place. Too hard to swallow my pride and go up and speak with them all, civilly, especially now, with the letter sent. But too shameful for me not to, as I am his mother, for God's sake. His mother. And too proud in any way to admit that the second marriage could fail someday—to acknowledge that one could be a two-time loser, attaching herself to someone whose power enthralls her

314

because she has a love-hate relationship with that power, and whom she wants and loves *because* he seems larger than the loving relationship she wants, and whom she needs *because* he is too cold to feel the same need. What does it mean to be yourself? He *is* what I want and now also what I don't want...but must want. And I love the way that Connor...that night at Jeanette's...my son.... His love for her like hers for him. No power games. But she wouldn't be there in that pew with Connor now if it weren't for me—or for what we gave sanction to and helped her get through. Simple as that. But best for me today, now, just to think of Jack, beautiful, beautiful boy, with his father's looks, who never did get to enjoy his freedom from a false obligation, inarguably false obligation, and of Mrs. Teague and her lost son, killed by the same killer, the two of us in our sisterhood of agony. Perhaps I will talk to her—and to Connor. Though I suspect not, even though I have come for this service, knowing they all would be here. And I will remain where I am...sitting next to...what? Every man's sex dream?

Ellie Shea knew she was over there, Jackie Riordan—and her presence, or just the thought of her, would always make Ellie question her right to come anywhere near the Riordans, no matter her love for Connor. What are love's rights? Still she asked herself this question. But she knew now, in her heart, that mistakes, contrasts—that they alone, indispensably, reveal the good and the real. Darkness necessary to the knowing of light. Emptiness to knowing fullness. From what it was and was not with the others, you know when you're in your loved one's arms. And no moments more sacred than those in which you come to know that difference—which is the difference between your body and your soul. But what of death? And in the arms of what god will Robert's soul find repose? We pray for the repose of the soul. But I don't. It is so very far beyond belief—that Watt would actually murder for his own freedom and safety—that he would just kill his way out of trouble. That anyone would. I am perfect, Tom Riordan said. Call him Tom, divisions between us all gone. Angel, he said, from the Greek for messenger. I am perfect. No I am not—in my easy freedom and safety. Even the forgiveness of Tom Riordan does not restore me. Think of all it would have been, Robert's life...or Jack's. And let the fact that, as Carolyn says, you are and are not what you have done, help you to extend your compassion to everyone, even to Watt. Forgive us our sins as we forgive those who trespass against us. Forgive Georgie armed, ready to end Watt's life.

IN THE PLACE OF AMERICAN PAIN AND SIN

The Reverend Mr. Griffin Ernest, Pastor of Olivet, spoke thoughtfully and compassionately about his parishioners the Teagues—about what unfailing effort it takes to break free from cycles of poverty, cycles of violence—about Maurice and Mary Tate's efforts in particular, efforts for the sake of hopefulness for all of us, for their children, for Robert, who was given the torch of hope to carry. And about the revelation that comes through tragedy—and the resolve that can be born from tragedy. He concluded with a prayer that Robert Teague would not have died in vain, that his blood would be that of a sacrifice—and for the end of violence in the violent city of Chicago. And all would have returned home touched by Reverend Ernest's words—feeling perhaps some of the resolve of which he spoke, some of the determination that he said could be born out of tragedy. And yet as a measure against a retreat, against a division, quick enough, of each person there back into his or her own self-preoccupations, the pastor's words would steadily fade in power as the retreat and separation of each and every one recovered its deeper determination.

Now, however, with the lifting of all those heads bowed in prayer,

IN THE PLACE OF AMERICAN PAIN AND SIN

and Pastor Ernest's then stepping down from the pulpit, Maurice Teague rose to give the eulogy for his son.

His walk was upright, stately. The strength of his person, expressed noticeably in his hands as he grasped the sides of the lectern—and, as he began to speak, the depth and tone of his voice, the deliberate pacing of his words—drew everyone, black, white, out immediately from his or her own separate world into a unity of attention, compassion, and respect.

"I bury the dead," he said, slowly, sonorously. "I prepare them for their final journey and carry them to their final resting place. Every day I do this. But nothing prepares the heart for the loss of one's own child, or one's own brother. One's own brother, Carolyn...and Dosey." He looked at his daughter, then bowed his head. Then, looking up and out, "And Connor."

He paused—a long moment. Then, in that deep, sonorous voice— "For over fifty years I kept a secret—a secret I swore to keep when my mother placed my hand on our family Bible in our cabin home in Artesia, Mississippi, and bound me to keep this secret—most especially from my father, who would be tortured and ruined by what I knew. I was not twelve years old."

Again he bowed, and then raised, his head. Then slowly, "I had an older brother, kind, and brave—and good. Jesse Teague was his name. My Robert, Robert Jesse, was named for him. But long ago he was killed, murdered—and, let it be known now, let the secret out—he was murdered by a white man, who hated his courage, his black strength— and I knew who this white man was. And I told my mother, who made me swear that I would never give that man's name to my father, or to any living soul—and that I never would say what I knew had happened to Jesse. For she knew that if my father ever were to find out—he would never in any futile exercise seek justice through the law but would exact his own revenge—though surely this would cost him his life. For the last thirty years of his life, I kept that secret from my father. And I kept the secret long after, watching my mother descend, too, into the grave, ten years later, knowing that still the two of us were the only ones who knew what we knew. I kept the secret until just these past few days, telling no one that my brother had been murdered, and by a white man. I bore the burden inside me—because I knew that to reveal my secret might well be to plant the seed of racial revenge, that dark American seed with such terrible power of growth, in the hearts of those I loved

317

DIVISION

more than my own life. I would lay down my life before laying down the burden of my secret. But I speak of it now—because, for reasons born of his dark experience of a terrible thing, I would come first to share the burden with my son, with Robert Teague—to share the secret with my Robert because I came to see in him a heart that, in the strength come from his own history of pain, could change his world—because I became certain that Robert Teague would on his soul's journey find through grace the way to lay the burden of that secret down—that, as he had known already the horror of bloodshed, my son would through knowing also my secret, discover, while still young, what it took me nearly the whole of a lifetime to discover."

He stood back now a moment from the lectern and half-spread his arms in an embracing gesture. He looked up to the balcony, then down again to those before him. "And it is in my son's name, and in the faith come upon me now that the strength of soul, and the *future,* that I found in Robert Jesse is there in all of you—that I open my heart with this secret now. And all of us—*all,* white and black—bear the burden of a secret. For peace, for civility, we keep our racial feelings secret, for years, for a lifetime. For the sake of civilization, we bear the inner burden and we keep our racial pain and anger, our American wound, a secret—and let it bleed in silence."

He paused—and took a slow, deep breath. "We find ourselves here today in a place of pain—of American agony. Olivet was a place of refuge for fleeing slaves; it was later a place of refuge for blacks fleeing the Jim Crow South. When my father, after Jesse had gone not to return, took us *here* to get us away from *there*—Olivet was the place in Chicago where we first came, as it was the place so many blacks came to first in their flight north, away from the impossible South."

He paused again, closing, then opening his eyes. Then, at first slowly, "But we find ourselves now, too, in the very place where some six thousand Southern soldiers, Confederates, died in the Federal Civil War prison, called Camp Douglas, which was here, *here* on this very ground—and they died of a hard, war-driven disrespect for their humanity—in what was the Andersonville of the North. But we who are black keep secret any feeling we might have that they received no worse than they deserved, and those of us here who are white must keep secret any feeling of remotest sympathy with the racist feeling of supremacy that produced slavery—and maintained it in America for a quarter of a millennium. All of us have placed our hands on our soul's inner Bible

318

and sworn for the sake of civilization, to keep secret our anger, our darkest urges toward vicious discrimination and division, or toward revenge."

He again closed his eyes a moment. "We keep our dark feelings secret, doing our duty, every day, for civilization and for peace." Keeping his eyes still closed, he lowered his head. At last then, looking out straight, "But we keep no secrets from ourselves—and we know what feelings, light, *and* dark, find life in our souls. And we feel the *weight* of our burden, of our duty. We feel exhausted as we strain to repress our own darkness—exhausted in the effort to fight against our inner original sin. Our eyes see black and white, see difference and division—and we want to go blind to what we see. All of us have eaten of the Tree of Knowledge, finding difference and division, and each of us wants to forget what we all know—and to make our way back to the Garden, innocent, and blind to differences that set us apart and against each other, that imprison us within lines of pride, lines of shame."

He paused, and his eyes, his face, sank in thought. Then, "Place, I told Robert Jesse—such a place as this in which we find ourselves, so fraught with history, with sorrow and pain.... When we are in such a place, it can concentrate our thought, our feelings, until they expand beyond all history and pain, sorrow and sin. I read in a book—that just as the Mt. Olivet Baptist Church, so too the Teague Funeral Home, my family's, stands on the very grounds of the now long-gone Camp Douglas. I bury the dead. I arrange last ceremonies of respect—for personhood, for humanity. And I read not only that those thousands died in the place where I perform my daily task but that they died of disrespect for their humanity—of not having been treated as persons but as animals, things. And I read that they were buried in the old city graveyard and that their bones were washed up by the lake and scattered, only to be picked up and heaped together and hauled away and placed in an undistinguishing mass grave at Oak Woods—Oak Woods, where today I will carry my son, my beautiful Robert Jesse, my hope, my life, to lay him to his final rest."

His face tightened now in a still deeper concentration. "Our secrets. Our burden. The darkness we all keep hidden but can never keep hidden from ourselves. Our American sin. Our bleeding wound. I found my brother, his death wounds terrible and obscene—not properly buried but lying in a shallow grave dug by his killer to hide his crime. Never buried with respect for what he was. And he was to me, his little brother

DIVISION

—everything. And so I gave my life, all the rest of my life, to a proper burying of the dead, taking care, as it were, every day, that my brother, who was all to me, was in my heart forever respected." Once more he bowed his head, breathed deeply, and then looked up. "Years after, I returned alone to the place where I found my brother. I was overwhelmed, trembling, as I stepped toward that place. Places of darkness, I told Robert Teague, Robert...Jesse...Teague, can expand the soul as can places of light. Auschwitz, Golgotha, can open up the spirit, perhaps more than can the mountain of the Transfiguration. But when I found that that place where daily I prepare the dead for their final journey, the place on which the Teague Funeral Home stood, was the place where six thousand fathers of the man who murdered my brother suffered death from disrespect for their humanity, I was brought, by a sudden influx of the grace of God, to a place, I was sure immediately, that had forever been prepared for me. Love thine enemy. Forgive us our trespasses as we forgive those who trespass against us." He paused —took then another deep breath. Then, "Our burden. Our cross. We must do our duty, for civilization. But our Lord did not come down and die to show us only how to bear our cross, to perform our duty, to hold up under our burden, to preserve civilization through the keeping of dark inner secrets—only how to reach out across divisions while ever, in our ineradicable original sin, remaining still divided."

He leaned forward and wrapped his powerful hands again a moment round the edges of the lectern. Then he stood back up and straight. "Our Lord came," he said, "rather to give us the key to the Kingdom of Heaven, not to be used at the end of our lives but now—for the Kingdom is within us, now. And when I came to that place, forever prepared for me, at which I arrived when I realized that the Teague Funeral Home stands on the very ground where six thousand forebears of my brother's murderer died of disrespect for their personhood—I knew that the key to the Kingdom of Heaven is forgiveness."

He for a moment quickened the pace of his words. "Because," he said, "I knew so well his beautiful anger, born of a hunger for justice, knew it as a God-given idealism that, in the fullness of his soul, would come to embrace its opposite, *transcendent love,* I would argue with my Robert, with Bishop Tutu, that without forgiveness there is no future, and, with Nelson Mandela, that unless I through forgiveness free myself from my desire for revenge, I remain in prison. Through forgiveness, I would say to my son, we can *change history*—the history of our

320

IN THE PLACE OF AMERICAN PAIN AND SIN

nation, and the history of our own individual souls. Just as we can give ourselves a future, we can change the quality of the past. We can free ourselves from the prison of anger and restore ourselves to health."

He for a moment removed again now into an abstraction of thought— at last then breaking out in a firm voice. "But forgiveness," he said, "is not just a restorative of the health of the self, not just a therapy for the soul, a sweet release from the prison of anger and the desire for revenge. Forgiveness must in the end rather be an *annihilation* of self. No complacent grand gesture of forbearance, no mere kind, generous condescension to the offender—but a recognition that anger and resentment and the desire for revenge all are forms of pride and that to forgive is to annihilate pride and eliminate all those divisions, those lines of pride, that separate you from loving the other's accomplishments and feeling compassion for the other's failings as if they were yours—feeling for the other's sins as if they were yours, your sins that you know are false to the real you, just as the other's sins, you now know, with your pride eliminated, are false to the real other. True equality is understood only when we pass beyond all pride and see all our goodness and all the distorted reality of our sins in the other—when we see in utter selfless forgiveness the full human soul in the soul of the other—when we know we are the other. The equality of our full humanity and the full humanity of the other is only perceivable to borderless, undivided selflessness—which *is* the Kingdom of Heaven, where we love our enemy, where pride is so fully overturned that when the first are made last and the last first, we feel in innocent love only the true human equality of every infinite soul, each and all untouched by false divisions, false distinctions, false limitations."

He paused again—and then once more slowly, in that full, deep voice. "*Love* thine enemy. All of you know what I did to show how I'd come to understand that every battle, every sin of my enemy, every accomplishment, was of me and in me. You know what flag I raised, and where. When I read that the Teague Funeral Home stood on the dark historic ground it stood on, I saw, torturingly, the face of the man who murdered my brother. I was haunted by his face, a man who had held me, too, at gunpoint—a man I saw shoot to death my brother's dog, who faithfully had kept post beside my brother's fallen body. Unless forgiveness, I told Robert Teague, appeared to the world a madness, it had not gone far enough. I thought I might let the funeral home go— that I would end my way of life and find another in a new place. But it

DIVISION

came to me in a burst of grace what I must do instead, though I knew
that it would appear to the world a madness."

He looked now down, for the first time, at his son's coffin, a long
moment, then up again. "Robert Teague," he said, "was certain that
my Christianity had brought me only to a disgraceful capitulation. He
was ashamed that that flag would fly above the funeral home that bore
our family name. He told me that my forgiveness was not just a madness but an insult to the personhood of all those who'd been enslaved
in America and whose personhood had been denied by the very souls
I would remember with that flag. He was infuriated. But whenever we
fought, it was always, always for me, with love—and with such a pride.
To have such a son, was for me such a pride. To have gone the journey
from that farm cabin in Mississippi to Robert Teague's graduation
from St. Ignatius—was to feel myself part of a changing history, of a
new birth. Robert's passion, his anger, made me proud—proud because
of its justice, its rightness. Even as we argued, even as he insulted me,
whom he had never before shown anything but love and respect—I
was so deeply proud of his passion—his righteous indignation—his
hatred of the wrongs of centuries—his *detestation* of the flag I had raised
in memory of the fallen fathers of the man who murdered my brother.
And of his belief that only in action, action driven by a sense of injustice, only in revolutionary action—would change ever come. But because I knew that the most real place in our souls—the Kingdom of
Heaven within us—the key to which is self-annihilating, seeming-mad
forgiveness—because through an inflow of grace I had come to this
place—I now stood my ground. I stood my ground because I knew
that were I to capitulate *here,* to give in to this call upon my sense of
shame, only another name for pride—that this would slow rather than
speed the journey of my son's soul to the gates of heaven, my son...in
whose name and soul...I appeal to you."

His face again tightened in concentration. And his voice carried
out to all there, to the last, highest row of the great balcony, to every
soul black and white, a sound and a feeling of pain. "But Robert now
left me. My son. My future. My love and pride. He couldn't bear the
shame. And it was at the end of three days gone from home that he ran
into his cousin, who—and surely, I would say, *because of* all that that
flag I raised represents—was in the company of the gangster. Robert
Teague and the gangster. Forgive my vanity—but truly all that Reverend Ernest said today is for me the truth. It is for my beloved Mary Tate

322

IN THE PLACE OF AMERICAN PAIN AND SIN

the truth. All that our son was—is the future, the beautiful future that someday we must come to after our history of pain. He is the light of hope—still he is. And he is all that the gangster is not. But that night, that terrible night for the Riordan family, for all of us, Robert Teague fell in with the gangster. And all that that terrible flag represents, explains it. And also, also, the fact that Robert could not yet raise that flag in forgiveness...explains it. But because he was the good and beautiful future—at the crucial moment, he did walk away, as did his cousin. At that crucial moment for young black men—and for all of us—for we *all* come to similar crossroads—Robert Jesse Teague and Marcus Sabbs divided themselves from the gangster, because in their hearts was lighted the light of compassion, and hope—the light that shines deepest inside us. And let us pray, all of us, that we will be washed in the blood of Jack Riordan and in the blood of Robert Teague—in the purifying blood of overwhelming sorrow—and compassion. In this place where we now find ourselves—the place of American pain and sin—let us pray that by grace we all of us move beyond divisions into fullest compassion, even if only for a moment, this moment of our gathering together. For a single moment can change a life."

Again he closed his eyes. He paused, seemingly waiting for an inspiration. "I told my secret," he said at last, "to Robert Teague. It was not long after the night when Jack Riordan died, and now with his cousin Marcus imprisoned, that I told Robert my secret. And someday the terrible secret of Jack Riordan's death will be told to a future generation of Riordans—with so much depending upon the way it is told. The Kingdom of Heaven is within you. And the key is forgiveness. Not just to be released from the prison of anger, to be restored to health, to enable ourselves to reach across divisions while remaining still divided. Rather finally we forgive to free ourselves from the sin of pride, to remove ourselves from that world of knowledge in which what we know is division, to raise the flag of the sins of the other while knowing that those sins are our sins and that any brave triumph over the weakness of self-protection that we see in the other is our brave triumph—and to know that in deepest truth, all any of us wants is to get back to the garden."

He looked again at his son's coffin. His eyes welled with tears, which, unashamed, he let fall. "My revolutionary son," he said. "My proud son, Robert...Jesse, who knew that only through determined action will the institutions of the world—so often so terrible in their divisive effects—ever be changed. I told him the secret—and every evening, I would have him lower and place respectfully in keeping that flag of the sins of the other, whose sins are also ours, whose desire for the garden is also ours. But I do not know where on his journey my Robert was when he died. I do not know where Jack Riordan was on his journey when he died. With what thoughts did they die? God help us in our pain. There are no signs in the mere natural world. That Robert Teague died while carrying that flag to its place of keeping, that the stain of his blood still remains on the threshold of the Teague Funeral Home, in this place of American pain and sin, and that by his murderer he was wrapped in that flag of all our sins, that flag also of our conquests over the timidities of self-protection, that flag of the other, who, in forgiveness, in the selfless nothingness of fullest equality, we realize is us—that Robert's murdered body was wrapped in its cloth—none of these things is a sign anywhere but in the human soul. Only on the line of division deep inside our souls—the line between unforgiving pride and the Kingdom of Heaven, can we know what signs these are, can we see the meaning—and feel the call."

Still Maurice Teague let his tears fall. But his voice was steady, strong. "I will never know," he said, "what point along his journey my proud, my beautiful revolutionary son had come to, what his last thoughts were—when his journey here ended. I know only that he has gone before us—and that we will in all our truest respect carry him now to his final rest—to the place where the division between two worlds reveals the soul's twin destiny to be both active in this world and at the same time, beyond pride, beyond shame, beyond the timid self's fear of seeming madness, always to be most deeply mindful of our call to the Kingdom of Heaven. And as we carry Robert Teague now to Oak Woods, let us all know in a most compassionate forgiveness that he has gone before us a person—a full human soul—that Robert Jesse Teague was all of us."

THE NAMES

Nearly two minutes having passed since Connor Riordan had hurried to beat the light at Cortland and Ashland, the long red at last turned green—and a car, nondescript, two-toned brown, maybe fifteen years old, bearing the license plate KTK0009, now pulled through the intersection, un-followed.

After he had crossed at Ashland, Connor, on his way toward Ellie Shea's, had come up from under the expressway overpass—and he'd seen then before him, standing outside the Leopard Lounge, George Rudkus and Detective John Touhy—these same two who together, four days past, had escorted him and his father and Ellie out to their car after the funeral services for Robert Teague and, both armed, had stood beside them at the burial at Oak Woods. As he'd emerged then into the afternoon light, Connor had waved at the two policemen. Then as he'd gotten close, before saying hello, he'd let them know, "No careless steps, I promise. I've kept my eyes out."

"Mr. Teague," George Rudkus had said, when Connor had at last come up beside them, "an incredible man—but the things we learn

325

from our eyes—they can make the difference between coming later to the Kingdom of Heaven—or sooner."

John Touhy, looking round from the moment he'd seen Connor, had said, while still casting his eyes out and beyond, and, if in a friendly tone, nonetheless not smiling, "Hungry, Con? George and I are stoppin' for a late lunch."

"Thanks, but I'll pass," Connor had then said, with a new resolution to stay out of the Leopard. Not mentioning where he was headed, because it was obvious and because he was sensitive to George's feelings, he had added (by way of explanation for a possibly uncivil-seeming abruptness), "Trying to stay clear of old ruts. Whether that would be a good idea or not, George can say."

George had smiled and nodded—and then had opened the Leopard's door and turned quickly away (thinking of how Ellie Shea would view it if he'd coaxed Connor Riordan in behind him). And John Touhy, still looking about, had just patted Connor on the shoulder—and then had followed George through the door. But before he'd let the door close behind him, turning his head, Touhy, his coat open on his shoulder-holstered service revolver, had looked Connor in the eye and said, "You take care."

After an early-February thaw, the streets and sidewalks were clear and dry, but with a return of the winter cold, the pack of snow on lawns had hardened solid. And now a half-block past the bar, having stepped over the ice-hard snow crust and out between two parked cars, Connor was beginning to cross Cortland. But as he came into the snowless street, that two-toned brown car, which had come out from the overpass shadows after Rudkus and Touhy had gone inside the bar, then had slowed, unnoticed, just west of the Leopard, and then had stood, idling, not fifty feet from where Connor had begun his crossing—now rose up with the thrust of what proved a powerful engine and, its tires screaming, bore down on Connor before he had a chance to make it off the street. Connor froze for a moment in the middle of Cortland— then, unthinking, impelled by some deepest instinct for life, leaped back between the two parked cars he'd come out from. He heard then the car spin in a screaming-loud U-turn at the intersection of Cortland and Honore—and then heard it roaring back. Watt! Here! He's come! Connor scurried back farther, out now from between the parked cars and up over the snow crust to the sidewalk behind them. Jesus God, don't let him stop!

326

THE NAMES

But now the car did brake to a screeching halt right beside where Connor stood exposed on the sidewalk. The door flew open. Shit Jesus! Fuckin' Christ! Jack! But now Connor broke out of a paralyzing fear and started to run, down the Cortland sidewalk, with the parked cars giving him a moment's cover, toward Honore. He could think of nowhere to go but toward Ellie. And now, as he looked back, he could see him. Shit, Christ, yes! Watt—with that gun!

But now—not his gun, or its rapid firecrack—instead Watt's voice. Hate all you motherfuckers forever! No—it was just "Got-damn SHIT!" And then it was Watt not coming toward him but getting back in the car, slamming the door and not backing up to pursue him but pulling away hard south on Wood St., his tires burning. And what Connor now saw as, in an exhaustion of dread, he looked back, was the uniformed, badged George Rudkus and John Touhy, their guns drawn, rushing down the Cortland sidewalk toward Wood—but then not firing, rather jumping in an unmarked police car, and now a magnetic police light placed on its roof, rotating blue—and at last, George, out its window, as they pulled onto Wood and began to pursue, shouting "Get to Ellie's! Get off the street!"

And as in sweating, bewildered exhaustion Connor, lead heavy, began to move as ordered, he could hear a siren—and he thought of what George Rudkus and John Touhy were doing, measuring it, with an even life-altering respect, from the perspective of his own stunned dread —which was now awakening in back-flashing imagination to the stink of sulfur and to his brother's torn-open face and his red blood.

Instantly shot through with adrenaline, John Touhy, at the wheel, tearing south down Wood, his mouth to his radio speaker, shouting to Dispatch, fearful of hitting motorists, pedestrians, patches of ice, watchful as Watt now, a block and a half ahead, was turning east—was that at Wabansia?—Touhy, for all this—knew who he was after. And in the depths of his mind, pushed down hard now out of sight and silenced beneath his complete conscious concentration, lived still the un-dismissible reality that he was in what could well be a life-ending pursuit of the one who'd gotten to that place he'd himself obsessed over getting to with Sandra—Sara Lee, whom he'd only kissed.

And George Rudkus, leaning, peering forward, listening to Detective Touhy yelling to Dispatch "Heading east now on Wabansia…"— feeling a familiar tension, too familiar these days, between his principles and a dark inclination toward a hatred of and rage against violent

327

criminals—between being not like them and, in moments of hardest confrontation, just like them—would, in some later moment of reflection upon it, have been able to discover, too, in this moment of total conscious concentration, infused with it invisibly, a feeling of confusion...as he was in a highest-risk pursuit of someone who'd just tried to murder the person who'd taken his place with the best woman he had ever cared for.

Hard turning onto Wabansia, his siren still blaring, Touhy saw the two-toned brown car now rocking up and over a speed bump a block and a half ahead. A school zone! Jonathan Burr Elementary. Touhy knew this school. Christ! Kids most likely still on the playground, maybe starting to walk home. And now Watt, un-slowing, at a violent speed taking the curve, listing hard, southbound. "Bosworth! Bosworth south!—toward North Ave.!!" Touhy still on with Dispatch, a moment later heard, "Patrol cars converging. Will try to set block at Bosworth and North."

But now Touhy must slow—the school, and yes, kids, dozens still on the playground, and on the sidewalks. If even one child's life was lost.... He took the speed bump slowly and headed slowly past Jonathan Burr and onto Bosworth, taking then the curve slowly southbound...only to see two patrol cars there indeed converged at North Ave., blue lights flashing, but no Watt caught in the net.

But no doubt! no doubt!—Watt had at North Ave. gotten on the southbound Kennedy! Touhy was sure—for not two hours before, he'd found a message left for him at the station, anonymous (it had been phoned in...in what tones?)—saying just that he, *he*...was living now on the South Side, somewhere near the District 3 station house, hiding in plain sight. "He's headed south on the Kennedy!" Touhy shouted out his window to the blue-and-whites. "Toward 67th!"

And now it was a train of flashing blue lights and sirens rising up onto the Kennedy ramp, southbound. Radios having reached also the U. S. Marshals, and, with Touhy providing specifics, the 3rd Precinct now on highest alert, the net soon was both expanding and dragging itself up into an exact readiness for entrapment and capture.

But Watt, having indeed gotten on the southbound Kennedy, immediately then, unseen, had slipped back off the expressway at Ogden. Then he'd turned east on Grand. And, as he'd come to a stop at the Halsted five-way and looked before him and behind—he felt more at ease, finding nowhere any CPD's on his tail. And as he turned south,

328

THE NAMES

breathing at last easily, having seemingly lost his pursuit, he at first for a moment found himself returning in flashes to thoughts—pictures— of the places he'd just been driven from—and then, as he drove on, beginning to ruminate variously, back and forth, on things that had happened, now, and things that would happen in time, and that had happened in the recent past.

Gentrifyin', turf-takin' motherfuckers. All their pretty places, whiter and whiter every year. Every hour. Get your nigga hands off what doesn't belong to you. No gettin' it done, no gettin' to that fuck-lucky white boy in a pretty white hood 'lest you say *Fuck dyin'!* And then you bury me in this gangsta city—but not you, Gravedigga Teague, Jesus-lovin' wanna-be white man. Who's gon' make the jails? All the story there ever is. But your boy—he chose. Sayin' he's sorrih. Prayin' f'forgiveness. WRONG. Without *supremacy* it's no true future f' th' American nigga. Without the streets goin' white to nigga, 'stead a nigga back to white. And got t'wrap your son all up in m'own white-man flag —and then lay the whole thing right at your doorstep, where it belongs. Sweet baby. Didn't say a thing when I put him to bed—jus' a few words made no sense.

Still un-followed, Watt turned east off Halsted onto Jackson Blvd. He wanted to lose the car, ditch this sombitch soon's I can, but he wanted, too, to get back fast to 7029 S. Rhodes, where for months he'd not only remained undiscovered but had headquartered his steadily expanding operation, which, having absorbed that of the now four-months departed Bennie Twin Bill, had, block by block in the now nearly everywhere divided gang world of Chicago, unified twice the territory ever to fall under the Twin Bill's sway. Call it *nation!*

Watt stayed on Jackson eastbound. He crossed the river and then came quickly, in now light traffic, to Michigan Ave., and then crossed through Grant Park, unnoticed, right to Lake Shore Drive, and headed south.

"He must have gotten off the Kennedy! We can't find him on the Ryan. But we'll find him! He's headed south! I know he is! And east! Keep the District 3 boys on highest alert! Got word he's been holed up within spitting distance of the station!" "Two-toned brown...mid-eighties GM something, Chevy, Buick...Still no plate number." "Copy that. And no doubt stolen. Likely just gonna ditch it. He's wearing glasses now, too. Wire-rimmed. And a brown winter jacket, and a black pullover turtleneck. Head's shaved. And he's heavily armed. Extended

329

DIVISION

mag semi-automatic, maybe automatic." So John Touhy, continuing with Dispatch—and from Dispatch the word still spreading—an APB out now on the car, and across District 3 an intense keening of every alerted eye. And the Marshals now fully engaged.

But now Touhy, exiting from the Ryan at 63rd, readying to head east, said to George Rudkus, as traffic slowed them...and then...stopped, "It was Sandra, who tipped me, left word a few hours ago. I'm guessing you noticed her—at the funeral, and the burial.... Looking the way I've said...." His voice, as he spoke, had slowed, had signaled thoughtfulness.... He began to pull again forward. "Such a bright, bright lady.... And so long a story how she's gotten to where she's gotten...consorting with the likes of Watt.... But I wasn't shocked...when she told me finally where he was."

"Yeah," George Rudkus said, one hand still on the dash, his eyes scanning the scene before him as Touhy now turned off of the empty street and headed for the expressway. He had seen her, beautiful woman, just as Touhy had described her, next to Mrs. Riordan at the funeral. And at the burial. Not near Mr. Riordan, and Connor, and Ellie.

East along the lake now, Watt exited the Drive at 57th, still un-followed, and swung south along the edge of Jackson Park to the Midway, where he turned west. More and more he wanted to rid himself of the car, which, since he'd carried in it the bloody body of Robert Teague, he'd been meaning to ditch and torch. But still he saw no blue-and-whites, so let this motherfucka roll me homeways a little longer. Then take it out Cal City way and smoke it f'good, like I shoulda done after carryin' and deliverin' Cousin Teague.

John Touhy, he and George Rudkus having crossed over MLK, headed now in more open traffic toward Cottage Grove. Touhy looked all about him still...for that car, two-toned brown...Watt's car.... But now he pressed down his window and reached up for his mag light, brought it in, turned it off. And in this temporary lull, as he drove on unobstructed in the lighter traffic, he could feel, more clearly, or even think, almost to the point of articulation, of how a woman, beautiful, once really inside your mind, or life, won't ever leave...maybe for the rest of your life. The daughter of two professors, one white, one black, using her sex as a weapon against marriage, their marriage...which somehow got betrayed. She was betrayed. But loyal to Watt...until now. *Where is he?* He'd said to her *Where is he?* The armed murderer. And George Rudkus, not relaxing his concentration, still scanned the

330

THE NAMES

sordid field—but, as they drove, he thought, looking out...these places, always the same look and feel to these places of the poor, the same sad eyesores, the streets of the American poor. Black. Ghetto things we see—and that become indelible impressions on the mind. Heading now to what could be one more deadly confrontation. The deaths we see. Don't let them weaken or change you. Let these things show you your strength...help you to know it. Ellie Shea...let that show it to you...make you know your strength. But maybe quit this job, this city. Move away. Arizona. The desert...not this city....

Watt, just as Touhy turned south at 63rd and Cottage, turned west off Drexel onto 63rd and prepared to turn south on Maryland. See that monster motherfucker stand up top those stairs tellin' the little bait grub he shoulda dropped his ass in the clinic bucket or cracked open his skull and pulled his brains out. She then lyin' there in her blood. But I'm never gon' capitulate—not for cops on my ass or white boy's three-times luck or no fuckin' acrobat's leaps and bounds. Time you bring in Jesus...always gon' be after you're wearin' the royal crown, not before. King's dead. Long live the king. United we stand. Divided we fall. Kingdom of fuckin' aristocrats! All, or nothin'. The Six reborn.

By 67th and Cottage, Touhy and Rudkus had begun to see blue-and-white wasps from the 3rd Precinct out circling the nest. At the light, Rudkus had pressed down his window to let a car next to them know who they were—and got it again confirmed that the watch was out everywhere. And at the same time, the driver of a blue-and-white heading north on Cottage, facing them across the intersection, as the light turned, looked over and nodded. They nodded back. But suddenly now Touhy, recognizing that they had come upon the walls of Oak Woods Cemetery, put on his blinker. And on an inarticulable hunch, he pulled east on 67th toward the cemetery's gate. But nothing immediately appeared. At Drexel then he turned north, meaning to take Marquette back west to Cottage and then head south again.

But as he turned off Drexel west onto Marquette, he could see ahead a car...Jesus Christ! Yes!—that two-toned brown fucking thing!—Right there! Crossing Marquette southbound at Maryland! Right there! Tip was right—her tip! "Marquette and Maryland! Suspect spotted! Southbound now on Maryland heading toward 67th! Suspect spotted!" So Touhy to Dispatch! But, as aroused, charged as he was, Detective Touhy now slowed on Marquette—let a divide widen between him and Watt's car—definitely Watt's!—so that maybe now the net could be cast that

DIVISION

Watt, unsuspecting, un-rushed, would swim into rather than slip past. And now from Dispatch, as Rudkus drew his gun: "Cars converging east and west on 67th. Backup moving in."

Where it's all or goddamn nothin'. Feel it in front a you. Feel it behind you. Feel every door closin'. Make it f'real, so it's all or nothin'—then see what's inside you you've never seen before. Let the kingdom come, on earth...as it is in hell. Watt smiled, as he rolled his fingers on his steering wheel, once, twice, three times.

But in the same instant, he caught in his rearview a glimpse of a ghost —Gotdamn fuckin' five-o's from back t'Cortland St.! Can tell it, light or no. And as he came up now onto 67th, out his side window looking west, blue-and-whites, two, three! Fuck me!—if it ain't true you think a thing jus' before you see it f'real! He turned east on 67th to keep from crossing paths with—and to keep out in front of—the blue-and-whites coming eastbound. But as he passed Drexel, he could see coming westbound, several blocks ahead on 67th, more blue-and-whites, two at least, maybe as many as four; and in his rearview he saw that car from Cortland St., now with that light again, sure as hell, swinging into formation with the blue-and-whites, and maybe another unmarked car, headed eastbound behind him. For a briefest instant then he recalled that tow truck coming off King Drive the night he took the life of Cousin Teague—and how it made him think his own death was approaching.

And now blue lights began to flash, before and behind him. And there were more cars—more than he'd seen before! And now the loud whooping sirens!—behind! in front! Blocked! Too much traffic!—he couldn't turn north! Fucking blocked! So here it is, motherfucka! HERE IT IS! Gon' find out what we're made of now! Watt grabbed his 19 from the seat beside him and laid it across his lap as he slammed on the accelerator, tearing, on a wild right turn, up into and through the gates of Oak Woods cemetery!—immediately bringing behind him a flooding dam-break of blue lights and whooping sirens, which with its violent cacophony, penetrating even the peace of the dead, would, for anyone who was there, alter the Oak Woods quiet forever after. Watt, as he screamed ahead on the cemetery's entrance road, all dry from the thaw, lost control, though, and spun hard onto the snow pack, but then slid out fast, while nearly knocking down several gravestones, and kept on tearing ahead as one group of his pursuit stayed right behind

332

THE NAMES

him and another broke to the right and a third broke left, lights still
flashing everywhere, sirens all whaling.

Pincered, trapped from behind and on both sides, with only the
twelve-foot, barbed-wire-topped back wall of the cemetery ahead, Watt
made a hard last decision. He slammed on the brakes, spinning the
car again out onto the snow pack, and, his tires at last having dug to
the dirt beneath the snow, got out. And fuck me if it isn't all too pretty,
Mistah Gravedigga! Your boy fresh under the ice here, and those cannons and cannonballs and that soldier-boy statue, stickin' up in the
sky a winter—him thinkin' a Miss'ippi and slave niggas bringin' him
Buffalo gotdamn Bourbon! Fuck me to blood!

He had ducked behind the driver's-side door—but suddenly now, 19
in hand, thirty-plus mag loaded in, he broke from the car, crunching
fast over the snow pack toward the nearest of the four cannons that,
each at a corner, defined the square ground of that gravesite of, and
memorial to, those more than six thousand Confederate dead, mass
buried here beneath the Northern snow—the exact place which Robert Teague had told him about and which he'd known from his own
reconnoitering.

Blue lights, last siren whoops, cars, twelve, thirteen now, skidding
to a halt on all sides of him, and Watt ducking low at the cannon. But
now suddenly he just rose up tall, his gun at his hip. And he began to
walk, deliberately, fully exposed across the wide-open snow pack toward the forty-foot-high pillared monument to the Confederate dead,
topped with a sculpture of that Southern soldier, his cap and the crook
of his arm iced white, and skirted at its wide, four-square, beveled base
by brass plates with the names and home states cut on them of all those
whose identities were not among the many forever lost.

DROP THE GUN AND PUT YOUR HANDS BEHIND YOUR HEAD!
Out from behind a swung-open door of one of the unmarked cars, a
member from the team of the U.S. Marshals had given the order
through a bullhorn.

But Watt, standing firm, tall, dark black against the snow, rather
than follow any white-man's command, raised his 19 over his head and
pointed it to the sky. "Think you got me! Think you fuckin' got the
one who did it all! Think you gon' tell this nigga what the fuck t'do!
Think he can't come up with nothin' 'cause you all closed the fuck in
on 'im—jus' gon' have t'give himself up! Well you think again, mother-

DIVISION

fuckas!" He now lowered his gun to the level of his temple and placed the barrel against his head.

Go on and do us the favor, you crazy fuckin' shine. A black-vested and helmeted CPD rifleman from the 3rd Precinct, his Remington 700 trained on Watt's chest, whispered to the stock of his gun, with his cheek pressed firm against it. And all around the police perimeter, a same whisper, terrible curse-driven, sin-driven American whisper, given the black skin of the hunted, was rising, inevitable, irrepressible, in the white minds of the hunters as from behind their car doors, they pointed the barrels of their pistols, rifles, and pump shotguns hard at Watt.

"Think he's jus' some dumb fuckin' animal! Some domestic fuckin' animal! Knowledge!—you peckerwood motherfuckers! I know you! You got jails and justice! Got Jesus on your side! None a you's guilty a nothin'! Got the law on your side! I know your motherfuckin' law—says get your hands off what don't belong to you, nigga! Responsibility! —word you love to shove up the nigga's ass! Nobody to blame for your nigga life but your nigga self! Your law says that too. And I gotdamn know you—how your shit goes everywhere! You're the ones in charge a what gets called what. But I've been down to where the names, they all c'n get changed around. YOU HEAR ME! YOU MOTHERFUCKIN' HEAR ME! AND I CHANGED 'EM! I CHANGED THE NAMES OF EVERYTHING THERE IS!"

"Watt!" John Touhy, feeling everything he'd ever felt about the man, crawling with him in his mother's blood, kissing the lips...he had kissed—now lowered his gun—and rose up, exposed, from behind the driver's-side door of his car. "Watt," he said, "put the gun down, man. There is more. More. Time to get past the past. Don't cut it off...your life. So much more is left." Touhy now tried to show how he had heard, listened. "Knowledge, you say. So much more, Watt, to be known. It is *never* too late to fix what needs to be fixed. Never too late. You're not through...changing things...your life...."

George Rudkus, his Smith and Wesson still locked on Watt's chest, stood up more now from where he had kept himself down low behind the car's passenger-side door. And he thought, no matter the words, the tones of his friend, that if this murdering, blood-shedding black bastard lowers and points that gun, he's capitally punished right here and now. Instant justice. But he thought of Ellie, too—and again of Arizona...and, then...of the mailboxes at Cabrini. None not broken. No mail ever delivered there.

334

THE NAMES

"All so personal, ain't it, Mr. Po-lice Man...." Watt, pressing the gun now hard against his temple, said now to John Touhy. "You know my name. Call me Watt, like we're friends. Well my *name,* motherfucker, it's Leonardo Sykes! And there ain't no mo' time to fix nothin'. Call me on back to your side, talk about value a life. Say there's time to fix what's broke. Say it's never too late—no line I can't come back acrost. BUT I'LL TELL EVERY ONE OF YOU MOTHERFUCKAS WHAT YOU WANT. YOU WANT ME TO BE EVERY GOTDAMN NIGGA EVER WAS AND ME TO PULL THIS TRIGGA AND GET IT DONE. CAPITAL PUNISHMENT FOR EVERY FUCKIN' NIGGA EVER LIVED OR EVER'S GON' LIVE! WELL HERE IT IS!"

Then with his eyes wide open, staring straight at John Touhy, Watt pulled the trigger of his 19, violently blasting back his head, shattering his skull, sending up, in shocking visibility, spatter of skull, and brain and blood. Then, all life gone in that instant, the gangster's once power-ful frame dropped slowly against the beveled base of the high-pillared memorial to the Confederate dead, and his darkening red blood, now pooling fast on a brass plate of names, began to drip over it to the ground and stain the hardened snow.

In the silence then, the police perimeter rose on all sides and began slowly to walk out from behind its protection and, cautiously, across the snow pack, to converge on the fallen body—no one of the over twenty officers saying a word, most still with guns drawn and trained. And now, as slowly they still came on, the flapping of the war memorial's American flag became audible in a rising winter breeze.

335

THE WHOLE TRUTH

For the third day in a row, Connor
Riordan, with his father and Ellie Shea, had made it—past the County
Sheriff's Officers yelling, barking out instructions in the vestibule—on
through security at the Cook County Criminal Courts Building at 26th
and California: a seven-story, cold-classical mass blockhouse, in which,
everywhere, entry hall to trial courts, clear as a Last-Judgment mural
showing the separation of the saved from the damned, Chicago white
is divided from Chicago not-white. Never once, upon advice, having
brought their cell phones, and now knowing better than to have had
anything metallic on them or to have waited even a moment and get
mocked by the barking Sheriff's officers for not stripping their belts off
fast enough, they had made their way, once the twenty-minute line had
brought them forward, without any wand search through the gauntlet
of detective devices, human and electronic, which, once it was determined none of them carried a weapon, stamped them approved. Still in
the end, three stories up, they would find themselves in that "fishbowl"
courtroom, twenty-five by forty-five feet, in which the judge's bench,
witness stand, jury box, and tables for the prosecution and defense

336

THE WHOLE TRUTH

would be divided from the gallery by a bulletproof-glass partition. Across this impenetrable division, the proceedings would be carried by a sound system that made it necessary, time and again, for all in the gallery, including nearly always, of course, families of the victim, and of the accused, to cup their ears.

Just off the elevator, Connor now took a look down out the third-story window at the prison city of ten thousand that stretched out for acres behind the courthouse, and he could feel the sweat beginning to pool in his palms as he imagined himself, not long from now, straining to hear if it was indeed his name that was being called, for what would then be the second and last time in the trial of Marcus Sabbs—over that sound system—from that other side of the bulletproof partition.

As he followed now his father and Ellie into Courtroom 302, Connor could see that his Aunt Bree was there again, first row, to sit with her sister, his mother...who was not there yet—though Connor knew that soon enough Jackie Riordan (not long to remain Riordan) would come through the door he'd just let shut behind him. But not here, today, the Starbuck's girl with the purple-streaked hair and piercings, her name Meghan Hoerster, who, after her testimony, had come back for her coat, looking first toward his mother and then, shaken, tears in her eyes, toward the other side of the gallery, searching for who knew what...before hurrying out clumsily, clearly distressed by her experience. But... yes...all four of the four corrections officers from Cook County Jail were there, as well as the arresting and interrogating Chicago cops... three today, and...not George Rudkus...but, yes, John Touhy.

Divided by an aisle from this group, which sat all on the right, and which Connor and his father and Ellie now joined, were, on the left, the Teague family, Mr. and Mrs., and Carolyn, not Robert...not Robert, Christ almighty...never again.... Robert Jesse.... So strange when into this soulless claustrophobic box reality would come—but when, for Connor, it came, it came. Watt—that fucking monster—now killed by the same gun he murdered with—by his own hand, his own brains shot out. Capital punishment, self-inflicted, a life, a human power, terrible human power, gone. Closure. Justice. We are all dead; and this absurd box is our coffin, which will open upon *nothing*...at the never-to-happen Day of Judgment? He would have killed me too—more than once he was ready—just one moment more was all he needed, more than once —and Marcus—he tried to have Marcus Sabbs killed. Where do you have to be—what history would you need—actually to kill someone?

337

DIVISION

To say that far-down-in *yes,* and pull the trigger? And Jack dead now so long, turned into blood. I'm his age now. He'll never be older than me again, my older brother.... He'll just grow younger and younger. I can't see his face. I might forget Jack's face.

Just Marcus Sabbs and I now are still in this world. And there she is, Dosey, whom I promised—who's been able to see nothing but her son's back—not in that prison jumpsuit...until proven—for these three days— in this coffin box where the word of God comes mumbled through that so-called sound system—as shit as some CPS intercom in some lost black high school. Like Wells. The winged W. The green pulse of the computer light. Her dress, subdued, tasteful—of course it's tasteful, it's Dosey Sabbs's dress. We have weddings, funerals, Sunday services —and clothes for every occasion. And blacks have weddings, funerals, Sunday services—and then also, thousands and thousands of black Chicago families—they have days in the Criminal Courts building, for which also they need the right clothes. Dosey couldn't wear the bright African print here, the colors, tasteful patterns.

And behind Dosey the woman, Renee Bean, who'd not been charged for harboring Marcus. And her two sons, Anthony and Rolando Trippett, different last names from their mother's. When that shit stops, Christ, so many other things would stop. One family, one fucking name! Riordan, not for long...my black white boy...with a name different from his mother's, no longer Riordan. Connor Olen. Give me a painful, drawn-out death first. And let none divide what God has joined.

But how am I remembering these names when there have been days when I could barely remember my own! And two names for one person—Sara Lee and Sandra Leyland, there in one person behind Ms. Bean, striking, beautiful. And the body. She'd make the preacher lay the Bible down, as the saying goes. But dressed today like she cared— maybe truly cared about the life of Marcus Sabbs, about the signals she would send, not sex signals—instead, today, quiet ones, respectful— because maybe she cared. And do I care? Or respect a single thing? Why? Or why not? Where's the truth, in this coffin of justice? Where, beneath the blood and the shit in my brain, is my judgment, my sense of justice, my conscience? Where do feelings go, when, for a *time,* even for the least division of an hour, they disappear? Will they come back when needed? And from where, from what place? Respect—where does it go? Can it just die and stay dead?

When I take the stand and look at Marcus's face, will I see another

338

THE WHOLE TRUTH

Watt, see all of 'em as one person, black, all the same—the prosecution wants me to see them all as the same, uniting all into one black criminal, when the defense would divide? Or will I, Ms. Christa Reese, see Marcus Sabbs, who was Watt's fellow gang member, his Disciple, who has the GD pitchfork tattooed on his arms (We've been shown the photo)—will I see him as *not* the same, as instead Dosey's son, and not another Johnnie B, dead for years, and *not* in one same gang, equal, equal with the addicted sisters in California? Not all one black family, one name?

He felt the touch of Ellie's hand on his hand—as behind them the door opened. Connor turned to see...not his mother.... But...in a dark blue, tent-like dress...still obese, still shuffling slow...Annabelle Lester...Mother Lester! "That's Annabelle," he said to Ellie, as he took her hand in his, "Watt's grandmother. That's her." But then before he could whisper to Ellie any thoughts, he now did see his own mother, coming in right behind Annabelle, who was taking a seat on the far back left, on the black side of the divide, while she, Jackie Riordan, her hair set severe, wearing a dark suit, blue, another courtroom-lawyer uniform, with no necklace this time, keeping her eyes to herself, now came up the aisle and took her seat in the first row, next to her sister. Sisters. Still, after a divorce, and remarriage, would Bree be his aunt? when his mother's, her sister's name was no longer Riordan? Who in the hell in this world *IS* anyone? Continuous personality. The immortal soul—*not*. Not for the least division of an hour. Succession, not duration. Nothing but blood, in the end. Blood running over a brass plate, with Confederate names engraved upon it, George said, as the American flag flapped in the wind.

He had been the first called, and he would be the last. Let the record show that the witness has identified the defendant as having been present at the scene and in the company of the shooter. That is all. Thank you, that is all. The witness may step down. But today there will be more. And not any witness to come after him. Not the Starbuck's girl, who followed him the first day—who said that Watt said to her y'all got it started already, which meant what? Watt meant what—by *it?* Got what started? And she said to him *Don't blame me.* For what? She said it was all about gentrification—about whites taking back the city that blacks had for so long been taking over. How did she know that? She did not, admitted she did not. Indefinite pronoun reference—*it*—meaning what? And *This:* obscure use of the demonstrative. Broad pronoun

339

DIVISION

reference, pointing back obscurely at a cluster of possibilities. Marcus said We don't want *this*. But then the pierced barrista, she said it was Marcus, under Watt's arm, an hour before the murder, brotha and brotha, all in one black gang. Sox caps and Raiders caps turned to the right, can't let you go, one way or the otha. The Jesse White Tumblers can't wear their red tumbling uniforms, not on the blue side of Division, the side of the Disciples. Jesse White and his Tumblers. Robert Jesse. Mr. Teague's murdered brother, his big brother.

Niggas gon' die. The smell of piss in the staircase of death. Sixteen stories of the poorest of the poor-refugee population of sharecropper Mississippi, and its essential representative, Watt—who slit his own father's throat. He said, *We do.* We do what? The way that that same Starbuck's girl smiled at me, her same purple-tinted hair, out on Division, talking to that cop, and then looking at me, as if to say isn't it good that we have a Starbuck's here, right on Division, pressing hard against the falling walls of Cabrini? We love it. Don't we. We do.

All of us the same, all of them the same. Gangs. You killed my brother! You kilt ma brotha! In the drunk tank, all together. But Marcus was put in protective custody. Separated. Not part of the gang, who tried to slash him to death. Christa Reese, hammering this fact home. Behind the Protective-Custody door, because Watt wanted to murder him, same as he wanted to murder you. Not a month ago. Or maybe a month ago. Today is the 2nd of March, three weeks 'til the anniversary of...the alley.

Watt said he hated all of us motherfuckers forever. And I'm a nigga right there with Annabelle. Trapped. Enslaved. Drunk. Paralyzed. How do you spell black? PTSD. And who am I to say a thing about people who can't get out? 1619. Crazy motherfucker fitna die. I went to find out where it all started—1619—and she said, You glad a nigga kilt yo brotha 'cause it prove you right about niggas all along. It satisfy you —line runnin' right out this door straight to yo brother's death. Ain't the first time you been drunk, neitha. Drunk when you call me. Gospel music playing on her radio as the heat pipes clanked, a smell everywhere of things unflushed, no mail delivered for years, the corridors pissed on to mark territory against hookers. Heart of Darkness. Crawling up the snake-like river. Indecipherable graffiti—what is the meaning? Watt crawled in his own mother's blood—ten years old—where the ambulances don't come. CHA ain't touch the elevator in years. Nothing but a sixteen-story shaft of vacant darkness, except for the rising garbage mound and the shit stink ascending to the top. The balconies all cage-wired, so people don't get hurled off, sixteen stories. Surly-as-death teenage reefer slant-caps manning the checkpoints, maybe toting firearms. And in that sixteenth-story steam box, I said her name —Annabelle—out of respect, for a person. Personhood—an embarrassment to say the word, except when it's not. I told her I was afraid. And she gave me her flashlight—and a guide, Isai. And told me to stop seeking my own death. And she got out. She came today, down from the top of Tha Jube, 1619, straight to here, sitting now behind the beautiful one.

Respectfully dressed, Sara Lee. She too had followed him that first day, called by the state. But she would come before him today, for the defense, he'd been told. Coming after the corrections officers, yesterday, before the state at last rested, it had been the arresting officers and then the interrogating, statement-taking cops, grillers, three—all with their red faces glistening from close morning shaves, skulls glistening beneath thinning hair—while Marcus was on the other side of the bulletproof glass, waiting to see what effect their words would have on his life.

When they took Marcus's statement, after his arrest, after those months in hiding, not turning himself in, staying with the Trippett-Beans, they got from him that yes he'd known Watt for a good time; that yes he was affiliated with the Disciples, that yes he was a *member;* that yes he'd planned to be with Watt that night. It was about business they were going to talk. Gang business? Yes. Yes. He said yes he knew what the business was. We do. Yes. We do. Brothas in arms. Collective guilt. You killed my brother. The last words I said to him were I wanted to kill him, my big brother, because of Ellie, because he knew what she meant to me—he knew—when he goddamned slept with her, the fucking sonofabitch, my brother.

Where are you when you can kill someone? I told him I wanted to kill him. I hated him. I despised him for selling out values important as life. Fucking *life!* And for sleeping with the girl...fucking her. Why did he *do* that! We do! And what all did I do to his mind to make him crazy enough to rage up against Watt—for property, for responsibility, for Watt's having nobody to blame for his life but his own black self? Marcus said yes he did know that Watt had a gun. Yes. And yes he did think something was up. He did think stealing the car was up. And yes he'd hidden for months. Yes. From the police. Yes.

But also no. No! Christa Reese came back at the witness, grilling

341

the griller, asking him-in-the-cop-suit did Marcus Sabbs not say it was pure coincidence that he ran into his cousin, did he not also say that NO he *didn't* know what the business with Watt was, and did he not say also that NO they did *not* talk about getting a car, and did he not say also that NO he did *not* know, really, that Watt had a gun, and did he not say that they were just going to see a lady, and did he not say that he RAN the second he saw the first sign of violent intent, and did he not say also that he had no *idea* that he had to inform the police against Watt, and that he had to turn himself in, in order to avoid an accomplice charge, and did he not say that he was just plain *scared* and that he was as afraid of Watt as he was of the police—and so he hid? And did you ever, Officer Smithson, at any time refer to Marcus Sabbs as a fucking animal? Never? Not at any time? Not right to his *face?* I remind you that you are under oath, Officer Smithson. And did you ever, Officer Smithson, at any time, call Marcus Sabbs a sub-human Cabrini bastard? You can't recall that? It doesn't ring a bell?—that phrase: *subhuman Cabrini bastard?*

Marcus. Named, no doubt, for Marcus Garvey. History and heroes. Black history month. QuaaaaanZA. The high-hatted, baton-pumping drum major and the drum-corps parade. And Marcus Sabbs. His room, neat as a pin. Those photos on the wall, of Marcus with Jesse White, of Marcus wearing his Tumbler's uniform, his colors, red, the pride, and the pro games, and Japan, the bridge over the lily pond. And that green light pulsing on that hard-drive tower. This is his place, not prison. This is his home, his starting place—from here he'll go into a future. His mother's life work, having lost all her others, Johnnie B, and the girls. And Mr. Sabbs gone so long ago.

What does *"this"* mean? We don't want *this!* Demonstratives. This, that, these, those. Always to be used with unambiguous precision. We don't want *this!* That's what Marcus shouted, as Watt pulled out the gun. Nothing is worth *this!* I told her I knew what *this* meant, but that then I got lost. I got drunk, and stayed lost. And didn't know anymore what I knew, or who I was. I turned away from those I loved. Dosey. I told her that I did know again what *this* means. And I did know again that Marcus chose not to join Watt, chose to divide, to separate—in the key moment of his life—because he was raised there, with Dosey. And I promised her I would be there when the time came, which meant *this—* that I would say that Marcus wanted no part of the killing of my brother. And then I asked her, out of the blue, if she *could* have, *would* she have

THE WHOLE TRUTH

chosen not to have Johnnie B at sixteen and so to have escaped, like
her brother Maurice, all this Cabrini life. Equal, equal, equal. Killing.
Murder. A person. She said she had thought lately, many times, that
she might have chosen not to have him. But if Marcus goes free…she
will, she said, just be grateful to the Lord for the path he put her on
long ago, starting pregnant at age fifteen, and for Mr. Sabbs, so long
gone…where? His people were from Arkansas. If Marcus goes free….
Because between him and Watt he put the sword of division….

Microphonic coughings, tappings, mumblings—the judge getting
ready now, setting his mic. And the jury coming back, neither all white
nor all black, but more white than black and more male than female
and more old than young—so the prosecution clearly won the battle
of voir dire, *verum dicere*. The jury pool was not asked in this case if it
could impose the death penalty. Christ. In the annals of deck-stacking
injustice maybe nothing more glaring than that only those not opposed
to the death penalty could sit on juries in death-penalty cases. Who
let *that* happen—let that question about prospective jurors' capital-
punishment feelings even get asked? But, question or not, the deck still
looks stacked enough here—those twelve poker faces notwithstanding.
And that my words, the words of the only one who was there in the alley,
could work their way into those brains and unlock, or lock, prison
doors—could make those twelve minds give or take a life, today, maybe
only an hour away, a life, started, or terminated. She chose termination.
What history must you have? And that that prosecutor could work me
—against my will…with my will, make me say what I don't want to say…
or what I want to say.

Want. Don't let *want* be part of it. Kill *want.* Do your duty!—and gun
down *want* wherever it raises its face—deep inside your head. Don't let
that prosecutor work on your darkest *want.* He'll find it. He'll create
it. You've seen his game. Instrument of justice, or rather minion of the
devil. Remember your promises. You've got to go deeper than *want.*
You—you have to. But you will take an oath today to tell the truth…the
whole truth, so help you God—or they'll let stand the oath you took
already, you still being you. Justice, the *lex talionis,* for your brother,
who died, while you lived, having just said you wanted to kill him, your
wish coming true. And what will come across through the bulletproof
glass, when you say what you say?

The defense calls Sandra Leyland.

And soon as that, she was gone. But then, after some measure of

343

DIVISION

time, having walked that connective passage with the armed bailiff, she again emerged, on the other side of the glass—and as she again took the stand, she was reminded that, yes, she remained under oath. Continuous, from yesterday. Yes. And now would the quiet elegance of that remarkable beauty, the softness of that voice, those shocking eyes, beautiful, and the sure intelligence in that respectful voice, make a difference—for Marcus Sabbs—for his life? Did she—yes, yes she did receive a call from Watt, from Leonardo Sykes, yes, on the night in question. About a date? Yes. With the two cousins—Marcus Sabbs and Robert Teague? Yes. And yes, *yes* Watt did say where he was and that he was with those cousins. And yes, yes for absolute certain she did ask were they coming straight over. And yes, she said then, yes Watt did say that they were coming straight over, straight, yes, and *no,* Watt did not mention any possible intervening business, no he did not. And would that not, given where they were, be about twenty minutes?—'til they got there, Robert and Marcus? And did she mark the exact time? She did. And it was? 6:55 P.M. And when the cousins did not arrive at 7:15 or thereabouts, was she surprised? Yes, she was. Did she think that, while Watt had anticipated no such thing, something unforeseen *had* come up? Yes, most definitely she did—and she was very surprised. Thank you, Miss Leyland, thank you very much. *Your witness.*

Thank you. A date, Miss Leyland? Yes. What kind of date? Some drinks, conversation, perhaps dancing. Um hmm. Dancing. Yes, you do dance professionally, Miss Leyland, sometimes Miss Sara Lee? Yes. And what kind of dancing would that be? Exotic. I dance at the V.I.P. Club. And would you dance exotically for these…dates? Objection! Relevance! Sustained. Had you had any dates with Marcus Sabbs before—dates set up by Watt? Yes. For such dates, would there be the expectation of sexual intimacy, on Watt's part—that is, would Watt expect you to perform in a sexual way, say to solidify a relationship? a connection? an affiliation? Objection! Relevance! Sustained! The jury will disregard…. That is all, your Honor. I have no further questions of this witness. Ms. Reese? No further questions, your Honor. Had she helped? Her respectfulness, her beauty? Her voice, her eyes? It was over so fast. If only they'd let her talk longer. Soft, respectful voice— and that striking beauty. Yes, it helped. Yes. And no. She was a dancer, an escort, an affiliate of Watt's. Always yes here, and then no. And in the end, *what? The defense will now call Detective John Touhy.*

Knowing that he would be next, after Detective Touhy, and that he

344

THE WHOLE TRUTH

would be last—that now *so* soon, in minutes, he would be bringing all
testimony to a close—Connor sank further into himself, swam apart,
floated even more alone in this unreal fishbowl, hearing whatever it
was that Touhy, still Touhy, still under oath, was saying, as if indeed
these words, sounds of Touhy's, came through water—even when they
were said to be recollections, restatements, of his *own* words, words that
Connor Riordan said on the night in question. Robert wasn't in it. You
have to separate! I'd be sorry for the rest of my life, if you did anything
to Robert. Not everything is the same! You have to separate. And the
other one—the other one said *We don't want this. Nothing is worth this!* And
he ran! And what did Detective Touhy, when later he questioned Robert Teague, hear about Marcus Sabbs's involvement? He heard things
from Robert Teague that did corroborate, yes, what Connor Riordan
had said. He did hear the same. The same. Yes. We don't want this.
Nothing is worth this. The sword of division at the defining moment
of his life. Thank you, Detective Touhy. Thank you. *Your witness.*

The prosecution, persecution, again he rises, now reading notes. Turning over notes. The direct, and now the cross. The choice-confusing, ad-
versarial, defense-canceling, doubt-creating cross. Indecision, and then
decision, coming from where and from what? Who and what decides,
in the end? Did Detective Touhy ask of Robert Teague how it was that
the three came to be at the house of someone known to Robert Teague?
Yes. And did this puzzle him? Yes, it did. He did wonder how that
came to be. And yes he did think that Robert Teague was holding back
somewhat. Did Detective Touhy question Robert Teague about conversations preceding the event?—conversations that took place at the
park? Did he discover if there had been any planning? Or any inspiration—of one party by the other? Any working up of one party by the
other? We do. Any thinking about gentrification, about animosities
against whites in general? Yes. No. We do. We don't want this. We do.
We fucking do. You kilt ma brotha! YOU KILLED MY BROTHER!
Marcus tatted up with the three-pronged pitchfork of the devil. Gang
business. All for one and one for all. Collective guilt. Social justice—
and injustice. Get your hands off what doesn't belong to you. That moment before the gun went off. And you have no one to blame for your
fucked-up life but your individually responsible self, black man. And
we're tired of your blaming anybody else—tired to the point of pulling the trigger, on *you.* And did Detective Touhy ask about anything
that might help account for the unbridled violence of this killing?—

345

DIVISION

anything that would make us think of this crime as a *hate crime?* A straight line from here to that alley, the American flag flapping in the wind, the Stars and Bars raised over the Teague Funeral Home, Watt's blood spreading over the plate of names. Y'all got it started. Don't blame me. But we do...blame you. Did he ask anyone about any history between the parties? Yes he did. And the answer was no there was not. No history. Two worlds. Worlds apart—that for some reason came together in that alley, on the night in question.

CLOSURE

The Defense calls Connor Riordan. Amidst the scratchings, the thonks from the microphone, he heard the sounds that were always coming, as time kept taking the shape appointed to it by human intent. He could see through the glass Christa Reese, and, in a slight beckoning turn of her mouth, discern a supplication. He felt the touch of Ellie's hand. He looked at her face, her hazel eyes. The sinner is not the sin. The division is not the whole. She was the choice of his heart—and is, and will be. Can't not want that. And for months she had held his arm through every step toward a full defending of Marcus Sabbs's innocence.

He touched Ellie's shoulder. He looked across to the black side at Dosey Sabbs—though Dosey couldn't look back—no more than she could wear today her Sunday dress. Then, with the armed bailiff, Connor took the walk he had taken once already, in this appointed procession of time leading—to *what?* What conclusion? What closure? Direct, and cross, and redirect, and recross. *This—We don't want this. We don't want this. We don't. Nothing is worth this.* How, tight and final, could he close up the meaning of these words? How to say what precisely they meant, for the sake of justice? The door at the corridor's end opened—and there again were the judge and jury, on this other side of the bulletproof glass, and the prosecution and defense, at their tables, and Marcus Sabbs, now face forward, though his head was bowed. Connor did it then—walked—made his way past them all—and, without falling, took the stand, and then, perhaps not visibly shaking, pulled the microphone's flexible stem to suit his need. He stated his name when asked to—and, when asked if he did, said that yes he understood he was still under oath.

He wouldn't let his mind sink into its mire of perverse potentialities. No. He knew he made her nervous, even afraid, this Christa Reese—because—he always could see—she was never for a moment sure she could count on him. Twice she'd come to the house, and maybe five times she'd called—and it never changed, that sound of uncertainty in her voice. So now it was blandishments at first, as she approached—Good morning, Connor, and how are you this morning? and good, she was glad to hear he was fine, and well rested. But her nervousness, her fear, which again he could hear and see, it was good—a good sign—because it all showed clear as sunlight that Christa Reese cared about the life of her client.

Yet just like that, her fear perversely empowered the darkness in Connor—the ever-ready dance of the devils. Instantly it made him aware of how he could kill, as her imploring look, her blandishments put immediately a Watt's pistol in his speaking mouth, which gun he could use to shoot death sounds into this Christa Reese and into Marcus Sabbs and into Dosey Sabbs. He had the full power of a gun—just like Watt. He could in insane blind vengeance kill a black man and his mother and every black life on the black side of the gallery. Hate *all* you motherfuckers forever! Only one side gets to say that? Just blacks get to say that?

He felt fine, he told Christa Reese, fine this morning, yes—but now, even as he said this, he felt the rising aura of a flashback—felt the sweat rising to the surface of his skin, as he looked up and saw Marcus Sabbs, his black face now lifted up, just as on that night in the alley, and could read beneath that shirt and suit jacket the pitchfork of the Disciples on both his arms. Marcus the trigger. He got tatted only to protect himself in prison, Christa Reese had insisted. Always an explanation. But Connor recalled now the glistening of the shackles round Marcus's wrists and ankles, at that hearing.

348

Not whiskey but water was there; and Connor reached now, shaking, and took a drink, in hopes of securing some composure. He knew tricks now that helped to chase back dark visions, had his breathing techniques, mental talismans, crucifixes against the fanged vampire. The water helped. So he would continue to hold the glass in his hand. And squeeze that.

Christa Reese had returned to her desk. She was bending over her papers. And now sat to read them, once more. The state, she had said to the jury in her opening statement—but Connor had felt then that he, directly, was being addressed—the state will want you *not* to use your intellect, she said—that decisive gift in your mind which can make distinctions, see differences, separate one thing, one person, from another. Instead the state will want you with an indiscriminate passion to paint with one brush of responsibility all three of the young men who came upon Jack Riordan and his brother, on the night of March 22nd of last year. Robert Teague, Marcus Sabbs, and Leonardo Sykes, or *Watt*—the state will try to relieve you of what is always the more difficult task and even at times the *disappointing* task of making distinctions and seeing separate individuals—disappointing at times because, and perhaps most especially when we are horrified and enraged, we sometimes just *want* the simplicities of painting with a single brush. And always it is the more *difficult* task, seeing individuals as different, rather than all of them as just one indistinguishable type, one indivisible *gang*—the more difficult task because it makes us think, each and every time, about who exactly, individually, it is we are considering, not allowing us ever just to say *they*—and then leap to the easy and often satisfying comforts of generalization. And the state will know both that you have every reason to feel horror and rage and also that in all of us there *is* that desire, when we are enraged, or devastated, shocked, horrified by a violence perpetrated by one individual in a group, just to make sweeping condemnations of that whole group, to spray the gun of our anger without even aiming and to keep firing until we get the dead silence that sometimes gets called *closure*.

She rose at last—Christa Reese—and approached the stand. Seeming, though, to Connor, not weak now, rather strong in her courtroom strength. And what was the strongest thing in him? Would there be anything deeper than the perversities that the devil, through the flesh-tearing gun of Watt, worked into his mind, changing him, making him into his own image, the devil's, altering his neurons because the fucking devil had the miraculous knowledge of how to alter the paths of atoms—and to set them on dark courses forever? PTSD, one of the chief fields of expertise of the Prince of Darkness.

"On that night, Connor, when your life changed," Christa Reese at last now said, "when you were right there, and you suffered the life-changing agonies that you suffered, you said to Detective Touhy, that if there was to be justice, there needed to be separation—that a line needed to be drawn. You said that you were sure that Robert Teague was not in it, not part of it, the theft, the violence. And the *other one,* you said—*he ran,* because *he* was not in it. You wanted, for justice, to make sure that Detective Touhy understood that. Am I right, Connor—am I right in saying that, even on that night when you suffered the worst thing that a loving brother can suffer—am I right that you wanted to draw that line of separation, for justice—and to divide Robert Teague and Marcus Sabbs from Leonardo Sykes?—from Watt? Am I right in saying that you told Detective Touhy that if this line weren't drawn, you would be sorry for the rest of your life?"

What history would it take—for one to kill? In a compact instant, Connor felt it all—felt every white frustration with the ignorance and entrenched poverty of blacks, felt sick of explanations, let alone justifications for black anger, felt every ounce of the weight of white anger at every instance of black urban violence, felt every satisfaction at every media report, over what seemed a million years, that once again for the ten millionth time the gunman, the killer in whatever the case might have been, was black, of course he was black, or, as expressed in the ever-perfectly understood Chicago code, was from an address known to be a black address, a South Side address, a West Side address, a Cabrini address—felt exactly why it would be that, if black men in prison got tattooed with pitchforks, white men would get tattooed with Confederate battle flags. He felt all of this.

But what he did was breathe. And take a drink from the glass he held, more loosely now, in his sweating hand. And all in an instant, too, even physically in his brain, along the capillaries beneath his skull, he felt the action of the invisible angels that he had from some invisible place in himself called upon, that he had prayed for (and would it be enough? the action of these angels, to win the war in heaven in his brain, to regain paradise for him, on the Milton St., Cambridge St. in his mind, like a back alley without the trash cans?)—and what he said was, "Yes. Yes I did. I did tell Detective Touhy that a line of separation

CLOSURE

needed to be drawn. And yes I did say that if it were not drawn I would be sorry for the rest of my life. Yes I said that. And yes I did say that Robert was not in it—and made it as clear as I could that Marcus Sabbs was not in it."

"And, Connor, do you still believe that—I mean that Marcus Sabbs was not in it?"

"Yes. I do. I do believe that."

"Connor, I must ask you—when you looked out from the car that night and you saw Robert Teague, did he look surprised to see you?"

"He did. Yes. He looked surprised. Very surprised."

"And had you, Connor, ever had either Robert Teague or his sister, Carolyn, over at your house on Lincoln Park West?"

"No. I never did."

"Had you, to the best of your recollection, ever discussed with either Robert or Carolyn Teague where you lived? Had you ever given them your address?"

"No. I never gave them my address. And I never discussed with them where I lived."

Connor never looked out across the separative glass. But, having spoken, having taken this action now with his mind, and his mouth, and feeling, at least for an instant, the closure that comes with a decisive commitment, he imagined the face of Dosey Sabbs…but in this same moment, also, the face of his mother, who raised him…. Jackie Riordan…at least for now, Riordan. Maybe she always loved Jack more…. And, because of the stink of matches, what you carry on your back, Connor Riordan, will forever be the weight of Chicago damnation.

"Connor," Christa Reese now said, "Connor…please help us to understand. Help us to understand, and to know…something crucial here. There were spoken words that night, in the alley." She moved still another step toward him. Duty. She had brought him back, to his duty. But the look on her face—was it in strength that she looked at him? Or in fear? How could that matter? He wouldn't let it matter—because it did not matter. "Would you say there is a difference between spoken words, words you hear—and written words, words you just see on a page? When we can hear and see a speaker, is it different from when we just read words on a page?"

"They are very different—the words we hear and the words we see on a page."

"The tones, the gestures of the speaker, the look on a speaker's face,

351

DIVISION

the actions a speaker takes—these things make the difference? They help us understand the speaker's real meaning, in ways words merely written cannot?"

"They can make all the difference."

"Yes, they can. And, Connor, first, can you recall what words you heard Marcus Sabbs say, just as Leonardo Sykes drew the gun he used to kill your brother?"

Connor felt himself moved in, and felt a pleasure in, the momentum he'd started in his soul, the rolling power of a good momentum. And he said now, "Yes, I do recall. Marcus Sabbs cried out the word 'No!' Then he shouted, 'It's not worth it!' and then 'Nothing is worth this!' and then 'We don't want this! We don't!'"

"Thank you, Connor. Thank you." Christa Reese nodded her head, closed her eyes, then opened them again. "And considering now, Connor, the tones, the manner in which Marcus cried out, as you say, *cried out,* would you say that Marcus Sabbs cried out in distress—distress—as well as in protest over the action that Watt appeared at that moment to be taking?"

"Ob-*jection!* Defense is leading the witness!"

"Sustained."

But now, feeling still his soul's good momentum, before Christa Reese ever altered her question, Connor answered, "Yes. I *would* say that the way in which he cried out made it clear he was in distress and that he wanted Watt not to do...what he did."

Disregard. Disregard. The jury will disregard the statement of the witness. And the witness will refrain. Now and in the future. *Will disregard...Will refrain.* Stricken from the record. Now, and in the future. Her question. His answer. But their words...maybe most un-containable when arrested, as they were, in trespass. No closure—in the imperatives, the words, of the judge. *His* words will be disregarded. Or would Connor Riordan be regarded as an over-determined witness? *I am sorry, your honor. I apologize. Sorry.*

Christa Reese, not re-phrasing her question, simply waited now...for a quiet to fall. At last then she nodded, smiled at Connor—briefly, restrainedly. She took a step toward the jury, then stepped back to where she'd been. *"This.* We don't want *this...."* She paused, let those words, that word, of Marcus Sabbs's hang in the air. Then, "Connor, knowing what you know from being there, from hearing Marcus Sabbs, from seeing Marcus Sabbs, what...would you say that the word *this* meant?"

352

CLOSURE

And now hearing, listening to his own voice almost as if he were listening to a recording of it, Connor said, "I would say that it meant using a gun against another person."

"And *Nothing is worth this*—And *We don't want this...We don't*—what would you say, Connor...knowing all you know from hearing them yourself, from seeing Marcus Sabbs yourself, from hearing the tones in his voice, from *being there* when he spoke—*what* would you say that Marcus Sabbs's words *Nothing is worth this* and *We don't want this...We don't*—what would say those words meant?"

Again now listening to himself, hearing himself, but now relieved, deeply, to be this speaking person, feeling the deep, good pleasure of it, Connor said, "I would say that what Marcus Sabbs's words meant is that there is nothing, *nothing* worth murdering a human being for. And that he wanted no part of any such act."

Christa Reese nodded, let her mouth—her face—express a quiet thankfulness. A quiet pleasure...of gratitude...could be read now in her eyes. At last, then, in a softer voice, "One final thing, Connor. One last thing. *What*—when he saw that gun being raised against your brother —what was it that Marcus Sabbs *did?*"

"He ran."

"Thank you. Thank you, Connor. That is all I wanted to know. You've helped us see and understand the crucial thing." Christa Reese now nodded a last time at Connor—and then, stepping toward her table to sit with Marcus Sabbs, she looked to the table of the prosecution and said the words: *"Your witness."*

Mid-forties. Un-grayed. Short hair—but not close cropped. Nothing overdone. A clean-pressed white shirt and charcoal suit with a monotone dark blue tie. Not handsome but powerful looking. Not that manufactured gym-toned look—rather that of the one you'd just know to place yourself behind when the fight broke out. You could see it all in his face—and in the black hairs on the back of his hands. The prosecutor with the strange name: Gerald Minister. Like a priest who'd get you down on your knees.

"Good morning, Connor." But no looking up, rather a last looking at notes, at the pad he carried, turning over now a page, licking his forefinger, turning over another. At last he raised his head. "Your intellect." He sniffed a laugh. "I won't, Connor, insult it. I know that you know it's just as hard to see links and to make connections—as it is to distinguish, separate, divide. We both know this, don't we.... And we know

353

DIVISION

that justice asks us either to separate people, or to link them, as the case requires."

He looked a moment again at his notes. Then, raising his head, "You saw, Connor—the photographs of the tattoos on the arms of Marcus Sabbs—tattoos placed after, not before the killing of your brother?"

"Yes. I saw them."

"Did they suggest to you that there was remorse on the part of Marcus Sabbs over the taking of a life—the taking of your brother's life? You have said that you see Marcus Sabbs as valuing the life of another person over anything. Do the tattoos of the Gangster Disciples cut on his arms after your brother's murder confirm your mind in that conviction?"

"I am satisfied with the explanation given for the tattoos—and for their being cut while Marcus Sabbs was imprisoned."

"Explanations. Justifications. Do you ever get tired of them?"

"I don't know what you mean."

"I think you do, Connor. I'm sure you do know what I mean. But let me ask—Did you hear the testimony of Ms. Meghan Hoerster, who was working at Starbuck's during the late afternoon of the day your brother was killed, murdered in cold blood, shot repeatedly in his face in a manner so ruthless that we do, Connor, *we do* think of your brother's murder as a hate crime—how can we not? Specifically, did you hear Ms. Hoerster say that not an hour and a half before your brother was violently and hatefully murdered, Marcus Sabbs stood under the arm of his friend, Watt, as that murderer, in an answer to Ms. Hoerster's saying *Don't blame me*—and she testified this was well understood by Watt to mean Don't blame me for the gentrification or white take-back of Chicago neighborhoods that had before gone ethnic—Did you hear Ms. Hoerster say that Watt said *We do?* We—*WE* do blame you for that, Watt said, with Marcus Sabbs, fellow gang member, brother in the Gangster Disciples, under his arm—which is to say *WE* blame whites in general for taking our neighborhoods back. Did you hear this testimony of Ms. Hoerster?"

"Yes."

"And did it put any doubt into your mind with respect to Marcus Sabbs's intent in roaming a white neighborhood, not an hour and a half later, on the night your brother was murdered?"

Connor, suddenly, and exactly as he had that night in the kitchen when he fought most fiercely with his mother, now felt himself keened for battle. He looked Gerald Minister straight in the face and said, "Did

354

CLOSURE

Ms. Hoerster's saying she couldn't say for sure what it was that Watt was referring to, when he said *We do,* put any doubt in your mind?"

"Answer the question I asked, Mr. Riordan. Did it put any doubt in your mind?"

"No."

"No what? No, it in fact left you *certain* that Marcus Sabbs was roaming a white neighborhood with aggressive racial animus?"

"No—it created no such certainty."

"And no doubt?"

"No."

"Do you believe, Mr. Riordan, that conversations taking place immediately or not long in advance of a confrontational situation can influence the nature or the outcome of that confrontation? Let me give you an instance, Mr. Riordan. Do you believe that the conversation you had with your brother in advance of the confrontation with Watt could have had an influence on your brother's behavior and hence on the outcome of the confrontation in the alley behind your house?"

His hands suddenly now pooling again with sweat, Connor feared that he would break the water glass, as he gripped it tighter. He loosened his hand on the glass—and lifted it, and drank. Then, still rattled, trying hard to hold himself together, he said simply, "Of course I have asked myself that question."

"So close, Connor, that night. So close that your brother's blood came to cover you. And yet you lived. You lived. Has there been a need in you to make sure that no one else dies or suffers? Fighting against a desire for vengeance, has there been a need in you to show mercy—to help you get free of all the bloodshed of that night? Of all the guilt? Has there been a need to forgive? To forgive everyone, no matter *what?*"

A thousand possible statements, answers. Who or what would decide what he would say? What grace gives energy to the search for the right thing to say? He bowed his head, breathed. Could he do his duty to the truth? What truth? He would be sorry for the rest of his life—if *what?* He looked up and said, at last, "I have had more needs than you will ever know, Mr. Minister. I have had a million *needs.* My mind has become a battleground of battling needs. But I have no need to forgive Marcus Sabbs. I do *not* forgive Marcus Sabbs—because forgiveness is for people who have done us wrong—and Marcus Sabbs has done me no wrong, nor done my family, nor my brother, Jack, any wrong."

"No need for forgiveness. I am sure you feel no such need and have

355

never felt any such need, with respect to Marcus Sabbs. I am certain. Yes. And, tell me, when you heard, as I'm sure you heard that Marcus Sabbs was out that night with his friend and fellow gang member Watt on *gang business,* were you left unshaken in your conviction that Marcus Sabbs played no part whatsoever in the attempted carjacking of your mother's car? Is that right, Mr. Riordan, you were unshaken in your conviction—that that gang business had nothing to do with getting a car and so Marcus Sabbs had no part in what happened to your brother? *Unshaken!?*"

Connor hid his hands. And what place was deeper than the source of his sweat? Unshaken. What place was deeper than all fear and trembling? Who or what could lead him to that place—so he could find the right answers to put into this Minister's face? He hoped the glass wouldn't slip from his sweating hand. He said, "I believe the attempt was unplanned. Unforeseen. Officer Smithson has testified as well that Marcus Sabbs said he did *not* know what that business was or would be. And Ms. Leyland confirms the statements of both Robert Teague and Marcus Sabbs that they were coming straight from Lincoln Park to her home, to see her, no intervening business anticipated, or mentioned."

"Saying and unsaying. First Mr. Sabbs said he did know what the business they were about was—and then he said he didn't know. He said he didn't know anything about going for a car. Then he said he did know that that was the intent. First he said he did know that Watt had a gun. Then he said he didn't know. And you, Mr. Riordan. You say you know. Have you always known what you say you know now? Or have there been any changes in your mind? Any changes at all? *ANY?* Could you, under oath, say that there have been no changes in your mind whatsoever about the involvement of Marcus Sabbs in the murder that night of your brother—the violent murder perpetrated by a member of the Gangster Disciples, while he was in the company of another member of the Gangster Disciples, out together with him on *gang* business! Could you say under oath that you have had not a single moment of doubt?!"

Connor wanted not to hesitate—for his hesitation might speak deadly volumes. But he found himself now looking up and out, not at Minister, rather at his mother, Jackie Riordan, who sat there still with her sister in the first row past the glass. She wore now on her face—what?—a pursed smile?—a thoughtful, concerned smile?—loving? What could he see there in her eyes? She had seen him looking out at her, and now

356

CLOSURE

she nodded, slightly. Was it a plea?—to do the right thing? Was it a request for love?—that turn of her mouth, into a smile? That nod?

"Mr. Riordan?"

"Are you asking me, Mr. Minister," Connor now said, turning his eyes on the prosecutor, and feeling again strength, feeling his mind grow hard and keen, "—are you asking me if there was no process whatsoever for me, in sorting out the truth? Are you asking me did I have no questions to sort out and answer before reaching certainty? You said you would respect my intellect. If you do respect it, you'll trust me when I say that if there were, yes, questions that my intellect, my mind had to answer, that nonetheless the sorting out it did as it brought me to the clear certainty that Marcus Sabbs is innocent was not difficult."

"He knew, Mr. Riordan, Marcus Sabbs knew, knew all night that night, that Watt was carrying a gun. He knew, and he did not separate himself from Watt, knowing that Watt had that gun, the gun that killed your brother. He knew it; he knew Watt had that gun as he came down that alley. He knew it as Watt made his move toward your mother's car. He knew Watt had that gun. And only when he got scared, *ONLY* when it was brought to the point of no return, did he say, 'We don't want this! We don't!' And what after all does that mean? We don't want now what we've said we wanted all along! That's what it means! And we don't want it because when it comes to the *point of no return,* I still want to go back—because suddenly I'm too scared to do what we all along *planned to do?* We don't! Have you, Mr. Riordan, had no suspicions that all that really means—all that means!—is that I am suddenly afraid, now that it has come to and *passed* the point of no return?"

The dark hairs of his wrists appearing darker against the bleached-clean white of his cuffs—in this passion, call it aggression now of the prosecutor, Minister, Gerald Minister, Connor found suddenly now, after all, a hard-as-ice disregard for the life of the person he would convict, and a hard-as-ice desire just to win, and no honest and true respect for justice, or for Jack Riordan, whose *brother* was on the stand!—so no love for the Riordans, no love, clear as hell on earth. *None!* And what Connor said now, in a calm voice, quiet, and strong, was this: "We do—the words Watt said in the Starbucks to Ms. Hoerster. You were certain, Mr. Minister, what they meant. You worked hard to show how those words could mean only one thing. But now *We don't*—you are working just as hard to show those words could mean just about anything. But there is this great difference between us, Mr. Minister. In neither

357

DIVISION

case were you there. But when Marcus Sabbs said *We don't*—I was. I *was* there. I was there, and I know what those words meant—and what they mean. And what they mean is that Marcus Sabbs is no Watt—and that he had no intention of doing my brother wrong, or me wrong, or my family wrong—and that he should be let go." And as soon as he'd said this, as soon as he'd stepped into this next and most firm life-determinative action, Connor looked up and out—to see across the glass division what look his mother now wore.

IN THE KINGDOM OF HEAVEN

" 'I am proud of him'—That's what she told Mary Tate when Mary thanked her for what you'd done for Marcus. Your mother is proud of you, son. Very proud. She told Mary Tate, too, how sorry she was that she hadn't talked to her at Robert's services—that she'd wanted to talk to her. But they just took each other's hands, the two mothers, and Mary said they didn't need to say another thing."

Connor Riordan, having told Maurice Teague, now three weeks past—when he saw Maurice in the gallery after Marcus Sabbs was acquitted and, right then and there, freed to leave in the coat and tie his mother had chosen—that he wanted, please, to come sometime and talk to Maurice—that he'd wanted ever since Maurice spoke out his name in his unforgettable eulogy for his son, to come and see him—now sat in Maurice's turret-room library, surrounded by the man's beautifully shelved collection, impressive, extensive as his own father's. It was a year and a day after Jack's death. "I had wondered...," he said, resistant against them and touched...and...pained by Maurice's words about his mother, "...wondered...what she might have said to Mrs. Teague." He paused. He lowered his eyes. "I don't see my mother.... I haven't talked to her...." He looked up again, now tilting back his head—then, changing the subject, "I saw Mrs. Teague talking, too, to Annabelle Lester, the grandmother...."

"Yes," Maurice said, wondering, disappointed. Clearly the boy, who'd mentioned it—and wanted it mentioned—was fighting his own desire...his need...to talk about the sad division in his family. Another moment—then Maurice said to him, "And for that, too, thank you, son. If not for you, Ms. Lester wouldn't have been there—and I...I am truly grateful." Again Maurice hesitated—but then, "It's been hard, for Mary Tate.... She never could agree with what I did with the flag. She'll never see any good reason for it...just the danger...and the foolishness, as she can't help but call it...and the vanity.... She can't separate the flag, son, from our Robert's death—the flag and the way...and the length of time it separated Robert and me at and around the time of your brother's death. And that has been hard for us.... But Ms. Lester —and again, thank you—she told Mary Tate that she knew past all doubt, from things she'd heard her grandson say just days before he died, that Watt had wanted to mislead—wanted it thought that somebody in the neighborhood, angered by the flying of the flag, had been responsible for Robert's death. She said she'd come to free Mary from any false suspicion—any anger turned in the wrong direction. Immediately, when Mary told me this, I tried to find Ms. Lester—but she was gone."

Connor could sense that Mr. Teague, with this confession that there were tensions in his own home, had invited him to talk more about his parents' divorce.... But he returned to Annabelle, pleased that she'd done what she did for the Teagues; and he nodded, smiling—though he wouldn't talk about the Teagues' troubles. "I brought Ellie over to meet her," he said. "She'd given me this flashlight, and Ellie told her that we keep it now in a special place. She called Ellie 'pretty lady' and told her to take good care of me. And she told me she was glad I was still in this world, not hurt by any foolish actions of my own...or of anybody else—and glad that it was all over now and done—glad that I'd finished it by helping Marcus. All over and done, I repeated —but looking at her as if to say that maybe things like what we've gone through won't ever be over and done. She just nodded. Then she touched Ellie's shoulder—told the pretty lady again to take good care of me. Then she left. I'd meant to ask her where she planned to go, once her building came down. But she was gone before I could."

IN THE KINGDOM OF HEAVEN

"Yes," Maurice said. "Yes...." Then, after a moment, "I've finally convinced Dosey to move over this way with Marcus. I've gotten them a place just a block over." He looked aside, then back at Connor. "Their coming helps me to convince Mary Tate, and myself, too, to stay...." He took a long, slow breath. "But where all the thousands and thousands of others still left in Cabrini, and in all the other slated projects, will go once the wrecking ball has struck the final blow...."

Connor, now sensitive immediately to Mr. Teague's wanting not to discuss his and Mrs. Teague's staying here...or leaving...picked up the thread again of Cabrini—of all the projects...slated...designated non-viable.... "*The* question," he said, in an instant now visiting all the perspectives he'd ever had upon it, "for Chicago...for the city's soul.... Annabelle Lester...Mother Lester, they call her.... She's the question.... And I don't know the answer. Not more of the same, but not nothing, either. There's got to be a true start, *somewhere,* past all the lies...before another entire generation, hundreds of thousands.... There are pictures of her dead young ones on Annabelle's wall.... And Johnnie B, your nephew, and Marcus's sisters...." He paused a moment. "But I'm so glad Dosey and Marcus are coming this way. Even though I know that Dosey took so much pride in her place on Cambridge St. Marcus's computer light in his room there—I told him I could see that green light pulsing before I took the witness stand—and the picture of him on a bridge in Japan. Perhaps you know it...." He lifted his eyes, saw book titles—Nietzsche, *Beyond Good and Evil;* Montesquieu, *The Laws.* And then down on the window shelf...the *Antigone* and the *Oedipus Tyrannus* of Sophocles.

Looking now out the window, Connor said, "She talked to me, too, Annabelle did, about what Cabrini was in the beginning...as it isn't now, and never will be again...." But now suddenly he went ahead, feeling a yet greater intimacy with Mr. Teague—and let his pain take him where it would. He turned once more to him. "It's hard to give up your place, especially when it seems like, after so many years, there's no other. It's like that for my father, too...our place.... It was the back door, not the front, at our house, the car pad, not the porch—where for us Watt left his calling card." He stopped again a moment, shut his eyelids over a starting of tears—then, "So much we have in common, Mr. Teague, both of us having lost brothers at the hands of someone of another race. Our older brothers.... And in having had Watt...come to our doors."

361

DIVISION

With his mind running over a hundred things, and feeling himself now invited to go anywhere, Maurice said to this white boy, St. Ignatius boy, "So much in common. Yes. So very much. And your father... Tom...you mention him. I met him at the services for Robert. How is he doing?"

Connor opened his eyes, wiped them, then looked again at Mr. Teague, strong, firm-postured in his chair, but his face tired, showing signs that no one wins forever over age, or grief. "He seemed for so long to be so much better off than me. But our house.... He was given the house, in the divorce. But *that*...the divorce, with its being final now...on top of Jack's being killed there—put all of it together, and he says he can't stay there much longer. And it's been over twenty years there, the only place we ever knew as a family. But too many hard memories for him now, with...my mother...her taste in things, everywhere in the house. He says the thing he most fears is anger...and that, for him, it lives there, and grows, without his being able to help it."

"To have heard me," Maurice said, "with my Robert, when he sat right where you sit, son, saying to him here what I said at his funeral services—telling him, when I tried to explain why the flag and the stone—telling him that powerful, soulful places, whether of glory or of grief and darkness, will, when we go to them, bring out the gifts of God in us, bring out the Lord's voices. To be, as I have, on the Mt. of Olives.... So we make pilgrimages, all of us, to our Meccas, our Wailing Walls. It's what we do.... But to have heard me—speaking as if *distance* away from places...weren't every bit as important—or that the sense of what the right distance is, or that the need for that right distance, weren't also gifts from God. Listening to our minds when they tell us to divide, separate ourselves from certain places.... Old Mississippi for me.... Please trust that I understand.... And that I feel for your father, son. And am sorry."

Connor, his mind now comforted in this intimacy, felt a sudden urge to explain his coming. "About all that you said...at Robert's...in your eulogy.... More than anything else...I've come to ask if you've found, I mean, through the forgiveness you spoke of...if you've found peace? I mean *lasting* peace? Not something that just comes and goes. Rather something so deeply healing that it gets your mind to just *change,* gets it past resentment and rage and grievance and the desire to vindicate or avenge yourself—avenge and vindicate yourself because you've come

362

IN THE KINGDOM OF HEAVEN

so deeply to doubt and devalue yourself...all because of what somebody *did* to you...whether with a gun, or with betrayals...betrayals
maybe of a whole shared moral history...that leave you with your past,
your future...your home base gone."

Maurice folded his hands in his lap. He looked closely at Connor.
"He understood.... Watt *knew* that his deception, his wrapping of Robert's body in that flag and then leaving him dead at our doorstep—he
knew, just as Annabelle Lester has said, that that might immediately
be seen as the act of someone here, some Bronzeville black man so
filled with rage at all that that flag stands for and so filled with vengeful rage against the Teagues for flying it that violently he would take
a life in retaliation, that he'd slit a beautiful and good young man's
throat over it and then take that boy dead to his mother and father's
doorstep. Watt knew that people naturally would think, as Mary has,
that someone here could have a darkness in him every bit as dark as
every dark thing that that flag has stood for. And of course someone
could. And there but for the grace of God go I, or you, Connor. All
blackness could go white; all whiteness black. None of us is without
the same dark potential. We all of us could kill the other in the name
of what we see ourselves as, with our eyes, white eyes, black eyes, all
the same. Racially we murder; always we murder *racially*—which is
to say after we've performed a discriminatory division between what,
because it looks like us, we judge to be good, from what, because it
doesn't, we judge to be evil. All murder is racial, is of the black-and-
white-seeing eyes, is of the skin of *definition,* is of judgmental *description*
—is responsive to a perceived threat, come from some visible other-
ness, to our visible *selves.* And we paint those who've done us wrong,
and whom we hate, with the colors, or the judgmental black and white,
that we find in our own selfishly encased, eyesight-imprisoned hearts
and minds. Watt slew Robert Teague on the threshold of our Funeral
Home, which I've tried to make into a place of soulful transcendence
—to dedicate it to the invisible and infinite, the beyond-description.
But when I heard that Watt's blood, when he killed himself, spilled
over the names on the name plate at Oak Woods, I was as satisfied as
any raging redneck who would have whooped in savagery had he seen
Watt spectacle-lynched, with his testicles and penis in his mouth and
his hanged and tarred body set afire—as satisfied, in other words, as
any abandoned, debased son of the souls named on that name plate.

DIVISION

And I haven't been able yet, in truth, to divide enough my wounded, bleeding self from the vision of what I saw when I opened that battle flag on my own doorstep. Not enough."

"I'm so sorry, Mr. Teague," Connor now said, feeling also, however, relieved that Maurice Teague had confessed to him all that he had. "So sorry that in this, too, we could be so much the same—I mean in the recurring bursts of irrepressible anger and resentment and fear. And that my dad, too—that for all his best efforts, he hasn't been able to keep from falling back into that place where it's an eye for an eye. I'm so sorry, and angry that we're the ones who suffer the life sentences— of flashbacks, of night sweats, of, in my case, the need to anaesthetize myself, by whatever means…. Though at least I can say I've gotten past the mind-numbing drinking. Small steps. And I sleep better, most nights. But did you…I mean, have you…over the years…found it hard to sleep at night, Mr. Teague? Seen white men in your dreams? Awakened in sweats? Watt twice had his gun raised at me. Twice I was seconds from death. And the only thing stopping the third time's coming is his death…. Is there someone you see in your dreams? Someone who's intruded and taken up residence in your brain, as if it's not yours but his? Some white man pointing a gun at you?"

"Yes, son—all of that. Yes. The white man with a gun, pointing it right at me—the white man of my nightmares. Yes. And recurring and recurring, my mad desire in dreams to find a gun, my frantic desire to do to him what he was about to do in my dreams to me, and in real life to me. And my waking in sweats, finding myself still alive, but still wanting in a lingering nightmare dread to find a gun and to do to him what he was about to do to me. Or to unload a shotgun's first barrel into his chest and its second into his genitals, as he did to my brother. Years of these nightmare desires—so much like yours." He stopped now a moment, took a long, slow breath—and looked most earnestly at this young white man sitting where Robert would sit. And he meant now more deeply still to relate, to connect, to this boy whose needs he did understand, whose needs he knew. "But my sufferings—they actually helped me, too, to strive for my future, for my life. And the sufferings, the rage and dread and nightmares helped me, too, to keep the secret that my mother swore me to…and so to save my father."

Maurice sighed. He folded his hands before his chest. He rested his elbows on the arms of his chair. He tapped his thumbs, looking down at them—but then, on his forearms, he lifted himself in his chair and

364

IN THE KINGDOM OF HEAVEN

leaned forward. "Both of us, in common, know—body and soul, we know, son; from our night sweats, we know; from our obsessions over another race, from the ways in which we've condemned en masse, sick-enjoying the easy sweeping logic that follows from stereotyping, uni-versalizing: All white men are the same; all black men are the same: *Therefore* we are always to think in the same unvarying and prejudged way about this one, and this one, and this one, none of them unique, none of them different, none of them an individual person—from the sick guilt induced by the fraud of this pseudo-logic, we *know;* from the deep sick feeling we get from taking nonetheless an angry pleasure in the holocaust of all these genocidal racist syllogisms, we know; and from the remorse we feel every time our anger is triggered, we know; from the acid in our stomachs, from the wild changes in our heart rate and the mad rushes of adrenaline and the inability to choose what we think, or to escape the hell's gallery of images that haunt us—from all this, we *know* that unforgiving anger is a deadly sickness determined to kill us. And yet we prefer this deadly sickness to forgiveness—because, somewhere deep inside our trembling selves, we are dead certain that forgiveness is another name for cowardly capitulation or for suicidal self-disrespect. To forgive, deep down we know, would take a radical elimination of self, of that thing we see and call *I;* and we would rather be sick, son, even unto death, than annihilate this angry, trembling thing, attached to it as we are, by our eyes, which we prefer to our souls."

Maurice now straightened himself in his chair again, and again folded his hands in his lap. He waited, then, looking again intently at the young white man who sat where his own son had sat, so many times, "I'm sure that I've thought through every challenge to forgiveness. And Robert, too, in his beautiful anger, his black man's anger, he brought the challenges against forgiveness all up again, both before and after your brother...Jack.... That forgiveness is always a sign of insufficient self-respect, that forgiveness is a capitulation to the idea that the offend-er's crime against us, which, as you say, devalues us—is justified. That when we forgive, we as much as say we *are* what the offender valued us at when he violated or abused...or betrayed us, treated us like dirt, like a non-person, like an animal."

Maurice had a clear memory flash through his soul. He could hear Robert's resistant voice, his angry reactions—and he missed his son in a spasm of agony—but felt a warm counter-rush of gratitude for the respectful listening of this young white man, not his son, who listened

365

DIVISION

with the respect of a non-son. He touched, for a moment, the forefinger of his closed right hand against his lip. "Forgiveness, Connor," he said, "or an insufficiency of natural resentment—is said to be a sign of mental *slavery*—of a morbid tendency, in the emotionally decaying mind of the victim, toward self-diminishment, even self-loathing."

As Connor still sat silent, respectful, Maurice rose from his chair and turned, stepping to the window that looked toward the Teague Funeral Home. In the happiness and confidence of a camaraderie of thought with this white boy, and of feeling and suffering, he would make his tone now even more clearly ironic. *"Resentment,"* he said, looking out the window, "that strong opposite of forgiveness, is given to us, it is said, to ensure that the score will be settled, that things will be evened up—the equality of all persons restored in justice."

He paused again a moment, but only to let the momentum of thoughts long familiar to him regather. "Forgiveness," he said, turning down his mouth in near scorn, "is the deep-felt letting go of resentment. But fully to let go of resentment is to take a first step toward the condoning of anything and everything—of Nazism, of slavery, of apartheid. Forgiveness makes tyranny permissible; it makes might be right."

He turned from the window toward Connor. "The mind of the forgiver tends, it has been said, toward a sick identification with the offender—no matter if it is the Nazi, or the slave master—and with the offender's crimes. The forgiving victim's softness sides morbidly with the offense...."

The signs of age, of grief, Connor could see them again. But the strength of this man, in his hands, his face, was all so clear as well. "The un-resentful softness of women, over the centuries," Maurice said, "the softness of long-oppressed and long un-rebellious working classes... the softness of older-generation blacks—like me. Uncle Toms. Doormats."

He stepped toward his chair. He held its back, tight. "No one, it is said, who has ever lived, is invulnerable to deep and terrible wounds to his or her sense of self-worth—and were it not for the deep impulse of resentment, there *never* would be the justice-cure that comes from getting even."

As now Maurice, stepping around his chair, sat again at last, Connor looked down, pressed his fingers together hard in his lap, then said, "This is my blood, which is shed for all, for the resentment of sins."

Robert, Maurice thought again of his son, Robert, my rebel son, angry and beautiful. Gone to rest. And may perpetual light.... Holding

IN THE KINGDOM OF HEAVEN

back another rush of intense grief, Maurice said to Connor Riordan, looking, nodding at him, Robert's schoolmate, one of the good ones, who'd made that sharp, fine sarcasm on the Last Supper of Christ, "I am sure that it starts, that grace is born, son, far back inside the Gates of Eden. If justice and equality depend upon unforgiving resentment, then unforgiving resentment has its work to do. And so be it. And let all the supine, all the uncomplaining workers, all the suppressed women, all the Uncle Toms start at last to feel it—let anger and resentment lead them to action and to revolution—until the last abuse has ended." He'd found indeed his full energy of mind. But he paused now, and once more breathed deep and slow. "Yet you asked me if I have found peace. And resentment, son, has nothing to do with peace. Nothing."

Maurice set his powerful hands over his knees. Truly, he thought, he could make a difference for this young white man listening to him. And not abandoning his train of thought, he drove it on, hard, with no irony now in his tone, only energized determination. "Those who speak of resentment, Connor, as being indispensable for order, or for personal or social justice, too often seem to think of resentment as some easily controllable emotion—as if its potential to develop into obsession or to create havoc in interpersonal relations, in *families,* in relations between entire ethnicities, races, nations—as if all this dark potential were easily enough manageable—as if resentment were never either lethal or epidemically contagious or historically immovable, again and again being passed on as a cultural inheritance, entrenching itself over centuries. Nor do they seem to have a sufficiently clear sense of the degree to which they speak facilely of this thing they call self-respect, which should in innumerable cases be understood as a possibly dangerous euphemism."

Connor knew he was journeying with someone down a road that truly they both knew. All that Mr. Teague was saying, he had said, thought, himself. But no matter. He was sure that this fellow traveler, Robert Teague's father, had in his longer, deeper life taken the road far closer to the end. He looked at the man, said nothing, letting him know that he meant still just to listen.

This boy, this boy here, Maurice felt once more...a difference could be made...and my Robert.... I told Robert my secret, told him of Jesse .... He said now to Connor, "It starts, for me, son, it *does,* with the flag I have raised at the Teague Funeral Home—with knowing that we are all sinners, that for all of us it is all one flag of murderous dehumanizing

367

DIVISION

darkness. We all ride under the banner of the Prince of Darkness. You and I are Watt, who, if a black slave, was also a white slave master. Moral equivalence. A million voices will scream against it—and let them— for in important, vital senses, moral equivalence must always be a lie. White pain, black pain—they are different in degree, in kind. But we all ride under the banner of the Prince of Darkness, equally. So judge not, lest ye be judged. There is a fierce economics in the gospels of Jesus, son—and it is all about the price you will pay if you think you are any better than the next man. So fly the flag. Drop the stone if you're not sinless—and you are not. Watt, Marcus has told me, had the face of the devil tattooed on his chest. And so do you. And so do I. Before we can in sympathetic love divide the sinner from his sin, we must know that we have sinned it ourselves. And then, Connor, we must ask, Who *was* he, Watt?"

"My friend," Connor did say now, countless things instantly concentrating in his mind, forcing themselves up, "George Rudkus, a policeman, he was there when Watt took his own life.... And that...that violent suicide, right before his eyes...and other things...personal.... They've all mounted up for him so that he's leaving the force, and leaving the city, moving to Arizona—for the distance—from Chicago, which as a cop he just can't take any more.... But he's told me that John Touhy said that Sandra Leyland, Sara Lee, must have loved Watt...and that this, for Touhy, when he came to know it, made Watt into a person for the first time...that it got him to stop seeing Watt as a cop out of the Eighteenth, as a Cabrini cop, he had seen him ever since he first heard of him. And George told me how Touhy told him things Sandra had said about Watt's father, whom Watt killed, his own father...God in heaven...that this man, Watt's father, was called the Gasoline Man— because of how many buildings he burned down during the Martin Luther King riots—and how this man, the Gasoline Man, in his raging anger, come deep out of Mississippi, Mr. Teague, like yours, just like yours, murdered Watt's mother, slit her throat, having supplied her with the heroin she became addicted to and then had to whore for, he her brutal pimp, who beat and abused Watt, too. And Annabelle told me that Watt was the one who found his mother dead, that he crawled to her through her blood...when he was ten years old.... And George, he was there; he heard Watt's last words...."

Connor bowed his head. He spread a hand over his brow, covering his eyes. "Jack's words, his exact words...telling Watt to get his hands

368

IN THE KINGDOM OF HEAVEN

off what didn't belong to him, and that there was no one to blame for his life but himself. Watt said these exact things, Mr.Teague, in raging anger, threw these exact words back at the white world, at the cops with their twenty guns trained on him. He roared out, too, that white men give the names to things...to what was good and what evil...but that he changed those names.... He changed all the names of things, what was good, what was evil, down where the names get changed.... Incredible, so incredible. And he shouted to all the cops around him— that ALL they wanted was the capital punishment of every black man who ever lived and who ever would live. The lynching! And then he said, 'HERE IT IS!' And he killed himself. Christ in heaven...with the same gun.... And my friend said that he couldn't take any more, after that. He had to leave Chicago, for good." Connor pressed his cupped hand down on his eyes. Then with his forefinger and thumb, he squeezed hard on his temples—till at last the pain made him roll the pressure back onto the bone over his eyes.

"Money, Mack, Murder—these words, too, Marcus has told me, Connor, were tattooed on Watt's chest. He had devoted himself to the devil."

Connor raised his face. And Maurice, leaning forward in his chair, looked at him, in intense concentration of thought. "Doctor King, Robert told me, was for Watt a man who while willing to die would never change history the way a man could who was also willing to kill. It was, Robert told me, a great and terrifying power that Watt had. It could convert you—all to that dark, wrong way he had chosen. He could make you his disciple. And there is that question, as deep and crucial as the question you said that Annabelle poses, as to whether Watt could have been himself a Martin Luther King had it not been for Cabrini and the Gasoline Man, who in Mississippi rage would burn Chicago down for what a white man did to Martin Luther King in Memphis—that white man who was born in the place of old slavery?"

Straight again in his chair, Maurice kept his look intensely on Connor and concentrated his mind upon a gathering together of the thoughts, the words, that truly might help this boy...as lost as ever he had been himself. "Marcus, who, I've promised the good Christ Jesus, will be a son to me now, has told me how Watt took him to the burned-out top of the Cabrini building that Watt had intended to make the headquarters of the kingdom he intended to build, and how Watt, alone, officiated there over Marcus's baptism into the Gangster Disciples."

369

DIVISION

A moment pausing, Maurice again let his thoughts gather around a center of what he hoped, yes, would be hope...though there must be a passage through darkness. "And Marcus told me that Watt told him that, in his baptism, his body would be cast into a lake of fire—that the night one is born a Disciple is the night he dies—that the gangster baptized in fire is the terror condemned in places of worship and worshipped in the scorned places of vice and abandonment—that he is the father and mother of sin, the heart of evil and darkness—the Gangster Everlasting and Evermore."

Maurice not wanting now to stop, rather to make quickly a point, *the* point he wanted Connor to see, fearing that, after all, the boy might not see it—still paused to breathe deeper, and to slow and deepen his voice. "Just as the son of God, Connor, took on humanity...and all the stain of human flesh—so you, I am sure—as sure as I am that I have needed, for my own soul's salvation, to ride under the battle flag of my enemy—that, for your salvation, you *need* to tattoo across your heart the banners of Watt, the double pitchfork of the Disciples—and to do this not just, son, as a confession of that darkness you share with him, but in a deep and true respect for those moments when Watt transcended all cowardly fear of death. Bury me in a gangster city, they say, and show no pity...."

Touching all his fingers together, Maurice now pressed them hard against each other. "Marcus has told me of a time when Watt stood alone and faced down an armed group of the most violent, ruthless men to come from any of the most violent and dark corners of God's creation—and Marcus told me it was for him a moment of conversion, a moment when he said that he knew that God himself must respect the magnitude of Watt's soul, a conversion that in some form, your friend might have undergone when he heard Watt's final words and saw him die, his words that were, some of them, the words of your own brother, now hurled back at the white world."

Maurice again slowed his voice. "And, for me—it would be those times when men in gray uniforms, those men of that slavery-South that my father had to take us away from—times when, here, where we sit now, those men suffered past the point where any lines of division will ever be found, past all partialities, all causes, all errors and sins of their souls, no matter how long they might have been accustomed to sinning their dark American sins—times in which they moved on to that point where they were in a final purity of soul brought back to

370

IN THE KINGDOM OF HEAVEN

their true father—these men who, too, were many of them capable, as we know, of giving under the terrible Stars and Bars, even to a final complete innocence, the same last full measure of devotion given by any of the best who died under the Stars and Stripes."

A longer moment now, of quiet—but still an urgency, thought now racing to meet thought in the invisible of Maurice Teague's mind. "Love your enemy," he said, "beyond all taking of an eye for an eye. It *is* madness, this love for your enemy—this forgiveness. And I explained to Robert that unless it is madness in the eyes of the world, it is not forgiveness. True loving forgiveness is inseparable from a mad respect for the soul of the enemy. Respect for your enemy, *respect,* born of compassion, born of selfless admiration. Respectful, loving forgiveness—this is the madness of Christ, which, son, I came to need for my life—to *need*—for my sweating, fearful, murderously angry life, guilt-ridden, rage-torn. My life so exactly like yours. The first shall be last and the last first. This is the greatest of all insults to that justice which the self looks to for settling the score, and it lies at the heart of the message— which finally is that we must reach the zero-point of the self, the radical end of all borders that divide us—the final crucifixion. What is exalted among men is abomination in the eyes of God. Saying this is the same for me as his saying Forgive and you will be forgiven;—for forgiveness, the end of resentment, is more truly the end of all worldly self-defense, all borders and divisions. Let resentment do its work. But mad forgiveness is the key to the kingdom of heaven. Whoever would save his life shall lose it, and whoever loses his life for my sake will find it. Saying this is the same for me as saying Forgive the offender, beyond all self-assertive resentment, seventy times seven. What will it profit a man, if he gains the whole world and forfeits his immortal soul? Saying this is only another way of saying Pray, beyond all resentment, Pray for those who persecute you, so that you may be sons of your Father who is in heaven; or of saying Take not an eye for an eye but instead, past all resentment, turn the other cheek as well, or give him your coat as well. Judge not lest ye be judged; condemn not and you will not be condemned. This all is the self-annihilating madness, beyond resentment, beyond law, beyond justice—the zero-point madness of Christ Jesus, which goes deeper, which did for me go deeper than the night sweats, than the source of racial murder and terrified judgmental, descriptive division, deeper than sin and death. Love the other as you love yourself—because you are the other as well as yourself. And in the truest, last equality, as sons of God, made in his image and likeness, neither of you is the mere description that you each might tremblingly protect or angrily condemn. I would say to my Robert, Connor, that this mad forgiveness, this insanity in the eyes of the world, is most surely the key to the Kingdom of Heaven—and I say the same to you."

As Maurice now paused, Connor...waited—then he said, in a counter-thought that he could not help—*"We don't want this. We don't.* Marcus's words to Watt as he drew his gun. We can still say, with all our souls, that we *don't?* We don't want this!?"

"After all is forgiven," Maurice said, calm, assured, "we still divide the sinner from the sin, the *this,* which no, we never want, and never condone. Always we will say with Marcus, *We don't."* Then he peered at Connor in such a way as to get him to look straight back at him. It was a long moment—and in the silence, Maurice's mind, in a new energy, found itself returning to a train of thought—to a set of strong feelings—feelings that for this boy bordered perhaps on the unbearable. Betrayal of a whole shared moral history, he had said.... As at last, now, they were eye to eye, Maurice said to him, "And your mother.... You will need her, son. She sits apart now. You need her in your life. Her too, you need to forgive. You don't see her now, you say. But that voice saying this, you need to kill that voice."

Maurice saw that he had torn open a deep living wound. Connor had now lowered his face and put his hand tight over his eyes. And he was crying, his shoulders now starting to heave up. Suddenly now, too, Maurice thought—another new filament extending over spaces in his mind—thought of things that that prosecutor, Minister, had said, when Connor was testifying—suggestions that probed the boy's need to get free of some kind of guilt—and that had disturbed him, almost made him stumble in his courage on the stand. "I have spent my life, Connor," Maurice said, "burying the dead...." Then, with his own voice suddenly faltering, "because I left him...my brother...I left him there without a proper grave, half-buried in the dirt.... So I know, son...I know what it means to be the brother who needs to forgive himself...to be the brother who was not killed."

Some good time later, after at last he had composed himself, and after, out of the deep truth of his heart, he had thanked Mr. Teague, for everything, the two of them walked down from the third floor of the Teagues' home. Connor saw Mrs. Teague in the dining room, arranging her table. What inflection to put into his voice as he said his good-

IN THE KINGDOM OF HEAVEN

bye? He did his best to make it wholly kind. He found himself a moment later, then, standing outside the Teagues' front door. And immediately he realized, even to the point of being overcome, as he turned now to thank Mr. Teague a last time, that he stood exactly where Watt had left Robert—exactly at that place where the Teagues had found their son...just like Jack...and his mother covered in blood...in the car.... His breath quickened. He wanted to tear away. And when he turned to say that last thank you and good-bye, he could see on Mr. Teague's face that this all was understood, and all felt...shared...the pain of it.... But Mr. Teague didn't close his door and turn away. Rather he said, as Connor still stood where he was, "In the kingdom of heaven, Connor Riordan, there is no property. Nothing is owned. There are no lines of division. In the kingdom of heaven, you also, would forever be my son."

WHAT WILL YOU DO?

Ellie Shea looked down on Honore and saw Connor Riordan pull up in his father's old Audi. It had been over a year now, but he was driving a car again—no longer afraid that, were he to take a car, anywhere, he'd find himself drunk behind the wheel before he'd ever make it home. Still a thing to get past, he said, was seeing the empty parking space on the car pad behind the house—but not much longer would he and his father live on Lincoln Park West, which could be another good thing. Reasonable fear, or morbid superstition—Ellie was afraid even to whisper in her mind the word *progress,* sensing still, a month and more past the trial of Marcus Sabbs, the possibility of some heartbreaking relapse. But as she saw Connor parking the Audi, then getting out looking healthier, fuller in his body, appearing more and more his old self and not the near street person he'd once become, she allowed herself the thought that, in a real sense, things had changed. And Mr. Teague—Carolyn said her father told her that he and Connor had in their hour together formed a bond, personal, real, father-son—and that in Connor Riordan her father saw a sincerest soul's need for a real peace—a need that seemed to him profound beyond all angry resistance against seeking such a peace.

The two of them sat now beside each other on Ellie's couch, beneath the painting of the swan, its iridescent feathers softer-seeming in the late afternoon. And speaking to Ellie of his visit to Mr. Teague, Connor began with Annabelle Lester. "Maurice told me he was grateful to me for Annabelle's coming to the trial. He said that when Annabelle told Mrs. Teague she could put it out of her mind that someone infuriated by Maurice's flying of the flag might have been the one who murdered Robert—that this had made a difference for the Teagues... a good difference. Not—I would guess—that Mrs. Teague ever really believed that it wasn't Watt. But, our minds being our property and also not, we sometimes construct our own thoughts, and sometimes don't. And thoughts that just come up on their own—trust an expert— can bring strong feelings with 'em, which there's no guarantee we'll shake off, no matter if we believe those self-generated, spontaneous thoughts or we don't."

"Carolyn," Ellie said, "so loves and admires her father—but it's been as hard for her as it's been for her mother, separating what her father did with the flag from Robert's death. All bound up together...so terribly. And so hard for her to untangle...even though she knows it's unfair to her father for her not to...and even though she's helped me, with such things.... But she can't help, as you say, thinking what she thinks, or feeling what she feels."

Connor didn't ask now what tangle of thoughts it might have been that Carolyn had helped Ellie with—for Maurice Teague was still much on his mind. "Driving just now past the Leopard and George's old place," he said, "and coming right to where Watt tried to run me down.... Right at that spot, they got detonated in me, E—thoughts about things Maurice said to me—about forgiveness. I mean that if I were ever truly to love my enemy and so to discover in myself the meaning, or the grace and freedom, of a true forgiveness of him, I'd have to know that I'd sinned his sins, *and* I'd have, somehow, to find the respectable and admirable in him—and actually then to respect and admire the goodness or power of soul I'd found. Even as I hated my enemy's sins as much as I hated Watt's murders, and attempted murders, I'd have, in some meaningful sense, to salute his colors. Love means *love* for Maurice Teague—that is, it means something, if never

375

entirely unqualified, still never so qualified and narrowed, either, that it has no deep and true meaning."

Connor pursed his lips tight a moment. Then, "The man's Christianity—and I understand Robert's resistance against it. But it is so real. Right out of the radical words of Christ. And born, too, out of the depths of its opposite—by which I mean a really sick anger...something both he and I have known—right down to the furious, raging dreams and the night sweats and the desire for a gun, and the insane condemnation of whole races of people because of what one man did to us.... To be with someone who knows the hell of this anger...and the sickness of living the lie of it...."

He breathed a series of short breaths, then slowed. At last then, "Self-crucifixion. Self-transcendence. It's not some book topic for the man, Ellie, or some meditative Buddhist exercise. For Maurice Teague, it's the only salvation from hell's sickness—from an unforgiving vengeance that would perpetrate sin after sin until it passed beyond the reach even of God's farthest-reaching mercies."

Neither of them said anything—a long moment. But now Connor's mouth bent hard in a look of scorn—though he shook his head, too, as if to concede something to some ineradicable reality. "But something he said—something he got from both Robert and Marcus—about Watt's ability to persuade—to win disciples—to convert.... Christ help me, it made me think, right as I was driving past that fucking spot just now, that maybe Watt *had* persuaded both Robert and Marcus in the park that night, that he *had* convinced them to come with him when he stole a car, and to stick with him, no matter what went down. And, so, exactly as I'm trying to love my enemy, and to respect him, and admire, and I'm feeling Maurice Teague's soul, and *knowing* he's right, about everything, about forgiveness...the very moment I'm thinking and feeling all this, the thought crosses my mind that on the stand I made Marcus out not to be Watt's disciple...when he was. And it's all the same, even if I don't believe a word of this sudden suspicion... which *I don't*."

Connor bowed his head and shook it back and forth. "Maybe if you're Maurice Teague, you come to a final, lasting conversion. But, me, I get so sick and tired, E, of opposites continuing to produce each other in my mind, beyond anything I might have to say about it. The incredible time with Maurice—and I am so grateful for your friendship with Carolyn...so I'll see Maurice—but those moments when I

376

WHAT WILL YOU DO?

was so changed...by such a man—all of this goodness, the real thing finding a real life in me, and yet nonetheless producing a reaction of wicked whispers, doubts, counter-statements. I mean, when in bleeding hell does all this back-and-forth brain shit just close itself down?"

She reached for his hand. She lifted it and touched her lips to the back of it—then turned it and kissed the palm. She took his hand then, warmed, moistened by her kiss, and placed it around the back of her neck, under her hair, and moved closer to him. But—and instantly this was so hard—he seemed to be moving away the more she came to him.

"I wonder where they put the flag," he said, his eyes turned to the floor, "...after Robert was found in it and taken out from it and brought to those catacombs at the county morgue, just like Jack.... George took my mother's bloody clothes that night. He told me he put them in a trash bag and took them down the alley, and buried them in a can...."

His hand had fallen, although on her lap she still held it, and more tightly, to try and bring him back. "A couple of those things in the mind and heart," she said, "that can't be helped—would be the way you love, and the one you love. I couldn't love George. I love you. Can't help it." She smiled, her warm lips beautiful, perfect against her fair skin— her hazel eyes, the dark red of her hair. She was trying so graciously now, and tenderly, to help him. She wanted to make love to him—to give him his peace—to take him inside her. To be lost with him. But he was distant, seeming even deaf to her.

"Maurice," Connor said, "told me he knew what it meant to be the brother...who lived...." He had taken his hand back again to himself. But by his own words he was moved. Again he shook his head. His breathing slowed into a quiet sighing. Then, "At their front door... right where Robert...Jesus...right there...he said to me there are no property lines in heaven...no divisions...and that in the kingdom of heaven, I, too...would forever be his son...."

Ellie touched her fingers to her eyes. Neither of them spoke. But now Connor wiped his hand quickly across his eyes, hard. He looked aside, at nothing, a long, silent moment. At last, then, "He told me that she sat apart...."

Ellie wanted now only to listen, but she must ask, "Who?"

"My mother."

"Where did he mean?"

"He meant everywhere. He said I needed to bring her back into my life."

DIVISION

Connor again went silent, tilted back his head, let his eyes shut a moment—then opened them to look again on nothing. But climbing up against her own disinclinations—given her own difficult feelings about Jackie Riordan—trying to be better than her reluctance, still sitting close, Ellie said, "You know I'm one with Mr. Teague on this. You know I think he's right. Please listen to him—the one who really knows every pain you've ever suffered." She moved now even closer to him—and would place herself under his arm.

But now absolutely he pulled away from her, far enough so that he could reach into his pocket. He pulled out a crumpled envelope and handed it across to Ellie.

It was a personal letter, sent to Connor Riordan at the Lincoln Park West address. And the return address was Jacqueline Riordan, 875 N. Michigan Ave., Chicago, IL, 60611, Apt. 72 C. The postmark, March 26, 2000, was for two days back. With a look of uncertainty—hopeful, and fearful—Ellie said to Connor, "What is this?"

"Read it," he said.

Ellie took from the envelope a folded, now crumpled sheet of stationery—close-written front and back. She held the letter before her now, straightened it, and read.

Dearest Con,

Forgive me for approaching you now only in a letter, when I failed—to come up to you at the services for Robert Teague and, again, at the trial of Marcus Sabbs—and when I failed, that night at Jeannette's, to follow you out of the restaurant and to tell you—I was sorry. I had whispered to you that night, after you had turned away, that I was sorry. Sorry for all that's happened. And for all I've done. But I had to do what I did—as I told you when we fought so terribly, for which, too, I am so sorry. Incredible to me now that in my self-defensive bitterness I told you I would never ask for forgiveness. But please do believe it— I had to do what I did—even as I knew as the closest, deepest personal truth that your father was *never* not good to me.

But I had to win my own life—which fight for oneself, however, can wound—very terribly—the lives of others. And when it does, you cannot just whisper some inaudible apology to the back of one you've badly injured. I am your mother. And I am *ashamed* that over so long a time, even over those months when we were still together and suffering together over Jack's heartbreaking death, which neither of us will

378

WHAT WILL YOU DO?

ever get over—that even as we shared this sorrow, I failed to open my heart to you in shared grief, and love. God forgive me, it was even with Bree telling me, Go to him, go to him and tell him—that I kept myself apart at the trial—kept myself, in the weakness of pride, or shame, from going up to you and telling you how proud I was of you. The trial, and those moments when we fought—these things all in retrospect bring it home to me. Really all your life I have not been for you what I always should have been—a good, good mother—the best. And the reason—it could be that while your life in books, that life-passion, is all from you father, the you who fought me, the you of that trial, was me. You are me, in a better and brighter form. You are the me I wished I had become. And so just envy? I think envy, yes. But so complex it all is. And you are. And Jacko was so much simpler, easier, so much less a challenge—and just like your father—in the pitch of his voice—in his beauty—in the way he moved in his body. And so, with Jack, I wasn't looking at myself. And—such an irony—I found it as easy to love Jack, as, for reasons only God will ever know, it was hard, too hard, for me to love your father. They grew in some dark breeding ground, my needs, my resentments. If I'd seen them, I would have stopped them, or tried, but they grew in the dark—and then one day they just came out. And it was too late. They had a life of their own. Still all that you said to me in your anger—the truth of it goes deep—will always, I know, go deep in me. Yet it can't change the way I had to go. And please, Con, forgive Jack—for any rivalry—and for all those terrible complications and all that happened. Let the two of us just hold him now in our memories, always—hold him in our arms—and remember him as a son, a brother, easy to love. And the explanation of so much, I think, is that, without your ever knowing it, you were too much for Jack—as you were for me. But as I watch your life now from afar (too far), and I learn, with more and more time passing, it seems *not* too much for Ellie Shea—so graceful, smart, beautiful a young woman. I can see—lucky you—that you may have met your match. And I won't speak, cannot speak of the selfish, self-protective failings that prevented my reaching out to her, when I *should* have. In some good hour—if you could ask, for me, her forgiveness. And now—and please believe that this is only to help our future, for we always will have a future—I want to ask you for something—though I promise that I ask it with no expectations. I need no answer. I expect none. I give you full freedom not only to reject what I ask but to do so in the confidence that, should

DIVISION

you find it impossible to say yes, I will rise above any trace of disappointment and will rest in the understanding that you have every right to say no—and in the faith that there will be another opportunity, at some later time, for us to make a new beginning. At 11 o'clock on Saturday morning, April 15th, at Fourth Presbyterian, Richard's church, I will marry, and start my new life with Richard. Ellie is most welcome to come with you, were you able to come and be with me. And please know that if for reasons I have confessed, you were the harder of my two sons for me to love—that this only serves as a preparation in my heart for my deepest love in the end.

With all my love,
Mom

Ellie closed her eyes, tight over a beginning of tears, as she held the letter down now on her lap. About it, she hoped, prayed that Connor would say something kind, forgiving, and that...yes, he would go... that he would see and feel the fullest meaning of his mother's confession, her remorse, her love...and that he would honor her request... please yes...and make a new start with her.... This letter, Ellie believed, *was* such a courageous gesture...an honest, heartfelt overture...from a mother who loved, and wanted to love more. But Ellie feared Connor would say something fierce, maybe call the letter some laying upon him of guilt, call it something his mother wrote to extract for herself an exoneration, a comforting pardon, from the son she said she hadn't yet loved the way she should have. And his father, Connor's loyalty to his father.... In no way now could she preach. Given all the complexities, she was even uneasy about the warmth of gratitude she felt for Jackie's kind words about her—and for the happy rush, yes, of confidence and strength they gave her—she was his match. His match— for her the word begot a happiness in the dark. She blinked her eyes drier, but still they were wet as she opened them. Then as she handed Connor back the letter, trying in no way to influence but only to respect his mind and the questions that had to be dividing his heart in two, she asked him, "What will you do?"

He refolded the letter, replaced it in the envelope and put it again in his pocket. He went silent, a long moment. Then he rose—and went to the kitchen and got from the refrigerator two Stellas, brought them back and, opening one, handed it to Ellie, opening the other for him-

380

WHAT WILL YOU DO?

self. "So," he said, taking a drink, "I'm not too much for you, with all that grace of yours, not to mention the beauty. I've met my match."

She felt again the happiness, the gratefulness for that touch of confidence, and strength. Jackie's words. His match. She felt it as a pleasure.... And no darkness—she liked that—in the smirk he wore now. And maybe...some circuitous route.... She hated to think a remarkable opportunity could be lost, this letter so great a chance—but maybe some roundabout way...it might take them back to the question of what he would do—the question that, as if it could be evaded, he now played at evading. And maybe...some tendentious indirection could even wind round to some good resolution, some good new place from which to see anew all the past. So with a ghost of it moving palpably in both their hearts, she too pretended to skirt round the inescapable question and, smiling, even coy, answered him, his match, "Oh, you're too much for me, mister, believe me, too difficult, too volatile, too... *entirely* too fucked up. Which reminds me.... I've been meaning to say, buddy, that, however, you do clean up good." She took a drink of her Stella, smiled, and with her free hand, touched...and ran a finger, softly, over the back of his.

He smiled back at her, as she touched him—but then became again abstracted. So for a while they just sipped their beers and sat, letting time pass. If the question again were to be broached, Ellie would let it be Connor who broached it. But he did not.

After some time, then, of unbroken quiet, she sat up straight and brought her calves up under her thighs. "Of course I've told you often enough," she said, again smiling warmly, feeling still that touch of happy confidence, "but did I ever really tell you, I mean in a specific and detailed manner, how much I hated your guts...I mean from the very first day at Ignatius, when you *claim* you fell for me." She took the bottle to her lips for a moment, not drinking but looking down the neck and cylinder, which she held now, one hand on each, and with the mouth of the bottle tapping her lips. She lowered the bottle and held it upright on her lap. "I mean," she said, now provokingly playful, "there I am with Carolyn and asking her who you are because there you are looking ever so cocky-cute and looking my way but then wearing this look of what anyone would call dismissive judgment—and then walking off as if to say I've made a swift but conclusive review of your assets, whoever you are, and my swift but conclusive determination is

381

that you're worth not a moment more of my ever-so-invaluable time."
Still playfully, she now gathered her breath—for more. "And then," she
said, "I find myself in Candelaria's algebra class not a dozen feet from
you, all that semester, but who's measuring or counting?—and...Mr.
Darcy...you are such...A...DICK...as you give the to-any-sensible-soul
unmistakable impression in a continuing refusal ever to look my way
that, as far as Connor Riordan is concerned, X=Eleanor Shea=o." She
took a full breath again, as if to say that that was the gathering—and
now *here comes the avalanche*. "Aaaaaaand *this*," she said, now starting
indeed a voluble rush of words, "over the years goes on through Pier-
son's social studies class, and Ryan's American history—but who's really
remembering what classes we actually took together?—and three years
of Latin with Schoendeinst, and two full years of English and American lit with Reston, the only—but who's even noticing?—discernible
difference in these two last-mentioned classes being that now and again
you did seem to notice my existence as you would every so often offer
an observation that was responsive to one of mine, if yours would be
generally of a, shall we say, more or less contradicting rather than cor-
roborative character—*however*, and again, WHO IS MEASURING?
I do recall that *one time* you did seem to agree with me that *Romeo and
Juliet* is a tragedy rather than a series of unfortunate accidents because
all the consequential mis-timings in the play seem by no means entirely
to be matters of mere chance but also, and to a significant degree, to
have been the outcomes of choices, decisions, made by individual persons or whole local cultures. *Yes,* you said, in agreement—not to the
teacher—not looking in any way of course toward yours truly—rather
speaking, or whispering to the wall—yet, nonetheless, it was *Yes* that you
did whisper—though who would recollect this barely audible mono-
syllable, addressed only to the thin air—to say nothing of remembering it not just all this time but quite likely for-ev-errrr?" She tilted her
head back now, smiled slyly, then took the bottle to her lips for a drink.

Laughing, at Ellie, at himself, Connor said now, "My dear Miss Bennett, you sorry and insufferable bitch." He held his Stella between his
thighs as now he turned to her more directly. "Did I ever tell you—I
mean really tell you how many and how various were the tortures of the
damned I suffered when in the years you speak of, and when up until
quite recently, you were anywhere near me, or, in fact, anywhere not
near me—the tortures, Miss Bennett!—because I wanted you so goddamned bad that it made me so terrified of losing you, or of being ter-

minally negged by your clearly-to-anyone-with-eyes-in-his-head stand-
offish self—so terrified, before I ever even approached you, that I never
approached you?! Oh the pride, Miss Bennett, oh the prejudice! Oh
the misunderstandings! misinterpretations! And the missteps...alas...
along the borderline of the tragic."

Words make their way, how, by what mysterious powers, to invisible
sensitivities that live where in the soul? Ellie wouldn't quit, not now,
maybe not ever, in her life task of being there for this soul-in-need—but
suddenly her face fell some, with his reference to missteps...along the
borderline of the tragic. Her night with Jack...and the consequences.
The whole complex of things she'd tangled together on the phone with
Carolyn...and in her mind.... That fight in the alley between brothers.
Jack's death, blaming herself. You are and are not what you have done.
She sat back. No longer playful—she took a drink.

But now she could see in Connor's face that he was aware that he had
with those last words...wounded.... She hesitated...then let her mind
just move on to a new...but not new...place. *"If,"* she said, "you were
to say—speaking of respect and admiration, as being, in the way that
Maurice Teague says, crucial to love...and to forgiveness...*what,* I have
wondered, would be the things you most respected and admired...in
your brother?" She took up her bottle again in her two hands, smiled,
took a drink, two-handed, then lowered the bottle, in such a way as,
she hoped, would say Don't give up, we are still in a place where good
lovemaking should happen.

Immediately Connor had known he'd given her pain—and had a
sense, struggling, of why it might be that Ellie was hurt—and why she'd
tried to change the subject away from their story.... Along the borders
of the tragic...not a series of accidents.... In any event the stupidity, or
worse, of having hurt her, again, made his mind search for whatever it
might find.... For some unnamable reason, then, with a blind instinct
that he might, somehow, in this way make up for his injuries, and feeling as well...a pleasure...of opening himself, of changing, toward her...
he recalled Jacqueline Riordan...Apartment 72C, and her letter. Not
knowing why, and speaking now slowly, as if trying to understand himself, he recalled his mother's words. "My brother, Jack, Ellie.... He was
easy to love.... As she said.... So easy to love...."

He stopped a long moment, moved again by the sounds of his own
voice—and seeing that his emotions touched Ellie. "But for *me,*" he
said—following his mother's words now suddenly down a swift, free

passageway into emotional territories where things he'd been keeping suppressed rose up immediately into life, "what made it so easy was the way that nothing between us ever mattered, *ever.* We could fight. Jack and I would argue about a million things. The idea that I didn't know that Jack had his jealousies. Not true. It was easy to see them. And there'd be tensions. Naturally. But nothing ever mattered for more than a second." Connor now found himself saying things that, fast as he said them, he knew he needed to say—he'd never known how much. "And I was *every bit* as jealous of Jack," he said. "If I'm the thinker, Jack was the *life.* And my brother was so much better in the classroom than I was on the football field, where he was a star. I saw *him,* Ellie, as having it all." He looked at Ellie intensely now, wanting her to understand. "But it wasn't—never was it in comparison that I found my respect and admiration for Jack. It was in the way...he would stand up for me. No matter what feelings, hidden rivalries, whatever on earth, Jack would stand up for me.... And he never, not one time *ever,* hit me, or in any way hurt me...all his life, not one time. Ask a thousand younger brothers if they could say the same.... Ask a million...." And now it was as if months of deepest feelings were coming suddenly in crowds, out from door after door into the streets of Connor's mind and heart. He could feel his brother's power, feel again, as when he was a kid, the way he always felt safe with Jack beside him, and later in life as well—anyplace— that happiness of being under his older brother's wing. And expressing his deepest feelings now without embarrassment, with his voice breaking, he said, "He was always...anywhere we went...my big brother...."

Little brother.... Ellie now heard in her mind those words. *Don't you wish this was you, little brother.* And, even as at the same time she felt urges to confess, to clear the air of more, and more—she determined that among the secrets she must forever carry deep inside her would be this of Jack Riordan's whispered words.... But now something else occurred to her, too—came to her heart, as a quiet moral happiness. She said, "Big brother.... Maurice Teague said that his big brother Jesse was everything to him...."

Connor closed his eyes a moment. All his feelings he let move through him simply as they would. At last he settled in a warm pleasure, come, he could tell, from an intertwining of all their futures. "Very easy thing to ask, E," he said, "but you and Carolyn have *got* to stay the friends you are...because I'm gonna *need* to keep up with Maurice."

The sun would go down and the room would darken enough so that

384

WHAT WILL YOU DO?

Ellie would stand and pull the string-switch to the accent light over the swan—before they would leave the couch. And while not yet returning to the question of what he would do about his mother's request, they would, as they sat together, turn their minds to many things, among them to the time, again, when Ellie had made her choice. For the real working out of difficult things will involve returns and repetitions, even over years, sometimes over all of a lifetime. It was all gesture, she said, with respect to the money. Clearly she hadn't needed the money. But Jack's providing it was a gesture—personal—that had a meaning for her strong enough so that she would accept the money, and in order, too, to give Jack the chance to give it. And as Connor could listen to her speak of these things, so she could listen to him—when he said that clearly the offer of the money was essentially gesture, and *statement,* on the part of his mother as well....

After a time, nearly nothing between them was getting hidden. And as the darkness deepened, Ellie, not rashly, she hoped, indeed pausing long to consider—yet feeling still a need to get things out—would confess that what had become the hardest thing for her conscience was that, after she had actually thought, that night, that the choice would be there for her should she need it, she went ahead and did what she did, without protection. She said that she feared at times she might be punishing herself by making this up. And maybe her thinking that way, at the time, was as invisible and silent as anything else taking place in her that night—but this, she said, didn't change its being as large as the whole new world of choice. But that I am no better, and no different, Connor would say to her, is as clear as the relief I felt, when Jack told me everything—the relief that you never in fact had a child with him.

Another trip to the refrigerator, another round of Stellas—and things grew lighthearted again—though they both spoke still in the spirit of confession, and still were working things out that would need to be worked out, one way or another. "So," Connor said, joking...and...also ...not..."exactly how good *was* it? The revenge sex, I mean, between you and my beloved brother?"

"You're such a fool," she said, with a smirk—even as she knew she would never be deterred in her determination to keep the secret of Jack's whispered words.... But now she shook her head and tilted it back, shaking it still in playful scorn. She held her beer before her, then looked at him, smiling...now laughing, mocking. "Oh my God!" she said aloud now, mocking him, farcical, and with a wisdom deep

385

as both their wounds, "Oh my God! I kept screaming it—*all…night…*
long—'It's so big! Oh my God!' It was the last time, little boy, that I
prayed. And it was a prayer of fullest gratitude. Heartfelt grrrratitude—
you pitiful loser!"

"Holy *shit* what a bitch you are!" he said, barely containing himself
as he laughed…despite his pain.

And so it went, and in one way or another they got to things, old,
and new, as they needed. But after a time, all the laughter dying down,
and things settling out, in the soft glow of the accent light, in the darkening room, they knew. The time had come. Ellie put her bottle down
on the glass coffee table, and Connor his. She rose up on her knees in
the soft light and moved across to him on the couch. Kneeling before
him then, she took his face in her hands warm, needing, loving, and
softly, slowly pulled him, her eyes now closed, into a passionate kiss,
breathless, deep—and then another. Then keeping a warm, moist lip
touched softly to his cheek as she moved her mouth sensually, slowly
across it, she touched her lips at last to his ear and whispered, soft and
low, "You're the one, mister, so don't you ever be a fool."

She would then reach beneath the couch, to what was its special
place, and take out their flashlight—and again lead him to her bedroom, which now was theirs. And as he lay naked on the bed, healed
back nearly into the fullness of a fine-muscled body, she stood at the
bed's end—and in the mysterious light of the flashlight, which she'd
nestled and set on the pulled-back blanket, she would undress for him,
feeling a love for her own beautiful, fair-skinned body, a joy of deep
sensual confidence as, looking only at him, she would unfasten for
him, slowly, the buttons of her gray, silken blouse, and then those of
her jeans, which she loosed then and let half-fall, to her knees. Standing before him still, then, with her eyes now closed, she ran her hand
beneath her lace, whispering things loving, sensual, to please him, as
she pleasured herself, some time. And at last then with a warm, slow
grace undressing herself fully, and clicking out the light, she came to
him across the bed on her knees and knelt over him, and as a gift for
herself, and a gift for him, she took him in her hands and, seeking for
them both to arouse fully every sense, placed him, and then took him,
slowly, inside her. And she would take and give then the fullest joy, still
kneeling up for him, until at last she came down, lay her breasts upon
his chest and continued to receive him while to him she whispered

WHAT WILL YOU DO?

words, again loving, sensual, private—and infused with a power of feeling she was now certain she would never in her life have for another.

They would make love late into the night. At last, tangled beautifully in one another's arms, with all the million things that resonated in it for both of them, endlessly, they would sleep on the question raised in Jackie Riordan's letter to her son.

WE DO

Two of Jackie Riordan's green-glass coasters set before them on the dark walnut, Tom Riordan in a DePaul t-shirt and Connor in a fresh white dress shirt but with loosened tie, sat together under the track lights at her kitchen table, each holding his cup of morning coffee. But now lifting his and sweeping it about him, Tom said, "Nothing these days markets your home and gets started that much-desired march of prospective buyers through it like a De Giulio kitchen." Without taking a sip, he set his cup on his glass coaster. Embittered, he turned his mouth down. "Got a feeling, though, Con, that the parade ends today. Couple coming back for the third time, between 11:30 and noon—and I'm told they're prepared to make an offer, which, if it's decent, I'll accept."

"You okay? Now that it's coming down to it?" Connor felt immediately the packed weight of his wording—for in sometime less, now, than an hour and a half, his mother, at the altar of Fourth Presbyterian, would become the wife of Richard Olen. As his father laughed a short, high-pitched false laugh and shook his head, Con could think only to say, "So stupid, Dad. That was so stupid of me."

WE DO

"It's okay." Tom shook his head again, then pressed a forefinger against his upper lip. Now he lowered his hand and reached for his cup—but didn't lift it. "You know," he said, staring at this coffee, "I've been thinking this morning of Mr. Teague's saying that you would be his son in heaven—and I've been jealous." He stared still at his cup. "Such a crazy thing—Maurice Teague and that flag. But he must be able to whisper to the Lord and feel that he's heard—that he's never alone, even when the whole world tells him he's out of his mind. And Mrs. Teague is still with him. Clearly she challenged the notion that there was any real conversation between Maurice Teague and the Lord above. I can hear her saying it was all just foolish self-delusion, as well as damned dangerous, that flag right out on MLK. But she stayed. And she will stay. He has that. He has her. And he hasn't lost his faith." Tom paused a long moment, tapping his cup. Barely above a whisper, then, he said, "And for that...I would give much."

He looked up at his son, and with pain written hard across his face, he added, "But this isn't heaven, Con." His face tensed still more in sorrow, and love. "And in this world, you are my son. And the feeling that you are *mine*—it's as powerful as the call to the kingdom of heaven. Every goddamned bit as powerful." He took his brow between his forefinger and thumb and pressed hard as he lowered his head.

Pain and pleasure divided against themselves, indecisive, here and there starting and then dying in his heart and mind, Connor, all through himself felt disloyal. Maurice Teague. His mother. His father. He felt choosing must be a crime. But seeing his father suffer, and finding force for, and committing it to, his words, he said, "I'm not going. I can't watch her stand there and go through with it with that sonofabitch —in a church."

"Ssshhhh," Tom said, his head still down in his hand. "Don't say that. For me—don't say it."

Not un-confused, with still nothing for him simplified, Connor said nothing.

Tom looked up again and wrapped his hands around his cup—still, however, not lifting it. "Never take this the wrong way, Con.... If I lost you...it would be the end of my life. The end. But today...her *wedding* day." He gripped the cup harder with his two hands, then took his hands away and formed them into fists. "This is harder...I don't know .... All the confusion following Jack's death—those things I came to know—and wish I hadn't. Hard—but truly not hard for me to forgive—

389

all long cleansed away now. And in truth Jack never did a thing in his life to injure me, not immediately. And with him so gone from me... all that life.... But this pain, today—I fear it might last even longer. Christ almighty. It's so hard to say it. So hard to have your conscience gut-wrenched as your grief over a son's death gets lost, even if it's just for an hour, in some different *thing*. Her with another man. It's been months...and before that...who in hell knows how long...but the finality today, of her saying *I do* to that choice."

His hands still clenched, Tom began rubbing his thumbs against the skin of his fisted forefingers. "When you have to pray, and to what god?—when you have to beg in prayer to someone, or something, just that you not become sick obsessed for the rest of your life." He stopped for a moment, shook his head, then, "It's a contemptible weakness. There'd be no need to forgive, if you were strong enough not to be injured. If you had that fundamental strength." He took a slow, deep breath, and then another. "But I'll find it—*that* faith, at least, I've got— the faith that with time I'll find the strength I need."

He waited, silent. At last then, "And if I say I love her—what does that really mean? That I would force myself down into her soul, carrying a whip, crack it hard at her innermost spirit, and tell her *This* is what you'll desire, forever, and *never that*. Chain her up and say You'll *be* what I goddamn say you'll be." He closed his eyes a moment. "Believe me—I've sunk to such imaginations."

As he heard his own father confess to him his sins, his weaknesses, and saw the man fighting himself, torn and tortured, Connor thought of the ease with which Jack spoke of his mother's leaving their father —of her finding another man—of her never having gotten over the feeling that she'd been trapped. As if she had no *obligation* to get over it— because it's called *marriage!* In her letter, she spoke of winning her life. And...today...today was to help their future. They would always have a future. And her remorse, acts of repentance, each word she wrote an act of repentance. But to win your life, you need to kill another's. He wished he could drag Jack up from the grave, and have him look at his father now. Shout in Jack's face that to justify his own actions, his own *choice,* he made everything of his mother's entrapment and nothing of his father's pain. But thinking suddenly, too, of how his father's loving care for him had evolved finally toward good tough love—and what difference that had made, he said to him, "You're stronger today, on your worst day, than for months and months I was on my best.

390

Choose to live. That's what you said to me. It's a start, choosing to live. And then things can happen. And they do. I *wasn't* trapped, you told me. I was not trapped."

"Fall out of your old love," Tom now said, having listened to his son, but still not looking his way, rather with his eyes just studying his own hands, now spread out on the table. "Let that cleansing process begin. And then find a new love. The degree to which I'm energy-less when it comes to starting that cleanse and renewal process..."—he lifted his head and turned to look at his son—"is surpassed only by the degree to which I'm instantly *re*-energized in that old love every time I do try to escape it." He thought, though, even as he said this, of the desperate-wayward inclinations he'd felt of late to call John Touhy, who knew her, who said she had some kind of a fine grudge against marriage, and see if Touhy might have an address, still, for the dancer. Just an evening...of relief...when all belief is gone. "And what crazy things," he said, however, trying now to assure his son that a sane caution was part of any reluctance of his to begin again, to venture in some new way his torn, sick heart, "what crazy things people will do on the rebound. That's part of it, too. Not wanting to seek merely for the sake of seeking, and ending up in a worse place—rather than feeling a real call, coming, I hope, next time, from a kindness more than anything else, some truly kind person, maybe, out there. One who needn't be...so beautiful."

Connor felt his watch now as an unwanted consciousness—an uncomfortably noticeable warmth, and weight, on his wrist. He wouldn't look at it. But he couldn't guess the time. He felt miserably that, while it had to be over an hour, it could still be, however, maybe only moments 'til the doorbell would sound and there would be Ellie, come in the cab. She couldn't be married in a Catholic church. So it was Fourth Presbyterian, Richard's church. Jesus Christ. "Crazy, all right," he said, finally, and then with an anticipatory regret, feeling sorry even before he would say them, for the words he now, however, did say—"crazier than hell the things, or the people, whom people will choose when they start over."

Tom Riordan sniffed, smirked—breathed a long, slow breath. "You know what he is for me, Con? Fair, or unfair—he's the compact embodiment of my loss of goddamn everything. Not just her—but my faith taken from me. I haven't been to Mass in eight months. I don't know if I'll ever go back. I feel so dead inside. And my resentment of this theft—it can get unmanageably intense." He stopped a moment, as his

391

resentments, with a life of their own, once more clarified, honed themselves. "So much goes, when the center of your life goes—and when *his* name takes its place. Olen—the name I can't separate from anything. And now never from your mother, after today—not 'til we're gone to the great beyond, where you shall not know each other as man and wife, which of course would be best for me, not having to look at the two of them together for eternity...assuming the start-over marriage is the one that counts, in the end."

Connor didn't know what to say. And what difference could words make? He *could* not go to the wedding—the blessed brand-new union. He could decide not to go. *Decide.* The word *kill* is right inside *decide.* Homicide. Fratricide. Matricide. Decide. Choose. But his father didn't want him not to go. He wanted him to go—even more than he didn't want him to go. No matter what he might now be saying and feeling about Olen, he wanted him to go. Yet to hear his own father confess to how deeply he'd been injured and to his faith having been stolen. He'd gone nearly his whole life without missing Mass. And to be divorced, the first divorce in his Catholic family. Not the same for her in her family —her sister Celeste, the trailblazer.

"I don't know, Con, if I ever told you this. But I had offers, coming out of Berkeley. And God help me, can I say it again?—you have to promise me you'll go back."

This he could, and would do. Connor even this instant let a growing need he'd been feeling mature toward a full imperative—and commitment. "Don't worry about that, Dad," he said, "I'm on that. Ellie and I have discussed her coming out to California. She's got only a semester more here. And after that, she could come out to Berkeley."

"Cannot, as a father, Con, when it comes to my son's relationships, say a word for, or against—because a father's words might just spin a son's heart against the father's wishes, simply *because*—because of the perversities of human nature and in a free society—that can happen. So this father will keep a wish of his a secret." Tom pursed, turned his lips now in a warm half-grin. But eventually he let his face fall more, and more, into a blank. Looking at last again at nothing, he said, "Good offers.... Tulane...Chapel Hill. You might have been a southerner. But I wanted to teach at a Catholic university. To give my life to that. So it was DePaul." He lifted his head—but with his eyes still kept downward. "Here in Chicago, too...home for us both. And she agreed. A Catholic university. It was a thing we shared. Our shared commitment

WE DO

to Catholicism really meant something...at that time." He looked up again—shook his head. "Jesus."

Connor was conscious still of the warmth of his wristwatch, the weight—under the cuff of his white shirt. His white shirt, his tie ready to be pulled up. He could see himself, feel his dressed appearance as irremovable, inescapable, unwanted. And yet traces of pleasure...thinking his going might help the future...which they would always have. Plezzzzzuuuure. Maurice said he would need to kill the voice that says you don't see her now. She sits apart. But what time had it been, really, when he'd come down? And what time would Ellie think of as early enough to get from here, to there? Offers. The choice of DePaul. Once, yes—nine years ago—it was when he was twelve, right near his Confirmation, he knew this—he'd heard his father speak of those job offers. Here in the kitchen...un-renovated. And his father's life-choice had affected—fortified for him—in a kind of second confirmation—his own Catholic commitment. He might have been a southerner.

"But what a joke it all is now." Tom, his anger and sorrow again finding life, sniffed cynically. "Yet even from the earliest days, late seventies, a Catholic university meant pretty much nothing, as far as Catholic principles are concerned. And I'm no Maurice Teague, Con, I'm ashamed to say. I keep my light under the bushel—never letting on what I believe. Silent as a goddamn mouse at DePaul, that Catholic university, which with moral determination I chose, but where in the English Department I found out it's just better for you—much better —if you never even whisper the word *personhood*. And so I am where I am, the one who let his feeble light shine only here...in the privacy of his own home."

Ellie—in utter sympathy—said she must remain impartial, knowing how this all must split his heart in two. She said she hoped so much that he would go but that she would understand if he couldn't. She said she had her hopes—but that, if it wasn't to be—they could take that cab anywhere....

"There's been no change, Con," Tom now said, his hands on the dark table, his fingers folded together at the tips, his thumbs now fast tapping against each other, *"none,* for me, when it comes to the arguments—that there's no person there. To say *this* is a person—and *that* isn't. The terrible history of this kind of anti-egalitarianism. And to stand Christ on his head and say that there is no obligation to be a Good Samaritan. To *start* with that!" He stopped tapping his thumbs—

and now folded his hands more fully, tightly together. "Like a shot," he said, "my mind will go through their every argument, tick every one off, with full moral and intellectual indignation and contempt." He squeezed his folded hands tighter, to the point of pain. But now, silent, feeling the pain in his hands, he considered...and couldn't *believe* he was returning to these things again...with Ellie Shea coming. How never to condone and yet ever to *forgive,* to forgive and yet never lose all that you ever were. ALL I want is still to be who I always was and yet to forgive, to love, with no anger. Please, Christ, no more anger. Not a day more. Not an hour. Not one...hour...more.

He loosened, softened the hold of his hands. "But all my rants now," he said, after a time, "all my inner rants—they all just turn into rages against your mom, whom I say I love. Whom I...love. She's always there before me in my imaginations, forced to listen as I rage on. And I am so sick of raging at your mom. So sick to death, no matter how quickly my godforsaken automatic mind might return, again and again, to all those arguments and then in imagination hold her there before me to take one more lashing." For a moment his lips quivered. He put his hand over them. Then, lowering his hand, he breathed again deeply, in a low sigh. "It makes me so sick of myself, and so tired."

He wore a look truly of weariness—of himself, of all the worn, rutted ways of his obsessions, and of his enslaving anger. He looked at his hands, which he had set again on the dark table. "And arguments," he said, "to state the obvious—not a single one works anymore, anywhere, anyhow. And all your father really has is his fading, faded Catholic anger, and his moral fatigue and his silence, in which he just finds a way to get along with it all. That's all I've got—that, and my contempt for those who do make noise and who do let their damnable light shine— the great, gun-totin' pack of the American pseudo-pious who claim for themselves a Bible whose Sermon on the Mount is as alien to their darkened spirits as water to oil and who are all stone blind to the fact that the culture war that the overturning of Roe v. Wade would start (and that they would lose) would (because this *is* where we are now) go every bit as deep and, in the truest spiritual sense, be every bit as bloody and divisive as the Civil War itself. It would bring on another raising of the Stars and Bars, all right."

Ellie Shea. The instant he said what he'd said, Tom thought of the actual girl, at the center of so much of his life. She made every issue so deeply personal, which altered so many things...its all being so per-

WE DO

sonal, and close. Jack, his own son. So, so close. On her way here, now, any minute. Her face hidden in her hands. Her fingers touching away her tears. He thought of Con's love for this beautiful girl, the depth, and the truth, and of her love, Ellie's, of their love. Equal. In an equality of love, is there a truer and a truly selfless strength, lasting, never bored, *not* ever bored? Why on earth couldn't this be true? Jackie...her utter and complete beauty, too, and also truly perfect. He thought of Jackie's eyes, the deep, rich blue, startling, of her mouth, the softness, the beauty of her mouth, the warmth of her kiss...the softness...of the touch of her lips. Jackie...my God.... He thought of her love for him, *never,* not once, equal to his, never for a single hour. If she weren't getting married, and if he took her back someday, she would feel contempt for his weakness in taking her back—he knew—because he felt it right now himself, just imagining...the no more possible. He fisted his hands again and touched his fists together on the table. He wanted to say something out loud. And yet in the end, fighting, suppressing his desire, he let himself say only silently, in his mind, "But never imagine, either, suggesting to the ones who deny personhood to the unborn, who it is that in the new Civil War would be riding under the Stars and Bars."

But now even just thinking this to himself, he felt, with Ellie Shea coming, a heaviness of guilt falling fast again over him, and a second strong wave of remorse; and he thought of Maurice—and of the memorial stone, of the six thousand names forgiven—and of the call, every bit as powerful as that of the world, to something beyond his anger, beyond him*self.* Like the mustard seed...the kingdom of heaven.... Let your light shine. William Blake. Ellie Shea.... In grace to live the life of that kingdom, which, unless you make yourself like one of these, you shall not enter. To feel these truths of the heart, as he felt them—to know forgiveness as a necessity, and its necessity as a matter of life and death. Even Olen forgiven, especially Olen. And never, ever let Con run toward death, toward resentment and unforgiving anger. Never let that happen. And yet still, was it worth it, that, in order for these truths about forgiveness to come alive as they had in his soul, worth it, that, in order for him to reach this understanding about the life-and-death necessity of the kingdom of heaven, he would have first to enter the double hell of racial and then jealous anger? Sex anger. And obsessive rage mastering, goddamn possessing you enslaved. Even Maurice, his brother Jesse gone so long ago, shotgunned...both barrels...that

395

DIVISION

white filth and psychotic brutality, and terror, and left there unburied, and now his son, Robert, his future, he said...gone forever.... Watt, without mercy or understanding...Christ...both Jack and Robert... our shared agony, Maurice, our joint baptism in the blood. Yet still, Maurice Teague...you have your wife.

Connor had let his father go, not interposing even with a nod or shake of his head. The man's anger, and those words his father couldn't hold back—like those expressions of his sickness of himself, his inner rants—all of it—the man simply could not now, in this final hour, not vent.

And now this silence—Connor, not looking at his watch, wouldn't break this long silence, knowing the hollowness of so-called healing words—and how they might well, in the perversity of human nature, even set the diseases of anger and of ongoing, living trauma running in the wrong direction, to the satisfaction of the Prince of Darkness. Partners. He had them. Maurice. And Ellie—the best of all partners in recovery...in discovery of real life, which might start, at last, when you reach that point where you know that if you try to take even one more step alone, you will die. Without a recovery partner, what chance that you will continue to live? And Marcus has Maurice now, too, a father. On to school. Southern Illinois. And Dosey out of Cabrini. And my father, too, so deep in my heart, my recovery partner, as I will be his, against the devil. But he has no one to touch. The one he wanted, now, today, gone with another. In no time now, standing with Olen in a church...at an altar.... And yet he wants with all his life for me not to lose my relationship with her—your mom, he keeps calling her. Your mom. The words he's choosing, deliberately. Separate the sinner—for the future.

Tom, his eyes again closed, his head tilted slightly back, now said, out of nowhere but *not*...out of nowhere, "California, Berkeley.... It's where it began for us, too, as of course you know." And now Tom squeezed his eyes tight again. "But don't be afraid. Don't be afraid of your love. Don't let your mother's and my divorce.... That would kill me.... So let Ellie come out to California." He opened his eyes, looked at his son. "Just now twenty-one, the two of you. And what does that mean in today's world? Ten more years before you'd marry? Fifteen? You don't have to fall for that. All that decade, and decade and a half, of *caution.*" He thought, as lately he had many times, of how girls who'd long avoided it might nowadays, as their biological

396

WE DO

clocks ticked, in the end seek pregnancy in a panic, maybe even to force a marriage out of someone who'd chosen his freedom so long that he couldn't give himself to anything. But again, then, he despised his own vain moralizing and self-defensive conceit—and his anger. He looked at his son. "And God forgive me," he said, "for saying this out loud. But what I see is the real thing. That incredible girl.... And how often does it ever come—the real thing? Or a girl like that?" And now he thought that if he said something else he might be forgiven as he forgave. But, still, how to forgive and not lose his moral soul—not lose himself? How still to be who he always was, before *she* changed? "Con," he said at last, "it's always an escape. Sin is always an escape from some difficulty. But I am so glad, let me confess it, as you have to me, so glad that Ellie never had a child with your brother. Glad for the way that this has given to the only son I have now in this world, a chance at the best thing there is."

Suddenly now, saying this, Tom felt again—unbearable—the pain of the utter love that he felt for his wife—and that agonizing energy in his passion that would become even more intense the more he tried to free himself from it—his passionate love—the best thing he'd ever known, but which had to be put out today...forever...for the sake of his own future. Still he wanted to rage in his hard, deepening pain. But what he said was, "Your mom was wrong, Con, when she told you that if you didn't go today, she would feel no disappointment and that she would understand and that there would be another time for you and her to start again. She was wrong. This is the day...that will make all the difference."

As his father paused now, in thought, ready, clearly, to say some further thing, Connor thought that—through the lintel-ed passageway and beyond the dining room and front room, out the front window, out on Lincoln Park West—he had caught the yellow of a cab.

And as Tom could now see his son—just for that moment—looking out toward the street, seeming as if he'd seen something, he felt yet another fierce pang. But he reached out to set his hand on, and to hold his son's forearm, tenderly. "She was wrong, Con. And Maurice Teague was right—about the key to the kingdom of heaven. Choose it, choose forgiveness. And for me, for my life, and not just for me—choose to go today."

The doorbell sounded. Father and son, saying nothing, reached for and held each other close and hard, in a completeness of love and

397

DIVISION

shared pain, some time. Then the bell sounded again. And now together they rose and went to the front door, Connor, as they passed, picking up his jacket from where he'd laid it over the back of a dining-room chair. Tom opened the door, and there she was, he felt again, sent— Ellie Shea. You are perfect...he had told her. And now, as he looked in her eyes, he had a sure faith that neither he nor she would ever forget either that moment or this. Tom again took Connor to him and held him—then, when at last he let his son go, he said to him and to Ellie Shea, "Promise me you'll go. Do you promise?"

And as together they looked at the man standing alone in his doorway, a thousand thoughts and feelings coming down for them both to a single simplicity, nearly in one voice, they said, "We do."

Patrick Creevy grew up on the South Side of Chicago, moving to the northern suburbs at age fourteen. He graduated from Holy Cross College in 1970, received his Ph.D. in English Literature from Harvard University in 1975, and has taught at Mississippi State University since 1976. For the last several years he has divided his time between his farm in Mississippi and his home in Wilmette, Illinois. He has five children and nine grandchildren and has been married to his wife, Susie, for forty-nine years.

Made in the USA
Columbia, SC
22 May 2020